EMPIRE

A SEVENTEEN SERIES NOVEL

A.D. STARRLING

COPYRIGHT

Empire (A Seventeen Series Novel) Book Three

Editors:

Invisible Ink Editing (www.invisibleinkediting.com)

Right Ink On The Wall (www.rightinkonthewall.com)

DEDICATION

To you, my readers

THE IMMORTALS

The Crovirs and the Bastians: two races of immortals that have lived side by side with humans since the beginning of civilization and once ruled an empire that stretched across Europe, Asia, and North Africa. Each possessing the capacity to survive up to sixteen deaths, they have been engaged in a bloody and savage war from the very dawn of their existence. This unholy battle has, for the most part, remained a well-guarded secret from the eyes of ordinary humans, despite the fact that they have been used as pawns in some of the most epic chapters of the immortal conflict. It was not until the late fourteenth century that the two races were forced to forge an uneasy truce, following a deadly plague that wiped out more than half of their numbers and made the majority of survivors infertile.

Each immortal society is ruled by a hierarchy of councils made up of nobles. The First Council consists of the heads of seven Immortal Sections: the Order of the Hunters, the Counter-Terrorism Group, Human Relations, Commerce, Immortal Legislations and Conventions, Research and Development, and Immortal Culture and History. The Head of the Order of the Hunters is the most powerful member of the First

Council. The Second Council, or the Assembly, comprises the regional division directors under each Head of Section, while the Congress of the Council is made up of local authority chiefs.

Though they have been instrumental to the most significant events in world history, religion, and culture, the Immortals' existence is known to only a select few humans, among them the political leaders of the most powerful states on Earth and the Secretary General of the United Nations.

PART ONE: RESONANCE

PROLOGUE

OCTOBER 1553. AMASYA. OTTOMAN EMPIRE.

THE MESSENGER HURRIED ALONG THE WIDE MARBLE HALLWAY, the leather soles of his dusty riding boots barely making a sound on the polished floor. Golden beams washed through open archways in the south walls of the palace and painted patterns of shadow and light across the colored tiles. The trickle of falling water carried from the fountains in the courtyards outside, where crystal jets sparkled like diamonds in the fading, yellow light. Dusk was falling fast across the Pontus Mountains and the narrow river valley that held the fortified city of Amasya.

It had taken the man the better part of a day to ride across Anatolia from the province of Konya. The document he carried inside his kaftan lay heavy against his breast during the long, solitary hours on the road, the weight matched by the growing despair in his heart.

He reached an imposing pair of gilded doors and halted in front of the armed guards who blocked his path.

'I need to speak to Her Highness,' he said in a low voice, ignoring the glances they cast at his Janissary uniform. He removed his bork hat and took the slim roll from his tunic. 'I bring urgent news from the south.'

A muscle twitched in his jaw while the guards carefully inspected the imperial seal on the parchment. He barged past them when they finally opened the golden doors.

The messenger's eyes darted around the lavish interior of the royal chamber before falling on the figure slowly rising from the ornate window seat overlooking the glimmering Yesilirmak River.

'Captain Rajkovic. What a pleasure to see you. I was not expecting a visit,' murmured Mahidevran Sultan.

Low and mellifluous, the older woman's voice matched her regal appearance. Gold and silver threads glittered in her garments as she crossed the floor toward him, the tips of her silk slippers peeking from beneath the hem of her dress. He caught the sweet scent of rose water drifting from her fair skin and auburn hair, and could not help but feel a flutter of admiration for the Sultan.

Despite the passage of time, the first concubine of Suleiman the Magnificent had retained the ageless beauty that had earned her the name of Gulbahar, the Rose Spring.

Rajkovic bowed. 'Your Highness.' He straightened and scanned the attendants lounging around the private quarters of the Sultan, before meeting the eyes of the woman he had traveled so far to see.

Mahidevran's steps faltered when she saw the expression he could no longer mask. She waved the other women away with brisk flicks of her hand, her gaze never leaving his face. Her attendants disappeared through a door at the rear of the chamber.

'You bring me news of my son?' she said stiffly, once they were alone.

He nodded wordlessly and handed her the sealed document. The Sultan's hands trembled as she unrolled the parchment. The color drained from her face when she read the message inscribed upon it. Rajkovic closed his eyes briefly at the sight of the raw anguish on her face. He knew the words already. He had been there when they were written.

Birdsong rose from the gardens outside the windows, the innocent sound at odds with the devastating tidings he had been ordered to bring to the woman before him. The parchment dropped from the Sultan's fingers and fluttered to the marble floor. She stared at him blindly, tears spilling over and rolling down her silken cheeks.

A single cry left her lips and she slowly folded to the ground, her sobs shattering the frozen silence. The door at the back of the chamber opened. Her attendants rushed in, their voices raised in alarm.

The guards at the main doors quickly followed. They staggered to a stop next to Rajkovic, their swords drawn. Confusion clouded their faces when they observed the women around the weeping Sultan.

'What happened?' said the closest man, his fingers whitening on the handle of his blade. He glanced anxiously at the captain.

'Prince Mustafa is dead,' Rajkovic replied, his tone leaden. As the words fell from his numb lips, the reality of the statement overwhelmed him once more. His shoulders sagged. 'Suleiman Sultan had him executed.'

The guard gasped.

His companion swore under his breath. 'The King killed his own son?'

Rajkovic dipped his chin.

As the wails of Mahidevran's attendants echoed around the royal chamber, the captain tore his gaze from the crying

Sultan. A slight motion drew his attention to the back of the room.

A young woman he had never seen before stood at the door. Her arms were wrapped around her midsection, and she hunched over as if she had received a blow to her body.

His breath caught in his throat.

Thick lashes fell to touch creamy, flawless skin, hiding her eyes. Tears trembled on the curved, velvet-black strands and dropped silently onto her pale cheeks. Her full, crimson lips glistened in the golden light as she pressed them together.

Despite the grief that shadowed the stranger's face, her beauty outshone even that of the Emperor's concubine.

Guilt and shame suddenly washed over the captain, drowning his dawning interest in the woman. He turned on his heels and exited the chamber.

In the chaos that followed, Branimir Rajkovic strode along the flame-lit corridors and halls of the palace and headed out into the city. As news of the death of the heir to Suleiman the Magnificent spread around him, a smoldering anger replaced the crushing pain inside his heart. Cries of 'The Lawgiver has killed Mustafa! Our Prince is no more!' soon reverberated across the narrow streets of Amasya. He stopped outside the forbidding gates of the Janissary barracks and stared at the moon rising over the valley, his hands fisting by his sides.

He had dedicated his whole life in service of the man who had been destined to become the next Sultan of the Ottoman Empire. Not only had Mustafa been a valiant warrior and much-loved Prince of Anatolia, he had also been the captain's closest friend since he joined the Janissary Corps twenty years earlier. He recalled the hours they had spent together, laughing and dreaming of the day they would rule the world and all the people within it. Although Mustafa spoke of such matters more in jest than in earnest, deep down, Rajkovic knew the prince was capable of achieving that vision and would be an even greater ruler than his father, Suleiman. The captain had wanted nothing more than to remain at Mustafa's side and help him realize that dream.

Images of his best friend's final moments flashed in front of the captain's eyes once more. He took a deep, shuddering breath and headed inside the barracks.

In the days that followed Prince Mustafa's wrongful execution, the rage simmering inside Rajkovic's veins grew stronger and was soon reflected by the civil unrest that broke out across Anatolia. News rapidly spread that Hurrem Sultan, Suleiman's wife, and her son-in-law, Rustem Pasha, had concocted a conspiracy to overthrow the rightful heir to the Ottoman throne. This caused further outrage from the Janissary Corps and Mustafa's soldiers, forcing Suleiman to remove Rustem from his position.

Two weeks after the death of the Prince, Rajkovic awoke in the middle of the night to the sound of knocking on the door of his quarters. He almost dropped the candleholder in his hand when he opened it and saw the two figures standing on the threshold.

Mahidevran Sultan observed him solemnly from beneath the hood of her cloak, her face ghostly pale in the flickering light of the flame. Standing behind her was the hauntingly beautiful young woman Rajkovic had first seen on that fateful day when he visited the palace to deliver the gruesome news of Prince Mustafa's death to the Sultan.

'May we come in?' said Mahidevran softly.

∼

CHAPTER ONE

S

JULY 1706. LONDON. KINGDOM OF ENGLAND.

CONRAD GREENE RAN ACROSS THE WET, SLOPING LEAD ROOF of the Banqueting House, his breath misting in the cool night air. Moonlight flashed on metal to his right. He caught a glimpse of a blade falling toward his neck and ducked.

The sword skimmed past his head with a faint hum. Feet skidding on the slick surface, he spun around, dropped to one knee, and lifted the short, silver-gilded staff in his hands.

A grunt sounded above him as the burly swordsman brought his weapon down once more. The edge of the blade struck the staff hard, raising sparks in the gloom.

The man's lips pulled back in a vicious grin, exposing two uneven rows of stained teeth. The muscles and veins in his neck and arms bulged with superhuman strength as he drove the sword into the staff.

Conrad's elbows slowly folded toward his chest. Air left his lips in a low hiss as the tip of the man's blade inched closer to his left eye. He pushed back with the staff with all his might, dark spots dancing across his vision.

A figure dashed past them on the left. Conrad caught a glimpse of soft, brown curls. His heart stuttered inside his chest. He swore, fell back, and rolled out of the way of the falling blade.

He landed close to the balustrade that ran around the top of the building and climbed swiftly to his feet. Ignoring the swordsman charging toward him, he peered through the rainfall at the dark shapes engaged in a fast-paced and deadly battle on the moonlit rooftop. His eyes sought and found the woman who had run by him.

She was almost at the north end of the terrace, where a young man with brown hair and eyes stood confronted by three armed attackers; blood from the wounds on his left shoulder and flank had already soaked through his long-sleeved, ruffle shirt and stained his leather jerkin.

'William!' the woman yelled, her voice edged with fear and desperation. She passed the weather vane on the sloping roof and unsheathed the rapier at her waist.

Relief darted across the younger man's face at the sound of his name. He glanced at the woman over his attackers' shoulders and raised his own blade to block another strike.

Conrad clenched his teeth. He turned to face his opponent and twisted one of the metal rings on his short staff. The weapon extended and a spear blade sprang out at either end. A loud battle cry preceded the attack of the burly swordsman a heartbeat later.

Conrad blocked his blade, kicked him in the groin, and hooked the staff behind his neck. He yanked the man's head down at the same time that he drove his knee up into his face. A guttural groan left his adversary's lips, and he slid to the ground, unconscious.

A flurry of activity to the right captured Conrad's attention.

Another group of men had rushed onto the rooftop terrace of the Banqueting House. He scanned the other fighters around him, anxiety twisting his stomach; he and his companions were now heavily outnumbered.

His eyes suddenly widened. The newcomers had drawn their swords and were heading resolutely for the running woman and the wounded man still fighting at the north end of the building. Knuckles whitening on his staff weapon, Conrad moved to intercept the men.

The woman reached the figures at the edge of the terrace. She stepped in front of the injured young man and swung her thin blade around in a flurry of strikes and blocks at his three attackers. Rage darkened her face and a roar left her lips. The men fell back under her fierce attack.

The wounded man sagged behind her and gripped his bleeding limb. Even from a distance, Conrad read the fear and confusion on his features. The man turned and flinched when he met Conrad's eyes.

The expression on his face left no doubt in his mind. William Hartwell was the one who had betrayed them. Bile flooded the back of Conrad's throat. Hartwell looked away. His lips moved, forming words that were lost in the stormy night as he shouted something at the men trying to kill him.

For an infinitesimal moment, the woman faltered, a flicker of incomprehension flashing across her face. She cast a quick look over her shoulder at the one she was trying to protect. Their closest assailant moved and brought down his sword. The blade arced across her left arm, carving a deep cut from her elbow to her wrist.

A cry escaped her lips. She took a step back and warded off another blow inches from her neck. Hartwell moved forward then, anger blazing across his face. He raised his sword and joined in the fray once more.

Conrad got to within twenty feet of them before he crossed

paths with the four men he was trying to head off. He raised the double-bladed spear staff and spun it through the air. The gilded wood deflected the silver swirl of swords that danced toward his body while the jagged tips blurred, slicing and stabbing through flesh. One man fell, his fingers rising to the spurting crimson stream pouring from the wound on his neck. Another followed him to the ground seconds later.

A single scream suddenly shattered the night.

The sound was a knife that cut straight through Conrad's soul. He blocked a blow to his head and looked to his left.

William Hartwell had backed up against the balustrade. Conrad froze and felt time slow down.

The young man tipped over the edge and fell from the terrace, dragging his three attackers with him. The woman leapt forward through the curtain of glittering rain, crystal drops crashing on her skin, her movements heavy and sluggish in that stolen moment of stillness. She leaned over the balcony, fingers clutching desperately at the figures plummeting toward the ground. Her hands closed on empty space.

The bodies struck the street three stories below with a dull thud.

Time unfroze in a cacophony of sounds and sensations. Thunder rumbled across the heavens, underscoring the battle cries around Conrad. Cold wetness drenched his hair and face, bringing the sharp scent of the storm to his nostrils and a tangy taste to his lips. Lightning tore a brilliant, jagged path across his vision and made him blink.

Heat suddenly erupted across his chest when a blade slashed his skin. Blood bloomed on his shirt. Conrad scowled and focused on his two remaining adversaries. By the time he had disposed of them, the woman had disappeared from the rooftop.

He looked at the other fighters around him and felt a rush

of relief at the sight that met his eyes; despite the odds, his men were winning.

'Go!' yelled someone to his right. The red-haired figure who had spoken danced nimbly out of the way of a blade and stabbed his opponent savagely in the chest. Pale eyes glanced at him for a second. 'We've got this, Greene!'

Conrad bobbed his head jerkily and twisted the ring that retracted the staff's spear blades. He raced for the door that led inside the building.

By the time he reached the ground floor, the wound on his chest had stopped bleeding. He knew without looking that the skin beneath his torn shirt was once more unblemished.

He found the woman on her knees by the pile of bodies that lay in an awkward tangle of broken limbs at the north base of the Banqueting House. She was leaning over William Hartwell, sobs shuddering through her as she stroked his pale face with shaking fingers; blood from the wound in her arm mingled with his where it seeped from the irregular depression on his temple. Hartwell's chest rose and fell shallowly with his breaths. He was unconscious.

The woman looked around at Conrad's footsteps, her hazel eyes wild with anguish.

'Do something, please!' she begged.

Conrad sank to the ground next to her, his voice frozen in his throat. He placed his left hand on the young man's head and closed his eyes.

A burst of energy flared inside his chest and pulsed down toward his elbow. It darted through the birthmark dancing along his forearm and flashed to the ends of his fingers. He inhaled deeply and guided the flow of his power inside the broken body of William Hartwell.

Bone popped beneath his hand. The young man's flesh slowly began to knit together.

Sweat broke across Conrad's brow. The battle had drained him of much of his strength; he could feel Hartwell's torn tissues resisting his ability to heal them. He ground his teeth together and willed his exhausted body to cooperate.

'What's happening?' said the woman. Panic raised the pitch of her voice. She grabbed Conrad's shoulders and shook him, her fingers biting into his skin. 'Why isn't he waking up?'

Conrad sagged as he felt his own life force start to ebb; he was nearing the limits of his ability. He blinked and swayed. Dark blotches clouded his vision. The woman's frantic words became a roar in his ears.

A moan suddenly broke through the rush of blood inside his head. He looked down and saw Hartwell's eyes open. Within the dark pupils of the man he had come to know and love as a brother, Conrad Greene read the words he could no longer utter.

William Hartwell wanted to die. He also yearned for something else.

Conrad gasped and slowly pulled his power back inside his own body, his fingers trembling on the cooling skin of the dying man. Hartwell shivered beneath his touch.

'Why are you stopping?' yelled the woman. '*Save him!*'

Conrad knew there were only seconds left; he could feel Death's shadow approaching through the thunderstorm raging across the city. He leaned down and brought his lips to Hartwell's ear.

'I forgive you,' he whispered, his vision blurring with tears. He pulled back slightly and saw Hartwell blink once. The young man's last breath left his mouth and caressed Conrad's cheek.

William Hartwell stared unseeingly at the rain falling from the night sky, his face serene and his body relaxing in death.

'No,' mumbled the woman. 'No, this isn't happening!' Her voice rose to a scream. 'Why did you let him die? Why?

Goddamn you—!' Grief overwhelmed her and she wept brokenly.

Conrad's heart shattered inside his chest as he looked at the woman he loved and saw hate dawn in the depths of her hazel eyes.

CHAPTER TWO

OCTOBER 2011. AMAZON RAINFOREST. BRAZIL.

MOSQUITOES BUZZED ABOVE THE SWAMP, THE NOISE OF THEIR beating wings a dull drone that overlaid the heavy stillness of the sweltering afternoon. Here and there, a bubble of marsh gas broke through to the top of the pond. The sporadic squawks of macaws and toucans sounded from the neighboring trees, the sounds stifled in the sultry air.

A breeze drifted through a narrow inlet from the southeast. It rustled the leaves in the rainforest canopy and danced across the dark waters below. Ripples broke across the glassy surface and rocked the small, wooden raft nestled in the living carpet of giant water lilies that covered the swamp.

Something shifted in the stern of the canoe. It settled down again and panted loudly in the heat. A moment later, it huffed and let out a low whine.

From where he lay in the bow of the raft, Conrad Greene raised his hand and lazily adjusted the faded planter's hat covering his face. He peeked out from under the chewed, frayed brim at the dog sitting at his feet.

'What's up, Rocky?' he murmured.

The German Shepherd mongrel wrinkled his brow. He looked at Conrad anxiously before turning his head to peer at the trees crowding the north bank of the swamp.

Conrad followed the dog's gaze to a black shape perched on the low-lying branch of a strangler fig some fifty feet away. The jaguar watched them unblinkingly, its golden irises shining eerily in the gloom under the canopy. The tip of its tail swung lazily from side to side in a hypnotic rhythm that swatted flies away from its lean, sinewy body.

The sudden lack of chatter from the boisterous group of squirrel monkeys who lived in the trees around the marsh should have alerted Conrad to the arrival of the predator. He observed the creature for silent seconds before acknowledging it with a brief nod. The jaguar's tail froze for a moment before resuming its idle dance.

It was almost nine months to the day since the big cat had started hanging out on his land, deep in the floodplains north-west of the town of Alvarães, in the Brazilian state of Amazonas. Conrad could recall their first encounter with vivid clarity. It hadn't gone so well.

During a stormy night in the rainy season, when lightning flashed across the skies and heavy squalls rattled the walls of his home, he had woken to Rocky's whimpers under his bed and the growls of the jaguar as she prowled the deck of the wood cabin. For the first time in almost seventy years, Conrad had had to draw his staff to defend himself. It was either that or have his throat ripped open by the wounded and desperately hungry predator, who he suspected had been preying on Rocky, still a puppy at the time.

Once he defeated the injured big cat, Conrad had used his unearthly immortal power to restore her to health. His reward had been a hail of angry hisses and a collection of scratches intended to disembowel him. Still, the jaguar seemed to have formed an uneasy connection with the immortal since the incident and kept returning to the swamp.

When he recounted this tale to his closest neighbor during one of their monthly drinking sessions, the old woman concluded the jaguar had a crush on him and burst out laughing until tears streamed down her tanned, leathery face. Conrad had to slap her on the back when her breath left her nicotine-stained lips in protracted wheezes. He decided to name the jaguar after her.

He turned to the dog. 'It's only Roxanne.'

Rocky whimpered, lowered his head on his forepaws, and hunched his shoulders. He had never forgotten the night the jaguar had intended to have him for dinner.

Conrad sighed. 'Seriously, you need to grow some balls, you big wuss. You're about ten times the size you were when you first met her. Where's your wolf pride?'

The dog's brown eyes drilled steadily into his face. The immortal resisted the soulful gaze for all of five seconds; he suspected a sheep lay somewhere in the dog's distant ancestry.

'All right. Let's give it another half hour and see if anything bites,' he muttered.

The dog lifted his head, bushy tail thumping the bottom of the canoe. Conrad adjusted the fishing rod on his lap, lay back down, and moved the hat over his face. Silence descended on the swamp once more.

Five minutes later, the raft rocked violently in the water.

'What the—?' started Conrad, jerking upright.

Rocky was up on all fours in the stern of the canoe. Head held high and ears pricked forward, he stared intently past Conrad at the sky to the west. A low hiss erupted from the branch of the strangler fig. The jaguar disappeared into the forest in a rustle of leaves.

Conrad inspected the patch of blue rising above the green rim of the canopy. Bar some popcorn-shaped clouds high up in the atmosphere, it was empty.

'What is it, boy?' he said, frowning at the dog. A soft growl rose from the throat of the German Shepherd mongrel.

As the agitated squeals and calls of monkeys erupted from the branches of giant mahogany and kapok trees around the swamp, Conrad finally heard the sound that had unnerved the dog and the jaguar. It was the faint buzz of an aircraft.

He put the fishing rod down and rose carefully to his feet. The raft swayed beneath him. He removed his hat and shaded his eyes as he gazed at the heavens.

There was an airport in Tefé, a city on the banks of the Rio Solimoes, just over ten miles south of Alvarães. Although the sight and sound of a plane were not exactly rare in the rainforest, Conrad knew his land did not lie below any direct flight paths. Which meant that the aircraft had to be a private charter.

The noise grew closer, the buzz changing into a stuttering, high-pitched whir. Conrad stiffened. There was something wrong with the plane's engine.

Rocky's growl grew louder. The dog let out a bark and jumped on his hind legs. The canoe lurched precariously beneath them. Conrad staggered sideways and almost fell overboard.

'Goddammit, Rocky, will you cut it—!' he snapped. It was as far as he got.

A growing shape blotted out the sun and darkened the sky. Trailing smoke and flames from its left wing, a twin-engine Cessna arrowed down toward him in a deafening roar that shook the canopy and eclipsed the dog's wild barks.

Conrad twisted on his heels, dove for the German Shepherd, and carried him over the gunwale of the canoe. The downdraft from the Cessna washed over them as they plunged beneath the cool surface of the swamp, engulfed in fleeting twilight by the shadow of the plane.

An explosion rocked the air. The pressure waves from the blast shook the floating water lilies and overturned the canoe. Conrad emerged from the water with a gasp. He coughed and wiped wet hair from his eyes while he looked around.

Rocky paddled the surface of the pond several feet away. The dog's ears flattened against his skull as he gazed despondently at the southeast bank of the swamp. A whimper escaped his jaws.

Conrad followed his line of sight and froze. 'You have got to be kidding me,' he muttered dully.

The space where his home had stood for sixty-five years was now occupied by a giant ball of fire. The Cessna had crashed into his cabin.

Conrad swore and started for the shore, his strokes carving the water deftly. Rocky followed, the planter hat clamped firmly in his jaws. The dog's forepaws scrabbled onto the pitted, scarred surface of the wooden jetty abutting the bank seconds before the immortal pulled himself out of the water.

Rocky climbed onto the rickety pier, dropped the hat, and shook himself energetically. Conrad barely noticed the spray of cool drops that splashed him from head to toe as he watched the conflagration some fifty feet away. Heat from the raging flames washed over him in waves that started to dry the moisture on his skin. The stench of kerosene was overwhelming. He headed toward the fire.

The Cessna's aft fuselage and tail were the only visible parts of the plane that had remained intact after the crash; rising from the center of the wreckage, they angled awkwardly toward the sky, silent witnesses to the wake of explosive destruction around them.

Conrad stopped and observed the burning debris that dotted the landscape. There were no signs of the flames threatening to spread to the shrubs and trees next to the swamp, a fact that was aided by the heavy humidity and waterlogged land. A frown dawned on his face as he slowly circumnavigated the remains of the aircraft and the ruins of his dwelling. He knew the chances of finding any survivors were remote at best. He soon spotted the body of the pilot.

The head and shoulders of the burning corpse could be seen sticking out from the rubble of what had once been his bedroom. If not at the moment of the collision, the man would have died during the explosion that followed.

Conrad grimaced. If the crash had happened at night, he and the dog would have been toast. His eyes followed the black fumes spiraling sluggishly toward the sky. It would only be a matter of minutes before someone in Alvarães spotted the smoke trail. Fear of a forest fire would have the authorities on his doorstep by the afternoon.

He turned and started to negotiate the area around the blast zone. Tail tucked firmly between his hind legs, Rocky padded silently next to him.

It was the dog who found the second body. About thirty feet south of the point of impact, at the end of a trail of flattened orchids and heliconias, a figure lay jammed between the buttress roots of a young kapok tree.

Conrad squatted and inspected the still shape held at an awkward angle in the timber embrace of the rainforest. The scent of the crushed flowers was at odds with the stench of burnt flesh rising from the dead man in the suit. The tilt of his head and legs indicated a broken back and neck.

Rocky whimpered and lowered his nose to the ground. He leaned forward cautiously and sniffed the area next to the body before rising with his forepaws against the buttress roots. He let out a sharp bark.

Conrad followed the dog's excited gaze to a branch some forty feet above the ground.

'Well, I'll be damned,' he muttered.

Caught on the hanging vines dripping from the moss-covered bough was a slim, metal briefcase. The immortal studied the line of Bala ants marching up the trunk of the tree. Climbing to retrieve the case was not an option; he had been stung by the giant ants too many times to even think about risking their painful wrath. After a moment's contemplation, he stood up, reached behind his back, and retrieved the gilded staff tucked in the waistband of his trousers.

'What d'you reckon?' he asked the dog, spinning the rod between his fingers. Rocky huffed approvingly.

Conrad twisted the second ring on the shaft and pulled on the ends of the weapon. The staff came apart to reveal a pair of gleaming short swords. The dog jumped back at the slick, metallic noise, a low whine escaping his jaws.

Conrad lifted his right arm behind his head and threw the blade in his hand. The sword cartwheeled in the air with a faint hum and sliced neatly through the creepers holding the briefcase prisoner. It fell to the fern-covered ground. The sword thudded into the earth next to it, gilded end vibrating to a slow stop.

The immortal bent and retrieved the case. Bar some superficial scratches, it was intact. He turned it and stared at the combination lock on the front. His gaze shifted to the dead man. He placed the briefcase on a giant root, walked over to the body, and patted it down under Rocky's anxious stare. His fingers closed on a wallet in the inside pocket of the suit jacket. He stood and flicked it open.

The dead man's surname was McPherson. He couldn't make out the rest of the details of the California driving license tucked inside the front holder; the wallet was heavily scorched. He raised an eyebrow when he found the burnt remains of a dozen hundred-dollar bills and a half-melted Amex card. The rest of the wallet was empty. There was no sign of a code for the combination lock.

Conrad turned and considered the briefcase. If the plane was indeed a charter as he suspected, a flight plan should have been filed with the airport where it took off. There would, however, have been no legal requirement on the part of the pilot to include the name of his passenger. The contents of the case might reveal the identity of the dead man.

He eyed the dog questioningly. Rocky barked once, his tail spinning furiously from side to side. Taking that as a sign of the canine's approval, Conrad wedged the briefcase between the roots of the kapok tree, raised a sword, and jabbed sharply at the combination lock. It broke after three blows.

He sheathed the twin blades, tucked the short staff inside his waistband, and picked up the case. Rocky trotted beside him as he headed for an open area of land away from the trees. He knelt down in the dirt, placed the briefcase on the ground, and unfastened the clasps. The dog's hot pants washed over his neck as he lifted the lid. His hands stilled on the metal.

The case contained two items. The first one was a thick envelope; the second was a 9mm semiautomatic Colt pistol lying atop it. Rocky lowered his head and sniffed at the gun. Conrad pushed the dog's muzzle aside and carefully picked up the weapon. He checked the chamber. It was loaded.

He removed the magazine, ejected the bullet from the port, and placed the gun on the ground. He reached for the envelope next. A loose sheaf of papers fell out and scattered across the rich, moist earth as he lifted it.

He scooped it up and examined the short, cryptic lines covering the top sheet. The next two papers were folded maps depicting the areas of a large outside space and the floor plans of an oval-shaped building. Sunlight gleamed on the glossy surfaces of the remaining ten sheets as he slowly thumbed through them.

They were all photographs, each depicting a different, solemn individual dressed in a conservative suit and wearing sunglasses. Although they all had loose-fitting jackets over their shirts, he spotted the strap of a gun holster and the curling wire of an earpiece on several of them. From their poses, they had all been unaware they were being snapped. His fingers froze on the last shot. Rocky huffed and licked the picture.

Coldness gripped Conrad as he stared at the hauntingly familiar features of Laura Hartwell.

CHAPTER THREE

THE LATE AFTERNOON SUN WAS BATHING THE SWAMP IN RED
light when Conrad finally departed the clearing where his home
once stood. As he suspected, officers from the Alvarães civil
police and the local branch of the military firefighter corps
arrived by boat barely an hour after the crash.

Rocky's barks alerted him to their approach. By the time
they reached the mouth of the small channel that snaked
through the rainforest floodplain from the lake next to
Alvarães, the fire had died down and only smoldering parts of
his cabin and the larger sections of the Cessna remained. He
watched the vessels chug steadily toward the jetty and strolled
down to meet them.

'Olá, Conrad,' said the olive-skinned man who stepped out
of the first motorboat.

'Matheus,' Conrad acknowledged with a brief nod.

Matheus Luiz Diaz was a senior officer of the Alvarães
District Police. Like his father before him, he had trained and
worked extensively in Manaus, the capital city of the state. Now
in his late forties and married with three children, he bore the

same wiry build Matheus senior had retained until an untimely death from a heart attack half a decade ago.

Conrad became aware of a pair of wary stares. He glanced at the two officers who had accompanied Diaz. The men lowered their eyes hastily and started chatting with the firefighters in the second boat, a hint of anxiety evident in their voices. The immortal swallowed a sigh. He could hardly blame the policemen. He was a legend among the superstitious locals.

Although Diaz used to regard him with the same guarded expression, the police officer appeared to have come to terms with the mystery that was Conrad's existence, despite the fact that they first met when the man was still in diapers.

There had been many tales and fables concerning Conrad bandied about in the area over the years. The immortal himself had been responsible for several of them. His all-time favorite was the story of how he had discovered the elusive Tree of Life while exploring the jungles of the Amazon sixty years ago, drank from it, and promptly burned it to the ground. The one he took the most offense to was about him being the reincarnation of an ancient demon god who feasted on the flesh of the sacred creatures of the forest, thus gaining longevity and eternal youth from the souls of his damned victims.

Though he was no vegetarian, Conrad humanely slaughtered and cooked the animals he ate. And last time he looked, he had failed to grow any horns, fangs, or claws to justify the first half of that particular myth. His birthmark had not helped matters. As far as the locals were concerned, someone with a black Aesculapian snake on his forearm was not exactly an ode to virtuousness.

'Well, that's not something you see everyday,' said Diaz in Portuguese. He stood next to Conrad on the bank of the swamp and contemplated the wreckage of the Cessna amidst the smoking ruins of the log cabin. 'What happened?' He bent and ruffled Rocky's ears. The dog whined and licked the police-man's face.

'A plane fell out of the sky and ruined my fishing day,' Conrad replied.

Diaz grunted and shook his head. He muttered something under his breath about now having seen it all and gestured to his men.

'You catch anything?' said the policeman as his officers lifted boxes of equipment out of the boat.

'I did,' said Conrad. 'It got dumped back in the water when the boat flipped.'

'That's tough,' murmured Diaz. 'Still, it could have been worse.'

Conrad stared mutely from him to the remains of the cabin.

'It could have crashed right on top of you is all I'm saying,' said Diaz with a shrug.

'Well, it kinda did,' retorted the immortal.

The officers took his statement and set to work quickly, examining and photographing the scene of the accident while daylight still remained. Forensic help from Manaus would not be dispatched for at least a couple days, and they could not leave the two corpses where they lay. The firefighters declared the area safe and left after half an hour, their vessel churning the waters of the swamp with a whiff of gasoline as it disappeared through the inlet toward Alvarães.

Conrad watched silently as Diaz's men zipped the two corpses in the body bags that had been brought across by a third boat. He had returned the passenger's wallet to the inside pocket of his charred suit and taken a close look at the man's hands minutes before the authorities arrived. The metal brief-case was at the bottom of the swamp.

Diaz and his officers left just after five. Conrad bade them goodbye and waited until the sound of their motorboats faded in the distance before he turned and strode into the forest, Rocky at his heels.

A giant sandbox tree stood some two hundred feet from the swamp. He squatted at the north base of the trunk and pulled at the vegetation on the ground. Concealed beneath the living camouflage he had arranged over the bulging roots was a dirt-colored trapdoor. Rocky nosed at his hands when he opened it and exposed the hollow space underneath.

The cavity measured four by three feet and was nearly half as deep. It contained a large, gray, army metal crate fastened with an industrial-sized padlock. He retrieved the key from a crack inside the sandbox tree and opened the container. Oiled hinges moved silently when he lifted the lid.

The envelope that had been in the dead man's briefcase lay near the top of the chest. He dropped it inside an empty, worn, military-issue rucksack. Rocky sniffed at the other contents of the container, crossed his eyes, and sneezed.

Conrad scratched the dog behind the ears as he contemplated the collection of firearms laid neatly in narrow compartments at the bottom of the crate. It had been a couple of months since he last cleaned them. He selected a Heckler & Koch P8 semiautomatic pistol and put it in the backpack along with some magazines.

Taped to the lid of the crate were half a dozen waterproof Ziploc bags. He removed the one that contained a passport, a wad of hundred-dollar bills, and some savings bonds, and tucked the whole thing inside his waistband.

Conrad locked the chest, closed the trapdoor, rearranged the green screen, and put the key back in its hiding place. He sniffed at his shirt. His clothes had long since dried in the permanent heat that lingered under the canopy of the rainforest. They now held the stench of smoke, sweat, and death. He wrinkled his nose; he seriously needed to change. Unfortunately, all his earthly belongings had gone up in flames in the explosion that followed the plane crash.

'Ah well, you'll just have to live with the smell, boy,' he told Rocky with a sigh.

The dog huffed and licked his hand. Conrad returned to the swamp, walked over to the jetty, and dropped the backpack in the stern of the canoe. The vessel rocked slightly, the puddles at the bottom gleaming in the crimson light.

Rocky hopped inside the raft, eyes shining and excited huffs leaving his jaws as his tail traced frantic circles in the air; he had been a hardcore fan of boat rides ever since he was a puppy.

Conrad turned and cast a final look at the place that had been his sanctuary for six decades. Although he was loath to leave it and return to the world he had willingly abandoned, he no longer had a choice in the matter. The contents of the dead man's briefcase had seen to that.

As the evening calls and cries of the rainforest wildlife rang out across the darkening canopy, he stepped inside the canoe, picked up the oar, and headed east into the forest toward the Rio Solimoes.

It was dark by the time they reached Roxanne's hut. The aroma of cooked cassava, fried green bananas, and grilled fish reached Conrad's nostrils well before he saw the flickering yellow flames of a fire between the trees. He guided the raft to a narrow landing abutting a bank that held a small house on stilts.

A short, stout shadow appeared in the doorway of the thatch and wood construct as they disembarked. Rocky scampered ahead, a friendly whine escaping his jaws. His claws clattered on worn hardwood as he climbed the steps to the shallow porch. The figure at the top leaned down and patted his head before straightening slowly with a crackle and pop of arthritic bones.

The orange glow of a tobacco roll flared in the gloom. The

heady, pungent smell of Roxanne's homemade mapacho cigarette drifted toward Conrad as he paused at the foot of the stairs.

'Olá, *Deus Demônio*,' said Roxanne in a parchment-dry voice.

'Olá, *Ela Diabo*,' muttered Conrad in response.

The old woman chuckled. Wispy tendrils of tobacco smoke escaped her lips and curved hazily in the warm air. Rocky sniffed at them and wrinkled his nose.

'What brings you to my doorstep tonight?' the old woman continued in Portuguese. She cast a glance at the shed behind the house. 'If it's moonshine you're after, you're a week early.'

Conrad mulled over the words that had been going through his head during the boat ride to the old woman's house.

Roxanne's rheumy gaze drifted from him to the treetops. 'I saw the smoke in the sky and heard the boats go by. Did something happen?'

'Yes.' He did not elaborate further. Knowing Roxanne, she would hear all the gory details before the next day's end. It never ceased to amaze him how much she knew of local affairs, given that she rarely left the hut.

The woman's wizened stare bore into his face. Although more than half a century had passed since Conrad first met her, she looked almost exactly the same now as she did then. He did not know how old she was and had never asked. Age was irrelevant to someone like him. He studied his neighbor and wondered not for the first time whether *she* was the one who had discovered the Tree of Life.

'I would invite you in, but I sense you're in a rush,' said Roxanne. 'Say your piece, my friend, for I can see the words pressing to get past your lips.'

Conrad smiled faintly. She knew him all too well. 'I have a favor to ask of you.' He hesitated. 'Can you look after Rocky?'

The dog's head rose at the mention of his name. His ears

pricked forward, as if aware of the somber tone of the conversation.

Roxanne replied with a question. 'You going on a trip?' She looked at the rucksack in the canoe. Conrad nodded.

The night crowded in around them while they watched each other. Monkeys chattered in the branches overshadowing the stilt house. Something howled in the distance and crashed through the undergrowth.

'You planning on coming back?' said Roxanne finally.

Conrad shrugged. 'I hope so.'

The woman scrutinized him for a while longer. 'All right. I'll look after him for you. But don't leave it too long. You know he'll pine after you, and there's nothing worse than a miserable dog.'

Conrad gave her a grateful smile and turned to Rocky. 'Come here.'

Rocky darted down the stairs and jumped up to rest his forepaws against Conrad's chest. He stretched his head and licked the immortal's face with slobbery enthusiasm.

'Good boy,' Conrad praised. He scratched him vigorously behind the ears. The dog whimpered and rolled his eyes in delight. 'You be good and stay with Roxanne, 'kay? I have to go somewhere.'

Rocky's expression turned wary. A small whine escaped his throat. Conrad ignored the ache in his chest and turned to walk away. The dog sank to the ground. He glanced anxiously between the hut and the boat, and loped after him.

Conrad stopped in his tracks. 'Stay,' he ordered in a hard voice over his shoulder.

Rocky skidded to a halt. He dropped his head, hunched his shoulders, and lowered his body toward the ground, his tail drooping between his hind legs. Large brown eyes gleamed in the faint light oozing through the open doorway of the stilt house.

Conrad sighed and twisted on his heels. He squatted in front of the dog, grabbed him behind the ears, and tugged him forward until their foreheads touched.

'I need to do this,' the immortal said softly. 'Consider it a temporary separation.' He paused. 'I *will* come back for you. After all, we are bound, you and I.' He lowered one hand and touched the dog's forechest.

Rocky stilled and peered unblinkingly into his eyes. A moment of silent communion passed between man and dog. Then, he huffed and licked Conrad's face.

The immortal rose reluctantly and headed toward the water. Rocky padded after him and stopped on the landing. The dog watched him climb inside the canoe.

Conrad picked up the oar, looked at the two silent figures on the bank, and dipped the paddle in the inky water. He rowed away into the darkness, his strokes strong and steady.

A howl tore through the night a short time later, the forlorn goodbye piercing his chest with the force of a well-aimed arrow. Unbidden, the immortal's hand rose to rub a spot over his heart.

CHAPTER FOUR

CONRAD REACHED ALVARÃES SHORTLY BEFORE SEVEN IN THE evening and hitched a ride in the back of a livestock truck for the five-mile trip to the village of Noguiera, on the north shore of Lake Tefé. By the time he arrived on the outskirts of the small settlement hedging an expanse of pale, sandy beach, Conrad was convinced he smelled worse than the animals he had shared the flatbed with.

Since the motorboats that would have taken him across the water to Tefé town itself only operated during daylight hours, he had to find someone disposed to make the journey at night. It took half an hour and a hundred-dollar bill to hunt down and persuade such a willing subject. By the anxious glances the man cast at the birthmark on Conrad's arm, the immortal's reputation had preceded him.

Shortly after landing at the docks in Tefé, Conrad walked inside a small, lean-to liquor store, slid some coins across the serving counter, and asked if he could make a call. The boy behind the till palmed the money and brought out an old rotary dial telephone from underneath the table.

The immortal rang the local airport. He placed the receiver

back in its cradle a couple of minutes later, thanked the boy, and walked out of the shack. The first scheduled flight to Manaus was not until the afternoon of the next day. His instincts told him he could not afford to wait that long.

He stood on the dirt road and looked out over the dark waters of the lake. Waves lapped against the wooden pilings of a floating pontoon some thirty feet away. An occasional bark of laughter broke the nighttime chatter rising from his left. He came to a decision, turned, and headed for the town's main strip.

Several drinks and a number of run-down bars later, Conrad tracked down the owner of a small propeller plane. The middle-aged man knocked back half a beer and spilled as much again as he listened to the immortal's request. Silence fell between them when Conrad finished talking. The pilot blinked bloodshot eyes and studied him with a glazed expression. Just when the immortal thought he should try and find someone else to broker a deal with, the man leaned across the table, which was nothing more than three stained planks balanced on a couple of empty oil drums, and admitted in a gruff, alcohol-laced breath that he would be open to taking on a private job for a suitable monetary incentive. The right price turned out to be an expensive bottle of whisky and four hundred dollars in cash.

They left the bar minutes after concluding their arrangement and headed for the man's truck, parked a couple of streets away. Conrad took one look at the way he staggered across the road and went in search of some strong coffee. He swapped the cup for the keys in the mumbling man's grasp and drove the vintage Ford pickup the short distance to the airport.

The pilot walked into the booking office in a comparatively straight line to file their flight plan to Manaus. Conrad waited outside the red-roofed building, his back against the hood of the vehicle as he gazed at the star-filled night sky. He wondered whether he would ever see it again from this place he had come to call home.

The plane turned out to be a 1965 two-seater Cessna 150F. It was in as good a state as the Ford truck, and a whole lot better condition than its owner. Half an hour after they arrived at Tefé airport, they were in the air. Since there was only one headset for the pilot, Conrad settled back in his seat, closed his eyes, and hoped to God he would get to Manaus in one piece. He really did not want to waste one of his remaining lives crashing in a blaze of fire in the middle of the rainforest. An image of the dead man with the briefcase flashed through his mind at the thought.

It was nearly midnight when they landed at a small aero club some three miles north of the center of the capital. The pilot bade him goodbye and headed off in search of a bar. Conrad walked out of the airport grounds and strolled down the road to a nearby motel. He booked a room for the night, took a long, cold shower, and rang for laundry service. He handed the maid who came to the room his clothes and a large tip, locked the door after her, and put the gilded staff on the nightstand next to the bed. He climbed naked under the thin cotton sheet and lay staring at the dark ceiling while he pondered the events of the day.

He had no doubt something nasty was about to go down. The loaded gun and the cryptic contents of the envelope aside, the dead man's bare wallet spoke of someone who did not want to be easily identified. He suspected the driving license was a fake. And, in his professional opinion, people engaged in scrupulous activities did not usually walk around with that much hard cash in hand and calluses on their fingers from heavy gun use.

The what, where, and when of the event, however, remained a total mystery. As to the who, the one woman on Earth least likely to be pleased about his involvement in the affair appeared to be right in the middle of it all.

Sleep proved to be an elusive beast. After the nocturnal lullaby of the rainforest, the alien sounds of the city jarred Conrad's nerves. He lay awake for a good couple of hours and finally dozed off at around three in the morning.

His freshly washed clothes were in a garment bag hanging outside his door when he got up the next day. He checked out of the motel shortly after nine and took a cab to the financial district of the city.

The vehicle's air con was broken and its driver unseasonably chatty. By the time the car pulled up along a busy road, sweat was running in rivulets down Conrad's back; not only had he caught up on the recent political scandals that had shaken the city's administration, he had also been brought up to speed on more local news and TV gossip than he had ever wanted to know.

He paid the cabbie and waited until the car disappeared in the heavy traffic before crossing the road to a sleek, glass and steel building. Beyond the discreet front door of the gleaming tower was the cool, monochrome lobby of a bank. An immaculately dressed young woman sat on a stool behind the reception. She regarded him politely as he crossed the marble floor toward her. Conrad stopped in front of the desk and spoke in a low voice.

The woman's eyebrows rose fractionally at his words. Her gaze skimmed over the birthmark on his left forearm and darted toward the tellers' counter behind him. Conrad gave her his best smile. Although he had showered again this morning, he suspected his two-day stubble and shabby clothes did not quite match up with the bold statement he had just made.

He reached inside the rear waistband of his trousers under the receptionist's increasingly anxious stare. His fingers brushed against the staff weapon tucked in the small of his back before closing on the Ziploc bag. He took out one of the savings bonds and placed it on the desk.

The receptionist paled when she saw the denomination and stamp date on the certificate. She stammered a profuse apology and swiftly dialed an extension.

Forty minutes later, Conrad strolled out of the building with more liquid assets than he had when he walked in. The bank's senior funds manager, a portly man with a receding hairline and sweaty hands, insisted he made full use of the establishment's facilities before he left. Conrad had thanked him and politely asked if he could use a phone in private. He was quickly ushered to an empty meeting room with a panoramic view of the city. The funds manager told him to take his time and closed the door on his way out.

Conrad leaned against the glossy, beech and chrome table that dominated the space and picked up the trim, modern phone that sat upon it. He made two calls.

The first was to a number in Rio de Janeiro. It went to voicemail after six rings. He listened to the message that followed, disconnected, and contemplated the glimmering waters of the Rio Negro in the far distance.

He picked up the phone again and dialed the number of a private jet charter company he had used in the past. After confirming the details of his reservation, he arranged the transfer of a substantial sum of money into their accounts.

The receptionist smiled graciously at him when he walked back into the lobby of the bank a couple of minutes later. He smiled back and saw her blush as he exited the building.

A shiny, black executive sedan with tinted windows pulled up at the curb as the door swung shut behind him. A man in a dark suit got out of the driver's seat and scanned him with a neutral expression.

'Mr. Greene?' he said with a hint of a Texan accent.

Conrad inclined his head.

'I'm the chauffeur from the charter company,' said the man.

The immortal raised his eyebrows. 'That was quick.'

'I was in the area,' the man explained with a civil smile. He opened the rear door of the vehicle. Conrad climbed inside the air-conditioned space and settled on the pristine, cream leather seat.

Fifteen minutes later, the car rolled to a stop next to a gleaming, white Learjet 31 parked on the tarmac of the private business zone of Manaus's main international airport. Conrad stepped out into the dazzling sunlight. He gave the Texan a tip and strolled toward the figure waiting at the bottom of the jet's steps. The man in the pilot's uniform walked forward and offered his hand.

'Hello, Mr. Greene,' he said in a broad Georgian accent. His smile furrowed the pale crow's feet fanning out from his eyes. 'This ain't your usual time of year to be making this trip.'

Conrad smiled and shook the man's hand. 'Hi, Bill. Yeah, something came up.'

The pilot observed the rucksack on the immortal's shoulder. 'Traveling light again, I see.'

The immortal shrugged noncommittally and followed him up the steps to the cabin. The pilot showed him to a table with a tray of complimentary food and drink, and headed for the cockpit. The jet got under way and lifted off moments later. Weather conditions permitting, their flight to Rio de Janeiro would take just under four hours.

Conrad helped himself to a delicious shrimp salad and a beer before moving to the large sofa at the back of the plane. He put his feet up, made himself comfortable, and opened the dead man's envelope.

The first sheet occupied his attention for half an hour. He studied the random, enigmatic text until his vision practically blurred and came to the conclusion that all of it was written in code. The first three lines intrigued him the most. Structured in the form of a haiku, a short Japanese poem, they read:

"On Freda's Dark Day
For the Rightful Blood to rise
The Falcon must fall"

It appeared to be some sort of message. As to what it stood for and for whom it was intended, he still had no clue. Next, he analyzed the floor plans of the oval building and the map of its exterior from every possible angle. He decided they would be impossible to interpret without a point of reference; considering most of his excursions from the rainforest in the last sixty-odd years had been restricted to his trips to Rio, he could have been staring at the latest Opera House in London for all he knew.

The photographs he left for last. It was obvious to him that the people featured on them worked for some sort of government agency. Whether they were CIA, MI5, or Mossad was difficult to ascertain from the limited details in the shots.

He was still staring at the picture of Laura Hartwell when the pilot's voice came over the intercom and informed him that they would be landing shortly. He put the envelope back in his bag, buckled up, and looked out of the nearest porthole just as the plane crossed the Serra do Mar mountain range.

The state of Rio de Janeiro spread out across the landscape through the thinning clouds below, a wide plateau of peaks and rainforests interspersed with coffee and sugar plantations that gradually gave way to coastal plains. Guanabara Bay appeared ahead, its glinting dark waters heralding the hazy, cobalt expanse of the Atlantic Ocean beyond.

Hugging the western shore of the bay was the state's namesake capital city. As the Learjet turned on its final approach to Galeão International Airport, the girder bridge that joined Rio to the neighboring municipality of Niterói drifted into view. Conrad caught glimpses of the iconic landmarks of Sugarloaf Mountain and the white, soapstone and concrete statue of Christ the Redeemer on Corcovado Mountain through the mantle of smog that blanketed the city.

His biennial pilgrimage to Rio had started some eighteen months after he retreated from civilization at the end of the Second World War. Although he had wanted nothing else but to spend the rest of his protracted immortal existence in the peace and solitude of the rainforest, three centuries of service as a senior intelligence operative in the Bastian First Council had instilled habits that were hard to break. Following an internal debate that lasted two weeks, Conrad concluded it wouldn't do any harm to keep up to date with world events and scientific developments once in a while. However good he was at covering his tracks, his instincts told him he would not be able to hide from the Bastian immortal society forever. He wanted to be ready if and when they came knocking at his door.

His trips to the city were one month long, and he spent most of that time catching up on global advances in the sciences and general technologies, particularly weapons and military engineering, as well as politics and the major cultural changes sweeping across the world. In the first forty or so years, this was achieved by reading newspapers in coffee shops, trawling through the city's libraries, and clandestinely touching base with the odd friend as well as old military connections. His voyages during the two decades spanning the mid 1960s to the early 1980s were often fraught with danger. With the country under the rule of a series of military dictatorships, the army aggressively pursued anyone they suspected of being a foreign political insurgent. His skills as a former agent kept him well beneath their radar during those years of autocracy.

Then came the advent of computers and the Internet. With his outings suddenly more streamlined, Conrad rediscovered the pleasures of the more physical pursuits of weapons and combat training. He had not realized how much he missed sparring with a skilled opponent until he knocked out his first man during a no-holds-barred fight in a seedy underground club in the city.

Since he rarely went anywhere without his staff weapon, he started to make his trips by private charter when airport security tightened up in the 1970s. Although it was technically legal to carry a bladed weapon in checked luggage, the last thing he wanted was attention from the authorities. Money was hardly an issue; despite the fact that he had donated most of his fortune to various charities when he went into self-imposed exile, there was still a considerable amount of it left in his accounts.

Forty minutes after landing at the airport, Conrad walked out of the men's toilet dressed in a newly purchased casual short-sleeved shirt, chinos, and Doc Martens. His backpack was bulkier from his purchases at one of the chain stores in the main terminal building.

He strolled into the offices of a local rental car company and booked a Ford Focus for the day. His old clothes and shoes went inside a trashcan in the parking lot. He climbed inside the vehicle, turned the air con to full power, and soon merged with the traffic headed south on the expressway.

Bottlenecks started to form shortly after he took the exit ramp for the neighborhood of Sao Cristovao. Horns blared and tires shrieked around him as cars, courier bikes, and pedestrians fought for space on the road. The sidewalks swarmed with the lunchtime crowd, droves of people milling around the food stands and snack bars that dotted the narrow space. The aroma of grilled meat and fried tapioca floated above the acrid stench of exhaust fumes.

He finally made it to the edges of the Manguiera shanty-town and stopped the Ford on a quiet street halfway down a hill. Just under a mile to the south and across an expanse of railway tracks, the pale facade of the Maracana stadium and its blue bracing pillars shimmered in the afternoon heat.

Conrad propped his elbows on the steering wheel and studied the dilapidated, two-story structure sitting on a corner plot two doors down and across the street from where he had parked. The drawn curtains on the first floor and the roller shutters across the front of the establishment projected an air of abandonment. The sign above the lintel read "Eterno Bar." The irony of it did not escape him.

He grabbed the backpack, exited the rental, and crossed the road to the building. A rust-stained, corrugated iron door stood in the wall around the side. He rapped his knuckles sharply on the metal sheet and waited.

Seconds ticked by. Nothing happened. Conrad sighed and knocked again. It took another couple of minutes of persistent banging to elicit a response from the inside of the edifice.

'All right, all right, I'm coming! Keep your goddamned panties on!' someone bellowed in Portuguese from the other side of the door. There was a shuffle of footsteps followed by the sound of a key turning in a lock. A bolt slid against metal and the portal creaked open.

A monstrous figure with a shock of disheveled, tawny hair and a beard loomed in the doorway. Eerie, pale eyes squinted sleepily in the bright sunlight. There was a sharp intake of breath. The eyes shrank into narrow slits.

'You!' the figure hissed.

Conrad gaped at the apparition. 'What's with the beard?'

The man snorted and slammed the door shut in his face. The bolt slid back in place.

'Hey!' shouted Conrad. He thumped loudly on the metal panel. 'What the hell's with that reaction?'

'Go away!' the giant yelled from the other side.

'I can do this all day, you know,' Conrad retorted grimly, still pounding on the door. Sweat pooled down the sides of his face and dripped onto his new shirt. He was aware of windows opening and people emerging on doorsteps further along the road.

'All right!' the man barked. 'Jeez, you're such a pain in the ass!'

Conrad lowered his fist. The footsteps returned. The door opened once more.

'Well, what are you standing there like a moron for? Come on in,' grumbled the orange-haired colossus.

Conrad followed the man down a cramped alley that gave way to a surprisingly pleasant, paved backyard. A metal grille swung shut behind them as they entered the cool interior of the building. They headed past a staircase and a galley kitchen to a large, dark space at the front. The giant disappeared in the gloom to the left, his steps heavy on the hardwood floor.

Conrad stopped in his tracks and blinked. It took a few seconds for his vision to adjust to the shadows. Dim shapes slowly materialized in front of him. There was a click from the left. Muted lights came on, illuminating the room.

Instead of the hovel that the exterior of the building suggested it would be, Eterno Bar was an unexpectedly clean and well-maintained drinking establishment. Period pieces from bygone eras dotted the floorboards and blended artfully with old furniture bearing elegant lines and a sheen of polish. Antique gaslights graced the ceiling and the pale walls, which held a scatter of faded black and white photographs.

'This place hasn't changed much.' Conrad strolled to the curved counter and climbed on one of the wooden stools arranged in a neat half circle beneath it.

The man with the orange hair grunted noncommittally and extracted two glasses and a dark bottle from a shelf behind the bar.

'So, what's with the grouchy attitude and the beard?' said Conrad.

The man glared at him. 'What the hell kinda time do you call this? And the beard's none of your beeswax.'

Conrad looked pointedly at his watch. 'It's one in the afternoon.' He inspected the giant's facial growth. 'You got bored of shaving or something?'

'I only went to bed at seven this morning,' the man retorted. 'I need my beauty sleep. I'm getting old.' He hesitated. 'The ladies say I look better with a beard,' he added in a low mumble. The tips of his ears went the same shade as his hair.

Conrad cocked an eyebrow at the Bastian immortal who had once been his colonel and third in command. At five hundred and sixty-odd years old, Horatio Cassius Gordian had almost an extra century on Conrad. Together with Gordian's cousin on his mother's side, they had enlisted in the Bastian corps in the mid-sixteen hundreds, during Europe's bloody Thirty Years' War. After a couple of decades working the field, Conrad advanced through the echelons of command and soon became responsible for an elite team of intelligence operatives, of which Gordian and his cousin were the first members and top colonels.

Although his otherworldly healing powers made him a figure to be revered by the Bastian councils, it was Conrad's fighting abilities and leadership skills that gained him the respect of the men and women in his charge, and they obeyed him with a steadfast loyalty that was scarce in the ranks at the time.

A whiff of strong liquor distracted him from his recollections. He watched Gordian pour two shots of the golden liquid sloshing inside the bottle. The giant slid one of the glasses toward him. Conrad closed his fingers around it and downed the drink in one go. The aged cachaça trailed a delicious, fiery path down his throat, leaving a velvety aftertaste.

'This is good,' he said, looking into the empty glass.

Gordian swallowed his, grunted in pleasure, and refilled both glasses. 'So, what brings you here? You're about a year early, aren't you?' The giant observed him guardedly.

Conrad twirled the shot glass and watched the amber liquid dance around the rim. He knocked back the second drink, placed the glass carefully on the counter, and looked steadily at Gordian. 'I need to know where she is.'

CHAPTER FIVE

Silence greeted Conrad's statement. Gordian lowered his glass to the bar.

'Why?' he asked gruffly.

'I think she's in trouble,' said Conrad.

Gordian snorted. 'So, what else is new? That woman is a magnet for disaster. Christ, remember that time in France when we were almost savaged by those wolves? And that assignment in North Africa when we practically drowned?'

Conrad sighed. He understood Gordian's reluctance on the subject. After all, the immortal had been around to witness the disastrous consequences of Conrad and Laura's breakup.

Never mix business with pleasure, his father once told him before his final end from the effects of the Red Death. It was a principle Conrad had abided by ever since he joined the Bastian corps. It went out of the window the day he met his soulmate.

Laura Hartwell had been one of a small and growing number of women who had joined the ranks of the Bastian Hunters in the sixteen hundreds. After twenty years in the Order, her fighting skills and sharp intellect brought her to the attention of Victor Dvorsky, the son and successor of the leader of the Bastian race. It was Victor who instigated the formation of the team of intelligence operatives that Conrad would one day command. It was also Victor who introduced Conrad to Laura.

The attraction between the two immortals was instantaneous and incendiary. Like moths to a flame, they could not help but gravitate to each other. To resist would have been akin to trying not to breathe. Within days of their meeting, they were spending their nights in each other's arms. Their passion was frightening, as was the sense that it would never stop growing. At times, Conrad feared he would lose himself in her.

By the end of that first week, he knew every inch of her body and face—every freckle, every mole, every strand of her coffee-colored hair, and every golden speckle in her hazel eyes. The way she moved, the laughter lines around her mouth, her irises darkening in anger or passion, her brow furrowing when she gave something her full attention—all of it was burned indelibly into his mind. Had he become blind, he would have recognized her just by her scent.

A year after they met, Laura brought her half-brother into the fold. It didn't take Conrad long to realize that William Hartwell was not an immortal. Laura finally admitted that he was a half-breed, the offspring of a tryst between her father and a mortal woman seventeen years previously. Her father's lover died in childbirth, and he followed her to the grave months later, another victim of the Red Death. Like many children conceived after the plague that wiped out more than half of the immortals on Earth, Laura became an orphan, left alone to raise her mortal, baby half-brother; for William was just like any other human, born without the self-healing abilities and sixteen extra lives of the immortals.

Conrad reluctantly agreed to keep William's origins a secret and recruited him into his regiment. But he warned Laura that the day would come when others in their squad would suspect the truth. When that time drew near, they decided William would retire from the Bastian corps.

The next decade was a blur of laughter-filled days and thrilling adventures. Conrad came to care for William Hartwell like a brother. Under Laura's tutelage, the young man became a skilled fighter who could hold his own against the immortals, even if he could not heal as fast as they did. Conrad was always heedful of the missions he assigned to him for fear William's secret would be revealed too soon as a result of a significant injury.

Then came that fateful night in London.

Shortly after taking the throne in the early 1700s, Queen Anne expressed her wish to bring about the union of two of her three realms, namely the Kingdom of England and that of Scotland, as well as their respective parliaments. Despite numerous failed attempts by her predecessors to achieve the same goal, the new queen was confident she could accomplish the impossible. There were many, both locally and across the Channel, who strongly opposed her plans and wished to see the consultation on the proposed unification fail. Most of the members of these rebellious factions were human. Some were not.

The Bastians supported the new queen's political views and ambitions. By 1703, a year after her ascension to the throne, the Bastian First Council dispatched a small group of immortal covert agents to infiltrate the corps of Westminster police constables and keep a watch on the evolving state of affairs.

Three years later, in April 1706, a large contingent of English and Scottish commissioners gathered in London to start negotiations for the treaty that would see the Kingdom of England and that of Scotland become united under a single entity known as Great Britain. The talks went on for several months, under the personal patronage of Queen Anne and her ministers.

It wasn't until July that rumors of an impending sabotage

first reached Conrad's ears, after one of his informants relayed a conversation overheard in an alehouse. At the time, it was clear the discussions between the English and Scottish commissioners were going well. At Conrad's request, Victor Dvorsky increased the number of immortal operatives in London.

The final details of the enemy's plan, which involved killing the main players in the negotiations and burning down the Royal Cockpit theatre, the scene of the crucial talks, only came to light at sunset on the day of the imminent attack, when two men broke into Conrad's quarters at the inn where he was staying and tried to kill him. While the clouds of a thunderstorm gathered over the city, the immortal clashed swords with his assassins and swiftly eliminated them.

Before Conrad disposed of the second man, he extracted the identity of the traitor who had sold him out, and whom he later discovered had been responsible for the murder of two other members of his team. Stunned by the name his would-be killer revealed, Conrad rallied his squad in time to intercept the group of human and immortal assassins assigned to the murderous task of stopping the treaty. At his command, relayed by half a dozen messengers, they converged on the Banqueting House, the meeting place of the enemy, from all over the city.

Conrad did not tell his men that William Hartwell had betrayed them; he wanted to be absolutely certain of the facts before he made such an accusation.

The battle took place on the rooftop of the building, with the summer storm raging around them. Less than five hundred feet from where Conrad and his men made their stand against their adversaries, the English and Scottish commissioners were in the final stages of concluding the Treaty of the Union.

One look at William's face was all it took to convince Conrad that the assassin had spoken the truth. Events unfolded too rapidly for the immortal to tell Laura of her brother's treachery. By the time the two of them found a moment to be alone, they were kneeling on the ground by the body of the dying William Hartwell.

Although she had heard William speak to the enemy as if he knew them, Laura refused to accept that her brother had betrayed them. Even after one of the captured assassins related how they had convinced the young man to double-cross the Bastians, she still clung to the hope that it was all a huge misunderstanding.

Only when the reason behind William Hartwell's deceit was revealed did Conrad see the truth start to register on her grief-stricken face. The young man's motive carved yet another scar in Conrad's soul. It had not been for money or power that William Hartwell had betrayed them.

It was for the love of his sister and the immortal he had come to regard as his brother.

Tears clouded Conrad's vision when the prisoner admitted that a Crovir noble had promised William the gift of immortality. It had been an empty pledge; no one could make a human immortal.

The prisoner also disclosed that William Hartwell had been unaware of the assassination attempt on Conrad's life and the other two immortals who had been executed. As far as the young man knew, the killers had been sent to keep Conrad and the others out of the way until the enemy's plan had played out.

The knowledge that William had only been disloyal so that he could live with his sister and her lover forever made the couple's subsequent breakup even more devastating. Laura Hartwell eventually came to accept her brother's treason, but she could never forgive Conrad for not healing the dying man.

The atmosphere in the squad rapidly became toxic, with Laura's resentment growing until she asked Victor to transfer her out of the team. Over the decades that followed, she refused all attempts at communication from Conrad; even when their paths would cross in the corridors of the Bastian

First Council, she never spoke to or looked at him. Two centuries later, at the end of the Second World War, Conrad finally parted ways with humans and immortals alike.

The loss of his soulmate was the primary reason behind his decision to seclude himself from the rest of the world.

The sound of fingers drumming a slow beat on the wooden countertop brought Conrad back to the present. Gordian was staring at him, lips pursed as he absentmindedly rapped on the bar.

'What kinda trouble?' he said with a grunt.

Conrad hid a smile as he extracted the envelope from his backpack; Gordian never could resist a challenge. He spilled the contents on the counter and related the circumstances under which he had acquired them.

'A plane crashed into your house?' said Gordian, eyebrows almost touching his hairline.

Conrad shrugged.

'Christ, you really do have the worst luck,' Gordian muttered. He moved the liquor bottle aside and leafed through the papers. A frown marred his brow. 'You weren't kidding.' He picked up the sheet with the puzzling quartet of passages and studied it. '"*On Freda's Dark Day, For the Rightful Blood to rise, The Falcon must fall.*" What the hell does that mean?'

'I think it's a message,' said Conrad.

'Still doesn't explain what it means,' countered Gordian. 'Or who it's intended for.'

They spent the next hour going over the rest of the encoded sentences, the maps, and pictures. Conrad realized then how much he had missed engaging in a discussion with another intelligence operative. The giant arrived at the same conclusions that he had.

'Whatever's going down, Laura's in the middle of it,' said Conrad. He put the papers back inside the envelope. 'If I talk to her, we may be able to unravel the meaning behind these documents.'

Gordian grimaced. 'You're willing to get involved in this, even after the way she's treated you? There's no guarantee that she'll even talk to you.'

Conrad shrugged. He had never had seconds thoughts on the matter; he would rather have his soulmate alive and hating him than in harm's way.

Gordian sighed. 'Wait here. I'll go make a call.' He left the room.

Floorboards creaked above Conrad's head a moment later. The low rumble of voices soon came through the ceiling. He helped himself to another shot of cachaca while he waited for Gordian's return.

'Who'd you ring?' he said curiously when the tawny-haired immortal strolled back into the bar.

'Who else?' replied Gordian with a derisive snort. 'Anatole, of course.'

Anatole Leon Vassili was Gordian's cousin and a close friend of Conrad's, as well as his second in command to the team of intelligence operatives he had once led. Shorter and thinner than Gordian, he had the same pale eyes and red hair that matched his fiery personality. At times known as 'The Maniac,' 'The Mad Immortal,' or simply, 'That Crazy Bastard Who Must Not Be Messed With,' his temper had been legendary in the Bastian ranks.

'What's he up to these days?' said Conrad with a faint smile.

He had always had a soft spot for Gordian's cousin. The immortal was undoubtedly a hothead, but he was also an excellent fighter and a great tactician. Strangely enough, aside from Conrad and Gordian, Laura Hartwell was the only other person who could pacify Anatole when he was in a foul mood. While Conrad and Gordian resorted to booze, a locked room, and the occasional female companion, Laura could actually talk him down. It was like watching a wild horse being tamed by a cheetah.

A scowl darkened Gordian's features. 'You'll never believe it. That crazy bastard became a bodyguard.'

'Oh.' Conrad was surprised. It was the last role on Earth he would ever have expected his old friend and fighting partner to take on. 'Who's he protecting?'

Gordian mumbled something unintelligible.

'What was that?' said Conrad.

'The Head of the Order of the Hunters,' Gordian admitted.

Conrad's eyebrows rose. 'You mean Roman Dvorsky?'

Gordian gawked at Conrad as if he had actually grown a pair of horns and a tail. His shoulders sagged. 'Christ, I forget how much time you spend in the jungle,' he muttered. 'Roman retired last year. It's Victor who's the current Head of the Order.'

Conrad drew in a sharp breath. That his old mentor was now the leader of the Bastian race came as another shock. Victor Dvorsky had always been destined to take over from his father one day; as far as Conrad was concerned, there was no other Bastian immortal better suited to the role. Still, he had not expected it to come about for at least another century.

'Did something happen?' he said.

Gordian leaned against the shelving behind the bar. 'Anatole mentioned an incident last year that resulted in a showdown between the Bastians and the Crovirs. I don't know all the details, but we were apparently on the verge of another immortal war.' He paused. 'Agatha Vellacrus and her heir, Felix Thorne, both died during the battle.'

'*The* Agatha Vellacrus? As in the Head of the Order of Crovir Hunters?' said Conrad, stunned.

'Yep, the old witch herself. And that bastard son of hers.'

Conrad gazed blindly at the empty glass in front of him. He

had met Vellacrus and Thorne on a couple of occasions in the past and had not liked either of the two Crovir nobles.

A lot had happened in the immortal world in the thirteen months since he had last been to Rio. Although it had been his decision to distance himself from that circle, it felt odd to be so out of the loop.

'So, what did Anatole say?'

Gordian crossed his arms and pulled at his beard. 'You're absolutely sure you want to get involved in this?' he repeated.

Conrad sighed. 'Yes, Hor. I am.' He could tell from Gordian's troubled expression that the news was not good.

The giant ran a hand through his disheveled hair. 'She's in Washington, working in President Westwood's security detail.'

A sinking feeling pooled in the pit of Conrad's stomach. 'You mean, she's a bodyguard?'

'Yes,' said Gordian. 'She's US Secret Service.'

CHAPTER SIX

THE RED-EYE FLIGHT FROM SÃO PAULO LANDED AT DULLES International Airport in Washington, D.C., just after six thirty a.m. the next day. Conrad went through airport security without a hitch, collected his two pieces of luggage from the conveyor belt, and went in search of a mobile phone shop. He walked out of the main terminal building with a prepaid cell in his pocket.

Fiery orange streaks raced across the horizon to the east as dawn broke over the land. At that time of the morning, the air was still chilly, a brisk wind blowing from the north helping keep temperatures down.

The immortal hailed a cab and helped load the bags in the boot. The driver, a short Hispanic man with a round face and toffee-colored skin, smiled at him curiously in the rearview mirror once they were inside the car.

'You here to play some golf, bro?' he said in a light tone.

Conrad shrugged and smiled back. 'Something like that.'

The previous day, he had made several purchases in Rio. First on his shopping list had been a small Pelican case for the

Heckler & Koch handgun, which he bought from one of Gordian's contacts. Next had been a suitcase and a golf bag.

Conrad had the private jet take him to São Paulo, where he booked a direct commercial flight to D.C. Although he could have paid the charter company to make the trip to the States, he decided it was an unnecessary expense. He zipped the staff weapon inside the golf bag, locked the Pelican case containing the gun and his magazines inside the suitcase, filled in a declaration form for the weapons, and checked everything in. The flight had been uneventful, and he had even managed about six hours sleep.

As the taxi rolled east onto State Route 267, Conrad instructed the driver to drop him off in Chinatown.

The man pulled a face and shook his head. 'Man, that's a bad idea.'

Conrad raised an eyebrow. 'Why?'

The cabbie gave him an incredulous look via the mirror. 'Bro, where you been? It's Columbus Day weekend. Most of downtown is still in lockdown.'

Conrad sat back in the seat. Lines puckered his brow as he contemplated the speeding motorway traffic and tower blocks dotting the landscape outside the window. He had not realized it was a federal holiday in the States. Survival in the rainforest did not exactly require a personal organizer. Although he was aware of the change of the seasons and important days like Christmas and New Year, he had not kept a calendar since he started living in the jungle more than half a century ago.

He recalled first seeing the Columbus Memorial Fountain outside Union Station in Washington a few years after it was erected. Twelve months later, he was on the Western Front in Europe, part of a five-thousand-strong regiment of Bastian immortals who joined the Allied Forces in their efforts to defeat the Germans and their associates in the First World War.

Conrad had never attended the Columbus Day celebrations

in D.C. or any other city. From the stories related to him by his father and other older immortals, Christopher Columbus had not exactly been a saint.

It wasn't until they entered Arlington that blue and white bunting, interspersed with the star-spangled banner, started to appear on the roads. The national flag was up atop every government building they drove past.

The taxi got him as far as Farragut Square before traffic ground to a halt. Conrad got the cabbie to pull over, took the HK P8 semiautomatic and the gilded staff out of the luggage, and gifted the cases and the golf bag to the bemused taxi driver. He walked the rest of the way to H Street NW.

Despite the day's festivities being concentrated near Pennsylvania and Constitution Avenue, it was still slow going. Street stands and temporary food pavilions had been set up on the sidewalks, and although it was too early for the crowds that would soon flock to the downtown area, there were plenty of people around.

By the time he reached a Starbucks some three hundred feet from the intersection of H Street NW and 10th Street NW, the temperature was nearing seventy degrees. Sweat dampened the back of his shirt, inches above the gun and staff weapon tucked inside his waistband. He went inside the coffeehouse, ordered an ice-cold drink, and took a seat near the window. He removed the prepaid cell from his pocket and stared at it for some time. He finally dialed the number Anatole had given to Gordian.

It rang three times before someone answered.

'Hartwell here,' said a female voice briskly. 'Who is this?'

Although Conrad had been mentally preparing himself for this moment from the second he saw her photograph inside the dead man's briefcase in Alvarães, his heart still stuttered painfully inside his chest at the sound of his soulmate's voice. The old, familiar rush of bittersweet emotions rose to the surface of his mind, threatening to drown him. His fingers clenched around the cell phone.

A pair of college students sat down in the booth in front of him. One of them bobbed his head at what his friend was saying and took an iPad out of his satchel.

'Hello? Is someone there?' snapped Laura Hartwell at the other end of the line. A low hubbub of conversation rose in the background behind her.

Conrad blinked and lowered his head. 'It's me,' he said quietly, cradling the phone close to his face. He was surprised at how composed his voice sounded.

He heard her inhale sharply. Frozen silence rose from the earpiece.

'What do you want?' Laura said finally.

Conrad looked out of the window at the heavy traffic clogging the avenue and steadied his nerves.

'Two days ago, a private plane crashed near my place in Brazil,' he said in a matter-of-fact voice. 'Both the pilot and the passenger died on impact. I found a briefcase in the debris. Inside it was a gun and an envelope containing an encoded sheet, maps, and photographs. One of the pictures was of you, dressed in what I assume are your work clothes. From your current job description, the other shots must be of your colleagues in the Secret Service.'

A lull followed his words. 'That's a great story,' Laura said coolly. 'How did you get this number?'

The guy with the iPad started to watch a TV show on the tablet. Conrad glanced around as music blared from its speakers. He turned away and tucked the phone closer to his ear.

'Anatole gave it to Gordian, who passed it on to me.' Conrad sighed and rubbed his forehead. 'Can you think of a single good reason why I would suddenly call you out of the blue and tell you such an elaborate story, after all this time?'

'I need to have a word with that bastard about who he gives

my number to,' Laura muttered. 'And no, I can't,' she added after a thoughtful silence. 'Since you know it's over between us, I seriously cannot imagine what you think you'll gain by making up something so ludicrous.'

A centuries-old pain stabbed through Conrad's heart at her words. He swallowed the painful lump in his throat.

'Where are you?' Laura demanded.

'Around the corner from your building,' he replied, struggling to keep his tone casual. He heard her breath catch.

'You're outside the office of the US Secret Service?' she said, incredulous.

'Yes,' said Conrad. 'I'm sitting within three hundred feet of it.' He thought he heard her swear under her breath. 'I've got the envelope with me. I thought you should see it.'

Someone called Laura's name in the background. 'Yeah, I'm coming,' she responded tersely. 'Look, I can't talk right now,' she continued in a low voice. 'I'm in the middle of something.'

Conrad tried to ignore the heavy feeling in the pit of his stomach. 'When can we meet?'

'By the end of today, maybe,' Laura replied distractedly.

Conrad looked to the booth where the two students now sat watching a local news channel. An anchorwoman spoke enthusiastically in the background while shots of the weekend celebrations flashed across the screen.

'Is there someone in your local office you would rather I show this to?'

Although he was loath to make the offer, Conrad felt he had to ask the question. He could almost see her frowning in the silence that followed.

'No. All my team are out here,' she said. 'I've got to go. I'll call you later to fix up a meet.'

The disconnect tone echoed in Conrad's ears. He ended the call and looked down at his hands. He was amazed they weren't shaking. He listened distractedly as a short musical tune from the young man's iPad heralded the weather section of the news bulletin. He tucked the cell phone inside his pocket, rose from the window seat with the rucksack on his shoulder, and was strolling past the college students' booth when he heard something that stopped him in his tracks.

'—so all in all, it's going to be a very warm and pleasant day for us, folks,' the reporter was saying in a lively voice. 'Elsewhere, there are fears that the system of low pressure in the Pacific Northwest might lead to a tropical cyclone in the next twelve hours. Forecasters are predicting that it won't be anywhere on the same scale as the Columbus Day storm of 1962—'

Conrad stiffened. A distant memory surfaced at the back of his mind; something about a storm. The feeling that he had just missed an important clue niggled at his subconscious. He stared blindly into space as he mentally went through the events of the last forty-eight hours.

An image of the encoded sheet flashed in front of his eyes. His breath froze in his lungs. Conrad twisted on his heels and stepped toward the booth.

'Excuse me, can I ask you guys to look something up?' He masked the urgency in his voice behind a smile.

The student with the iPad raised his head, looked at him from head to toe, and shrugged. 'Sure, dude. What did you wanna know?'

'Can you tell me the name of the 1962 Columbus Day storm?' said Conrad. He waited tensely while the kid tapped on the tablet screen.

'Yeah. It was called Typhoon Freda,' said the college student.

Conrad thanked him numbly, the words from the Japanese poem screaming in his mind.

"On Freda's Dark Day

For the Rightful Blood to rise
The Falcon must fall"

A sudden premonition made the hairs on the back of his neck stand up. Conrad grabbed his cell and frantically dialed Laura Hartwell's number again.

She picked up after the second ring. 'Yes?' she hissed.

'What's your codename for President Westwood?' said Conrad, his knuckles whitening on the phone.

Static crackled down the line. 'What—that?—breaking up —' came the disjointed reply.

Conrad swore and looked at the cell's signal. He had four bars; the problem had to be at Hartwell's end. 'The codename! What's the codename for the president?' he barked into the mouthpiece, aware of the frightened looks he was receiving from the two college students and a nearby Starbucks cleaner.

The line fizzled for a couple of seconds. Laura's voice suddenly came through, clear as a bell in between the garbled sounds from the low signal. '—Falcon. His codename is Falcon—'

Icy fingers gripped Conrad's heart. 'Listen! I think something big is going to go down with the president today!' He saw a female employee reach for the phone behind the counter, alarm evident on her face. 'Are you with him?'

There was silence at the end of the line for a couple of beats before a busy tone sounded.

'Laura? Laura, can you hear me? Where are you?' Conrad shouted desperately into the mouthpiece of the cell. The busy signal continued to mock him. 'Shit!'

He dialed again, his fingers almost striking the wrong keys in his haste. This time, a computerized voice stated that the person he was trying to contact could not be reached. He spun toward the college students. They shrank back in the booth.

'Can I borrow that?' he demanded, extending his hand to the iPad.

The kid practically threw the tablet at him. 'Dude, take whatever you want! Just...don't hurt us, 'kay?'

The coffeehouse was emptying fast, the customers eyeing him fearfully as they streamed through the exit; Conrad got the distinct impression they were committing his face to memory in case he made the six o'clock news.

He tapped on the tablet, typed something into a search engine, and opened the first web page that came up. He scanned the information swiftly. Seconds later, his finger froze on the screen. Conrad went back to the search engine, punched in directions for an address, and scrutinized the map that came up until he had it memorized. He tossed the tablet on the lap of the stunned college student, shouted a quick 'Thanks!' and raced for the door.

From the White House schedule he had just looked up, President Westwood was attending a special Columbus Day fundraiser at FedEx Field, home of the Washington Redskins football team, in Prince George's County, Maryland. He was due to give a speech at ten thirty to an audience of approximately 85,000 spectators.

Conrad skidded to a stop on the sidewalk outside the Starbucks and glanced at his watch. It was five to nine; he had ninety-five minutes to get to the stadium and stop a possible assassination attempt on the president of the United States.

He looked around, spotted a suitable target coming up to the intersection on the left, and dashed out into the middle of the avenue. Brakes squealed and tires screeched in the eastbound lanes as traffic swung wildly around him. The horns blasting in the air were interspersed with waves of profanity.

Conrad ignored the yelling and general clamor, and stood facing the black Ford SUV barreling down the road toward him.

A man in a suit was talking on a Bluetooth headset behind

the wheel. It took him a couple of seconds to notice Conrad. He gaped and slammed on his brakes. The SUV screamed to a stop a foot from the immortal's shins. The driver's head whiplashed violently against the steering wheel.

Conrad strode around to the side of the vehicle, yanked the door open, and swept the HK P8 out of his waistband. He gestured with the gun. 'Out!'

'Hey—hey, ta—take it easy!' the guy stammered, face ashen but for the rapidly growing red mark on his forehead.

Conrad grabbed him by the scruff of his neck and hauled him out onto the blacktop. He ignored the man's shocked cry, climbed behind the wheel, and threw his rucksack onto the passenger seat. He smiled grimly when he spotted the manual transmission. His gaze alighted on a briefcase in the passenger footwell as he buckled himself in. He chucked it out of the window in the direction of the slack-jawed man sitting on the asphalt, shifted into first, and stepped on the gas pedal.

The Ford shot forward. A cacophony of blares exploded around him as the SUV accelerated. Conrad swerved across the orange centerlines and steered sharply around the traffic headed east on the avenue. Two thousand feet later, he hung a tight left on 6th Street before swinging the vehicle in a sharp right onto New York Avenue.

As signs for Interstates 95 and 495 started to flash past, Conrad took his cell out and dialed 911, his spare hand alternating between the steering wheel and the transmission.

'Operator. What's your emergency?' said a female voice.

'My name is Conrad Greene! I need you to get a message to US Secret Service agent Laura Hartwell!' he barked into the mouthpiece. 'She's at the FedEx Field stadium in Maryland! Tell her there will be an assassination attempt on President Westwood during the fundraiser event today!'

For a moment, he thought he'd lost the call. Then, the operator's voice came through.

'Sir, you do realize threatening the president of the United States is a Class D felony offense which is punishable by a prison sentence and $250,000 fine—' the woman said frostily.

'Listen, lady, I'm not threatening the president, I'm trying to save his sorry ass!' Conrad shouted. 'Just get that message to Agent Hartwell! And let state and county law enforcement on the ground know that there's an imminent threat!'

CHAPTER SEVEN

CONRAD DISCONNECTED, THREW THE PHONE ONTO THE passenger seat, and dug inside his backpack until he found the envelope. His eyes moved to the speedometer; the SUV had just hit seventy miles per hour. He slammed his hand on the horn to clear the sluggish traffic in his path and emptied the contents of the envelope onto his lap.

His fingers had just closed over the encoded sheet with the haiku when a deafening sound thundered down the motorway and rattled his teeth.

Conrad looked up and saw that the Ford had crossed the centerline in the same instant that a red and silver eighteen-wheeler filled his view through the windshield. He swore and spun the steering wheel to the right.

The SUV clipped the edge of the truck's bumper just as the rig's driver started to brake.

The shriek of heavy tires roared in Conrad's ears as he shot past the giant semi. He smelled burnt rubber and glanced in the side mirror in time to see the end of the trailer start to jack-knife toward the concrete barrier of a flyover.

'Oh shit,' he whispered.

The truck wobbled, accelerated slightly, and finally corrected itself as the driver gradually steered the trailer out of the deadly angle. Air whooshed out of Conrad's lips. He pinned the sheet with the cryptic lines to the steering wheel with one hand and peered at it briefly while he drove.

By the time he crossed the Anacostia River, he thought he had an idea what the cipher was. Unfortunately, he wasn't in a position to decrypt it while traveling at eighty miles per hour.

Conrad tried to recall the little he knew of President Westwood. He had caught a glimpse of the man's face on TV the year he was voted in as president, while he was on one of his rare outings to Rio. From what he'd gathered since, although Westwood's popularity poll remained good with voters, it wasn't so with Congress. This was because the new president was adamant that he was going to follow through with all the policy changes he had promised during his run for office, even if he had to, as he'd stated, "wade in the blood of the opposition" to do so. Conrad suspected Westwood was the kind of leader Victor Dvorsky would respect.

The buzz of rotors rose somewhere in the sky behind him. He looked in the side mirror and spotted a black police helicopter heading rapidly in his direction. His gaze shifted to the phone on the passenger seat. That the authorities had managed to locate the coordinates of the cell in such a short time was no small feat. He had their attention now.

He was about to throw the phone out the window when he stopped and frowned. The more cops he brought to the target site, the better it would act as a deterrent to the assassins.

Conrad got within two miles of the stadium before traffic started to pile up again. The SUV's speed quickly dropped to under twenty miles per hour. The helicopter was now only a few thousand feet behind him and closing fast. Police sirens sounded in the distance.

He saw an exit ramp on the right, hit the horn in short,

violent bursts, and forced his way across two lanes of crawling cars. The front wheels of the Ford hit the curb, and the vehicle climbed onto a path. Clods of earth and grass churned under the passenger side wheels as he headed down the embankment toward the slip road.

He hit a highway heading southwest and hurtled along it until he spotted an intersection. A queue of stationary traffic sat patiently behind the red lights. Conrad passed the vehicles and took a sharp left into the contraflow.

The Ford shot through a gap between two cars, glanced off the rear bumper of a van, and darted onto a road with a thirty-miles-per-hour speed limit to the sound of angry horns. Residential areas hedged by woods and parkland appeared on either side of a low hill.

He reached another intersection and turned left, the chopper close on his tail. Relief flashed through him when he saw the distant lines of the stadium's upper levels through the treetops. A second later, he swore and stomped on the brakes. The Ford slewed to a stop a couple of feet from the back of a bus.

Conrad stuck his head out of the window. The eddies from the helicopter rotors whipped his hair as he scowled at the static column of traffic ahead. He looked over his shoulder, switched into reverse, and stepped on the accelerator.

The Ford shot back up the road. A car coming up behind him stopped abruptly, the elderly driver's face a mask of horror. The chopper rose and pivoted sharply in the sky.

Conrad caught the far-off reflection of flashing blue and red lights, braked after fifty feet, changed into first gear, and took a tight right onto a small paved road with a "no entry" sign. He crashed through a low metal barrier and accelerated.

The Ford bolted onto the blacktop of one of the car parks of the FedEx Field seconds later. The chopper followed at the head of three patrol units. Conrad kept his foot on the gas and steered sharply around the rows of parked vehicles and the processions of cars trying to find a space in the stadium grounds. He crossed a second parking lot and saw police vehicles barreling toward him from several directions. He braked violently.

The Ford skidded through a one-eighty spin and juddered to a stop two hundred feet from a stadium gate. Conrad jerked against the belt and slammed back in the seat, a grunt leaving his lips.

Three state trooper and four county police patrol cars screeched to a halt in a half circle, yards from the SUV's front bumper. The officers leapt out of their vehicles with their guns drawn and aimed the weapons steadily at Conrad's chest through the windshield. The immortal's eyes flicked to his watch. It was fifteen minutes to ten.

'Sir, keep your hands on the wheel where we can see them and do *not* make a move!' shouted a middle-aged sergeant on the left. The man's voice was muffled by the clatter of rotors as a Maryland State Police chopper joined the DC Met Police helicopter.

A muscle clenched in Conrad's jaw as he waited for four uniformed officers to draw close to the vehicle. The sergeant reached the driver's door first and opened it carefully.

'I'm armed,' said Conrad. He turned his head slightly so he could meet the officer's eyes. 'The weapon's on the passenger seat.'

Although his expression remained professionally detached, the sergeant visibly stiffened. 'Is it loaded?'

'Yes,' said Conrad.

The sergeant directed one of the other officers to retrieve the gun. As the policeman opened the door, Conrad heard the noise of the large crowd already gathered in the stadium complex. A mob was forming beyond the circle of police vehicles, people stopping to gawk at the unfolding drama. Sunlight flashed on mobile phones as some took shots of the scene. The second officer retrieved the HK P8, passed it carefully to a colleague, and kept his Glock on the immortal.

The high-pitched wails of sirens and the roar of engines suddenly rose in the distance and grew louder. Conrad tensed at the telltale sounds of a motorcade. His eyes darted to his watch. The speech was not scheduled for another forty-five minutes. He hadn't expected Westwood to get here until well after ten. He turned to the sergeant.

'There's a US Secret Service agent called Laura Hartwell inside that stadium right now.' Conrad's fingers clenched on the steering wheel. 'I was talking to her on the phone before I got cut off. You need to tell her there's going to be an assassination attempt on the president during today's fundraiser. They need to abort this visit and get him the hell out of here right now!'

The sergeant's grip tightened on his gun.

'Speak to one of the agents inside and ask them to get Hartwell down here,' the immortal continued in a strained voice. 'Tell them Conrad Greene wants to see her.'

The sergeant stood still for several seconds, his expression unreadable. Conrad let out the breath he had been holding when the man finally reached for the radio clipped to his uniform and requested to be put through to the US Secret Service on a coded frequency.

A female voice came across the radio channel a moment later. 'Hartwell here. What can I do for you, officer?'

For the second time that day, Conrad's heart throbbed inside his chest.

'Ma'am, DC Met Police followed up on a threatening 911 call made from a prepaid mobile phone about forty minutes ago,' the sergeant explained after identifying himself. 'The call was located to a stolen Ford SUV traveling at high speed on Interstate 495. We've just apprehended the driver of the vehicle on the grounds of the stadium. He's insisting he has important information to convey to you about an impending threat to the person of the president. Says his name is Conrad Greene.'

A silent beat followed. 'Describe him!' barked the voice.

The state trooper scrutinized Conrad. 'White male, six foot two, one eighty, dark brown hair, gray-blue eyes, snake tattoo on the left fore—'

A colorful expletive erupted on the airwaves. The sergeant's eyebrows rose slightly. Surprise darted across the stony faces of the police officers close enough to have heard the exchange.

Conrad suppressed a smile. Though she could act every inch a lady when she wanted to, Laura Hartwell could swear, fight, and drink with the best of them. It was one of the reasons she had fitted in so well with his team.

'It's not a tattoo,' he heard her mutter darkly, 'it's a birthmark. What's your position?'

'We're outside the main ticket office,' replied the sergeant. 'We're kinda hard to miss.'

'Wait there. I'm on my way,' she commanded.

Conrad followed the state trooper's orders to step out of the vehicle and lean against the hood. He was aware of the eyes of the crowd drilling into his back as the officers cuffed him. One of the policemen retrieved the staff weapon tucked in his waistband.

He was being marched to a squad car when running footsteps rose from the direction of the stadium gate.

'Hold up!' a female voice shouted.

Conrad froze in his tracks.

The sergeant looked around. 'Agent Hartwell?' he asked with a small frown.

'Yes,' said Laura Hartwell.

Conrad saw her appear out of the corner of his eye and remove her sunglasses. The immortal turned slowly and beheld his soulmate for the first time in a hundred years.

As his gaze swept over her lightly freckled skin, high cheekbones, full lips, and hazel eyes, emotions old and new welled up inside him. Love, desire, resentment, regret, and sadness were sentiments he had lived with for a long time.

The shock was a bolt from the blue. Before her expression shut down into a cold, businesslike mask, Conrad thought he detected a flash of some nameless emotion in the golden-green depths. It caused him to wonder.

'Do you know this man?' asked the sergeant.

Laura's gaze moved to the state trooper. 'Yes, I—'

'We have about thirty minutes to figure out the positions of the killers,' Conrad interrupted urgently. He ignored the racing of his heart, which he knew had as much to do with the physical proximity of his mate as with the looming danger, and pressed on. 'The envelope I was telling you about is on the passenger seat of the SUV. The maps are floor plans of the stadium. I think I know how to decrypt the encoded passages.' His voice hardened. 'You guys should still evacuate the president.'

Laura's eyes narrowed at his words. 'This is a National Special Security Event,' she stated frostily. 'Our teams went over every inch of this place in the last few weeks to design and coordinate the optimal operational security plan. We did it all over again last night with the K-9 teams. All the checkpoints were established and have been maintained since zero six hundred hours. There are metal detectors on the gates and the stadium staff has been security cleared. We've looked at every potential threat scenario during the site surveys.'

The cuffs clinked around Conrad's wrists as he shifted on the warm asphalt, apprehension making him restless. 'Have you received any intelligence of an impending threat?'

'No,' Laura replied.

'Did you come across anything odd during your search?' he questioned insistently.

'Negative.'

'Then you've missed the assassins,' said Conrad.

Laura cocked an eyebrow. 'Or there is no threat.'

Conrad quelled the tide of dread rising inside him as precious seconds ticked past. 'Are you willing to take that risk?'

She went still at the question. The state trooper looked curiously between the two of them.

'Goddammit!' Laura exclaimed. She exhaled sharply. 'Fine! Let's take a look at what you've got.'

Conrad waited tensely while Laura assumed custody of his person from the state troopers.

'I need my weapons,' he said when she returned and removed his cuffs.

Laura muttered something unsavory under her breath and headed back to the sergeant. She spoke to the man briefly and came back a minute later with his gun and the gilded staff.

'I didn't expect that to go so smoothly,' said Conrad, glancing at the frowning sergeant.

'I assured him nothing would give me greater pleasure than to personally shoot you if you tried anything,' Laura replied with a mirthless smile. 'Besides, the US Secret Service is the lead agency for this kind of event. What we say goes.'

Conrad suspected the shooting comment had not been made in jest. He retrieved the envelope from the Ford and followed her as she jogged back to the stadium.

'Where's your command post?'

'We're on the second level, in the Owner's Club,' came the curt reply.

They left the slow-moving crowds behind and entered a brightly lit lobby patrolled by officers from the local and state police. Dozens of watchful eyes scanned them as they entered a lift.

The elevator opened onto a small atrium that led to a glass-walled concourse. Conrad followed Laura down the corridor and glanced at her curiously as they entered a luxurious lounge and headed for the back. Though she wore the same conservative, two-piece suit and earpiece as the rest of the agents they had crossed paths with, it was evident from the way they deferred to her that she was their senior.

'I thought you were part of the president's personal detail,' he said.

'I am,' she replied, her expression aloof. 'My boss wanted me on the shop floor today.'

Conrad digested this information for a couple of seconds. 'Are there more immortals among your ranks?'

She opened a door, a look of irritation darting across her face. He stifled a sigh and walked in behind her.

The command center was in one of the executive suites of the Owner's Club. The floor had been stripped of its opulent furnishings and replaced with a business-like bank of tables holding computer monitors and telephones in front of the panoramic bay windows looking out over the football field. Detailed maps and charts were pinned to a series of boards on the left. Two men and a woman hovered next to them.

Laura strode toward the tall, black man looming over the group.

'Clint, this is the guy I was telling you about,' she said, interrupting the low hubbub of conversation. She looked between Conrad and the black man. 'Clint Woods, Assistant Special Agent in charge of the Office of Protective Operations. Conrad Greene.'

Conrad acknowledged the senior agent with a curt nod. Woods observed him woodenly while Laura introduced the Lieutenant Colonel in charge of the Special Operations Bureau of the Maryland State Police and the Deputy Chief of the county police Special Operations Division.

'So, Greene,' said Woods, 'what was so urgent that you had to get everybody's panties in a bunch?' His disgruntled voice boomed across the room. A couple of the Secret Service techs glanced over their shoulders. The Deputy Chief of county police blew a sigh through her lips and rolled her eyes.

Conrad looked at the clock on the wall. It was eight minutes past the hour. He walked wordlessly to the table next to the boards, upended the envelope, and spread the contents across the surface. Silence fell over the group as they scrutinized the photographs and floor plans of the FedEx Field stadium.

'What's this?' said the Deputy Chief quietly.

Conrad briefly retold the story of how he had come across the envelope. He did not elaborate on the details of his trip from Alvarães to Washington.

The Lieutenant Colonel raised an eyebrow. 'And you didn't report this to the local authorities in Brazil?'

'No,' retorted Conrad. 'I didn't know who I could trust.'

'What makes you think there will be an assassination attempt on the president today?' said Woods. He was frowning at the pictures of the agents. Laura smoothed out the maps and studied them intently.

'Because of the haiku at the top of the first sheet,' said Conrad. He tapped a finger on the paper in question.

'"*On Freda's Dark Day, For the Rightful Blood to rise, The Falcon must fall,*"' quoted the Lieutenant Colonel. He shrugged. 'So?'

'"*Freda's Dark Day*" refers to Typhoon Freda,' Conrad explained. 'And "*Falcon*" is the codename for President Westwood.'

Understanding dawned on Woods's face. 'The 1962 Columbus Day storm,' he breathed.

'Exactly,' Conrad concurred. 'We've got less than twenty minutes left to find the two killers.'

Laura's head jerked up. 'What makes you think there are two of them?'

'Because of the other nine lines,' Conrad replied. He pointed them out. 'I think each paragraph is a message to an assassin about where they should position themselves for the shot.'

Laura frowned. 'There are three paragraphs.'

'The third killer was the guy who died in the plane crash,' said Conrad steadily. 'He had calluses between his thumb and forefinger from using a sniper rifle.'

Laura turned to Woods in the taut lull that followed, her expression troubled. 'Although I hate to admit this, Clint, Greene is right. We should abort the visit now.'

Relief flashed through Conrad at her words. She believed him.

Woods ran a hand through his receding hair and sighed. 'You know as well as I do what he'll say to that. He's gonna want to see an act of God before he changes his mind.'

Laura chewed her lip and remained silent.

Conrad looked between the two agents. 'It's your call, isn't it?' he said, making no attempt to mask his surprise. 'He shouldn't have a say in his personal security matters.'

Woods cast Conrad a mocking look. 'We do not order our commander-in-chief. We only advise him. We sometimes have to do it loudly and vehemently, but still, we can only recommend a course of action.' He lowered his voice a notch. 'I can tell you don't know *this* president.'

Laura pulled a face. 'He's a stubborn bastard.'

The Maryland Lieutenant straightened, his back rigid. 'You *are* talking about our Head of State here!'

Laura eyed him coolly. 'I'm sorry. The president is a stubborn bastard, *sir*.' She ignored the man's disapproving glare and turned to Conrad. 'You said you could decode the passages?'

'Yes,' he replied with a quick nod. 'I think they might have used a stacked cipher combining a date shift and the Vigenère square. The keyword is Falcon. The date is—'

'10-12-1962,' Woods cut in. 'The day of the storm.'

'Yes,' said Conrad.

The Maryland Lieutenant threw his hands in the air. 'What the hell is a Vigenère square?' he exclaimed.

'It's a polyalphabetic substitution cipher, Bob,' muttered the county police Deputy Chief. She shrugged at the man's expression. 'So sue me. I took a course on cryptography.'

Laura got one of the techs to print out a Vigenère table while Conrad wrote out the nine encoded lines on a fresh sheet of paper. They used the table, followed by the date shift, to painstakingly recreate the original text. Five minutes later, they examined the new words he had written out.

'That still doesn't make any sense,' said Laura with a frustrated sigh.

Conrad's heart sunk as he studied the incomprehensible text; he had been certain that he was on the right track.

The Deputy Chief had been gazing at the paper as intently as the rest of them when she suddenly gasped. 'There's a third cipher!'

She snatched a couple of blank sheets from a printer tray and drew a different sized concentric circle on each piece of paper. She marked out sections on the circumference of the two rings and filled them in with all the letters of the alphabet and the numbers 0-9.

'Dammit!' swore Conrad as the policewoman grabbed a pair of scissors and started to cut out the smaller circle. 'The Alberti disk!'

'It's another encryption tool, Bob,' snapped the Deputy Chief, preempting the question hovering on the Maryland Lieutenant's lips. 'In fact, it was the first mechanical cipher device ever invented.' She placed the small disk inside the large one, stuck a pin in the middle, and stared at Conrad's partly decoded text. 'What's the key?'

'Try the date,' urged the immortal. He glanced anxiously at the clock.

The Deputy Chief started scribbling on the paper. Conrad

followed the fast movements of the pencil with his eyes, his gaze occasionally skipping to the disk to double-check the decryption as she rotated the inner ring to align the ciphertext with the plaintext.

They ended up with a jumble of thirty-six numbers and six letters. The Deputy Chief's eyes grew round at the same time that Conrad's heart plummeted. The answer to the riddle stared him in the face.

'Holy shit!' whispered the policewoman, the color draining from her face.

CHAPTER EIGHT

WOODS WAS ALREADY BARKING INTO HIS RADIO UNIT.

'Sniper teams, we have possible hostile subjects at the following locations! I repeat, we have possible hostile subjects at the following locations!' He gave out the three sets of geographic coordinates scrawled on the paper and snapped out instructions to the agents and law enforcement agencies on the ground and in the air. 'Get ready to abort and extract the president on my command!' he shouted into the mouthpiece. 'And tell him if he doesn't do as I say, I'm walking out the door!' he added with a growl.

Laura grabbed the sheet bearing the decoded text and shoved it in front of one of the Secret Service techs. 'Get those numbers on the screen!' she snarled.

Sweat beaded the guy's forehead as he brought up the digital map of the stadium and typed in the coordinates. Three dots appeared on the display. Laura studied the monitor for a couple of beats, took out her FN Five-seveN semiautomatic pistol, and yelled out orders into her handheld microphone as she raced for the exit.

She skidded to a halt in the corridor outside and whirled around. 'Where the hell do you think you're going?'

Conrad slowed, his gun in hand. He had followed her out of the room. 'I haven't come this far just to sit back on my ass now!' he retorted. 'Besides, I have a bone to pick with these guys.'

Laura opened her mouth, hesitated, and let out a snort of disgust. 'Fine! Just don't get in our way!'

They met up with a company of agents in the stairwell next to the lifts and divided into three groups. Laura introduced Conrad briefly and gave out his description over the agency's coded frequency so he wouldn't get targeted by friendly fire.

'We'll take the third and fourth levels,' she commanded. Her eyes moved to Conrad and the four armed agents with him. 'You take the first.'

Conrad led the two men and women down the steps. A long-forgotten emotion coursed through him as they raced along the main concourse in the direction of one of the three possible locations of the assassins. It felt good to be part of a team again.

They slowed when they reached one of the corner end seat sections on the lower level. Here, the sound of the crowd was almost deafening.

'The subject will very likely be somewhere at the back,' said Conrad. 'Look for anyone with a bulky jacket. They'll be on their own.'

The agents bobbed their heads. Conrad checked his gun, gripped it low in his hands, and entered the stadium. The noise almost rocked him back on his heels. He did his best to ignore it and spread out along the rows with the other agents.

THE KILLER LISTENED TO THE INFORMATION STREAMING

across the US Secret Service coded frequency through a tiny earpiece and smiled at the swarms of people strolling past on their way to their seats.

'Good morning. Thank you for coming. Here's a complimentary discount voucher for our concession stands for your next visit. Have a nice day.'

Most smiled back as they took the flyers the killer offered.

It was Conrad who spotted the man first. His clothes and hands gave him away.

Whereas the majority of spectators ambling and standing along the seat rows had their arms bared to the warm weather, the suspect wore a long-sleeved, quilt-lined, hooded jacket branded with the word "Staff." His tanned skin and features suggested a Middle Eastern or Mediterranean origin. He was dispensing leaflets to the Redskins fans, a ready smile on his face; there were band-aids wrapped around the thumb and forefinger of his right hand.

Conrad stopped fifteen feet from the suspect and studied him for a few seconds. He looked around, caught the eye of one of the female agents, and cocked his head slightly toward the man in the long-sleeved jacket. The woman lowered her head and shifted to speak discreetly in her microphone.

Conrad caught movement on the skyline to the right and saw sunlight glint on the scope of a rifle as a Secret Service sniper swung his weapon in their direction. Then, two gunshots erupted from the opposite side of the field. Had he not been listening out for the sounds, he would have mistaken them for the stick balloons filling the air with their explosive racket.

He scanned the stands on the northwest side of the stadium and saw a commotion near one of the doors on the third level. From the distance, it looked like several Secret Service agents converging on a figure on the ground. Laura and her team had caught the first killer.

∼

THE ASSASSIN HEARD THE DISTANT BLASTS OF GUNFIRE, looked around, and moved.

∼

CONRAD SAW THE KILLER GLANCE AT THE DISTURBANCE ON the other side of the stadium. The man turned, spotted the two agents closing in on his left, took a step back, and dashed down the aisle toward the field. He threw the stacks of brochures in his hand up in the air and reached inside his jacket. Flyers rained down like confetti on the heads of spectators as he pulled out a pale, shiny gun. Conrad bolted after him.

The man looked over his shoulder, pointed the pistol, and squeezed the trigger twice. The immortal ducked. The shots went wild and zinged off a concrete wall and a metal railing. Alarmed cries erupted across the section as the crowd started to panic. Conrad saw the guy smirk as he sprinted along one of the rows toward an exit.

'Oh no you don't, you bastard!' the immortal hissed.

He shoved his gun in his waistband and slipped the staff weapon out as he ran past the fleeing fans. He bounded onto the top of a seat backrest and vaulted precariously from row to row toward the running figure. Eight feet from the killer, Conrad took a flying leap in the air.

The assassin spotted his swooping shadow and started to turn. The immortal slammed into him and took him to the ground.

The gun clattered out of the killer's hand and was lost in the footfall of the press of people streaming toward the exit.

He slipped out from under Conrad, rolled over, and flicked a pocketknife out from under the wrist of his jacket as he jumped up.

Conrad sprung to his feet and rotated the first ring on the gilded staff. The spear blades sprung out at the ends. The killer's eyes shrunk into narrow slits. He moved, the sharp end of the knife flicking toward the immortal's groin.

Conrad hopped back and spun the double-bladed spear in a series of rapid strikes. The first one smashed the killer's nose. The next two broke his right wrist and shattered his left patella. The knife fell from the man's grasp and a choked cry escaped his lips.

Conrad kicked him in the face, dropped down knee first onto his chest, and pinned him to the ground with the staff wedged against his neck. The assassin's eyes rolled back in his head and he let out a throaty gurgle.

Running footsteps rose to his left.

'I think you broke his jaw, Batman,' drawled a blonde female agent as she jogged down the aisle toward them.

Conrad looked around. The Secret Service agents had cleared most of the seats in the adjacent stands on the lower level. Uniformed police stood at the exits and calmly guided the agitated crowd to safety.

'Did Laura—?' Conrad started to ask.

'Yeah. Hartwell got the other killer,' confirmed the blonde agent. Two of her colleagues rolled the assassin onto his stomach and cuffed him.

The immortal rose to his feet and twisted the ring on the staff. The spear blades disappeared with a slick, metallic noise. He gazed toward the other side of the field and let out the breath he had been holding. Incredible as it seemed, he had made it in time to avert the assassination attempt on Westwood's life.

'Those were quite some moves you pulled there.' The

female agent was staring at the gilded weapon in his hands. 'I've never seen a spear staff like that. Where'd you get it?'

Conrad hesitated. 'It's...a family heirloom.'

'Cool,' said the agent. She smiled. 'It's Conrad, right?'

'Yes.' He saw the blatant invitation in her blue eyes and looked to where the assassin was disappearing in the midst of a group of agents and state troopers. 'Shall we head ba—?' A gasp interrupted him. His gaze shifted to the female agent. He froze.

She stood motionless, her face ashen as she stared blindly past him. She raised a trembling hand to her earpiece.

'What?' said Conrad harshly. He took a step toward her and scanned the other agents' faces. They were similarly pale and stood transfixed as they listened to words he could not hear.

A sudden foreboding made the immortal's heart accelerate. 'What's happening? Talk to me, goddammit!' he snapped. Conrad grabbed the female agent by the shoulders.

The action jolted her out of her state of shock. 'The president is down,' she said shakily. 'He's been shot!'

THE ASSASSIN LOWERED THE CUSTOM-MADE, CARBON-FIBER-reinforced plastic rifle and scope, dismantled the weapon, and placed it on the ground. She stripped off her FedEx Field usher uniform, slipped on a Redskins jersey over her running shorts, and tucked her long, glossy black curls under a sports cap.

She collected the weapon parts and exited the four-and-a-half-foot-wide, triangular space enclosed by a flexible banner stand advertising the Redskins' premium club membership. The location was perfectly positioned to target the president's evacuation path. The fatal strike had been delivered through a small, resealable flap in the vinyl wall facing the exterior of the stadium.

The assassin merged with the hordes of people racing for

the exits on the second level concourse and discreetly tossed the pieces of the sniper rifle beneath their panicked, stampeding feet.

The firearm and its ammunition had been specially manufactured in Europe and cost millions of dollars. Along with the rifles and guns that had been successfully delivered to the other assassins, it was never meant to survive more than a few dozen rounds.

The weapons had been made for only two purposes: to evade detection by metal sensors and to be accurate enough to take out the president of the United States and any bodyguards who stood in the way of the bullets.

Soon, the assassin was just another Redskins fan in the rapidly moving crowd.

～

CONRAD SPRINTED ALONG THE CONCOURSE, THE FEMALE agent close on his heels.

'Where?' he shouted over his shoulder.

'To your left!'

He took the corner and pounded down a corridor in the basement of the stadium, anger and self-reproach warring inside his heart.

The enemy had never meant for there to be just three assassins. They had always planned for a fourth one. And it was that last assassin who had delivered the deadly shots that had killed two US Secret Service bodyguards and almost certainly fatally wounded the president just as they extracted him from the north field tunnel to the waiting motorcade.

Conrad scowled. Had the coordinates of the fourth assassin's position been in the haiku?

There was no more time to think. He saw the crowd of agents and police amassed in front of the mouth of the passage twenty feet ahead and barreled toward the sunlit opening.

The county police Deputy Chief stood outside, her gaze frozen on the two agents lying on the ground a few yards away. The paramedics had stopped working on the men and were sat back on their heels, their expressions as stunned as everyone else's. The roar of sirens faded to the north.

'So much blood,' the Deputy Chief whispered.

Conrad grasped her shoulders. 'Which hospital are they taking him to?' he demanded, desperation hardening his voice. For a second, he thought she hadn't heard him.

'The—the Prince George's Hospital Center, in Cheverly,' the policewoman finally stammered, her gaze shifting from the dead men on the asphalt. Tears brimmed in her eyes. 'Oh God, there's so much blood!'

'Conrad!' someone shouted from behind.

He spun around and saw Laura racing out of the tunnel.

'I need to get to him!' he yelled, his heart hammering painfully against his ribs.

'I know!' she replied, her expression grim. 'I'm already on it!'

The squeal of tires rose from the left. A black Suburban raced down the road and pulled up sharply next to the curb. An agent leapt out from behind the wheel and tossed the car keys to Laura. She snatched them from the air and dashed around the hood to the driver's side. Conrad yanked the passenger door open and leapt inside a second before she floored the gas pedal.

The Suburban shot down the stadium's main avenue, lights flashing and siren blaring. The fast lane had been cleared by the passing motorcade, and they rapidly overtook the stationary traffic on the right.

Conrad glanced at Laura. 'You catch your guy?' he asked tensely.

A muscle jumped in her jaw. 'He resisted arrest. He won't survive the gunshot wounds.'

Conrad frowned. Three miles later, he braced himself against the dashboard and roof of the vehicle as she took a sharp left onto a highway. The tires on the passenger side lifted off the blacktop briefly and dropped back down with a jolt.

'Shit, shit, shit!' Laura suddenly shouted. Her fist slammed repeatedly on the wheel, underscoring her cries.

'What?' snapped Conrad.

Laura had gone pale. Sweat beaded her forehead as she listened to the stream of communication coming through her earpiece. 'He's bleeding out.' Her lips pressed tightly together. 'His pulse has slowed right down. He's about to arrest.'

Conrad stared at the road, his knuckles whitening on the dashboard. Lights flashed in the distance. They were about a minute behind the motorcade.

Twenty seconds later, Laura's grip slackened on the wheel. Her breath hitched in her throat. Up ahead, the town cars and Suburbans making up the rear of the convoy were coming into view.

'Laura?' Conrad asked in a low voice.

'He's dead,' she whispered. Her voice shook. 'Oh God, he's dead.'

Fear squeezed Conrad's chest and contracted the air in his lungs. He inhaled sharply and yelled, 'Get me to him!'

Laura looked at him dazedly, confusion replacing the distress on her face. 'Didn't you hear me? He's dead! There's nothing you can do!'

'Yes, there is!' Conrad barked. His nails dug into his palms. 'Just get me there, Laura!'

She observed him for a stunned moment, her hazel eyes filled with anguish and uncertainty. She dipped her chin sharply, gripped the steering wheel, and spat out a terse message into her microphone to all the agents, state troopers, and county police officers in the motorcade.

'Clint, pull over!' she ordered. 'I have an urgent package to deliver.' She broke off for a beat. 'Yes!' she shouted. 'I know he's dead, but please, just do this, Woods! We have nothing to lose!'

A couple of seconds passed. Laura's shoulders sagged. She closed her eyes briefly.

'Thank you,' she whispered in the mouthpiece. She seemed to recall something and suddenly stiffened. 'Who else is in the car with you?' Her face cleared when she heard the answer. 'Good.'

The Suburban darted past the line of speeding vehicles. The heavily armored presidential limousine came in sight in the middle of the convoy. Laura maneuvered the Suburban behind it and flashed her headlights. The Cadillac responded by pulling off the highway and rolling to a stop in a lay-by overlooking an empty, overgrown field.

Laura followed and braked inches from the vehicle's bumper. 'Form a security perimeter around us!' she instructed through the microphone.

Conrad bolted out of the Suburban and ran toward the limousine. The rest of the motorcade screeched to a halt around them and blocked off the lanes of the highway. He reached the Cadillac and yanked open the armor-plated back door. The fresh, coppery smell of blood hit his nostrils. He lowered his head and looked inside.

'Shut down all the roads, stations, and airports!' Woods was bellowing into his radio unit from the front passenger seat. 'Goddammit, I don't care what you have to do! I want this state in lockdown! These bastards are not getting away!'

The glass partition that separated the back of the limousine from the driver's compartment had been lowered. President Westwood lay in a pool of blood on the rear-facing seats below it.

A woman in her forties with shoulder-length blonde hair and what would normally be a charismatic face knelt next to his head. Scarlet blotches darkened her gray dress suit. She held an oxygen mask between her crimson-stained fingers, her expression numb.

An equally blood-splattered agent sat paralyzed to her right, a used adrenaline pre-filled syringe discarded on his lap. His fingers were still clenched around the blood pack connected to an IV line in Westwood's right arm. An empty bag floated in the congealing puddles covering the floor of the limo.

A middle-aged man with a receding hairline slouched, slack-jawed, where the president normally sat. The other seat had been pulled down to access the emergency blood bank and resus equipment routinely stored in the trunk of the presidential limo.

Conrad climbed inside the vehicle and gently pushed the shocked agent out of the way. He knelt by Westwood. His presence seemed to bring everyone out of their stupor. The agent looked up sharply and automatically reached for his gun.

'It's all right, Harry. He's with me,' said Laura.

The agent looked over his shoulder to where she stood in the doorway of the limo. He gulped and nodded shakily. Conrad studied the still, waxen features of the president. He raised his left hand and placed it on the dead man's chest.

'What the hell is this?' barked the middle-aged man in the back. Out of the corner of his eye, Conrad saw the guy's head turn sharply to Laura and Woods. 'What's that man doing?'

'Shut up, Bill!' snapped the woman in the gray suit. She ignored the older man's shocked gasp and scrutinized Conrad. 'Is he one of you?' she demanded, glancing briefly at Laura.

Laura hesitated. 'Yes.'

It was Woods's turn to gape between Laura and the woman in the suit. 'One of who?' His eyes locked onto Conrad's hand. 'What the hell *is* he doing?'

'I don't know,' said Laura softly. 'I really don't know.'

Conrad closed his eyes and tuned them out. In the seconds since he had laid his fingers on Westwood, he had identified the extensive damage caused by the bullet that had penetrated the man's left armpit and punched through his lung and aorta before lodging just beneath his fourth rib.

The immortal's healing powers sparked down his left arm and flashed along the body of the snake birthmark before streaking out of its forked tongue toward his fingertips. He steered the unearthly energy inside the dead man and slowly pushed the bullet back along its path of entry until it plopped out from under his arm.

Conrad opened his eyes and looked at the strange slug lying in the pool of blood. He concentrated on closing the jagged tears in the dead man's artery. As he moved to the torn tissues of his lung, the immortal's gaze shifted to the blood pack attached to the IV line.

'You got any more of those?' he asked the agent next to him.

The man bobbed his head jerkily. 'Yes, in the trunk!'

'Get them,' Conrad ordered between clenched teeth. 'And start squeezing!'

The agent scrambled to the back of the limo and grabbed the blood bags. Conrad was aware of Laura's hot stare on the side of his face. A fine sheen of perspiration coated his brow as tendrils of his power continued to snake through the president's body. The agent attached the next blood pack to the IV and pumped it with both hands.

The immortal felt the dead man's heart and vessels slowly fill up. He stopped just shy of fully repairing the entry wound in his chest and took a deep breath to steel himself for what was to come. A moment later, he unleashed the full force of his immortal legacy.

It was like opening the tap on a dam. Within seconds, sweat dripped down Conrad's face and soaked his back. He curled over, his breath leaving his lips in short, sharp pants as heat exploded inside his chest. Heart racing like a high-speed train and blood thundering in his ears, Conrad reached deep inside himself until he located the source of his ungodly powers. Slowly, carefully, he wrapped the fingers of his consciousness around the shimmering mass and tugged.

'No,' Laura whispered behind him. 'No, stop it! You can't! You'll die!' Her voice rose in urgency as she reached inside the limo and grabbed his shoulder.

Conrad shuddered. It was the first time she had willingly touched him in more than three hundred years. He resisted her attempts to pull him away and focused all his energy on the pulsing, golden lines around his heart. He lifted his tortured face to the sky, the muscles and tendons in his neck tensing to breaking point.

A hoarse cry left his lips as he tore away a piece of his soul.

Conrad's world went supernova. He was dimly aware of his life force scorching a burning path along his birthmark as it departed his heart. He sagged and took deep, shuddering gasps. Black spots blurred his vision as his numbed senses slowly recovered from the incandescent explosion that had rocked his very being.

The body beneath his fingers jerked. A second later, the dead man's eyes slammed open.

Westwood gasped and sat up.

CHAPTER NINE

'WHAT IN THE NAME OF HELL WAS THAT?'

The Director of National Intelligence rested her chin on the back of her interlocked fingers and scrutinized Conrad across the shiny, polished wood of the conference table.

Conrad returned the woman's steely stare and absentmindedly rubbed his left arm. Even though several hours had passed since the incident with the president, his birthmark still tingled and throbbed; for all the immortal knew it was a trick of his weary imagination, he thought the black Aesculapian snake looked pretty pissed after what it had endured.

He glanced at the clock on the mantelpiece as it struck one p.m. before turning to watch the Director of National Intelligence once more. They were inside the Roosevelt Room, on the first floor of the West Wing, about a dozen feet or so from the Oval Office. The immortal stifled a sigh. He wished his first visit to the White House had taken place under more auspicious circumstances.

Sarah Connelly had changed out of the stained, gray dress suit she had been wearing that morning. There was no evidence of the bloodied and grim individual who had taken control of the chaotic situation that had followed Westwood's assassination and revival. In between ensuring the safe delivery of her commander-in-chief to the state hospital and his subsequent extraction to the White House via helicopter, Connelly had the press secretary issue a short statement to the media to the effect that the president had survived an attempt on his life and all law enforcement agencies were working closely together to hunt down the escaped assassin. She had also organized the treatment and interrogation of the injured killer Conrad had captured earlier that day at an undisclosed facility outside D.C. Her features now schooled in the cool, business-like expression that had no doubt helped her attain her current position, Connelly projected an almost palpable aura of authority.

Conrad was unfazed. All he wanted was a hot meal and a bed to crash in for the night. Despite his focused training in the last ten months, using his powers to their limits had drained him. Still, he had fared better than the first time he had done it.

'Yeah, Greene, what did you do?' demanded Woods. The Assistant Special Agent was sitting to the right of Connelly.

Laura stood behind Woods. By the look on her face and the way her fingers occasionally twitched at her sides, Conrad suspected she was struggling with a visceral urge to kill him. He swallowed another sigh and slouched in the chair.

'Sarah, do you know this man?' said Bill Sullivan. The National Security Advisor occupied the chair on the other side of the Director of National Intelligence. It was the middle-aged man with the receding hairline who had been in the back of the limo.

'No,' said Connelly. She regarded Laura with a critical expression. 'I didn't know your—*kind* could do that sort of thing.'

'"*Kind?*"' repeated Woods. He looked between Laura and Connelly, suspicion darkening his features once more. 'What "*kind?*" You said the same thing back in the limo! What are you talking about?'

'They can't,' Conrad stated. He ignored Woods's incensed scowl and gazed steadily at Connelly. 'As far as I know, I'm the only one alive today who possesses that ability.' He hesitated. 'It runs in my bloodline.'

Sullivan's lips were pinched in a white line. Before the National Security Advisor could utter the protest threatening to explode past his lips, Woods pushed his chair back and rose stiffly to his feet. A vein throbbed in the agent's forehead.

'If someone doesn't start answering my questions in the next five seconds, I swear to God, I'll—' he ground out between clenched teeth.

A door clattered open at the back of the room. Conrad looked over his shoulder and froze when he saw the group of men who walked in. He cursed under his breath.

'It's nice to see you too, Conrad,' drawled Victor Dvorsky.

The Head of the Order of Bastian Hunters and leader of the Bastian immortal race paused inside the room, his dark eyes assessing the people at the table.

'How the hell did you get here so fast?' snapped Conrad. 'Weren't you in Europe?'

'I was in Virginia, actually,' Victor replied blithely. He acknowledged Connelly with a brief nod. 'Sarah.'

'Victor.' Connelly's expression remained guarded.

With his tailored three-piece suit, silver-streaked dark hair, trim goatee, and lean build, Victor Dvorsky was the poster child for Capitol Hill politicians. In a sense, he was a truer statesman than any past or current member of Congress. Born into one of the most powerful noble families of Bastian society, Dvorsky had negotiated the treacherous corridors of the world's greatest powers for more than seven hundred years. He had survived countless political squabbles and blood-soaked battlefields in that time.

The four Bastians who made up his escort fanned out around him.

'Long time no see, Greene,' said one of the bodyguards. The red-haired immortal winked at him, an impish smile lighting up his face.

Conrad sighed. 'Anatole.'

Anatole Vassili looked across the room and grinned. 'Hey Laura.'

Laura gave him a dirty look. 'I have a bone to pick with you.'

The red-haired immortal raised an eyebrow and shrugged his shoulders in a 'What'd I do?' gesture.

Woods sagged. He turned to Connelly, his expression deflated. 'Who the hell are these people?' he said, waving his hand vaguely at the Bastian immortals.

Before she could answer, the door facing the Oval Office swung back forcefully on its hinges. The president strode in with two members of his detail. Connelly, Woods, and Sullivan rose respectfully to their feet, while the US Secret Service agents took up position next to the door. Conrad did not move.

James Anthony Westwood did not look like a man who had died two hours previously. In fact, bar the telltale bulge of the dressing covering the wound on his chest, he seemed to be the definition of health.

At just over six feet, he had a lanky build that projected a wiry, restless energy. Though not classically handsome, his features were nonetheless arresting and were dominated by piercing brown eyes that hinted at his distant Italian ancestry.

Now that he was in the presence of the man when he was upright and breathing, Conrad noticed the strong-willed light in the president's expression. He felt a flash of pity for the men and women of the US Secret Service; Westwood looked like the kind of guy who would have them dancing to his tune whether they liked it or not.

'Mr. President,' Victor greeted politely.

Westwood's gaze slipped briefly from Conrad's face. 'Victor.'

'Can we have a moment?' said the Bastian leader, his tone still relaxed.

Sullivan took a step toward the president. 'Really, James! What's the meaning of all—?'

Westwood cut his eyes to Sullivan. The National Security Advisor fell silent, his posture rigid.

'Could the five of you leave?' Westwood's gaze swung to encompass Sullivan, Connelly, Woods, and the two agents. 'I need to speak with these gentlemen in private.' He glanced at Laura. 'Agent Hartwell can stay.'

Connelly opened her mouth to voice a protest, thought better of it, and clamped her lips shut for a second. 'As you wish, sir,' she said in a tightly controlled voice. She hesitated. 'May I interject something?'

Westwood indicated she could speak.

'In view of what Woods and Sullivan witnessed back there,' said Connelly, 'I feel it would be wise if I updated them about the—*unusual* circumstances of this situation.'

Westwood looked at Victor. 'Do you have any objections?'

The Bastian leader shrugged. 'As long as they're aware of the conditions surrounding that information and what could happen if they breach them, I have none.' Although his tone remained friendly, no one could miss the underlying veneer of steel that coated his words.

Connelly acknowledged the Bastian noble's words with a stiff nod and departed the room with Woods and Sullivan in tow. Westwood waited until the door closed behind the Secret Service bodyguards. He pulled up a chair, sat down, and leaned forward with his elbows on the table, his probing gaze focused on Conrad once more.

'What did you do to me?' he asked in a low voice.

The immortal ran a hand through his hair and rubbed the

back of his neck. He was starting to wish he'd stayed in the goddamned rainforest after all. 'I gave you one of my lives.'

Shocked silence descended on the room.

'You did *what?*' said Victor in a hard voice.

Conrad sighed and glanced at his old mentor. 'He died before I could heal his injuries. The only way to bring him back was to gift him one of my seventeen lives.'

'Is that even possible?' said Westwood after a pause. He glanced at the bloodstains on Conrad's clothes and directed a wary look at Victor. 'I know you people have...*abilities*, but I didn't know reviving the dead was one of them.'

'It isn't,' Victor retorted gruffly. 'At least, it's never happened before, to my knowledge.' The Bastian leader's eyes shifted to Conrad's birthmark. An unreadable emotion darted across his face. 'How long have you been able to do this?' he asked in an accusing tone.

Conrad was aware of Laura's heated gaze as he studied his hands. 'This is only the second time I've gifted one of my lives.' He hesitated. 'The first time was eleven months ago, when I brought Rocky back.' He looked up, saw their blank expressions, and suppressed another sigh. This was the part he was going to struggle to explain.

'Who's Rocky?' Westwood asked, nonplussed.

Conrad shifted uneasily in the chair. 'My dog,' he mumbled.

This time, the silence that followed was deafening.

'Your what?' said Anatole, slack jawed.

'Rocky is my dog,' retorted Conrad. He was unable to stop the defensive note that crept into his voice.

Westwood opened and closed his mouth soundlessly. Conrad suspected it wasn't everyday the president was rendered speechless.

'Let me get this straight,' said Victor dully. 'You suddenly develop this hitherto unknown immortal ability, and the first thing you do is use it to give one of your lives to your *dog?*'

'It was an accident,' Conrad admitted grudgingly.

He hoped they would buy the blatant lie. For although the event had indeed started out with a tragic mishap, it had been his decision to kill himself that had enabled him to unlock his greatest power.

Thirteen months ago, on an unusually hot night during the wet season, when heavy rains had pounded the forests for weeks and inundated the floodplains of the Amazon, Conrad had woken at dawn to the sound of yelping coming from the swamp outside his cabin. He'd walked out into a faint morning mist, stopped on the bank of the pond, and spotted something floating in the water.

It turned out to be a wet, bedraggled puppy clinging to a log of wood that had drifted down the bloated channel feeding the marshland.

Surprised that the creature had survived the deadly caimans that inhabited this part of the rainforest, Conrad took the canoe out and went to rescue the shivering dog. When he lifted the animal up from the log for a closer inspection, it gave him a long, assessing look from soulful, chocolate eyes.

Conrad brought the dog inside the cabin, dried it with an old towel, and fed it the stew he'd made the night before. The puppy wolfed the food down, licked the bowl clean, released a giant burp, and promptly fell asleep.

The next day, Conrad went to Alvarães to make enquiries about any missing pets. Two weeks later, no one had come to claim the animal. The immortal was unexpectedly relieved. In the short time they had spent together, the puppy had completely won over his heart. He named him Rocky.

For the next two months, man and dog were inseparable. Although he knew the animal's life span would be a blip in the night compared to his own long and insufferable existence, Conrad was nonetheless grateful for the canine's company.

One night, when they were sitting outside the cabin

watching a thunderstorm dance across the dark skies, Rocky bolted from the deck and disappeared into the trees crowding the banks of the swamp. Conrad heard him growl before emitting a single, high-pitched yelp and falling silent.

He grabbed a fire torch from the hearth and raced into the jungle, where he found the dog lying by the water's edge. The fading rattle of a bushmaster snake sounded in the undergrowth close by. In the flickering light of the flames, Conrad spotted the pale body of the deadly creature, with its diamond-shaped patterns of darker colors, disappearing along the forest floor.

Rocky had been bitten twice, on the head and on the neck. Already, the puppy's face was swollen and his breathing labored. Faint whimpers escaped his slack jaws. Within seconds, he was vomiting and drooling uncontrollably.

As fat raindrops cascaded from the storm-tossed clouds and extinguished the torch by his side, Conrad fought desperately to save the dog. Kneeling in the mud, in an inky darkness that was lit by the occasional bolt of lightning, he cradled Rocky's head to his chest and unfurled the ungodly powers that he had inherited from the male predecessors of his pureblood lineage, all of whom were nobles directly descended from the original forefathers of their race.

His attempts to reverse the advancing effects of the venom were in vain. When he felt the dog's life force start to ebb from the tiny body quivering in his arms, centuries of loneliness and despair erupted to the surface of Conrad's consciousness with a vengeance. He threw his head back and raged at the heavens. No one answered his broken cries.

What the hell am I doing? he finally thought wretchedly. *I live alone in the middle of nowhere. Nobody knows I'm here. Nobody cares if I live or I die.*

Rocky went limp in his grasp. As he gazed into the puppy's unseeing eyes, his vision blurring with raindrops and tears, Conrad suddenly resolved to end it all there and then.

His father had warned him about what happened when an immortal with their healing abilities went too far; if he ever exerted his power beyond its breaking point, if he dared stretch it past the natural ceiling he could sense when he utilized it, he would suffer not just one death but lose all his lives in one go, the pieces of his soul shattered in an instant. It had happened twice before in their bloodline.

Knowing that releasing the brakes on his immortal energy would lead to his final demise, Conrad took a deep shuddering breath and let go. The next sixty seconds were the most terrifying and exhilarating of the immortal's entire existence.

As he forced his healing powers into the puppy's dead body to bring about his own end and waited for the telltale symptoms that would indicate he was nearing his limits, Conrad bid a silent farewell to Laura Hartwell.

When his heart finally thudded irregularly inside his chest and his vision tunneled into a shrinking dark circle, the immortal took giant, quivering gulps and welcomed Death's looming shadow with open arms. But it seemed Death had other plans that night.

In that penultimate moment of consciousness, as his lips parted for what he presumed was his final gasp, something raw and hot exploded inside him. What followed was a singular moment of clarity and insight. Though it lasted seconds, the instant felt like hours to the immortal. And in that indiscernible period of suspended time, Conrad grasped what no one in his bloodline had likely perceived. He saw the unearthly lines of energy that mapped out the contours of his heart.

Before he realized what was happening, he felt his mind grasp one of the shimmering threads and pull. The next thing he knew, he was waking up on the forest floor, in the dark and the rain. Rocky was crouched on his chest and licked his face anxiously, his moist breath warming the immortal's skin.

In the days and weeks that followed, Conrad came to understand and accept what had happened. He had no choice in the matter, for he could feel himself changing in ways he could never have anticipated. It was as if he had unlocked a door he never even knew existed. His powers were evolving. They were stronger, more focused, more...aware.

For one thing, he knew exactly how many pieces of his soul remained, not just through a normal death tally, but because he could feel them. It was as if they were extensions of his body, like his arms and legs.

The wounded jaguar was the first creature he healed after that fateful night. Conrad was amazed when he realized how much more he could sense about the creature's injuries when he laid his hand on it. It was as if his fingertips provided a detailed 3D map for his mind, complete with directions and flashing danger signs. He also learned the precise degree to which he could fine-tune the energy he delivered into the injured jaguar's body.

After that incident, he thought it wise to explore the evolution of his newfound abilities. With the abundance of wildlife on offer in the jungle around him, he took every opportunity he could find to practice his powers; be it sick or dying creatures, he trained until he had his skills refined to an art form, but never went as far as to give away another piece of his soul.

All this he now recounted to the attentive group inside the Roosevelt Room. He withheld the part about how he had originally attempted to end his existence. Judging by the haunted expression that dawned in Laura's eyes, Conrad suspected she had an inkling about what had actually transpired that fateful night. Had his heart not already shattered a thousand times over in the last three centuries, he would almost have chuckled then. The one person in the world who knew him the best also loathed him the most.

'Does this mean I'm different now?' Westwood asked stiffly. He stared unblinkingly at Conrad. 'I need to know if I can still carry on in my duties as Head of State. Otherwise, I'll have to abdicate my—'

'You're fine,' interrupted Conrad. 'All I did was jumpstart your body. The piece of my soul is only there to keep you alive.'

'Are you sure?' demanded Westwood.

Conrad studied the president closely. He sensed there was more behind the question than a simple need for reassurance. 'Yes. Why do you ask?'

Westwood hesitated. 'Because I can feel you.'

Conrad went still. 'What do you mean?'

Westwood looked like he was choosing his next words carefully. 'I knew a set of twins when I was growing up. They always claimed to know exactly where the other was or if the other one got injured. It's like that, except...different.' His eyes never moved from Conrad's face. 'Before I came into this room, I knew you were here. Not because I was told.' He faltered. 'I could sense it. It was as if you were a radio beacon and I was homing in on your signal.'

Conrad blinked and straightened in his seat. The shock of Westwood's revelation resonated through him.

'I didn't know that,' he said slowly. He recalled the pain he had felt in his chest when he and Rocky had parted, and how the ache had slowly faded over the past two days. 'It gets better with time, I think. Still, it should have no influence on your abilities to act as Head of State.'

'A goddamned dog,' Anatole muttered under his breath. 'Un-freakin' believable.'

Conrad ignored his old friend's comment and studied the figures around the table. He caught the looks dawning on the faces of his former mentor and the president, and rose to his feet.

'Well, I think my work here is done,' he said briskly. He glanced at Laura and turned to Westwood. 'Your agents have the envelope I retrieved from the plane. The bodies of the pilot and the third assassin are with the medical examiner in Manaus. I hope you find the people responsible for this.'

He walked toward the exit and had just closed his fingers on the door handle when Westwood and Victor spoke simultaneously.

'Stop!' they barked.

Conrad closed his eyes. *Shit. Almost made it.*

CHAPTER TEN

Nadica Rajkovic climbed over the gunwale of the custom-made Zodiac RIB and stepped onto the side dock of a sleek super yacht. The two crewmen waiting to maneuver the inflatable back into its storage space on the upper level of the seventy-five-foot, diesel-powered vessel bowed their heads respectfully when she walked past. Nadica ignored them and climbed the passerelle to the port walkway. She followed the teak-laid passage to the main deck aft.

A woman dressed in a flawless, white pantsuit stood in front of the railing that overlooked the swimming platform at the stern of the yacht. Beyond it, foam-tipped waves rippled across the dark blue waters of Chesapeake Bay. She was gazing out over the estuary, her red-nailed fingers resting lightly on the steel bar. Nadica removed her sunglasses and studied the silent figure.

Ariana Rajkovic's profile was a work of beauty that Nadica never tired of contemplating. With her pale complexion and natural rose-cheeked tint, the older woman's face was as unblemished as in the first memories Nadica could recall of her. Long, curved lashes graced eyes she knew were an identical smoky gray to hers. Below the Grecian nose, her plump, bow-shaped lips could curve in a heart-stopping smile, or just as easily compress in a tight line of fury.

Nadica crossed the deck and planted a soft kiss on the woman's velvety cheek.

Ariana turned. 'It is done?' she said, her fingers unconsciously clenching on the railing.

'Yes, Ama,' Nadica replied with a dutiful nod. 'He's dead.'

Satisfaction flared in Ariana's eyes and her shoulders visibly relaxed. She raised a hand to the back of Nadica's head, pulled her forward, and pressed her lips to her brow.

'Well done, child,' she murmured. 'Come. Sit.'

Nadica removed her cap and shook out her hair. She shrugged off the Redskins jersey covering her running shorts and T-shirt, and curled up on one of the overstuffed, padded seats that lined the gunwale. Ariana joined her and wrapped her arm around Nadica's shoulders. They leaned into each other.

'No one saw you?' Ariana asked.

'No,' Nadica replied. Her fingers rose unconsciously to touch the amulet at the base of her throat. To any onlookers, the two of them would have looked like sisters.

There was a noise from the opposite end of the deck. Nadica turned her head and saw the doors to the main salon slide open. A man walked out, a cell phone in hand. His face visibly brightened when he saw her.

'Nadica,' he said in a husky voice. He headed toward them.

'Hello, brother.' Nadica rose and hugged the man.

Zoran Rajkovic stepped back, his arms looped loosely around her waist. A smile broke across his tanned, sculptured face, and an amulet identical to hers gleamed at the opening of his shirt. 'I'm glad to see you made it back safely.'

'I will always return to you,' said Nadica, her lips curving in an answering grin. An achingly familiar, age-old love blossomed inside her chest as she beheld her brother's handsome features.

There was no one else she cherished more in this world than her older sibling. She would do anything for him.

The sudden blare of a phone broke the comfortable silence between them.

'Excuse me,' said Zoran. He touched the screen of his cell and brought it to his ear. 'Rajkovic here.' A frown dawned on his face as he listened to words she could not hear.

Nadica went still in his embrace.

'Okay,' said Zoran finally. A muscle quivered in his cheek. 'Find out where they took the prisoner and keep me updated.' He ended the call abruptly.

'What's wrong?' Nadica asked in the taut hush that ensued.

'You said you killed him when you called.' Zoran's voice was smooth and controlled. His hand dropped from her waist.

Ariana straightened in her seat. 'Nadica?'

'I did,' Nadica retorted, her voice hardening. 'It was a perfect shot. There's no way Westwood could have survived it.'

Zoran's hand tightened around the cell. 'That was our source. Although it's yet to be officially announced, the president was discharged from the hospital an hour ago.' His slate-gray eyes glittered dangerously. 'He walked out of the building.'

'That's impossible!' snapped Nadica. 'I saw the bullet strike him. It was a lethal wound!'

'Are you sure, child?' interjected Ariana. The older woman's lips were pursed in a pale line.

'Yes, Ama.' Nadica's nails dug into her palms. 'I swear on our bloodline,' she hissed.

The yacht's twin diesel engines rumbled into life in the frozen stillness.

'If that's the case, then something is very wrong,' Ariana finally said, her features set in a steely mask. 'We need to find out how the president survived Nadica's shot.' She glanced between the two siblings. 'We cannot let this interfere with the rest of our plans.' She focused on Zoran. 'Is everything else proceeding according to schedule?'

'Yes,' he replied. 'Our operations are almost complete. The agents in Europe and Asia should be reporting back to me in the coming hours.'

'The devices will be ready in the next few days,' added Nadica. 'I'll personally be taking delivery of them.'

'Good.' Ariana turned and looked out over the water. The yacht was underway. White backwash foamed in its wake as it powered smoothly toward the Atlantic. 'It would have been better if President Westwood had died today,' she said stonily. 'Still, if we are successful, he will be more vulnerable in the days that will follow. We'll have another chance to get rid of him.'

'Yes, Ama,' said Nadica through gritted teeth. 'I will not fail you again.'

Lines creased Zoran's brow. 'We should take care of our hired help. Even if he doesn't know enough to implicate us, I don't like loose ends.'

'I'll see to it,' said Nadica.

'Take the helicopter,' ordered Zoran. 'I'll phone the location through to you.'

Nadica went to her cabin for a change of clothes and headed toward the super yacht's landing pad.

A HUNDRED MILES AWAY, CONRAD FROZE WITH HIS HAND ON the door of the Roosevelt Room.

'Get back here,' commanded Westwood.

'Sit down,' ordered Victor.

The immortal hung his head and examined the fine wood grain in front of him. He contemplated the likelihood of evading the hordes of US Secret Service agents currently inside the White House.

Laura could still read him. 'Your chances are zero, Greene,' she scoffed.

Conrad cursed under his breath and returned to the table. Westwood waited until he sat down before he dropped his bombshell.

'I want you to find out who's behind this,' the president declared. He observed him unwaveringly across the polished surface.

The immortal bestowed a blank look upon him in return. He wondered fleetingly whether giving the man one of his lives had done something to his brain.

'You have a whole army of law enforcement agencies on the task right now,' Conrad pointed out. 'Never mind the half dozen international organizations they're presently coordinating with. I don't see what else I can contribute to this endeavor.'

'You're the one who uncovered the plot,' said Westwood, his tone uncompromising. 'You're one step ahead of everyone else. Dammit, Greene, you saved my life!' He banged his fist on the table. 'No, you *gave* me back my life!'

Conrad watched Westwood steadily in the hush that followed. 'If you really want to thank me, I'll accept a case of beer.'

A strangled sound escaped Anatole's lips.

'You seem to be forgetting something.' Victor's dark gaze swung from Westwood to Conrad. 'The immortals also have a vested interest in this matter. As the representative of the Bastian First Council at the UN, albeit secretly, I have a responsibility to assist the head of state of the most powerful nation on Earth, if I feel this is the right path to follow.' His tone hardened. 'The death of the president would have resulted in huge political unrest across the world, especially with the current volatile situation in the Middle East and with North Korea. Whoever is behind this needs to be stopped.'

Conrad tensed at the expression in the Bastian noble's eyes.

'I have already conferred with the other members of the Bastian First Council on this subject, and we're all in agreement,' Victor continued, confirming the reluctant immortal's worst fears. 'We want you on the investigation team.'

Conrad felt his last hope slip away. He silently cursed the fate that had brought the dead pilot of the Cessna and his passenger to his doorstep. 'And if I refuse?' he challenged grimly.

Victor's lips curved in a thin, humorless smile. 'Technically speaking, you're a deserter, Conrad. I know you've been away for a while, but you remember what happens to deserters, don't you?'

Conrad glared at the Bastian leader. He knew all too well what immortals did to those they deemed to be traitors. 'I didn't run away from the Bastian ranks, I just—'

'Left your home one day and disappeared without telling your superior officer of your intentions and future whereabouts?' Victor interrupted coldly. 'Did you seriously think I'd count the last six decades as an extended leave of absence?'

'You know exactly why I left!' Conrad spat.

Victor's eyes flickered to Laura. He remained visibly unmoved. 'Still not good enough.'

Conrad's hands curled into fists under the table. He had known Victor long enough to realize that his former mentor was going to use every single trick in the book to get his own way; the immortal noble's reputation as a silver-tongued, bull-headed bastard had preceded him through the ages.

'If I do this, we're even,' he finally ground out.

He felt a searing stare on his skin and looked around in time to see Laura pale. She flinched when she met his gaze and steeled her features into an aloof expression once more.

Before Conrad could fathom what the emotion was that he had glimpsed in her eyes, a knock sounded at the main door.

Westwood signaled at Laura. She crossed the floor and opened it.

Connelly walked in with Woods and Sullivan in tow. The two men looked gray under their skin. They stopped just inside the room and watched the immortals guardedly, a hint of fear evident in their posture.

Woods masked his apprehension and turned to Laura. 'Is that why you always refused the promotions I offered you?'

Laura gave him a pained look. 'Sorry, Clint. It would have been impossible for me to accept. Only the president, the VP, and Director Connelly were aware of my background.'

Sullivan startled at her words. He turned to Westwood. 'The vice president knows?'

'Yes,' acknowledged Westwood.

'How long have there been...immortals in the service?' Woods asked after a short lull. He could not completely disguise his distress at the magnitude of the deception that had been played out.

'Ever since President Kennedy's assassination,' Laura replied in a low voice. Her eyes moved briefly to Victor. 'Both the Bastian and Crovir First Councils offered their protective services to the US government's commander-in-chief, as well as other important heads of state around the world.'

'Are there many of you working as agents?' said Woods gruffly.

Laura shrugged and gave him a tired smile. 'A few. We rotate out of the law enforcement agencies every ten years.'

'Agencies?' said Woods. Laura winced.

Westwood broke the ensuing silence.

'I want Greene on the primary team investigating my assassination,' he told Connelly and Sullivan. He checked himself and muttered, 'Christ, I can't believe I just said that. Let's call it my *attempted* assassination from now on, shall we?'

Connelly's expression grew thunderous. 'What?'

'Honestly, James, what the hell's gotten into you?' snapped Sullivan. He turned to the Director of National Intelligence. 'Sarah, we should talk to the Cabinet about invoking Section Four of the 25th Amendment and—'

'And what, Bill?' interrupted Westwood. He rose and leaned forward with his palms down on the table. 'On what grounds are you going to invoke the 25th? The Senate and the Speaker of the House will clearly see that I am more than capable of performing the duties of my office. The vice president and I will deny all knowledge about the existence of the immortals, and you will only end up looking like a goddamned fool. And don't even think about telling them you saw me come back from the dead. That will *guarantee* your confinement to a psychiatric hospital.' He stopped and straightened, his posture rigid. 'Bill, I want to get the bastards who did this. By attacking me, they've declared war on the United States.' He looked at Conrad briefly. 'If not for Greene, I wouldn't be here right now, and this country would be shot to hell. He's the only one who picked up on the threat. And he traveled halfway across the world to stop it.'

'To be fair, I didn't know this was about killing you until I got to Washington,' Conrad admitted.

Woods's expression fell at the president's words.

'I'm not blaming the Service, Clint,' said Westwood. 'But I still want Greene on this investigation. In fact, I think he should lead it.'

'What?' barked Conrad.

'You can't be serious, James!' snarled Connelly.

'Christ, this is just so—' said Sullivan.

'I know,' Westwood cut in. He observed his National Security Advisor with a steadfast gaze. 'Bill, I *need* you with me on this. You too, Sarah,' he added, glancing at the Director of National Intelligence.

Despite the anger thrumming through him, Conrad had to

admire Westwood. He was as devious a bastard as Victor Dvorsky.

Tense seconds passed. Sullivan's shoulders finally sagged. 'I can't believe we're asking a complete outsider to lead on this,' he murmured. Connelly remained silent, her expression stony.

Conrad stared down the man opposite him. 'I seem to recall agreeing to assist you on this matter, not be at the helm of the entire goddamned investigation,' he said icily.

Westwood's headstrong expression never wavered. 'Think of it as a promotion.'

Conrad inhaled sharply and was about to launch into an angry tirade when Victor cut in.

'I agree with the president,' the Bastian leader interjected. 'You should lead.'

Conrad stared aghast at his former mentor. 'Have you lost your mind? I've not been in the field for decades!' he roared.

'That didn't seem to stop you today,' Victor responded calmly.

Conrad's knuckles whitened on the table. It didn't take a genius to realize he didn't have any options left. He closed his eyes briefly, a defeated sigh escaping his lips. There were no two ways about it. He was going to have to see this whole damn thing through to its bitter end.

'Is he even capable of overseeing such a large operation?' said Connelly. The Director of National Intelligence still appeared unconvinced by her commander-in-chief's decision.

Victor shrugged. 'If not for Conrad, the United Kingdom of Great Britain may not have come into existence.' He ignored the shocked expressions and gasps around the room. 'He was my best general and the greatest team leader I've ever had in my section. I trust him implicitly.'

'Thanks for the vote of confidence,' Conrad said bitterly. A last surge of defiance made him straighten from the table. 'I do have a couple of conditions.'

The Bastian leader cast a slow, appraising look his way and arched an eyebrow. 'And those would be?'

'I want Anatole on the team,' Conrad demanded.

The red-haired immortal startled where he leaned against the wall. 'Huh? Me?' he exclaimed, his eyes round.

Surprise darted across Victor's face. His expression grew shuttered.

'Yeah, you,' scoffed Conrad. He directed a mocking smile at his old friend.

Anatole's eyes shrunk into slits. 'Oh, you son of a—'

'Agreed,' Victor interrupted. He ignored Anatole's choked protest and considered Laura and Woods. 'I believe the US Secret Service would appreciate having one of their members on the team. Hartwell should be in as well.'

'What?' said Laura.

'No,' Conrad stated adamantly.

She glared at him. 'Oh yeah? Why not?'

A wave of lassitude swept through Conrad. The events of the day were catching up with him.

'By your reaction just now, I deduce you weren't exactly craving the role,' he said in a worn-out voice. 'Besides, I thought you never wanted to have anything to do with me again.'

Stony silence fell between them.

'That's beside the point,' Laura stated frostily.

Westwood looked pointedly between them. 'Is there some history between the two of you I should be aware of?'

Conrad caught the faintest glimmer of amusement in the president's eyes. He was starting to wish he'd never revived the stubborn bastard.

'Yeah,' Anatole said, his tone sullen. 'They used to get like a house on fire. *Literally*.'

Westwood's face grew grave. 'I hope you won't let your

personal feelings interfere with this investigation,' he told Laura.

She bristled at the president's words. 'No, sir.'

Conrad ran a hand through his hair, too exhausted to argue. He turned to Westwood. 'My second condition is that you provide me with Top Secret clearance to national security and counterintelligence data. On a need-to-know basis, obviously.'

This time, the hush that followed was short-lived.

'James, if you agree to this—' Connelly started in a strained voice.

'How vital is it that you have this access?' said Westwood, his eyes not moving from Conrad's face.

'Very,' replied the immortal. 'I need to use all the available resources at my disposal if you want me to have a shot at finding these people.'

Westwood mulled this over for several seconds. He turned to Connelly. 'Do it.'

Connelly's lips tightened in a grim line. 'Jesus, James, the background investigation itself takes about a year—'

'Just get it done, Sarah!' Westwood barked. 'We don't have a goddamned year. I want these bastards found yesterday!'

CHAPTER ELEVEN

AN HOUR LATER, CONRAD STOOD AT THE HEAD OF THE White House Situation Room, in the basement of the West Wing. He studied the sea of hostile faces in front of him while Sarah Connelly spoke by his side.

'Conrad Greene is a special operative assigned by President Westwood to lead the investigation on the assassination attempt that took place at the FedEx Field today,' announced the Director of National Intelligence in a stilted voice. 'He has been given emergency TS clearance for the duration of this mission.'

Although it was evident that Connelly begrudged having had to violate internal regulations to grant him the classified information access Conrad had asked for, the immortal sensed she would cooperate with him as long as he did nothing to threaten the interests of the president and the United States government. She had introduced him briefly to the chief National Security Staff and the Sit Room Director ahead of the meeting of the special, multi-agency task force that had been put together to tackle the crisis.

'Why an external investigator, Connelly? And a civilian at

that,' said the FBI National Security Branch Special Agent in a hard voice. 'Does the president think this is an inside job?'

'No,' retorted Connelly. 'Greene was the one who identified the threat.' She hesitated. 'Had it not been for him, the assassination attempt would have been successful. He saved the president's life, Lewis.'

Despite her inscrutable expression, Conrad detected the flicker of tension in the woman's posture; the Director of National Intelligence could hardly announce that the enemy's mission had been a positive success.

'The floor is yours, Greene,' Connelly said curtly. She stepped aside and took a seat at the head of the table dominating the crowded conference room.

Conrad ignored the palpable resentment permeating the air. He recalled the last assignment he had spearheaded for the Bastian First Council. Although he never sought the admiration and deference the immortals under his charge so readily showed him, he was used to his commands being obeyed to the letter. This was going to be a completely different ball game.

He waited until the low mutters died down. 'Three things. First, I'm sorry the Service lost two men today. I wish their deaths could have been avoided,' he said in a cold, clear voice. 'What is done is done. Dwelling on it won't achieve anything.' He observed the guarded glances being exchanged around the room.

'Second, I'm just as pissed as you at my having been put in charge of this investigation. Trust me, I don't want to be here.' Conrad felt the animosity level drop a notch. 'However, now that I've committed to this mission,' he added, his tone hardening, 'make no mistake, I *will* give it my all. And I expect no less from you.'

The FBI lead agent grunted, his irritation plain to see. Conrad ignored him.

'Third and final point.' The immortal looked to the two

figures standing silently behind him. 'Agent Laura Hartwell of the US Secret Service and Special Operative Anatole Vassili will be my seconds in command for the duration of this assignment.'

The red-haired immortal lifted a hand in a small wave and grinned. 'Hi. Call me Anatole.'

Laura rolled her eyes. Conrad stifled a sigh. Angry murmurs rose from the men and women crowded in the room.

'Connelly, what the hell is going on here?' snapped the CIA representative, a woman with auburn hair and gray eyes. 'Who *are* these men?'

The Director of National Intelligence straightened in her seat, her eyes glittering with thinly veiled anger. 'This is what our commander-in-chief has dictated, Donaghy. As to who they are, I'm afraid that's classified information for which none of you have clearance.' She faltered for a beat. 'Although I have similar reservations on the subject, I've seen Greene in action and I trust Westwood's judgment. Squabbling amongst ourselves is only wasting precious time we do not have.'

Conrad watched the assembled agents closely in the taut silence that followed. 'Hartwell, Vassili, and I have worked together in the past. Although we have suffered casualties along the way, our squad has had a one hundred percent mission success rate.' He frowned. 'Let me be clear on one thing. *You* are now part of *our* team.' He paused. 'Any questions?'

Grudging respect appeared on some of the faces in the room. There was a general shaking of heads. Although he knew it would take time to win the agents' trust, Conrad saw the lack of queries as a good sign.

'Good,' he said with a curt nod. 'Let's get down to business.' He looked at the communications technician standing at the head of the room. 'Bring it up.'

The man typed on the keyboard in front of him. One of the large wall monitors flashed on.

'This investigation will have three stems, all of them targeted at finding out who was behind this assassination attempt and apprehending them,' Conrad explained. 'Number one: we need to identify the individual who shot the president and killed the two bodyguards at the FedEx Field.' Satellite images and photographs of the stadium appeared on the screen. 'Despite the emergency closure of all transport routes out of Maryland, state and county law enforcement have yet to locate a possible suspect. We can only assume the killer got away. Finding out the who and how will give us information about the organization responsible for this.'

A voice chimed in, its tone skeptic.

'What makes you think this is an organization rather than a couple of radicals who had it in for the president?' said the Homeland Security lead agent, a guy called Petersen.

'This was a sophisticated plan,' said Laura. 'President Westwood has made many enemies since he came into office, both on the domestic and international scenes. The list of possible suspects is long.' She glanced at Conrad with a neutral expression. 'What Greene hasn't told you yet is that he came across an envelope recovered from a plane crash in Brazil two days ago. It was inside a briefcase that belonged to one of the four killers who had been assigned to this assassination and contained encoded information and detailed maps of the stadium.' She indicated the second display terminal that lit up next to the first one. 'Greene also found ten photographs inside that briefcase. They were all of US Secret Service agents assigned to the president's security detail.' Surprised mumbles erupted around the room when pictures of the envelope's contents appeared on the screen.

'Is that the encoded information that led you to the killers' positions?' said Petersen.

'Yes,' said Conrad. 'Though it never gave us the location of the fourth killer.'

'Hmm,' murmured Donaghy. 'It seems an elaborate way to get the information across.'

'We believe the assassins were hired to work independently of each other,' said Laura. 'Hence the need to get the message through to each of them in an encoded format for which they would already have been given a key and an indication of which of the passages to take as their position. We think the haiku was written specifically to indicate the date the attempt should take place.'

Conrad's gaze darted over the assembled agents. He chose his next words prudently. 'The format of these instructions tells us something about the enemy we are facing: they like theatrics.' He paused, deliberately. 'And they didn't know when they were going to act until a few days ago.'

He watched the meaning behind his words sink in.

Donaghy's face darkened. 'That means we have a mole, doesn't it?'

'How so?' said Petersen, the Homeland Security agent.

'The security details for the FedEx Field fundraiser were only confirmed last week,' said Laura in a flinty tone. 'They included the exact routes we were going to take to deliver President Westwood and extract him in an emergency.'

'Shit,' muttered Lewis. The FBI agent's eyes scanned the faces of his colleagues, his posture stiff.

'Rest assured, we're looking for the traitor in our midst,' said Connelly. 'In the meantime, we continue to work as a team.' Her voice held a hint of a warning.

'I agree,' said Conrad. 'Our focus needs to remain on finding out the identities of these people.'

Knowing that they were going to have to watch their backs because of the possible double agent inside their circle would make cooperation between the different organizations involved in the investigation fraught. Conrad felt a sudden rush of gratitude for Connelly's presence.

'The body of the killer who died in the plane crash is with the medical examiner in Manaus,' the immortal continued. 'We need to retrieve it and get it examined by our people, along with the body of the assassin who was killed at the stadium today. We have to ID these two men fast. Although we believe them to be contract killers, their associates may be able to help with our investigation.' His gaze flickered to the Director of National Intelligence. 'The assassin who was captured has had his injuries treated and is being held at a secure location. So far, he's refusing to talk.'

The NSA agent, a man called Franklin, raised an eyebrow. 'Haven't we been able to establish who they are from their biometrics?' he said, incredulous.

Anatole shook his head. 'Nope. Both the dead guy and the prisoner were wearing artificial skin membranes imprinted with fake prints taken off US soldiers who died in combat in Afghanistan. The killers' palms and own fingertips looked like they've been surgically modified. Even if these guys were on any databases, you wouldn't be able to identify them now. So far, we've had zero hits on TIDE, NCIC, hell, even Interpol.' He grimaced. 'The facial recognition software gave us zilch as well. We believe they went under the knife to have their features altered.'

'So we know they may have connections in Asia,' said Donaghy. 'It'd be difficult to get our dead soldiers' prints without someone doing it locally.' The CIA agent's eyes grew narrow. 'Of course, they could have broken into the US Armed Forces database to obtain that information, but I seriously doubt it. The security protocols and firewalls have been heavily enhanced in the last ten years.'

'There have been no intelligence reports from the NCC, the NSA, the TTIC, the NIC, or the DIA to suggest there was an impending domestic or international threat,' said Connelly. She rubbed the back of her neck and sighed. 'As much as I hate to admit it, we're working blind here, people.'

A taut silence ensued. Conrad did the math and unraveled the acronyms. The enemy was seriously sophisticated if they had managed to coordinate this assassination without hitting the radar of the National Counterterrorism Center, the National Security Agency, the Terrorist Threat Integration Center, the National Intelligence Council, or the Defense Intelligence Agency.

Donaghy leaned forward, her eyes bright as she stared at Conrad. 'You said there were three stems to this investigation. What are the other two?'

The immortal smiled faintly. He liked the CIA representative's zeal. 'Our second priority is to analyze and trace the origins of the weapons and ammunitions the killers used.' A third screen flared brightly into life, and several forensic photographs appeared across the screen. 'These are no ordinary guns,' he explained as excited whispers rang across the table. 'As far as we're aware, there is no patent in existence for these firearms, and they are not in production or circulation in any country in the world. Initial inspection shows that they are made of some sort of carbon-fiber-reinforced plastic. The bullets are ceramic, encased in a malleable jacket for grip in the rifling. Both the weapons and the ammunition were designed for easy assembly and dismantling, and created explicitly to evade metal detectors.' He frowned at the display. 'Judging from their composition, they were very expensive to make and were likely never intended to last hundreds of shots, which means that the enemy has the funds and the ability to either manufacture such firearms or outsource the job to specialists.'

The assembled agents digested this information with a range of wary looks that mirrored the immortal's own apprehension, which had doubled when he'd come to that conclusion a short while ago.

'The third element of this investigation is the most complex,' said Laura. 'Despite what Director Connelly has stated about the lack of information from the intelligence community, we need to look at all the available data again.' A low groan escaped the NSA guy's lips. Laura glanced at him with a frown. 'We're looking for isolated events that may suggest a pattern of threat against the United States and, in particular, the person of the president. Spread the word to your individual teams. However insignificant a detail may seem to the analysts assigned to this task force, I want to know about it.'

'Vassili and I are going to talk to the suspect,' said Conrad. 'Agent Hartwell will start looking at the surveillance data and the findings of the preliminary site investigation at the FedEx field. CIA and NSA, you're on intel. FBI and Homeland have the bodies and the guns.' His eyes shifted briefly to the Sit Room Director. 'The president is allowing us to use this place as our command post. All incoming data is to be pooled here.' He stood back from the table. 'Meeting's over. Let's go, people.'

The agents dispersed rapidly, their movements full of urgency and purpose as they headed out the room amidst a low rumble of conversation. Someone spoke quietly behind Conrad as he started toward the door with Anatole.

'I may have underestimated you, Greene,' said Sarah Connelly.

Conrad stopped and turned to observe the inscrutable look on the face of the Director of National Intelligence. 'Look, I don't blame you,' he said bluntly. 'I would have reacted the same way if I were in your shoes.'

A faint smile flashed across Connelly's lips. 'Agent Stevens will take you to the facility where the prisoner is being held.' Her expression hardened. 'Don't disappoint me, Greene.'

The two immortals walked out of the room and made for the flight of stairs at the end of the corridor.

'I think she likes you.' Anatole grinned and waggled an eyebrow. 'You always did have a way with the ladies.'

'Not all the ladies,' retorted Conrad.

Anatole sobered. 'That's true.' He sighed. 'It breaks my heart to see the two of you still like this. Christ, it's been three hundred years already! Don't you think it's about time you kissed and made up?'

'Some things are hard to forgive,' said Conrad quietly. Following the earth-shattering discovery of his hitherto unknown ability thirteen months ago, the immortal had often reflected bitterly on how different his life and that of the woman he loved would have been had he possessed that wondrous skill at the time they both needed it the most.

A sad light flitted in Anatole's eyes. He opened his mouth for a riposte, thought better of it, and remained silent. They emerged through the West Wing basement entrance and crossed a sunlit car park to a stationary black Suburban. The US Secret Service agent who had been in the back of the president's limo stood waiting for them in a fresh suit, his expression concealed behind a pair of sunglasses.

'Stevens,' Conrad acknowledged with a nod.

The man turned wordlessly and climbed behind the steering wheel. Conrad took the seat beside him and Anatole got in the back. The agent guided the SUV to one of the West Executive Avenue security gates.

'How far is this place?' said Conrad.

'It's four miles southwest of our current location,' Stevens replied in a clipped tone.

They left the White House grounds and turned south on 17th St. Stevens drove toward Independence Avenue and took the ramp onto Interstate 395 South. The waters of the Potomac River glittered below them as they crossed the George Mason Memorial Bridge into Arlington County.

Conrad studied the limestone facade of the Pentagon rising

pallidly against the sky in the distance to their right, its walls foreboding in the brilliant daylight.

Stevens took the exit toward Alexandria and came off the highway. He turned left at a busy junction and guided the Suburban through the network of high-rise buildings and avenues that made up the urban village of Crystal City. He took a couple more corners before entering a narrow service road. They slowed outside the back of a nondescript, multistory complex and entered the dark mouth of an underground tunnel.

A security barrier appeared in the Chevy's headlights. It was manned by an armed guard in a booth. Stevens braked and lowered the window. He flashed his Secret Service ID at the sentinel and indicated Conrad and Anatole cursorily. 'They're with me.'

The two immortals held up the temporary badges they had been granted by the White House security staff. The guard scrutinized the cards closely before operating the barrier. Stevens drove down the ramp and parked the Suburban at the end of a large underground garage. The immortals exited the vehicle after the agent and followed him across the concrete floor toward a lift.

Conrad glanced around the sub-basement as he walked in Stevens's steps. The parking lot was full of government cars and SUVs. The agent punched a code into the biometric security display in the wall next to the elevator and pressed his hand against the electronic window on the screen. A beep sounded from the panel and the lift doors opened. They entered the metal cage.

'Have you got similar security on the ground floor entrances of the building?' said Conrad as the steel panels closed with a metallic whoosh.

'Bar the main reception and the fire exits, yes,' replied Stevens. 'There's a private medical center on the third level. It's where the suspect's injuries got treated. The holding cells and interview rooms are higher up.'

The elevator opened on the top floor. They exited the cabin and walked out into an airy lobby. A glass wall overlooked the George Washington Memorial Parkway and the Ronald Reagan National Airport to the east.

An armed woman in a suit sat behind the security station at the far end of the foyer. A pair of metal doors framed the wall on either side of her.

Stevens removed his sunglasses and strolled toward the desk. 'We're here to see the prisoner.'

The woman wordlessly passed them a digital tablet. They scanned their badges across the ID reader at the top. She checked the data that came up on the monitor in front of her and entered a code on the keyboard.

'Go through,' she said in a crisp tone. 'He's in the last interview room.' The door on the left swung open with a faint pneumatic hiss.

Conrad and Anatole headed through the opening after Stevens. A wide, windowless corridor lit with fluorescent strips lay on the other side. Touch-sensitive keypads guarded the locks on the doors lining the passage.

Anatole eyed the security system with a grin. 'Cool. I kinda feel like I'm in a spy movie.'

Stevens gave him a look.

'What? It's a compliment,' said Anatole, shrugging at Conrad's expression.

A door opened near the end of the corridor. A woman in gray nurse's scrubs and a stethoscope around her neck stepped out with a digital blood pressure monitor in hand. She acknowledged the three men with a dip of her chin and started to walk past them.

Stevens moved into her path. 'How's he doing?'

The woman stopped and looked up with a small smile. 'He's

a bit woozy from the pain meds, but his obs are stable.'

A man in a suit appeared in the doorway of the room the nurse had just exited. 'Oh. It's you,' he said when he spotted Stevens. 'Come on in.'

'Excuse me,' murmured the nurse. She sidestepped around them and headed for the security door they had come through.

The assassin Conrad had overpowered at the FedEx field was slouched in a metal chair behind a table in the middle of a stark interview chamber. His right foot was shackled to the floor and his left hand had been cuffed to the armrest. His other hand and leg were in casts.

His expression changed when he saw Conrad. The ugly bruise and swelling over his fractured nose and around his eyes distorted with his scowl.

The female agent on the near side of the desk looked over. 'Gee, that's the first reaction we've had from the guy since he got here,' she drawled. 'You the one who beat the shit out of his sorry ass?'

'Yes,' said Conrad, his gaze shifting from the prisoner.

The agent grinned. 'Swell.'

Conrad joined her and took the third chair at the table. He leaned forward with his hands folded together and watched the assassin for a long, silent moment.

'What's your name?' the immortal said finally.

The man returned his look blankly.

'Who are you working for?' asked Conrad.

Silence followed his question.

'When were you hired for this job?'

The assassin absentmindedly scratched at his cuffed arm with his free hand, his expression clearly disinterested.

'Where did you get the gun we found on you?' Conrad persevered.

The man remained resolutely mute.

The female agent sighed. 'We've been asking him the same questions for the last two hours.'

'And?' said Anatole.

'Zip. Zilch. Nada,' she replied. 'The wall's got more personality than this guy.'

Conrad leaned back in the chair and studied the tight-lipped prisoner with a critical eye. He doubted the man would talk so easily.

'If you cooperate with the authorities, your sentence will be reduced,' he stated in a passionless voice. 'If you don't, there are ways and means to make you talk. They will be painful and unpleasant. After that, you will disappear. I will personally see to it that no one finds your remains.'

The assassin blinked. He glanced at his left arm where it lay restrained to the chair. Conrad followed the path of the man's eyes with his gaze.

The female agent suddenly straightened in her seat. 'Hey, are you okay?' she said sharply to the prisoner.

Conrad looked up. The assassin's eyes bulged in his skull, his pupils growing black circles in a sea of reddening white as blood vessels popped in his sclerae. Sweat beaded his skin and his features contorted in an expression of shock and pain. He swung his injured arm to clutch violently at his chest and collapsed face down on the table, his forehead smacking the surface with a thud.

~

CHAPTER TWELVE

'SHIT!'

The metal chair rattled and fell on the floor as Conrad sprang to his feet and moved around the table. He heaved the man upright in his seat and felt frantically for the pulse in his throat as the female agent joined him from the other side.

The killer's head lolled backward on his neck, and he stared unseeingly at the ceiling. Alarm shot through the immortal.

'Get a medical team here! We have a man down!' the male agent at the door shouted into his radio unit before storming across the room toward them.

Conrad swore when he felt the absence of the steady heartbeat he had been expecting.

'He's arrested! Let's get him on the floor!'

Anatole and Stevens helped the female agent undo the prisoner's restraints and lower him to the ground.

Conrad kneeled by the unconscious man and placed his hand on his forehead.

'Start CPR!' he ordered grimly as he cast his healing energy down his birthmark.

The female agent pinched the prisoner's nose and blew air

into his mouth. Anatole put his interlocked hands over the man's breastbone and started to pump vigorously.

'Let the White House know we have a situation!' Conrad barked at Stevens. The agent took out his cell phone.

'What the hell is that on his arm?' grunted Anatole, his upper body moving rhythmically as he compressed the killer's chest.

Conrad looked down and saw a small, round, red blister on the killer's left bicep. His alarm turned to fear.

'Don't touch it!' he shouted when the female agent reached out with her fingers.

She snatched her hand back millimeters from the dead man's skin.

A door opened in the distance. Footsteps pounded the concrete passage outside the room. The male agent strode out into the corridor.

'In here!' He beckoned the people running down the hallway.

Conrad's gaze focused on the discolored circle of skin on the prisoner's flesh.

'Did that nurse give him any pills?' he asked urgently.

'No!' replied the female agent. 'All she did was measure his blood pressure!'

Conrad went still.

'On his left arm?'

'Yes,' she confirmed. She froze and stared wide-eyed at the blister, realization dawning on her face.

Beneath his fingertips, Conrad could sense the presence of a strange chemical in the assassin's blood stream. The damage to the man's heart muscles and nerve fibers had been done. Though he could reverse the physical effects of the toxin, he would be unable to bring the killer back to life without giving away a piece of his soul. He clenched his teeth.

Fingers closed around his wrist in a steely grip. He looked up into Anatole's scowling face.

'I hope you're not thinking of doing what I think you are?' the red-haired immortal muttered as a group of doctors and nurses rushed inside the room. 'He's *not* worth it.'

'No, I wasn't.' Conrad was aware of Stevens's uneasy stare on the side of his face. 'And no, he's not.' He rose and started toward the door as the medical team took over resuscitating the dead man. 'Shut down the building!' he called out to the two agents who had been with the prisoner. 'We need to find that nurse!'

Conrad exited the room and sprinted up the corridor. He emerged in the security lobby with Anatole and Stevens on his heels. The woman behind the desk looked up, a phone receiver tucked against her ear; she was speaking urgently in the mouthpiece while typing on the keyboard of her computer.

Conrad strode around the station and studied the security monitors.

'Can you see the woman who came through that door a few minutes ago?'

'You mean the nurse?' said the agent sharply. She placed the phone down on its cradle.

'Yes!'

She clicked on a mouse and brought up more feeds from the security cameras in the complex.

'The building's in lockdown. If she's still here, she won't be able to get out.'

'There!' Anatole exclaimed. He stabbed a finger at the bottom left corner of the screen.

A slim figure in gray scrubs was disappearing swiftly down a flight of stairs.

Anger blazed through Conrad. His nails bit into his palms. 'Where is that?'

'It's the northwest service stairs,' said the female agent. 'She's on the fourth floor!'

'How do we get to it?'

'There's a shortcut through there!' The woman's fingers clattered on the computer keyboard. The security door on the right popped open. 'Go straight down and take a left. I'll override the fire door!'

Conrad ran for the opening and heard the woman bark instructions into her radio as he disappeared over the threshold. Another passage dotted with harsh light strips stretched out in front of him. Curious faces appeared in the narrow, glass windows of some of the holding cells lining it.

He skidded round the corner at the end and bolted for the fire door ahead. It clicked ajar just as he reached it. Conrad pushed through and entered a narrow stairwell. He staggered to a halt and peered over the metal banister. Eight floors below, a shadow was moving swiftly down the stairs.

The immortal's pulse ratcheted up a notch. 'Shit! She's almost at the bottom!'

He started rapidly down the concrete stairs, Anatole and Stevens following in his footsteps.

'She's trapped!' shouted the agent. 'There's no way she can escape!'

'Tell me that when we've got cuffs on her!' retorted Conrad.

The sharp staccato of gunfire suddenly rose from the stairwell. The immortal stopped and looked over the handrail.

A couple of agents had cut off the woman's exit route on the ground. She shot at them steadily as she raced back up toward the upper floors of the building. One of the men cried out and fell.

Conrad swore. He braced his hands against the wall and the banister, and swung down the stairs three steps at a time. Shots sounded one level down; it was echoed by the sharp pings of bullets striking metal. He jumped to the next landing, turned the corner, and spotted the woman on the floor below just as she kicked down a fire door.

Conrad scowled and vaulted onto the railing. The woman looked around when she glimpsed him sliding obliquely toward her. She glared and disappeared over the threshold of the fire escape. The immortal's feet struck the ground a couple of seconds later. He went after her.

The door opened onto a corridor at the back of the medical center. He raced past a couple of operating rooms and emerged into a recovery area. A couple of startled nurses in gray scrubs shrank back against one of the beds lining the walls, where an unconscious man lay with an oxygen mask on his face.

Conrad scanned their faces, heard a clatter on his left, and saw a pair of doors flutter close. He ran toward them and pushed through the panels. There was a faint click to his right. He dove to the ground.

Bullets slammed into the metal door above him, raining sparks on his head. Conrad whipped out his gun and aimed it toward the slim figure racing down the length of an open wing. His finger froze on the trigger when he registered the patients and staff in the bay. He swore, rose to his feet, and bounded after the fleeing woman.

Panicked screams shattered the air as he chased her through the clinic. She turned another corner and disappeared from view.

Conrad made a low, guttural noise in the back of his throat and accelerated. He skidded around the bend, bounced off the opposite wall, and saw her vanish inside a cleaner's supplies closet at the end of a narrow corridor.

The door slammed shut in his face seconds before he reached it. The lock turned. A dull scrape followed from the other side as something was dragged and jammed against the closet entrance.

Conrad twisted the handle frantically and slammed his

shoulder against the wood. It refused to budge. He swore and rammed into it again. Footsteps rose behind him. Stevens appeared at his side. Anatole was nowhere to be seen.

'She's in there!' Conrad bellowed.

He raised his semiautomatic at the lock and squeezed the trigger repeatedly. Stevens took out his FN Five-seveN and joined him. An echo of shots accompanied the barrage of bullets from their guns. Conrad thought he heard glass shattering inside.

The lock fell off. They jammed their shoulders against the door and pushed. Something heavy ground across the floor on the other side. It gave away without warning. They stumbled into the closet.

Conrad's eyes locked on the blinds fluttering in a mild breeze. He dashed to the broken window and looked outside. The woman was rolling off a canvas awning three floors below. She landed nimbly on the ground and sprinted toward a car park at the front of the building.

Stevens staggered to a stop at the immortal's side, glass crunching beneath his shoes. 'Shit!'

Conrad tucked his gun in his rear waistband and climbed over the windowsill. The jagged pieces around the frame bit into his palms as he balanced on the outer ledge.

'Hey, what the—?' started Stevens in a choked voice.

Conrad jumped.

His body dented the awning a couple of heartbeats later. Air left his lips in a harsh exhale. He twisted to the end of the green canopy, grabbed the edge, and flipped down. His boots touched the asphalt just as the powerful growl of a motorcycle erupted from the left. He looked around.

A black Ducati superbike emerged from the shadows under the trees. Conrad's eyes widened when he saw the figure atop it. He cursed and started to run.

The motorcycle flashed past yards ahead of him. Conrad

caught a glimpse of the woman's narrowed gray eyes through her open, black helmet before she brought the visor down. The superbike roared, the front tire lifting briefly off the ground. Its rider leaned into the corner and headed for the avenue.

Conrad angled toward the park in front of the building. He bounded over a row of seats and raced across an expanse of freshly mown grass, his heart thundering inside his chest. He hit the blacktop seconds later.

The Ducati was moving rapidly up the road on his right. He bolted after it. The woman spotted him in her side mirror. She glanced over her shoulder, gunned the engine, and accelerated. Conrad's stomach lurched as the distance between them widened. He clenched his teeth and willed his legs to move faster, his breath coming in hard, hot gasps.

Tires suddenly squealed somewhere on his right. Stevens's black Suburban appeared on a service road running parallel to the avenue. The SUV climbed a narrow embankment and plowed through a hedge. It rocked on its suspension before shooting out onto the road a dozen feet ahead of him. The brake lights came on and the passenger door popped open.

'Get in!' Anatole shouted from behind the wheel as Conrad came abreast of the vehicle.

He grabbed the interior armrest and hopped inside just as Anatole hit the gas. The Suburban lurched forward.

'You got the keys off Stevens?' Conrad panted.

'Didn't have time! I hot-wired it!' Anatole glowered at the road. 'Dammit! Where'd she go?' He maneuvered sharply around a bus.

A grunt left Conrad's lips as he slammed into the window. He slid back into the seat, clipped his belt in, and looked through the windshield. The Suburban was hurtling toward a junction with the signals on red. The bike had disappeared.

Anatole switched on the SUV's flashing forward lights and siren, clutched the steering wheel, and weaved violently between two braking cars. They shot across the intersection to a blast of horns and shocked screams.

Conrad caught a flash of black out the corner of his eye. He looked to the right. 'She's cutting across the park!'

The Ducati was disappearing between the trees at the south end of a green area containing an elaborate central water feature and fountains. He spotted a signpost on a pole.

'There's a bike trail to the east! That's where she's headed,' he said grimly, his gaze focused on the back of the woman's helmet.

'Hang on!' yelled Anatole.

Conrad's eyes shifted to the avenue in front. 'Oh fu—!' he started and braced himself against the dashboard and roof of the vehicle.

The shriek of tires drowned out the rest of his words. The Suburban cut through a flock of scattering pedestrians in the middle of a crosswalk, sending several people hurtling to the ground as they leapt out of the way.

A driveway materialized on the right. Anatole took a tight turn into it. Another signpost appeared up ahead. He jumped the curb, twisted the steering wheel, and sent the Suburban careening down a short walkway toward a train station entrance. The crowd standing on the concourse moved back in a horrified wave. The vehicle streaked through the open gates and drove off the edge of the platform.

Conrad picked up a shrill screech of metal amidst the terrified shouts of the commuters. A shadow eclipsed the sky on their left. His knuckles whitened on the dashboard as he looked past Anatole and saw the train heading inexorably toward them.

The Suburban sailed a few feet past the leading edge of the locomotive before bouncing down on the far side rail track. Anatole revved the engine, drove onto an overgrown trail, and turned right.

Conrad tasted bile at the back of his throat. 'Next time you decide to pull a stunt like that, warn me,' he muttered, his heart thumping erratically against his ribs. 'In writing, preferably.'

Anatole grinned and accelerated. The biking trail appeared on their left after several hundred feet. He guided the Suburban onto it and drove down a steep embankment. Riders veered out of their way as the vehicle shot along a path between the trees. They emerged from the coppice and went under the George Washington Memorial Parkway.

Conrad spotted the black Ducati winding up a trail through some trees to the south. He gripped the dashboard, his nails digging into the plastic cover.

The woman hunkered low over the handlebars of the super-bike. She looked around at the sound of their engine, her black helmet gleaming in the sunlight. She swung the Ducati to the right and came off the track, the tires biting sharply into dirt and grass.

Anatole yanked the steering wheel and drove onto the turf. A grim smile twisted his lips as he gave chase. 'This chick is seriously starting to push my buttons!'

He sent the SUV hurtling up the incline and darted beneath an overpass. They emerged into sunlight and curved sharply back onto the path at the top of the slope.

Metal shrieked and sparks rose from their left as the Suburban scraped along the guard rail separating them from the expressway. Anatole righted the vehicle and headed for a narrow bridge crossing over one of the motorway exits.

Alarm froze Conrad to his seat when he saw the figure in their path. 'Watch out!' he bellowed.

The man in the running shorts and T-shirt looked around at the blare of the siren. He gaped when he saw the Suburban barreling toward him, grabbed the guardrail, and vaulted up the brick wall on the side of the bridge.

Conrad looked back as they flashed past and saw the guy fall onto the grass embankment next to the motorway. He glared at Anatole.

The immortal glanced at him. 'I wish you'd stop bitching about these close calls. It's not like I ran him over.'

The trail turned between some trees and climbed toward another overpass. The Ducati was disappearing over the rise. The SUV bolted onto the concrete bridge and headed over a motorway entrance. The north end of Ronald Reagan Airport appeared on their right as they neared the peak of the incline.

By the time they bounced back onto the ground on the other side, the bike was nowhere in sight.

Anatole cursed. 'Where the hell did she—?'

'There!' Conrad indicated the fresh tire tracks carved in the ground to the right.

Anatole rotated the steering wheel and sent the Suburban into a hairpin skid. The tires screamed before finally gripping the asphalt, the smell of burning rubber flooding the air. The vehicle shot onto the side trail heading into the airport grounds.

The Ducati was already halfway across the parking lot that lay beyond the path. It curved sharply around the fence at the end. Anatole raced onto the blacktop and followed speedily, his fingers white on the steering wheel. He negotiated the turn, swore, and slammed on the brakes. Conrad grunted as he jerked forward against the seat belt.

The Suburban screeched to a halt an inch from a security barrier. The Ducati had slipped through a gap at the edge of the roadblock and was racing across the airport vehicle lanes beyond.

'Oh no, you don't!' snarled Anatole.

He reversed sharply, spun the wheel, and aimed for an opening on the right. They headed past a row of emergency vehicles parked in the shadow of a hangar and bolted onto the tarmac.

Up ahead, the superbike shot under a taxiing airplane and accelerated toward a wide grass belt north of the airport grounds. A runway shimmered beyond it.

Tension suddenly knotted Conrad's stomach. 'Shit.'

A roar from the right rattled the windows of the Suburban. He looked around and saw a large Airbus jet making its way up the strip for takeoff.

'Anatole!' he barked warningly.

The red-haired immortal glanced at the approaching plane, a muscle jumping in his jawline. He clenched the steering wheel and stamped the gas pedal to the floor of the vehicle. The Suburban juddered onto the grass.

The Ducati crossed the strip of green and hurtled over the tarmac some five hundred feet in front of the airliner.

Conrad's mouth went dry. 'Oh God!' he whispered. His words were drowned by the growing boom of the approaching aircraft.

Anatole swore viciously. He stepped on the brakes and twisted the wheel. Chunks of dirt and grass rose in violent arcs around them as the tires tore through the earth. The Suburban spun through a one-eighty revolution and slipped onto the tarmac. It shuddered to a halt on the edge of the runway.

The Airbus thundered past less than a hundred feet from the SUV, its port wing casting them in brief twilight. The vehicle rocked violently on its suspension in the downdraft from the plane's powerful engines.

Conrad's fingers ached where they braced against the dash-board and the door. He twisted around and made out the vanishing shape of the Ducati and its rider in the distance. Movement in the sky drew his gaze. His pulse stuttered.

A black helicopter was dropping down ahead of the super-bike. It landed on a ribbon of land bordering the Potomac River. The woman braked and jumped off the motorcycle. She

threw her helmet on the ground and ran toward the aircraft.
The two immortals watched her climb inside.

Anatole glowered. 'I am officially pissed off.'

They ignored the emergency vehicles converging on them
from across the airport grounds and stared at the helicopter as
it rose and turned toward the river.

PART TWO: FREEFALL

CHAPTER THIRTEEN

'WE GOT ANYTHING ON THE BIKE?' SNAPPED CONNELLY.

'It's a 848 Evo Ducati,' said the Sit Room communications assistant. 'It was hired from a bike shop in Arlington at 14:55 today. We've got a picture of the person who leased it on the store's security camera.'

A video rolled on one of the screens on the walls. The communications assistant froze the clip. Conrad stared at the image of a slender figure in a black biker's suit and sunglasses in mid-stride on the floor of a brightly lit show room. His hands fisted at his sides when he registered her face.

Although a sports cap obscured half her features, there was no mistaking the woman who had infiltrated the US Secret Service holding facility in Arlington just over an hour ago and killed the assassin he had captured at the FedEx Field.

'Information's coming through from Crystal City,' said Stevens. He was talking to someone on a Sit Room phone. 'They just found the body of a female nurse shoved inside a locker in the clinic's changing rooms.' His eyes darkened. 'She had her throat cut.'

Stony silence followed. Although it was anger that turned Conrad's blood cold, he was alarmed at the speed with which the enemy was moving. That they had gotten so close so fast not only indicated the enormous resources they had at hand, but also that their spy was deep inside the task force.

'How are we doing with finding our mole?' he asked Connelly stiffly.

'We're going through the list of people who may have had access to President Westwood's itinerary,' replied the Director of National Intelligence. 'Considering the number of agencies involved, it's going to take a while to check everyone's background.'

'You need to be looking closer to home,' Conrad said in a low voice. 'I think their informant might be someone in our immediate team.'

Connelly observed him for silent seconds before nodding.

'What about the helicopter?' said Anatole.

Conrad glanced at the red-haired immortal. It had been a long time since he last heard such thinly veiled fury in his friend's voice.

'From your description of the tail boom, we know it's an MD aircraft, likely the 520N or the 600N model,' replied the Sit Room intelligence analyst. 'The company that makes them is based in Arizona.' He made a face. 'Unfortunately, without the registration number, it would be damn near impossible to identify it.'

Conrad frowned. 'Get a list of all the helicopters fitting that design from the manufacturer. I want to know who owns the ones currently licensed for use inside the US.'

The agent picked up a phone. Sarah Connelly turned to Conrad.

'That was some stunt you guys pulled at the airport,' she said through pinched lips, her cool gaze swinging to encompass Anatole. 'I had the FAA Administrator shouting in my ear for almost ten minutes. The guy almost had a coronary. He demanded I fire the, I quote, "two assholes who almost caused one of the worst accidents in US aviation history." She glared at them. 'I sure as hell hope this is not a taste of things to come.'

Anatole shrugged. 'Hey, we almost caught the suspect.'

Connelly's expression grew stormy.

Conrad raised a hand in a pacifying gesture. 'Look, I'm sorry we—' he started to say.

The Sit Room door opened. Laura walked in ahead of the FBI and CIA lead agents.

'We got something interesting from the stadium,' she announced without preamble.

A phone rang on the other side of the room. The communications assistant lifted the receiver.

Laura's eyes gleamed with ill-concealed animation. 'We found the rifle used by the fourth assassin. It was on the second level concourse.' She smiled, a forbidding flash of white teeth. 'It's identical to the one we got off the sniper who died at the scene. She took the shot from inside a banner stand about two hundred feet from the north field tunnel.'

Conrad tensed. A dark intuition shot through him. 'She?'

A low mumble of conversation rose from the front end of the Sit Room. The communications assistant clutched the phone and bent over the console.

'Yes, "she,"' said Laura. 'We caught an image of her on one of the stadium cameras.'

Conrad's misgivings deepened. 'What does this woman look—?'

'Director Connelly, I think you should see this,' interrupted the communications assistant shakily.

The man had risen to his feet. He clasped the telephone receiver to his ear and lifted a remote control toward the monitor that took up most of the wall at the head of the conference room. The screen flashed on. A patchwork of live feeds appeared across it.

Stunned silence fell over the room as they stared at the images being broadcast over several major, international news channels. Icy fear filled Conrad's veins when his brain finally registered what he was seeing. He felt Laura stiffen on the other side of the table.

'Turn up the volume,' Connelly ordered, her face ashen.

'—although information is still coming through from our sources, the authorities have yet to confirm the veracity of the reports being relayed by local reporters in London.' An anchorman's voice overlaid the video on the far left display. 'Once again, John Cunnington, the prime minister of the United Kingdom, was the victim of an assassination attempt during a dinner held in honor of wounded British soldiers who served in the Afghan Civil War. The prime minister insisted on attending the event despite rumors that the president of the United States was himself the victim of a terrorist act this afternoon. The prime minister was allegedly shot in the chest as he left the building and is said to be in a critical condition in one of the major trauma centers in the city—'

The camera had captured the scenes of chaos outside one of London's iconic Victorian establishments. In the middle of the screen, an ambulance raced away into the night, surrounded by a protective police escort. Vehicles from the London Metropolitan Police occupied the cobbled road in front of the brightly lit edifice. Grim-faced officers in tactical gear were on the ground, their postures tense as they clutched their firearms. Crowds of onlookers gawked at them from behind a line of barricades.

The communications assistant increased the sound on the second feed. Conrad felt his limbs go numb as the newscaster's voice rose above the British anchorman's ongoing announcement.

'—I repeat, Chancellor Dressler has been admitted to the UKB, the emergency trauma center in Berlin,' the man blurted out in German, his pale face shining in the studio spotlights. English subtitles flashed at the bottom of the window. The background image showed the exterior of a large hospital. 'The chancellor's armored Audi A8 was damaged by a rocket-propelled grenade launched from an unidentified vehicle as it left Bellevue Palace, the official residence of President Hoefler. The two leaders had been holding an emergency meeting after reports that the US president had been injured during as assassination attempt—'

'Oh God,' whispered Donaghy, her hand rising to her lips. Lewis gripped the seat next to her with white-knuckled fingers. Petersen and Franklin walked through the door behind them and stopped dead in their tracks.

The third news channel broadcaster's voice swelled above the frozen stillness that shrouded the chamber just as Westwood stormed inside the Sit Room with a horde of bodyguards.

'—Russian President Gorokhov has been shot in the head by a member of his own Security Service,' the woman was saying. She could barely mask the distress in her trembling voice. The camera feed behind her displayed pictures of the exterior of the Kremlin. 'The officer, named as one Sergei Bortnik, took his own life seconds after the incident by ingesting a powerful poison that killed him instantly. President Gorokhov is currently having emergency surgery—'

'Enough!' bellowed Westwood. He placed his hands palms down on the table and leaned forward rigidly. 'Mute them all!'

The communications analyst pressed a key on the remote control, his hand quivering. The news channels fell silent.

A muscle throbbed in Westwood's cheek. 'I've just heard from France and China,' he announced in the sudden hush. 'The French president and the general secretary of the Chinese

Communist Party have just narrowly escaped assassination attempts on their lives.'

'Holy shit,' Anatole murmured, his eyes glued to the videos playing across the monitor. The information streaming across the remaining news channels confirmed the president's words.

Westwood glanced at the immortal. 'Yes, "holy shit" indeed,' he commented darkly.

Connelly ran a hand through her hair. Her skin was waxy, her expression distracted. 'What the hell is going on, James?'

Westwood ignored his Director of National Intelligence and turned to Conrad.

'This investigation has just taken on a whole new meaning,' he said. 'The timing of these incidents cannot be a coincidence.' His face grew shuttered. 'Your people are going to be assisting the authorities on the ground in Europe and Asia.'

Conrad stirred, still struggling to come to grips with the events unfolding around the globe. His stomach dropped as the meaning behind the president's words sank in. The immortal societies were being caught up in the conflict.

'Under Victor?' he asked Westwood.

'Yes. And the head of the other group.'

Conrad frowned. He didn't know whether to be pleased or alarmed at the news of the Crovirs' involvement in the situation.

'Who are you talking about?' said the NSA agent. He flushed slightly at the president's expression. 'I mean, who is this...*group* you mentioned, sir?'

Connelly regained some color and glared at the man. 'It's nothing you should concern yourself with, Franklin!'

'It's all right, Sarah.' Westwood scrutinized the members of the task force gathered in the room. 'I'm truly grateful for all the hard work you people are doing. However, there are some things best left unsaid.' He hesitated. 'We have powerful allies working with us on this matter.' His eyes flickered to Conrad and his voice hardened. 'For the sake of our national security, their identity must remain a secret.'

The agents exchanged wary glances in the uneasy silence that followed. Conrad suppressed a sigh. The covert participation of immortals in the investigation would undoubtedly complicate things. Gaining his team's trust after this was not going to be easy.

'Sir, we think we've identified the assassin who shot you,' said Laura.

Westwood stiffened. 'Show me.'

Laura signaled to the communications assistant. 'Pull up the feeds we sent from the FedEx Field.'

The man punched some keys on the computer in front of him. One of the sidewall monitors lit up. The recording from a security camera started to play across the screen. It showed a crowded concourse inside the FedEx Field.

'Roll forward to six minutes before the president was shot,' Laura ordered.

The monochrome images blurred and the time on the film counter accelerated. It soon dropped back to normal.

'Zoom in on the top left corner,' said Laura.

The image closed in on a large, curved, advertising banner next to a safety rail overlooking the road encircling the stadium. Standing next to it was a young woman in an usher's uniform. Though the picture was grainy, Conrad made out long, dark hair framing her face and spilling past her slim shoulders. She was handing out what looked like pamphlets to the Redskins fans strolling past her. A minute later, she turned and disappeared around the banner.

The counter ticked down the time. Though the camera feed carried no sound, Conrad could tell exactly when the fatal shot was fired by the way the people on the concourse suddenly froze in their tracks and hunched over protectively. He saw Westwood blanch out of the corner of his eye.

Half a minute passed before the woman stepped out from the cover of the stand. She had a sports cap on her head and had changed into running shorts and a Redskins jersey. There were several tubular, pale objects in her hands. She joined the mass of people fleeing down the concourse and tossed the items she was holding on the ground.

'Freeze it!' barked Laura.

The camera stilled on a relatively clear shot of the woman's face. Anatole swore and took an involuntary step forward.

'What?' said Laura.

'It's her,' Anatole said in clipped tones.

Conrad's nails bit into his palms as he stared at the picture of the president's killer. His instincts had been right.

'It's who?' Laura asked with a puzzled frown.

Anatole indicated the opposite wall, where a screen portrayed the still of the woman captured by the security camera in the motorcycle store in Arlington.

'That's the suspect Conrad and I just chased from the holding facility in Arlington,' the immortal responded darkly. 'We think she poisoned the assassin Conrad captured at the stadium.'

Shocked murmurs erupted around the room.

'It's the same woman.' Anatole's lips thinned in a grim line. 'She got away from us.'

Westwood's troubled gaze swung between Anatole and Conrad. 'Is the prisoner dead?'

'I'm afraid so.' Anatole's eyes darted to Conrad for a split second. 'We couldn't help.'

'Damn,' muttered Lewis.

'That's a pity,' said Petersen. The Homeland Security agent shook his head ruefully.

Anger clouded Westwood's features. 'We have got to find these people!' he spat. He looked at Connelly. 'I'm raising the National Terrorism threat to imminent and ordering the FAA to ground all domestic and international flights. The US Border Patrol is being placed on high alert. As of now, the United States is in lockdown.'

Several of the assembled agents inhaled sharply at this news. The Director of National Intelligence rose and leaned across the table, her palms flat on the polished surface as she faced down her commander-in-chief.

'James, do you realize what this will do to the country?' Connelly asked in a strained voice.

'She's right,' Conrad told the president. The immortal masked his growing anxiety behind an even tone. 'You're playing right into their hands if you do this.'

Westwood looked between the two of them. 'Do you see any other option?' he challenged.

Conrad and Connelly exchanged troubled glances.

'No,' the immortal muttered at the same time that the Director of National Intelligence shook her head in a defeated gesture. 'They've set the rules of this game—for the time being,' he added.

Westwood exhaled sharply. 'Let me know if you find anything that could be useful to the other governments who have suffered at the hands of these criminals. Although some of them are not our NATO allies, we appear to have a common enemy at present. It's in all our interests to bring down this adversary.' He pulled a face. 'I'm returning to the Oval Office to field the queue of calls no doubt awaiting me.'

Everyone breathed more easily once the president left the room with his retinue of guards.

Conrad ran a hand through his disheveled hair and turned to Laura. 'Did you find anything else at the stadium?' he said, irritation sharpening his voice.

A flicker of what looked like concern darted in her eyes before she nodded. Conrad blinked and wondered whether he had imagined the emotion.

'We think we caught another picture of the woman when she was leaving the grounds,' said Laura. 'We lost all traces of her beyond that, although we did find her FedEx Field ID and uniform.' A trace of bitterness underscored her voice. 'The badge was a fake.'

She turned to the communications assistant at the Sit Room console. 'Bring up the next feed.'

The clip that appeared on the monitor showed a panicked crowd fleeing across a parking lot to the west of the stadium. Laura guided the agent controlling the video to zoom in on a quadrant of the screen.

The shot closed on the back of a hazy figure wearing a Redskins jersey, running shorts, and a cap. They followed the silhouette's convoluted path through the press of bodies until it disappeared from view.

'We haven't worked out how she got away yet,' said Laura, her frustration evident in the creases of her brow.

Conrad stared at the clip. His eyes unfocused slightly as he recalled the map he had seen on the student's tablet in the coffeehouse on H Street NW earlier that day. He couldn't help but feel that they were missing something.

'Where is that exactly?' he said.

The communications assistant turned and typed on a keyboard. A satellite image of the FedEx Field appeared next to the frozen image.

Conrad tilted his head. 'Zoom out.'

The man pressed another key. The stadium shrank until D.C. appeared on the screen.

The immortal studied the monitor for some time. His heart sank when he spotted their mistake. 'We were watching the roads, airports, and train stations, right?'

Laura straightened at his dismayed tone. Her eyes swung between his face and the map. 'Yes. You heard Woods give the orders.'

'We missed something big,' said Conrad leadenly.

'What?' she demanded.

He sighed. 'It's staring us right in the face.'

They all scrutinized the screen.

'Ah,' said Anatole. His face brightened. 'The river.'

'Yes, the river,' Conrad concurred amidst a storm of perturbed murmurs.

Laura gripped the back of a chair tightly, her nails digging into the leather. 'Shit! She must have jogged the five miles to the Anacostia!'

Connelly blew out an angry sigh. 'How the hell did we miss that?'

Conrad looked at the Director of National Intelligence. 'Any chance our satellites may have captured a shot of a boat on the water?' he asked in clipped tones.

Connelly's scowling gaze switched from the monitor to him. 'It's worth a shot,' she said with a curt nod. 'Get the NGA on the line and see if any of the satellites covering the area around Washington this morning caught something,' she instructed the Sit Room communications assistant. The agent picked up the telephone receiver and started to dial a number.

Conrad turned to the other agencies' leads as they waited. 'You got anything for us?'

'Homeland is flying the body of the guy from the plane crash across from Manaus as we speak,' said Petersen gruffly.

'Good,' the immortal murmured.

'We've got our people at the FBI's forensics lab in Quantico examining the guns and bullets the killers used at the FedEx Field,' said Lewis. 'The weapon Agent Hartwell retrieved from the stadium is en route to Virginia.'

Laura made a face. 'Chances are they won't find any prints on it.'

Conrad arched an eyebrow questioningly.

'It looks like she wiped down everything at the scene,' Laura explained. She shrugged. 'Even if there are any, they're bound to be fakes.'

Conrad looked at Donaghy.

'NSA and CIA haven't detected any obvious patterns in the intelligence data we've gathered so far,' said the CIA agent, glancing at Franklin. 'Nothing that's screaming assassination plot at us yet anyway.' The woman hesitated and bit her lip. 'However...'

'What is it?' said Laura with a frown.

Donaghy ran a hand through her hair, her face projecting unease. 'I picked up on something strange.'

Conrad turned to face her fully, his curiosity aroused. 'Strange how?'

'It's to do with some unusual disappearances in the criminal underworld. Several prominent warlords and cartel leaders have vanished off the face of the planet in the last twenty months, along with the substantial troops under their command,' the CIA agent explained. 'We're not just talking South America here, but also Africa, the Middle East, and Asia. We have no idea as to why or how this has happened.' She sighed. 'The whole thing has been a goddamned puzzle for the international intelligence communities. We've never seen anything like it.'

'It's true,' Franklin said with a nod. 'Intel on the ground has been unusually slow as well. We've lost contact with several of our sources.'

Conrad furrowed his brow as he digested this enigmatic information, uncertain whether it bore any relevance to their current predicament.

Footsteps sounded at the door. An FBI agent rushed into the room.

'I've got some news!' the woman announced breathlessly. 'We found a strand of hair in the helmet the suspect abandoned at the airport.'

Excited murmurs broke out among the assembled agents.

Conrad tried not to let the sudden thrill get to him. 'Good work,' he said tersely. 'Get it analyzed straightaway.'

The woman made for the bank of phones on the other side of the room; with stringent Sit Room restrictions in place, none of them were allowed to use mobile devices inside the emergency operations center.

The immortal stilled as another thought came to him. 'Speaking of which, I would get your forensic examiner to look at the blood chemistry of the prisoner who died in Arlington,' he told Lewis with a tiny frown. 'The poison used to kill him was pretty unique.'

Lewis raised an eyebrow. 'Really?'

'Yes,' said Conrad. 'I'd bet my life on it.'

He ignored Stevens's perturbed expression and looked at the monitor at the head of the room. International news channels were still playing across the screen.

'It might be interesting to compare notes with the Russians,' Conrad added reflectively. 'The bodyguard who shot their president also used a poison to kill himself.'

A phone rang loudly, startling everyone. The communications assistant took the call. He listened for a couple of seconds and looked over at Conrad. 'It's for you.'

Surprise shot through the immortal. He crossed the floor and took the receiver from the man's grasp. 'Hello?'

'You guys got anything yet?' said Victor Dvorsky at the other end of the line.

'We have a couple of leads,' Conrad replied. He turned to face the wall and cupped the mouthpiece in his hand. He briefed the Bastian leader on the events of the last three hours in a low voice. 'What's going on at your end?' he asked finally.

'The Bastian Councils just met,' said Victor.

Conrad frowned at the noble's somber tone.

'There are some in our ranks who feel our enemies of old may still be behind this,' Victor continued. A sigh travelled over the connection. 'The Crovir First Council has vehemently denied any involvement in these incidents. I believe them.'

Conrad rubbed the back of his neck. He was aware of Anatole and Laura hovering close by, their faces puzzled. 'You talked to Reznak,' he murmured into the mouthpiece.

Dimitri Reznak was a Crovir noble and a member of the Crovir First Council. Along with a small group of influential Bastian and Crovir immortals which included Victor and Roman Dvorsky, he spent several decades of the latter half of the fourteenth century instituting an aggressive campaign to end the war that had consumed the immortal races for several millennia. Since he hated being in the limelight, he had chosen to keep the instrumental role he played in the final talks that resulted in the peace treaty a secret. It was therefore hardly unsurprising that Victor Dvorsky and he were good friends.

Conrad thought back to the couple of occasions when he had met the man. Whereas Victor projected a visible aura of strength and authority that marked him as the natural-born leader he was, Dimitri Reznak had come across as relaxed and amiable. Conrad had not been fooled; he suspected the Crovir noble was a sleeping lion who would bare his fangs if the situation called for it.

'Yes, I did,' Victor admitted presently. 'Dimitri is convinced the Crovirs have nothing to do with this.' Tension lowered the pitch of his voice. 'I'm attending a special meeting of the UN Security Council tonight, along with the current leader of the Crovirs. We *have* to convince the humans that the immortals are not behind this. Both the Bastians and the Crovirs are sending agents to assist the local investigators in Europe and Asia.'

Conrad's stomach fluttered as he absorbed this latest news. He was not surprised that the UN was holding an impromptu assembly. From Victor's tone, however, it seemed the immortals had been summoned there.

'Yes. Westwood told me you would be helping out on the ground,' he acknowledged.

'Tell Laura to send us the pictures of that female suspect and a sample of the hair the FBI found,' Victor requested. 'We'll get the Bastian and Crovir techs working on them as well.' There was a short lull. 'Get me the bastards who did this, Conrad,' the Bastian leader added darkly. 'I'm counting on you.'

CHAPTER FOURTEEN

THE WORDS OF HIS FORMER MENTOR WERE STILL RINGING IN Conrad's ears when they made their next breakthrough.

Disappointingly, the National Geospatial Intelligence Agency's GEOINT satellites had only yielded a couple of stills showing the female assassin boarding a Zodiac boat where the Beaverdam Creek met the Anacostia River, before making her way south past Kingman Island. Though it helped them draw up the assassin's escape route, it had been impossible to deduce any useful information from the limited imagery. It was the FBI's labs in Quantico that came up with a crucial lead.

'I've got good news and bad news,' announced Lewis. The FBI agent had just returned from a trip to Virginia. 'The bad news is that we have no match on the DNA from the hair sample we obtained at the Ronald Reagan Airport.' He let out a frustrated sigh. 'Whoever this woman is, she's not on any criminal or intelligence database in the world.'

A groan of disbelief swept across the Sit Room at his words. The rest of the task force had reconvened at the White House as night fell across the capital. It was now six in the evening, and the conference table was littered with sandwich wraps and disposable coffee cups.

Conrad stared at the FBI agent. The fact that they hadn't gotten a hit on the suspect's DNA bothered him greatly. It could not fail but give him yet another inkling of how powerful the enemy they faced was. He saw the same concern displayed on Connelly's face.

'What's the good news?' the immortal asked bluntly.

A gleam appeared in Lewis's eyes. 'The techs looking at the guns and the jackets framing the ceramic bullets think they've identified the plastic polymer used in their manufacturing process,' he said with barely veiled excitement.

An animated rumble rose in the room.

'This material apparently has a distinctive microstructure,' Lewis continued. 'We got a lucky break.' The agent's teeth flashed briefly. 'One of our guys has an interest in macromolecular science. He's built up quite a database on synthetic polymers over the last fifteen years.'

'Get to the point, Lewis!' snapped Connelly.

'He's traced this particular product to a company in Germany,' said Lewis, unfazed.

Conrad observed the FBI agent with a guarded expression. 'How confident is your man about this?'

Lewis grinned. 'Very.'

Ten minutes later, they were looking at the German firm's details on a wall monitor.

'The Obenhaus Group is a multibillion dollar corporation founded by Franz Obenhaus in the mid-1940s, just outside the town of Arnstadt, in central Germany,' said the Sit Room intelligence analyst. 'The current president of the board of directors is one Maximilian Obenhaus, the first-born son of Franz Obenhaus. That's his picture.'

The professional photograph next to the intelligence summary featured a charismatic, middle-aged man with a shock of white hair and piercing blue eyes. The patriarch of the Oben-haus dynasty looked relaxed as he leaned against a desk in an ultra modern, white-walled office. Behind him, a floor-to-ceiling glass wall offered spectacular views over acres of forested land.

'Almost all the board members are related in one way or another to the Obenhaus dynasty,' continued the intelligence analyst. 'The company originally started out making vulcanized rubber products for the car industry. It expanded rapidly in the decades following the end of the Second World War and has since placed a particularly heavy emphasis on polymer science research and development. To that aim, the group has substan-tial, state-of-the-art labs across several of their sites, all using the latest technologies in chemistry, physics, and engineering. The materials they've produced over the years have had far-reaching applications, from transplant medicine and car manu-facturing to the building and aviation industries. Their silicone seals even made it on several rockets.'

Connelly drummed her fingers on the table. 'How big is this group? Could they be the ones behind these assassination attempts?'

'They have an extensive global presence, with offices and production plants on every continent,' said the Sit Room analyst. 'However, there's no intelligence data to suggest that they're the front of a terrorist organization.' He shrugged. 'All in all, they seem pretty above board.'

Conrad inspected the facts and figures next to the photo-graph. 'Do they have any political affiliations or strong ideolo-gies?' he said pensively.

The analyst scrolled down the screen. 'The Obenhaus dynasty is firmly left wing. The family's made significant contri-butions to the Social Democratic Party over the years and appears to favor the idea of social capitalism. They fund several art, science, and cultural projects around the world and are generous contributors to a number of local and international charities. There's even an Obenhaus Innovation and Technology Prize aimed at university graduates in Europe. The Obenhaus Group itself regularly features on the Forbes 100 Most Innovative Companies.'

Laura crossed her arms, lines crinkling her brow. 'They *must* have skeletons in their closet,' she muttered. 'Is there anything in their background checks that might give us an idea why one of their products ended up in our assassins' guns?'

The Sit Room agent turned to the computer and tapped some keys. Fresh data streamed across the screen. 'Hmm,' he murmured after a few seconds.

Laura straightened. 'What?'

'The company's had an exemplary audit trail except for a red flag in the annual report produced by an external inspector eighteen months ago.' The analyst highlighted a small paragraph on the monitor. 'Says here there was some sort of irregularity in their records traced to one of their company directors. The matter was dealt with by Maximilian Obenhaus himself, and the case was later closed by the auditor.'

Conrad leaned forward, his interest piqued. 'Who was the director in question?'

The analyst brought up the names of the Obenhaus Group board. 'The report mentioned a Luther Obenhaus as the culprit.' He typed swiftly on the keyboard.

A photograph flashed up next to the list on the screen. The picture showed a thin man with graying hair. He was bundled in a heavy winter coat and was stepping inside a car in front of a tall, Neoclassical apartment building. Sunglasses obscured his eyes and a scarf covered his lower face. Light gleamed on a thick ring on his left middle finger. The shot looked to have been taken covertly.

'How is he related to the president of the board?' said Connelly.

'He's Maximilian Obenhaus's younger brother,' replied the

analyst. He panned down the screen, a faint frown dawning on his face. 'There isn't a lot of information available on the man. According to the data the European intelligence community has on him, he's a notorious recluse and hasn't engaged in the public life of the Obenhaus dynasty for some years.'

A contemplative silence descended on the room.

Conrad turned to Lewis. 'Is your guy in Quantico positive this polymer could only originate from the Obenhaus Group?'

'Absolutely,' replied Lewis. 'The stuff is called OG1140. Like I said, it has a unique composition and morphology. Our tech tells me it's only recently come on the market. He also mentioned that although the polymer is present in many products readily available to the public, the unique way it has been bonded with the carbon fibers in the guns indicates it was used in its pure form. The only way to get your hands on the original material is directly from the company's manufacturing plant.'

'Have they ever reported any thefts from their factories or security breaches at their research facilities?' asked Laura.

The man turned to the computer. 'No,' he said after a while. 'They employ one of the largest corporate security firms in the world. Their safety measures are pretty tight. Even their computer networks are well protected.'

Anatole scratched his head, a puzzled expression on his face. 'If they have production plants all over the world, then the polymer could have come from any of them, right?'

Lewis grinned. 'Wrong. Our guy at Quantico tells me this OG1140 is pretty hot stuff. As such, it's being manufactured by a single Obenhaus site.' He signaled to the Sit Room analyst. 'Bring up the address of the first Obenhaus plant.'

A satellite image popped up on the wall monitor.

'That's their factory outside Arnstadt,' said Lewis. 'The company's headquarters are also located there, as is their biggest R&D lab.'

Conrad studied the extensive complex featured on the

monitor. The Obenhaus primary operational facility occupied approximately one square mile of land south west of the town and was surrounded by pristine countryside. A network of service roads crisscrossed the site and linked several industrial-scale, rectangular buildings. An array of medium-sized constructions separated by areas of parkland dotted the grounds around them.

A landscaped garden featuring a large, central fountain stood at the southern periphery of the compound. Sunlight reflected off the glass facades and roofs of a pair of round structures in the middle of the green plot. A transparent sky-bridge connected the two buildings.

Conrad's pulse picked up. His instincts told him that they were on to something.

'How fast can you get us to Germany?' he asked Connelly.

The woman raised her eyebrows, her gaze swinging between his face and the wall monitor. 'You want to go to the site?'

'It's the only clue we've got,' said Conrad. 'I want to see this place.'

Connelly watched him for a moment, her face unreadable. 'I can have a jet ready at the Baltimore-Washington airport in forty minutes,' she said finally. She leaned back in her chair and spoke to the Sit Room communications assistant. 'Get the FAA Administrator on the line.'

Conrad rose to his feet. A thrill of nervous energy was building up inside him. The hunt was finally starting.

He turned to Donaghy and Franklin. 'Start talks with the Obenhaus Group president,' he ordered. 'And let the German foreign intelligence and domestic security agencies know we're on our way. They should cooperate with us after what happened to their chancellor.' He started toward the door, stopped, and looked over his shoulder. 'Oh, and see if they can dig up any more information about Luther Obenhaus and the company.'

Ten minutes later, he was in the back of a black Suburban

headed for the airport. Stevens drove. Laura had comman-deered the passenger seat.

The two agents occasionally spoke in low voices. Conrad could not help the pang of jealousy that rushed through him as he observed their casual interaction. He wondered whether their relationship went beyond the professional.

'This is nice,' said Anatole from where he sat next to Conrad.

Conrad looked at him. 'What is?'

Anatole waved his hand in a gesture that encompassed the immortals in the vehicle. 'This. The three of us together. It's been ages since we've worked as a team. We should do it more often.'

Laura glanced at him in the rear-view mirror. 'You're treading on thin ice, Vassili,' she said warningly.

Anatole's smile faded. 'Seriously, the two of you need to take a chill pill. All this tension is bad for your sex lives.'

Stevens almost lost his grip on the steering wheel.

A government-owned Learjet 75 stood waiting on the tarmac when they reached the airport half an hour later. A cold drizzle poured out of the clouded night sky. They exited the vehicle and jogged toward the plane.

Anatole stopped halfway up the cabin steps. 'This sure is spooky,' he murmured.

Laura frowned. 'What is?'

'Look around you. You ever seen the place so dead?'

Conrad turned. He had been so preoccupied with his own thoughts that it had taken until now for the eerie silence prevailing across the airfield to register.

Although the lights of the runways shone brightly in the darkness, not a single aircraft was lifting off or landing at the normally bustling international airport. The sky was similarly bereft of circling planes. It was like gazing at the aftermath of the end of the world.

Half a mile to the west, the shapes of dozens of jets crowded around the terminal buildings where thousands of passengers had become stranded as a result of the presidential order announced that afternoon.

Conrad dragged his eyes from the uncanny spectacle and followed the others inside the cabin of the Learjet, his heart full of misgivings. They stowed their bags away and settled into leather executive chairs as the jet taxied toward a runway.

A third of the way into their ten-hour flight to Germany, Connelly called them on the video link on the aircraft's onboard computer.

'Prime Minister Cunnington and Chancellor Dressler both made it through surgery,' said the Director of National Intelligence. 'They're currently in ICU.'

Conrad's elation at this news was short-lived. He observed her tight-lipped expression with a sinking feeling. 'What about President Gorokhov?'

Connelly shook her head slowly.

'Damn,' muttered Anatole.

'Westwood is talking to Russian Prime Minister Ivchenko, who is now the acting president,' Connelly continued. She sighed. 'Things aren't going well. The Russians suspect we had something to do with their president's assassination.'

Laura scowled. 'That's bullshit! They know full well Westwood was the victim of a similar attempt. We could accuse them of the same thing!'

'Anti-US members of the Russian Federation are whispering in Ivchenko's ears that it was all just a smokescreen to hide our nefarious plans,' Connelly explained grimly. She rubbed her temple. 'Westwood and the Secretary of Defense just increased the alert state of the US Armed Forces to DEFCON 4. This situation is getting uglier by the hour, Greene. I hope you come up with some concrete proof that an external force is at work here, before we're all nuked to hell.'

Connelly ended the connection abruptly. Conrad stared at the blank screen and let out the breath he had been holding. His darkest fears were being realized. Instead of combining their forces to find the real culprit behind these alarming events, the countries involved were starting to fight with each other. He wondered if the enemy had also anticipated this. He tried to shake off the wave of pessimism threatening to swamp him. It wasn't like him to be so negative.

Maybe I'm losing my touch, he thought. A mirthless chuckle almost escaped his lips at that notion. If so, he had chosen absolutely the worst mission of his immortal existence to do so.

Conrad felt an intense stare on his face. He looked up into Laura's golden-green eyes. She blinked and lowered her gaze. He considered her for a beat before glancing at the two men.

'Get some sleep,' he ordered, an edge of steel returning to his voice. 'We're gonna have to up our game if we want to catch these bastards.'

Laura slid into the seat across the aisle some time later.

'You sure seem pissed off with these guys,' she said after a short silence.

Conrad swiveled his head and observed her steadily. Her eyes were hooded, their expression concealed by the dimmed cabin lights. 'Remember when I said that the plane crashed near my place?' he muttered.

Puzzled lines puckered her brow. 'Uh-huh.'

Conrad sighed. 'It landed on my house.'

Laura stared. Her lips twitched.

Conrad raised his eyebrows, incredulous. 'Are you laughing at me?'

A strangled sound escaped her. 'No.' A snort contradicted her weak denial.

'You are, aren't you?'

She bit her lip.

Conrad could hardly believe she was talking to him so easily, after three hundred years of stony silence. Not for the first time, he wondered what the emotion was he had glimpsed on her face in the parking lot at the FedEx Field earlier that day.

'How well do you know Connelly and Donaghy?' he asked.

Surprise darted across her face. She arched an eyebrow. 'Are you wondering if one of them is the mole?'

Conrad remained silent.

Laura studied him for a moment. 'Sarah Connelly is the daughter of US Senator Connelly,' she said finally. 'She worked in the State Department for a number of years, first in the Foreign Service, then the Bureau of Intelligence and Research. She was the Deputy National Security Advisor before she was promoted to Director of National Intelligence a year ago.'

'And Donaghy?' said Conrad.

Laura sighed. 'Claire Donaghy is an ex-army brat. Her father is a decorated war veteran and her mother worked for the US Air Force. The woman would quite literally bite a bullet rather than betray her country. I doubt either of them is our double agent.'

'Seems you did your research,' said Conrad.

'I like to know who I'm working with.'

He looked over his shoulder to where Stevens sat at the back of the plane.

Laura followed his gaze. She stiffened. 'I can vouch for Harry,' she said in a hard voice. 'I've known him since he joined the service.'

'The two of you seem close,' Conrad said with a neutral inflection.

Laura leaned back in her seat. 'I've been his mentor for the last five years. His wife asked me to be a bridesmaid at their wedding.'

Conrad felt guilty at the wave of relief that shot through him. 'Were you?'

'Was I what?'

'A bridesmaid?'

Her lips curved in a faint smile. 'Yes, I was.' Her expression sobered. She hesitated. 'Conrad?'

'Uh-huh?'

'I trust Harry with my life,' Laura murmured.

Conrad's breath caught at the tortured look that clouded her features. She turned to face the window.

He knew exactly when she drifted off from the way her breathing slowed and her ribcage rose and fell more steadily. The immortal watched his soulmate for a long time, a lump clogging his throat as he allowed the flicker of hope that had been living in the very depths of his soul since that morning to burst into bright flames.

He finally closed his eyes and let sleep claim him.

IT WAS NOON THE FOLLOWING DAY WHEN THEY LANDED AT the airport just outside the town of Erfurt, in central Germany.

Conrad was the last to exit the aircraft. He stopped at the top of the cabin steps and shivered. A bitter wind coursed across the tarmac and stung the exposed skin of his face. The sun was a pale orb in the overcast sky, the heavy clouds holding the promise of early snow. The immortal sighed. After sixty years in the Amazon, he was finding it hard to acclimate to the continental weather. He stretched out the kinks in his neck and joined the others on the ground.

A pair of black BMW four-by-fours pulled out of the shadow of an aircraft hangar and slowed to a stop twenty feet from the Learjet. Two men in dark suits stepped out of the vehicles and headed their way.

'Agent Hartwell?' said the blond guy in the lead in accented English. He extended a welcoming hand.

'Yes,' said Laura. She shook his hand firmly.

'Jonas Schulze, German security agency,' said the man. He indicated the guy behind him. 'This is my colleague, Karl Bauer, from the Criminal Police.'

Laura introduced their team.

'So, you in charge of the investigation?' Bauer asked Greene, his tone belligerent.

Conrad observed him with a neutral expression. 'Yes.'

A bleak smile stretched Bauer's lips. 'I hope you know what you're doing. Your government appears to have ruffled feathers in the Ministry of Interior this morning. From what I hear, the Russians aren't too pleased with the way you guys are throwing your weight around either.'

Conrad narrowed his eyes at the German policeman in the tense silence that followed. 'I am well aware of the scope of my task, Mr. Bauer. Quite frankly, I don't give a damn if some of your politicians don't like the way we're doing things. I'm not here to indulge them or their precious sensibilities.'

A choked noise erupted from Anatole. Bauer stared stonily at Conrad before turning on his heels and striding toward one of the vehicles.

Schulze sighed. 'Don't mind him,' said the German agent with an apologetic shrug. 'He doesn't like US Intelligence interfering in our domestic affairs.'

'In that case, he might be pleased to know Greene is local,' said Anatole with a smile. His expression sobered at Laura's and Conrad's expressions. 'What? It's not exactly a state secret, is it?'

'I swear to God, one of these days,' Laura muttered. She stormed off after Bauer. Stevens followed.

Schulze regarded Conrad curiously. 'You're from Germany?' he said in German.

The immortal fought back a sigh. 'Yes, I am,' he admitted reluctantly in his birth tongue.

'That's funny.' The agent frowned. 'I can't place your accent.'

'I've not been here for a while,' Conrad said dismissively as they walked to the second four-by-four.

He caught a barely audible, 'Yeah, like try three hundred and sixty odd years,' behind him and frowned at Anatole over his shoulder.

'All right, all right. My lips are sealed. See?' Anatole made a zipping motion across his mouth. Conrad rolled his eyes and got into the seat next to Schulze.

The drive to Arnstadt lasted just under a quarter of an hour and took them through an undulating terrain of low elevations and open countryside. Snow capped the summits of bluffs and dusted the canopies of woodland covering the foothills of far-off mountains. Winter had arrived early in this part of the continent.

Sunlight finally broke through the low cloud cover as they drove past the town on their way to the Obenhaus site. It bathed the gray spires and red roofs of churches in streams of golden light and highlighted the autumnal leaves clinging to the trees and shrubs rising up the slopes of the hills framing the settlement to the south and west.

Three miles after they entered a valley outside Arnstadt, a dense wall of conifers appeared to their right. A discreet road sign announcing the Obenhaus plant materialized shortly afterward. The four-by-fours turned next to it and headed onto a driveway that cut through the banks of towering trees. Conrad spotted a small notice announcing that they were entering private grounds owned by the Obenhaus Group.

The conifers formed an extensive windbreak, their overhanging branches creating a shadowy tunnel that muffled the sound of the vehicles' tires rolling across the asphalt. Two thousand feet after they left the main road, a pair of steel gates came into view up ahead. A perimeter fence topped by rolls of barbed wire stretched out on either side of the entrance and disappeared between the trees.

Schulze braked by a security booth and lowered his window.

'Mr. Obenhaus is expecting us,' the agent told the sentry inside in German. He showed the man his badge.

The guard checked the computer tablet in front of him and picked up a phone.

'They've got good surveillance,' said Anatole in a low voice.

Conrad followed his second-in-command's pensive gaze to the cameras atop the entrance.

'You noticed the ones on the drive?' said Anatole.

'Yes,' Conrad replied.

'Fence looks electrified as well,' the red-haired immortal remarked.

The sentry lowered the phone back into its cradle. He typed a code in a security panel and engaged a switch. The gates swung open smoothly.

'Go straight through,' the man said with a heavy Thuringian accent. 'Take the first left, then a right. Someone will be waiting for you in the main reception.'

They drove onto a road lined with mature fir trees and reached the first crossroads seconds later. The plant's main factories appeared at the far end of the compound. The other constructions Conrad had seen on the satellite feed were partially obscured by further windbreaks.

Schulze followed the directions the guard had given him and turned onto a circular drive fronting a pair of globe-shaped, glass and steel buildings rising in the middle of a landscaped garden. He parked opposite a water fountain.

They climbed out of the vehicle just as Bauer's BMW braked behind them. The German policeman and the two Secret Service agents joined them on the steps leading up to the entrance of the first building. They walked through the revolving doors at the top and entered a large, airy reception.

Anatole looked around and cocked an eyebrow. 'Nice digs.'

'Thank you,' came a voice from the left in polished English.

Conrad turned and saw a man striding across the marble floor from a bank of lifts.

Maximilian Obenhaus was taller than he appeared to be in the picture they had seen of him the previous day. His white hair was combed back elegantly from his tanned face, and his casually stylish clothes fit his frame with an effortless ease that hinted at their costly price tag.

He walked up to Conrad and offered his hand. 'Mr. Greene? Agent Donaghy told me you were coming.'

Conrad grasped the man's fingers. The German's grip was warm and firm. The immortal appraised the Obenhaus Group president's steady, blue eyes and found them to be as shrewd as they had seemed in his photograph. He introduced the rest of his team and the Germans.

'Criminal Police?' Maximilian Obenhaus repeated in a pleasant tone. His gaze shifted from Bauer to Conrad. 'Should I be concerned?'

'As Donaghy no doubt explained, we believe you can assist us in our investigation,' said Conrad.

He scanned the lobby and the smartly dressed figures navigating the extensive space. His eyes skimmed over the abstract sculpture in the middle of the floor and rose to the glass ceiling of the atrium above them. Another bank of lifts stood at the far side of the hall, the parallel shafts ascending through the three galleries running circumferentially around the building.

'The matter we wish to discuss is somewhat sensitive,' Conrad added in a low voice. 'Can we talk in private?'

The Obenhaus Group president hesitated before inclining his head graciously. 'Follow me.'

He twisted on his heels and led them to one of the elevators. They crowded inside the glass cabin and watched while he pressed his hand against a biometric display on the operating panel. The doors closed soundlessly.

'This lift opens directly into my office,' the man explained at their expressions.

'Cool,' said Anatole.

Maximilian Obenhaus grinned, seemingly oblivious to Laura's chagrined expression.

Though he had only just met the man, Conrad's instincts told him that the Obenhaus Group president had no affiliations with the enemy they were seeking. But someone in his company quite likely did.

CHAPTER FIFTEEN

'Are you absolutely certain of this?'

Obenhaus leaned back in the sleek, white-leather executive chair and raised his pressed hands to his lips. Sunlight streamed through the glass wall behind him. Beyond it was the vista of woodland that graced his official company photograph. The blue eyes that had been friendly up until ten minutes ago now watched them guardedly.

'Yes,' said Conrad. He glanced at the scattering of picture frames on the top of a sideboard to the left, his eyes skimming over the figures in the photographs. His gaze switched to the man on the other side of the glass desk. 'The FBI technician who made the connection has triple-checked his findings and had his data confirmed overnight by a further two specialists in the field,' he continued steadily. 'One of them is based in Frankfurt.' He leaned forward with his elbows on his knees. 'They are in no doubt that the polymer in the weapons and ammunitions used in the assassination attempt on the president of the United States yesterday is OG1140.'

A strained silence followed this statement.

'This is a serious accusation indeed,' Obenhaus said gravely.

His brow puckered. 'I should really be seeking legal advice instead of talking to you.'

Conrad studied him with a neutral expression. Lawyers would definitely complicate matters. For one thing, they would delay his team's access to the plant. He had to convince Obenhaus to cooperate.

'You are well within your rights to do so,' the immortal admitted. 'But allow me to say something. This has as much to do with the other grave events that have transpired around the world in the last twenty-four hours as it does with US security matters.'

Obenhaus's eyes grew wide. He straightened in the chair. 'Are you talking about the attempt on our chancellor's life?'

Conrad glanced at the German agents. 'Yes,' he confirmed with a brief nod. 'The US believes that the same group is behind the unsuccessful attempts on the British, French, and Chinese premiers, as well as the execution of the Russian president.'

Obenhaus had gone pale. 'I heard the news this morning.' His expression suddenly hardened. 'I know our chancellor personally. What can I do to help?'

Conrad swallowed a sigh of relief. 'We'd like to take a look at the plant where this polymer is being manufactured.'

Obenhaus hesitated. 'All right,' he said. 'But can I ask that you leave any mobile devices with inbuilt cameras in my office? The place I'm taking you to is highly secure.' He looked apologetic. 'I wouldn't want our trade secrets to get into the hands of our competitors.'

Conrad looked at the Secret Service and German agents.

Laura shrugged. 'Sure.'

'We understand,' said Schulze.

Bauer's lips tightened in a thin line. He opened his mouth, paused, and nodded curtly.

Obenhaus locked their phones in his personal safe and led

them through the main door of his office. His secretary startled when they passed her desk.

'Mr. Obenhaus! Sir, I didn't know your guests had arrived,' she said, flushing.

'It's all right, Elsa.' Obenhaus smiled. 'I took the liberty of greeting them myself. Can you warn Ulrich that we're on our way?'

The secretary nodded. 'As you wish, sir.'

Obenhaus took them down a flight of stairs to the next floor. They strolled past a row of offices and conference rooms and came to an opening in the west wall of the gallery. The glass and steel skywalk lay beyond. They entered the tubular bridge and crossed the one-hundred-foot gap to the second building.

Obenhaus stopped in front of a curved, glass door and pressed his hand against another biometric display. 'Welcome to the main R&D section of the Obenhaus Group,' he said as the door slid open.

They followed him into a wide, brightly lit corridor. Airy labs appeared on either side of the passage. White-coated figures worked at counters crowded with complex instruments and machines inside them.

'The building has four levels, each dedicated to a different aspect of macromolecular science, as well as the technological applications of our polymer materials,' Obenhaus explained. 'The production of our most valuable invention takes place in the basement of this facility.'

Conrad raised an eyebrow. 'You mean it isn't in one of the factories in the compound?'

Obenhaus shook his head. 'The security measures in place inside this building are far superior to the ones we use for our other plants.' His tone grew guarded. 'We have data-sensitive contracts with a number of foreign governments. The nature of the work we're carrying out for them requires added protection.'

He turned the corner and proceeded to a service elevator. They entered the cabin after him and walked out onto a metal mezzanine fifty feet below ground.

'*This* is the heart of the Obenhaus Group.' A note of pride crept into the voice of the company president. 'My father had this facility built in the 1980s, just months before his death.'

Conrad walked to the edge of the steel walkway and looked down onto a vast space that extended a good five hundred feet ahead of them.

Towering rows of industrial-scale, automated machinery and workstations populated the factory below. A chain of airtight doors lined its western wall, the gaps between them interspersed with thick piping that fed into the machines. Roller doors hedged a staging area packed with pallets of boxes and crates at the other end of the plant. Cranes and forklifts dotted the floor, while extraction fans and airshafts populated the ceiling and walls.

Despite the dozens of people working below them, the plant was remarkably quiet but for the drone and clank of the machines. It also reeked of efficiency. The immortal was impressed.

'I find excessive noise to be counterproductive,' Obenhaus explained with a faint smile at Conrad's expression. 'Come, I'll show you where the polymer exits the production chain.' He guided them to a metal staircase at the end of the walkway.

A man in white overalls and a hard hat came striding across the concrete floor toward them when they reached the bottom of the steps.

'Ah, Ulrich!' Obenhaus exclaimed. He made the introductions. 'This is Ulrich Voigt, the operations manager for this plant. Ulrich, the gentlemen and lady would like to see where product OG1140 is being made.'

Voigt lifted his hat and scratched his forehead, surprise evident in his eyes. 'I didn't know we were having the auditors today, Mr. Obenhaus,' he mumbled. 'I thought they weren't due to visit until next month.'

'They're not from the audit office,' Obenhaus said pleasantly.

Voigt waited for his employer to elaborate. When he realized no further information would be forthcoming, he cleared his throat and turned on his heels. 'Follow me.'

They crossed the floor to the west wall of the plant and stopped in front of one of the sealed doors. A glazed window occupied the top half of the metal panel. Conrad peered curiously through the glass. Several enormous steel vats and man-sized tanks occupied a large room on the other side; a figure in a protective suit sat manning the computerized control panel in front of them.

Voigt gestured to the chamber. 'This is one of five units where OG1140 is synthesized,' he explained. 'As you can see, the original constituents are undergoing high performance compounding using a process unique to the Obenhaus Group.' He indicated the large, hermetic tubes above their heads. 'OG1140 then makes its way to the next processing steps, where degassing, devolatilization, additives, coating, and coloring take place, depending on the end product required.'

They followed him as he strolled along one of the production chains. The operations manager pointed out more complex instruments and systems. Conrad shifted restlessly as he listened to the man.

'In what forms is OG1140 available as a pure product?' the immortal said finally, trying not to show his growing impatience.

'The polymer comes as a pellet and a pure melt solution,' Voigt replied. 'We also do direct extrusion into plates, films, rolls, or tubes.'

He stopped next to one of the machines and smiled

distractedly at the woman supervising the packing of boxfuls of pea-sized, round balls of clear plastic.

'This is OG1140 in its pellet structure,' said the operations manager.

Conrad picked up one of the transparent globules and raised it to eye level. He examined the material for a moment, his mind racing.

'If you wanted to combine high-strength carbon fibers to this and mold it into a specific design, what form would you choose?' he said.

The operations manager glanced at Obenhaus, unease dawning in his eyes.

'The liquid solution would be easiest to work with,' Voigt admitted reluctantly. 'You wouldn't need to remelt OG1140 and reprocess the copolymer.'

'We've been informed that the Obenhaus Group has never suffered any security breaches or thefts at its production plants,' said Laura matter-of-factly. 'Does that hold true for this facility as well?'

Voigt opened his mouth to reply, hesitated, and looked at Obenhaus again.

The company president observed Laura shrewdly. 'You did your research,' he commented in an even tone.

She shrugged. 'It's part of the job description, I'm afraid.'

Obenhaus nodded and turned to the operations manager. 'You can tell them, Ulrich.'

'Eighteen months ago, the auditor discovered that a batch of OG1140 had gone missing from this plant,' said Voigt. A guilty expression flashed across his face, as if he somehow blamed himself for the incident. 'The polymer was just out of its experimental phase at the time.'

Alarms bells rang in Conrad's head. He exchanged troubled glances with Anatole and the two Secret Service agents.

Schulze frowned at their expressions. 'What is it?'

Conrad turned to Obenhaus. 'Is he talking about the incident involving Luther Obenhaus?'

The company president went still. 'You know about that?'

'We also checked the Obenhaus Group finances and audit trails,' Conrad stated grimly. 'That was the only red flag your company has received since its inception.'

'We assumed the infraction was a misappropriation of shares or embezzlement,' said Laura as Obenhaus paled. 'Obviously, we were wrong.' An undercurrent of frustration tempered her voice.

Bauer's face had gone red. He exhaled explosively and threw his arms in the air. 'What the hell are you people talking about?'

Laura regarded the irate policeman coolly. She summarized their findings on the Obenhaus Group.

Understanding dawned on Schulze's face. 'That incident also came up during our intelligence gathering.' His eyebrows rose as he indicated the box at the end of the production line. 'Still, that auditor must have had hawk eyes to have picked up on a missing consignment this size.'

Voigt startled. He gaped at them for a moment, too shocked to speak. 'I don't think you understand,' he said finally. 'The batch I'm referring to was 150 gallons of liquid OG1140.'

'What?' Laura exclaimed.

Conrad turned to Obenhaus. 'What did your brother need that much polymer for?' he asked accusingly. 'And how did you manage to settle this with the auditor?'

A flush of embarrassment darkened Obenhaus's cheeks. 'Luther took the material to experiment with a new laser cutting and welding technology he had devised,' he said, a defensive note creeping into his voice as he met Conrad's gaze. 'He returned the product and was suspended as a director, with his shares and company assets frozen. Those were the conditions the board demanded. They satisfied the external auditor enough to close the case.'

A stilted silence fell on the group.

Anatole cocked an eyebrow. 'Christ, he got expelled from the family business just for that?'

Obenhaus hesitated. 'No, there was more to the decision. Luther had been a disruptive figure in the company for well over a decade. There have been prior incidents when he behaved in ways and engaged in activities that threatened the Obenhaus dynasty's reputation, his ongoing gambling addiction being one example.' The company president's shoulders suddenly drooped. A sigh left his lips. 'The theft was the last straw as far as the board was concerned.'

'And he just gave you back the stuff he took?' said Laura skeptically.

'Yes,' said Obenhaus. 'He made a sculpture out of the polymer to demonstrate the practical application of the laser system he had been working on. It was his..."parting gift" to the company.' His voice turned bitter with his last words.

Conrad's pulse jumped. 'What do you mean, he made a sculpture?' he said uneasily.

'You saw it when you came into the Obenhaus Group head-quarters,' the company president explained. 'It's the one in the atrium.'

Five minutes later, they were standing inside the lobby of the first building. The sculpture was eight feet tall and balanced on a steel base inset in the middle of the floor. Shaped like a teardrop, it had been dyed a brilliant white, the geometric twists and curves along its contours creating an eye-catching pattern of light and shadow. A sliver of a hunch blossomed at the back of Conrad's mind as he studied the structure.

'I'm kinda curious about something,' said Anatole. 'How come your brother can create this stuff?'

A blank expression washed across Obenhaus's face. 'Oh. Of course,' he muttered. 'Your investigation may not have revealed this.' He ran his fingers through his hair. 'Luther is a developmental engineer with PhDs in polymer processing and applied chemistry. He didn't want the Obenhaus name to create any negative preconceptions when he attended university, so he graduated with our mother's maiden name, Brandt.'

Conrad's mouth went dry at the company president's words. He stared at the teardrop-shaped sculpture. 'Are you sure this is made from OG1140?'

Obenhaus frowned. 'Yes, of course.'

'How can you be certain?' Conrad challenged.

Obenhaus's gaze shifted to the sculpture. 'I—I didn't have any reason to believe Luther would lie to me,' he stammered.

Conrad bit back a curse. 'How fast can you get this thing analyzed?' he demanded.

Obenhaus had gone pale once more. 'It shouldn't take long once we obtain a sample. I'll get one of the technicians to come down and take a specimen.' He turned and started hurriedly across the lobby.

'You know, there's a faster way to do this,' said Anatole.

Obenhaus stopped and turned. 'What do you mean?'

Conrad saw motion out of the corner of his eye. He opened his mouth to shout out a warning.

Anatole raised the gun and fired. The bullet chipped the sculpture and struck the marble floor with a soft ping. He retrieved the small, white fragment and handed it to the shocked Obenhaus Group president.

'Will this do?' he asked brightly.

'And here I thought you'd mellowed,' Conrad grumbled under his breath.

Stevens, Schulze, and Bauer stood paralyzed around him, their hands halfway to their guns. Laura was not as indecisive. She strode up to Anatole and smacked him on the side of the head.

'*You ass!* How could you be so reckless?' she hissed.

'But I used the suppressor,' the immortal protested. He indicated the barrel of his gun. 'Besides, this will speed this up, won't it, Pres?'

Maximilian Obenhaus observed the damage to the sculpture and his expensive marble floor. His staff went about their business some twenty feet away, oblivious to the muffled gunshot. 'Let's get this over with,' he managed stoically.

They followed him back to the R&D building and up some stairs to a lab on the top floor. Half an hour later, the polymer chemist Obenhaus had tasked to analyze the chip from the sculpture looked up from her workstation and shook her head.

'This is not OG1140,' the woman said, chagrined.

Conrad's stomach sank. His suspicions had been confirmed once more.

'What?' Obenhaus's shocked gaze shifted from the sample on the counter to the scientist. 'Are you certain?'

'Yes, sir,' the woman replied. 'This is a plastic polymer that's widely available on the market. It's not even one of ours.'

'Luther, what have you done?' Obenhaus mumbled to himself after a stunned silence. The company president stared blindly at the floor.

Despite the sense of urgency flowing through him, Conrad felt a stab of sympathy for the man. 'We need to talk to your brother.'

Obenhaus looked up and nodded slowly, a haunted expression in his eyes. 'Let's go to my office.'

They returned to his room and retrieved their phones from his safe. Obenhaus sat at his desk and called his brother on the office line. A frown puckered his brow after a couple of minutes. He pressed the hook switch and dialed another number.

'He's not answering his home phone or his mobile,' Obenhaus murmured. A trace of anxiety laced his voice. 'I'll call his building.' He disconnected again and punched in a third number. 'Jürgen? This is Maximilian Obenhaus,' he said after a few seconds. 'Have you seen my brother today?' His lips compressed in a thin line as he listened.

Conrad tensed.

Obenhaus studied the immortal with a perturbed expression. 'Did he mention if he was going anywhere?' he said into the phone. 'No? Okay. Thank you, Jürgen.'

Conrad watched the company president place the phone carefully down in its cradle.

'The concierge of Luther's apartment building in Leipzig hasn't seen my brother since Sunday morning,' Maximilian Obenhaus announced.

Conrad shared anxious glances with the immortals and the assembled agents. This was not good news. 'Can you think of anywhere he could have gone?' he asked.

Obenhaus hesitated for a beat. 'He has a cabin in the Thüringer Forest, about twenty-five miles from here. It's...his sanctuary.' He frowned. 'But he usually lets the concierge know he's going there.'

'Can you give us directions?' said Conrad.

'Yes,' Obenhaus said reluctantly.

They left the company headquarters minutes later with instructions on how to get to the lodge.

'Mr. Greene?' Maximilian Obenhaus called out from the steps of the building.

Conrad stopped and turned.

'Though it appears Luther may be involved in something criminal, he's still my brother,' said the company president, his shoulders drooping.

Conrad considered the forlorn man for several seconds. 'As long as he cooperates, I'll see that no harm comes to him.'

~

CHAPTER SIXTEEN

THEY LEFT ARNSTADT AND HEADED SOUTH TOWARD THE hazy, snow-capped Thüringer mountain range. The road soon climbed through the foothills of the peaks, taking them past narrow river valleys and undulating plateaus dotted with villages. Rocky outcrops and bluffs topped with ancient stone castles broke the vista of dense spruce and pine forests covering the slopes and vales.

One mile after passing a sleepy hamlet of slate-tiled dwellings, they turned onto a private track between the trees. Sunlight broke through the soaring canopy and painted the forest in strips of light and shade.

A rusted metal gate appeared in their path after a thousand feet. Schulze got out of the vehicle and opened it. They drove through the opening and soon reached a snow-dusted field of heather and wood sorrel. Shadowy woodland appeared on the other side. The track meandered between the trees and tapered to a rutted, overgrown trail. Conrad braced himself against the dashboard and the roof as the four-by-four bumped along the uneven ground.

A mile later, the land dipped into a large bowl ringed by

towering conifers. A meadow stood at the bottom of the shallow depression. Sunlight danced on the stream running along its western boundary, where a wooden barn, bleached a pale gray by the weather, stood some hundred feet from a shallow creek. Ice patches gleamed on the surface of the water.

Squatting in the middle of the clearing was a chalet-style cabin. Smoke curled from one of its chimneys. A black Freelander stood parked on the graveled area at the side of the building.

'Looks like we found Obenhaus,' murmured Schulze.

The German agent guided the four-by-four down the path leading to the meadow and parked next to the Freelander. They had just stepped out of the vehicle when shouts suddenly erupted from inside the building.

Conrad stiffened as he registered the panic in the male voice. His stomach lurched when the sharp reports of three gunshots issued from the interior of the lodge in rapid succession.

He yanked his gun out and leapt up the steps to the porch, his heart hammering against his ribs. His fingers had just closed on the handle of the screen covering the front door when a high-pitched rumble rose from his left.

A dark-clad figure on a green dirt bike shot out from around the corner of the building. The man looked over his shoulder at the sound of Bauer's vehicle slowing on the gravel. His eyes shrunk through the open visor of his helmet. He gunned the bike's engine.

'Stop him!' Conrad shouted to the others as he sprinted along the porch.

He vaulted over the railing at the end, landed hard on the ground, and raced after the fleeing biker. Schulze and Anatole gave chase behind him. Bauer accelerated and followed in the four-by-four.

The man rose on the foot pegs of the dirt bike seconds

before he hit the slope of the bowl. Soil and grass spun up behind the tires as he ascended toward the trees.

Conrad raised his gun and fired. The first two bullets went wild and struck the ground. The third pinged off the bike's tail panel. The immortal cursed and jammed the gun in his waist-band as he neared the incline. He started to scale the embankment, his breaths coming in hard, fast pants. Anatole and Schulze followed in his steps.

An engine roared to their left. Bauer's four-by-four overtook them a second later. The two immortals and the German agent reached the summit of the rise just as further gunfire echoed to the skies.

The four-by-four had slewed to a stop in front of a wall of dense undergrowth. Three of the vehicle's doors were open. Fifteen feet in front of the bumper, Bauer, Laura, and Stevens slowly lowered their weapons as they watched the dirt bike disappear in the gloom of the crowded forest.

'Goddammit!' Conrad gasped as he reached their side. His hands dropped to his knees as he caught his breath. Frustration gnawed at his insides. The enemy had bested them once more.

A flush of anger darkened Laura's cheeks. 'Let's go back!' she ordered. 'Obenhaus is probably still in the chalet.' She turned on her heels.

Bauer took the vehicle while the rest of them headed swiftly toward the meadow on foot.

'Looks like the bastards were one step ahead of us again,' Anatole said darkly as they scrambled down the incline.

Conrad scowled. 'Ye—'

Incandescent light bloomed up ahead. The thumps of two powerful explosions ripped through the clearing and drowned out his voice. The force of the blasts washed over the slope and lifted them off their feet.

As he soared helplessly through the air, heat scorching his skin and throat, Conrad saw Bauer's four-by-four judder backward on its suspension. The vehicle skidded and started to flip.

The immortal slammed into the ground a heartbeat later. His head struck something hard. Stars exploded in front of his eyes. The impact knocked the breath out of his lungs. A dull buzz filled his ears, dampening all sound. Clouds of black smoke billowed past his vision. Ash and debris started to rain down around him.

Conrad gritted his teeth and turned on his side. Fear lanced through his heart at the sight that met his eyes.

'Laura!' he cried out, his voice a muffled echo inside his skull.

She lay on her back some twenty feet away. Her eyes were closed and blood stained her skin from a gash on her temple.

Conrad crawled to his knees and shook his head dazedly. His ears popped as he staggered to his feet. Sound returned in a painful clamor. The crackle and roar of raging flames finally registered. He looked over his shoulder.

The lodge and barn were engulfed in fierce blazes, as were the wrecks of the Freelander and Schulze's vehicle.

His eyes shifted to the unconscious woman a short distance from where he stood. He stumbled across the ground and sank to his knees by her side just as she blinked and opened her eyes.

'Are you okay?' Conrad asked shakily. He ran his hands lightly over her body.

Laura groaned and nodded slowly. She pushed herself up on her elbows.

Relief flooded Conrad. He took her arm and helped her gently into a sitting position.

She looked up, the hazel gaze sweeping over him. 'And you?'

'I'm fine,' Conrad murmured.

Anatole, Schulze, and Stevens were slowly rising to their feet. Except for some cuts and grazes, they seemed unharmed.

Schulze suddenly froze. 'Bauer!' he shouted weakly.

Conrad followed the German agent's horrified gaze to the four-by-four lying on its roof at the bottom of the incline. He pulled Laura up and they joined the men stumbling down the slope. Tempered glass from the vehicle's smashed windows crunched under their feet as they reached it. They found Bauer unconscious inside.

Blood drained from Schulze's face. 'Shit,' he whispered hoarsely, reverting to German.

Conrad stared. A jagged pole of timber had pierced the windscreen of the vehicle and impaled Bauer's left shoulder, pinning him to his seat. He lay suspended at an awkward angle, his long legs jammed underneath the wheel. A scarlet stain had soaked through his shirt and jacket, and a dark rivulet was slowly trickling along the length of wood. There was a wound on his temple where his head had struck something.

Schulze fumbled for his phone and punched in a number. A beeping tone sounded from the receiver. He gaped at the screen. 'Damn it! There's no signal!'

Laura lobbed her cell at him. 'It's a satellite phone! You should be able to get through!'

The agent nodded shakily and dialed again.

Trepidation filled Conrad as he knelt by the vehicle. He reached through the broken window and probed Bauer's neck gently. A small sigh of relief left his lips when he felt a strong, thrumming pulse. The police officer moaned. His eyes fluttered open.

'Bauer? Bauer, listen to me! Keep still! You're bleeding heavily,' Conrad ordered. The beat beneath his fingers was turning thready.

The man blinked at him, his gaze unfocused. He saw the wooden pole in the windscreen and followed its path to his shoulder. Alarm distorted his features. He started to flail. A crimson pool bloomed from his wound.

Conrad cursed and pinned him down. 'Help me keep him

still!' he shouted at Laura. She ran round to the other side of the car. He glanced over his shoulder at Anatole and Stevens. 'You two, get that thing out of his shoulder!'

'We shouldn't move him!' said Stevens.

'If we don't do something *now*, he'll die!' Conrad shouted. 'That's arterial blood!'

Stevens bit his lip. Laura scrambled wordlessly through the passenger window and murmured reassuring words to the thrashing man as she immobilized him against the seat.

Shadows played across the cracked windscreen. Anatole and Stevens positioned themselves in front of the vehicle and gripped the end of the jagged shaft piercing Bauer's shoulder.

'This is going to hurt,' Laura warned Bauer. 'Just hold on to me!'

Her voice finally broke through the German officer's panic. His eyes cleared and he focused on her. Bauer gritted his teeth and grunted, his face ashen. Schulze ended the call to the local emergency services; the agent joined Anatole and Stevens.

Conrad placed his left hand next to the wound on Bauer's shoulder. His brow creased when he detected the underlying fractured clavicle and ruptured major vessels beneath the man's skin.

'What?' said Laura.

Conrad closed his eyes briefly. 'There's a lot of damage,' he murmured. He took a deep breath, concentrated, and released his healing power. 'On the count of three!' he shouted to the men outside. 'One, two, *three*!'

They pulled on the pole. Bauer screamed as the jagged shaft slowly came out of the seat and his flesh. Conrad ground his teeth together and controlled the flow of blood escaping the man's torn artery and vein. The policeman went limp and collapsed in the immortals' arms a moment later.

'Let's get him out!' barked Conrad.

They maneuvered Bauer out of the vehicle and lowered him

to the ground, Conrad keeping his hand on the unconscious man's shoulder the entire time. Once the officer lay supine, the immortal swiftly extracted the fragments of wood embedded inside the flesh beneath his fingers. He fixed Bauer's broken clavicle and lacerated blood vessels, and moved to the damaged muscles.

'What are you doing?' said Schulze.

Conrad ignored the agent and inspected the wound on the policeman's temple. He healed the linear skull fracture in the left temporal bone and the underlying small, subdural hematoma, before stemming the bleeding from the vessels in the man's scalp. Once again, he did not completely repair the skin and subcutaneous tissues.

Seconds later, he sat back on the ground and released the breath he had been holding. His hands shook from the rush of adrenaline surging through his veins.

'Is he okay?' said Schulze.

Conrad looked up into the security agent's anxious face.

'He'll be fine,' said the immortal. He caught sight of Stevens's troubled expression.

'Are you all right?' Laura asked quietly, her gaze shifting from Conrad's trembling fingers to his face.

Conrad nodded and gave her a weak smile. Her eyes flashed. His heart stuttered in his chest when he glimpsed an emotion he never thought he would see again in her gaze. Before he could wonder whether he had been imagining it, Bauer stirred on the ground between them.

The policeman opened his eyes and blinked slowly. 'What just happened?' He tried to sit up.

'Hey, don't move! You're injured!' Schulze exclaimed. He pushed the man to the ground.

Bauer looked at his left shoulder. He fingered his bloodied clothes and wound with a wince. 'It's just a bit sore,' he muttered, his tone reflecting mild puzzlement. 'I feel fine.'

Schulze gaped as the police officer started to climb shakily to his feet.

Conrad rose and gave him a hand. 'Be careful. You lost a lot of blood.'

Bauer watched him for a beat and inclined his head. His eyes moved to the conflagrations consuming the buildings in the clearing.

'Well, I think we can officially tell the suspicious assholes in the Ministry of Interior that the US is not being behind this,' the policeman said bitterly.

Conrad's heart sank as he stared at the fires. He thought of his words to Maximilian Obenhaus. He was not going to be able to keep his promise to the company president.

It was four thirty in the afternoon when the flames were finally doused by firefighters from the forest authorities and the local brigades. By the time the scene investigator completed a preliminary inspection of the buildings and declared them safe for entry, the sun was sinking in a reddening sky.

Bauer allowed paramedics to dress his wounds but refused to go to the hospital. He followed Conrad and the others when they slipped on protective crime scene gear and entered the lodge.

The explosion had originated from a study at the rear of the building. The force of the blast had removed parts of the external walls and a section of the roof. A deer head mounted above a stone fireplace dominated the space, miraculously unscathed but for a layer of soot. The animal's dead eyes seemed to follow Conrad as he walked to the mangled, charred body partially visible under a pile of rubble next to the hearth. Blackened floorboards creaked beneath the immortal's feet as he squatted to inspect the corpse.

'We'll have to wait for analysis of the dental records to confirm whether this is our man,' said Schulze.

'It's Luther Obenhaus,' Conrad stated flatly.

A grunt escaped Bauer. 'How can you tell?'

'Because of the ring on his finger,' said Laura before Conrad could reply.

Schulze and Bauer stared at the smoke-stained band on the body's left hand.

'He was wearing it in the intelligence photograph we had of him and in the pictures in Maximilian Obenhaus's office.' Laura met Conrad's gaze. 'You're not the only one who notices things,' she muttered.

Conrad rose and observed the damaged display cabinets and bookcases around the room. The glass had cracked and shattered in the doors of most of the units. A grimy clock above the mantelpiece had stopped with its hands on ten past two.

It was Anatole who found the remains of a computer and a cell phone under some debris on the far side of the room. Conrad joined him and stared at the distorted plastic frames, his hands fisting at his sides. He tried the power button on the phone. The fractured screen remained black.

'We might be able to recover data from the card and the hard drive,' said Schulze. Conrad remained silent. It would be a miracle if they retrieved anything useful from the devices.

They left the cabin and headed for the barn. Though night had fallen, they were bathed in the artificial brightness of dozens of spotlights dotting the perimeter of the clearing. The hum of generators echoed against the trees.

The old farm building had once been used to store hay and house livestock. Although it had been damaged by the fire, it was structurally sounder than the lodge, with its walls and roof still intact.

'That's because most of the explosive force took place downstairs,' explained the investigator.

'Downstairs?' Conrad repeated with a puzzled frown.

'Yes,' said the investigator, jerking his head toward a stall at the end of the building. 'In the bunker.'

'A bunker?' said Laura, skeptical.

The investigator shrugged and led them to the enclosure. A heat-distorted, metal trapdoor lay on the ground some ten feet from a rectangular opening in the floor. An acrid stench rose from the dimly lit depths beneath it.

'I recommend you wear face masks,' the investigator told them. He slipped on a respirator and indicated the box of gear on the floor. 'It's nasty down there.'

'I sure as hell hope that's not dead rats we're smelling,' Anatole muttered as they followed the man down a stepladder.

The metal stairs originally connecting the barn to the basement lay in a buckled heap on the floor of a narrow passage. A containment door stood ajar at one end. The security display under the handle was flashing an alert.

The investigator pulled the damaged panel open. Illumination from a pair of spotlights on stands washed across a metal landing.

'Watch the floor,' the man warned. 'It's a bit unsteady.'

Conrad could not quell the feeling of dread knotting his stomach as he stepped onto the narrow mezzanine. The bright beams cut through smoky blackness and revealed the interior of a large, subterranean chamber some ten feet below. The ceiling and walls were bare concrete that had originally been painted a brilliant white. Soot and other chemical stains now streaked across the pale surfaces. Two rows of worktops had occupied the extensive floor space; the shapes of blackened, warped machinery and melted instrument coverings lay scattered around the damaged counters.

The bunker had served as a lab.

'The sprinklers that weren't damaged in the explosion managed to dampen the blaze somewhat,' said the investigator in a matter-of-fact voice. He indicated the round, metal heads screwed into the concrete ceiling. 'I'm afraid the stairs are too unstable,' he added, pointing to the twisted structure to their right. 'We'll have to wait for a more secure—' He broke off suddenly. '*Hey*! What are you doing?'

Conrad had slipped under the railing of the platform. He lowered himself over the edge and dropped down to the floor below. His boots squelched when he landed in a film of water.

'You're going to contaminate the scene!' the investigator shouted from above. The man gaped when the others ducked under the railing. 'What the—? Hey, where the hell are you guys going? *Come back here!*'

'They'll be careful,' Bauer murmured reassuringly next to the man. With his arm in a sling, the policeman couldn't follow them.

Glass and debris crunched under their feet as they started to explore the room. It was Laura who discovered the laser workstation at the other end of the bunker. Conrad stopped at her side and stared at the device. It bore a faint resemblance to the machines he had seen in the Obenhaus Group labs earlier that day. Attached to it was a computer with a shattered monitor and a buckled hard drive damaged by the blast. Anatole stepped across the aisle and carefully lifted an object from a grimy work surface.

'Hey, does this remind you guys of something?' he asked, his cold voice slightly muffled by his mask.

Conrad turned and examined the frame in the immortal's hands. His pulse accelerated when he recognized the shape.

Laura frowned. 'Yes. It looks exactly like the casting template for the sniper rifles we recovered from the FedEx Field.'

They found the mangled molds for the other weapon parts and the ceramic bullets under the rubble of the next workstation. By the time they finished exploring the lab, Bauer and the investigator had maneuvered another ladder to the bunker floor. Conrad's head filled with a single, disturbing thought as he climbed the rungs.

Had the enemy known they were coming here? If so, did that mean the mole was a member of his immediate team? His eyes darted to Harry Stevens. Laura had never once doubted the US Secret Service agent. Although Conrad liked the young man, they had both once been wrong about someone they had put their trust in.

Conrad breathed in the fresh night air outside the barn and related their findings to the German policeman and the scene investigator. Bauer's expression was grim by the time the immortal finished talking.

'We'll get this place processed as fast as we can,' he promised. 'This is now a matter of national security.'

'Thank you.' Conrad gazed steadily at the German officer. 'Will you let me tell Obenhaus?'

Bauer hesitated. 'We should really wait for confirmation.' A loud exhale escaped his lips. 'But hell, the way things are looking, that body *has* to be that of Luther Obenhaus.'

Conrad used Laura's phone and dialed the number Maximilian Obenhaus had given them when they left the company headquarters that afternoon. There was a click after the third ring.

'Hello?' said a tense voice.

Conrad stared at the dark sky beyond the trees. 'Mr. Obenhaus, this is Conrad Greene,' he said quietly. 'I'm afraid I've got some bad news.'

'THAT'S HIM!' EXCLAIMED NADICA RAJKOVIC. 'THAT'S THE man who was at the facility in Crystal City!'

Zoran Rajkovic froze the image and slowly leaned back in his seat.

They stared at the picture of a grim-faced figure on the ninety-inch monitor on the wall. It was a clip from the dozens of videos that had been uploaded to the Internet by the Redskins fans who had been at the FedEx Field the previous day. The man was stepping out of a vehicle surrounded by armed police and state troopers on a road outside the stadium, his hands behind his head.

'According to our source, his name is Conrad Greene,' said Zoran, his tone cool despite the anger thrumming through him. 'President Westwood has put him in charge of the multi-agency investigation into his assassination attempt. No one knows anything about the man. He just appeared out of the blue in Maryland yesterday morning and helped the Secret Service locate the positions of the other two assassins. Rumor is he got involved when our missing contractor's plane crashed near his house in Brazil.' He scowled. 'He's currently in Germany with a team of agents.'

'Germany?' Nadica asked sharply.

'Yes.' Zoran glanced at Ariana. 'One of the FBI scientists in Quantico identified the polymer we used for the guns. They wanted to check out the Obenhaus factory outside Arnstadt.'

'They won't find anything there,' said Nadica. Satisfaction tinged her voice. 'Even if they make the link with Luther Oben-haus, that trail will soon be cold.'

Ariana Rajkovic studied the shot of Conrad Greene with a forbidding expression.

'Still, for them to have made the connection to Germany is something that should concern us,' she stated in a steely tone. 'We need to slow them down. No, not you, Nadica,' she added tersely at the young woman's hungry expression. 'I know the man has angered you, but you have more important tasks at hand.' She looked at Zoran. 'Send one of our other contractors in Europe.'

'Yes, Ama,' he replied with a dutiful nod. He watched her disappear through the doors of the main salon and turned to scrutinize the still image on the screen.

He would not let Conrad Greene get in their way. Not after all the hardship Ariana Rajkovic had suffered to see this scheme come to fruition. The events currently being played out around the world were part of a plan that had been set in motion a long time ago. Too much blood had been spilled along the way for it to fail now.

Zoran looked at his sister and saw the same defiant light in her eyes. They would see this through to the end. They owed it to the woman who meant the whole world to them.

ARIANA STROLLED ALONG THE TEAK-LINED PASSAGE TO THE master cabin on the upper deck and closed the door of the luxurious room behind her. Sunlight glowed on the waters of the Atlantic outside the windows overlooking the balcony.

She ignored the mesmerizing sight and crossed the floor to the bulkhead opposite her bed. Soft glowing spotlights illuminated the oil portraits of two men inside gold-lacquered frames.

Ariana stopped and gazed lovingly at the first painting. 'Soon, my love,' she whispered, raising her fingers to touch the man's face. 'Soon, I will fulfill your long-held dream. Your bloodline will rule this wretched world, as it was always meant to do.'

She turned to the other painting and similarly brushed the lips of the second man, her heart aching all over again. 'Thank you for giving me the strength to carry on, husband.'

CHAPTER SEVENTEEN

'HE'S DEAD?' CONNELLY SAID SHARPLY.

'Unfortunately,' muttered Conrad. Anger and sadness still coursed through the immortal following his difficult conversation with Maximilian Obenhaus. 'They got to him before we did. The Germans just sent us some preliminary reports. Luther Obenhaus was shot in the head and chest and died instantly.' He clenched his teeth. 'This will be small comfort for his brother, but at least the Obenhaus family will know he didn't suffer the agony of being burned alive.'

A heavy frown dawned on the face of the Director of National Intelligence.

An hour had passed since they returned from the Thüringer Forest. Conrad had called the Sit Room for an update the minute they reached the Learjet parked on the tarmac in Erfurt.

'And the motive for his involvement in this affair?' asked Connelly finally.

'We suspect it's going to boil down to money,' said Conrad. 'The authorities are going to check out Obenhaus's apartment in Leipzig. We're waiting to hear if they'll let us join the team doing the search.'

'Good,' said Connelly with a firm nod.

Laura stirred next to Conrad. 'How's Westwood getting on with the Russian PM?'

Connelly rubbed her forehead and sighed. Exhaustion lined her face. 'This incident in Germany will certainly help ease things. We're still at DEFCON 4, but I anticipate the alert state might be downgraded in the next few hours once the Russians receive confirmation on the intelligence coming out of Berlin.'

'Have the other investigation paths yielded anything of interest?' said Conrad.

Connelly's face brightened slightly. 'The dead guy from Brazil had his face and prints modified as well, same as the other two assassins,' she said. 'The medical examiner did however uncover the traces of a laser-treated tattoo under his hairline.'

An image flashed up next to Connelly's face on the video link. Conrad inhaled sharply as he stared at the faint image of a snake's head that had been etched in ink on the shaved skin covering the back of the dead man's skull. He recognized the symbol.

'Fer-de-Lance,' he whispered, his mind racing.

'What?' asked Laura, puzzled.

Conrad glanced at her, excitement flushing through him. 'Fer-de-Lance. The common lancehead,' he explained. 'It's a venomous viper found in South America.' He gazed at Connelly. 'If I remember correctly, it's also the symbol of someone who belongs to the Barba Amarilla drug cartel.'

'Exactly.' Connelly's eyes gleamed. 'Forensics have performed a high-resolution, three-dimensional facial recon-struction based on the guy's skull structure.'

The computerized model of what the man from Brazil

would have originally looked like appeared below the image of the tattoo.

'We believe the third assassin was one Julio Vargas, the Barba Amarilla group's top hitman,' Connelly continued. 'He's currently wanted on four continents.'

Conrad frowned. 'Did you check with Donaghy—?'

'Yes,' Connelly cut in. 'CIA's confirmed that the Barba Amarilla cartel is one of the groups that recently disappeared from the intelligence community's radar. Donaghy's currently talking to an operative who just emerged from an undercover operation in Africa.'

Conrad could feel pieces of the puzzle starting to coalesce.

'What about the MD helicopter?' Anatole asked Connelly.

'We're still going through the list provided by the manufacturer,' replied the Director of National Intelligence. 'We've ruled out all government agencies who purchased either of the two suspected models. That leaves us with forty private organizations and individuals. The ones we've looked into so far are all above board.' Connelly sighed. 'There's not a whiff of scandal or criminal activity about them.'

The sound of a commotion suddenly rose in the background on the video link. Creases wrinkled Connelly's forehead. She turned and spoke to someone off the screen. 'What is it?'

'We've got something on the stuff that killed the prisoner in Crystal City,' someone said excitedly.

Conrad recognized the FBI agent's voice. Lewis stormed into view behind Connelly a second later.

'You were on the right track about that poison,' the man told Conrad with a fierce smile. 'We didn't find anything in the dead guy's blood chemistry, but we got something on the skin and muscle biopsy taken from his arm. Our forensic toxicologists believe the substance might be a neurotoxic alkaloid. It degraded too rapidly for them to be able to determine its exact molecular structure, although they think it was co-crystallized with another compound to increase its bioavailability. Moscow just confirmed that the poison used by the secret service agent who killed their president has a similar chemical profile.'

Laura ran a hand through her hair and exhaled sharply. 'What does that tell us though?'

Some of the animation faded from the FBI agent's face. 'Well, not much at the moment,' he admitted. 'But if we could get our hands on a sample of the original product before it has a chance to break down, we might be able to figure out its ori—'

'Hang on!' Connelly interrupted. She was scowling at something to her right. 'I've got Donaghy on a separate video channel.' She glanced at the camera projecting to the Learjet. 'I'll link everyone up.'

A second window opened on the aircraft's computer monitor. The CIA agent's face appeared in the center of it. She was speaking through her cell phone in what looked to be the back of a moving vehicle.

'Can you hear me, Greene?' she said.

Tension tightened the muscles in Conrad's neck at her expression. 'Yes, we hear you fine.'

'I'm on my way to the White House right now, but this thing was too big not to let you guys know about straightaway,' said Donaghy brusquely. 'I've just finished debriefing one of our undercover agents. If what he says is true, we may be about to have a war on our hands!'

Shocked silence resonated across the communication channels.

'What do you mean, Claire?' said Connelly guardedly.

Donaghy's eyes grew stormy. 'It seems someone's been busy raising an army.'

Conrad went still at her words.

'Three days ago, our operative came across evidence of what looks like dozens of training camps across the globe,' the CIA agent continued. 'He saw pictures of four of the missing warlords and cartel leaders we'd been concerned about. One of them was the Barba Amarilla drug lord. Our agent wasn't able to glean any more intel. It took the poor guy forty-eight hours to exfiltrate through a war zone. He reckoned they were on to him.' Lines puckered her brow. 'Whoever our mole is, he or she may very well be responsible for the disappearance of our other undercover agents and sources in the last couple of years.'

Sweat dampened Conrad's palms. Connelly's face was frozen.

Lewis straightened. 'What are you worried about, Donaghy?' he said, his tone dismissive. 'The US army can take on a bunch of guerrilla fighters with their arms tied behind their backs.'

The CIA agent was silent for a beat. 'Lewis, can you see my face clearly?'

'Uh-huh,' the FBI agent confirmed with a puzzled frown.

'Do I look like I'm goddamn joking to you?' snarled Donaghy.

'Enough, the both of you!' barked Connelly.

'The details that our operative glimpsed before he took off suggest the enemy is incredibly well-equipped,' Donaghy continued in the chilly silence that followed. 'Their soldiers have the latest combat gear and weapons.' She hesitated. 'There's some pretty heavy money behind these operations. The people providing the training to the men and women recruited in these troops were professional mercenaries. If our operative is right in his assumption, God only knows how big this army could be. It's pretty clear they are preparing for a battle.'

'What makes you think this has anything to do with our current investigation?' said someone out of sight of the Sit Room camera.

Conrad recognized the Homeland Security agent's voice.

Connelly looked to her right. 'We'd have to be complete

fools to ignore this, Petersen!' snapped the Director of National Intelligence.

'I don't understand how the hell an army that size could stay hidden,' said Lewis, his doubt plainly displayed on his face. 'And where would all the people they enlisted have come from?'

Conrad had just asked himself the same questions. The answers had been frighteningly easy to come across.

'The world is a big place, Lewis,' the immortal said quietly. 'Whole cultures and species once rose and vanished from the face of the Earth without us having the faintest inkling it was happening.' He broke off for a beat. 'Think about it—there are currently millions of disgruntled individuals out there who blame their dire existences on this planet's most powerful nations, be it through those countries' direct actions in wars or inaction, which create abject poverty, famine, and disease. Angry, disillusioned people are easy targets for extremists. From the heads of state who were attacked yesterday, it's clear someone doesn't like the political and economic dominance of these nations. And the fact that Russia and China were also targeted tells us that this is not simply an East-West divide.'

A glum silence descended on the comms lines.

'I have to let the President and the Joint Chiefs know about this,' said Connelly finally. Her eyes flitted to the other individuals in the Sit Room before falling on Conrad through the video link. 'Will you tell the other man who assigned you this task about these latest events?' she added quietly.

'Sure,' said Conrad.

The connection ended. The screen went dark.

'Holy crap,' Stevens murmured shakily.

A sudden ringing broke the leaden silence in the cabin.

Anatole reached inside his suit pocket and took out a cell. His eyebrows rose when he looked at the screen. 'Speak of the devil,' he said wryly. 'It's Dvorsky.' He answered and passed the phone to Conrad.

'Hi,' Conrad said into the mouthpiece.

'This situation is turning out to be more complex than I originally anticipated,' the leader of the Bastians announced in a strained voice. 'I'm not looking forward to telling Westwood and the UN Security Council about the latest finding from our end.'

Conrad tensed. 'What is it?'

'Our people had a look at the hair sample you sent us. We didn't get any match on the Bastian databases,' said Victor.

'Why should that—?' Conrad started, perplexed.

'We uncovered something far more worrying,' Victor cut in. 'That woman you chased in Crystal City? She's a human-immortal half-breed.'

Conrad's fingers whitened on the cell. Laura took a step toward him, alarm dawning on her face. He made a reassuring gesture with his other hand. Relief replaced her anxiety.

'A half-breed?' he repeated.

'Yes,' said Victor. 'And we're not just talking any immortal lineage here. She's the descendant of a pureblood Crovir. As such, she is a rare species indeed. There are only a handful of immortals alive today who can claim to be the direct descendants of the original beings who created our races.'

Blood thundered deafeningly in Conrad's ears. He could never have foreseen something of this magnitude coming out of this investigation. 'How is that possible?' he said with a frown. 'I thought the offspring of an immortal and a human—'

'Dimitri Reznak crossed path with a sect of similar origins eleven months ago,' Victor interjected. 'We're liaising with his scientists to cross-check the genetic data from this woman in case there's a link.' There was a short lull. 'The descendants of a pureblood immortal-human offspring do not possess the number of lives we do, but they share our other abilities, namely faster healing and an extended life span.'

Conrad was aware of a barrage of anxious stares as he gazed

blindly into space and started to come to grips with the over-reaching ramifications of this latest development. 'You're right. This puts a whole other light on this situation.'

He told the Bastian leader about their findings in Germany and the recent leads coming out of Washington.

'It seems we've seriously underestimated the enemy,' Conrad concluded grimly. 'Whoever they are, they may have been planning this thing for years, if not decades.'

'And now they're getting ready for a war,' Victor concurred in a deadly voice. 'The political and economic upheaval caused by the assassination of the world's most powerful leaders would have created the perfect window of opportunity for them to strike. The affected governments would invariably have been too slow to mobilize their military in the face of a fresh attack.'

The Bastian leader paused. Conrad could picture the frown darkening his mentor's face.

'But still,' Victor continued pensively, 'however big their army is, they could not hope to win against the combined forces of the humans and immortals.'

'True,' Conrad muttered. The same thought had crossed his mind. 'That's *if* they know about the existence of the immortal societies. We must be missing something.'

'I agree,' Victor said after a short silence. 'And I suspect it's something big. I'll be in touch if I find out anything more.' The Bastian leader ended the call.

Conrad returned the cell to Anatole and apprised the others of the immortals' discovery.

Anatole pulled a face. 'Yeah, I heard about that sect. According to Reznak, they were a bunch of unholy fanatics.'

Headlights flashed through the windows of the Learjet. A transporter van braked to a stop next to the plane.

Laura stepped to a porthole. 'It's Schulze.'

The German security agent met them at the bottom of the aircraft's steps.

'It was hard going getting a deal out of my superiors and Bauer's boss, but you're in,' he announced with a grin. 'We're on our way to Leipzig now. Another team's already at the site.'

A rush of gratitude flowed through Conrad. 'Thanks, Schulze.'

They climbed in the van and set off into the night. The clock on the transporter's console was reading nine pm when they reached Leipzig. Schulze pulled up behind an unmarked police car and a mobile crime scene investigation unit parked outside an imposing, Neoclassical corner building overlooking a dark park. Conrad recognized the exterior of the edifice from Luther Obenhaus's intelligence photograph.

Schulze stepped out and went to confer with the police officer in the car. He returned a moment later. 'Obenhaus's condo is on the top floor. Criminal Police and Crime Scene are already up there.'

They headed inside the building and walked past the distraught night superintendent to an old, black and gold cage elevator on the far side of the lobby. The metal doors clinked behind them. A faint rattle shook the floor of the cabin as they ascended to the sixth floor.

A policewoman guarded a pair of oak doors at the end of a silent corridor. She checked Schulze's ID and studied Conrad and his team cursorily before letting them through.

Luther Obenhaus's apartment took up the top east corner of the complex. It was filled with an eclectic mix of old and modern furnishings and reeked of luxury. Conrad studied the original artworks gracing the wood-paneled walls of the hallway and reception rooms. He caught a glimpse of an opulent, Italian-marble kitchen and a similarly styled bathroom.

Despite his gambling problems, it was evident Obenhaus had not spared any expense when it came to his personal comfort.

A team of detectives and crime scene technicians were busy

working the place. Schulze found the investigator in charge and made the introductions in English.

'Bauer told me about you guys,' said the female detective, whose name was Peters. She had a hint of a Berlin accent. 'Thanks for saving him.' She flashed a smile at Conrad. 'From what we've determined of the place so far, you're gonna want to see the study.'

Obenhaus's home office was one of the larger rooms in the apartment. It featured floor-to-ceiling windows that overlooked the communal gardens. A grand piano dominated a corner of the carpeted floor.

Peters indicated the computer on a walnut desk. 'We've had a look at that already. There isn't much on it. Looks like our guy was using a portable hard drive.'

Conrad's heart sank at her words. He recalled the damaged equipment they had discovered at the dead man's lodge.

'Don't worry,' Peters added. 'There are still plenty of files to go through.' She gestured to the folders lining the bookcases along the walls.

A technician appeared in the doorway of the study. 'Excuse me. I think you guys should take a look at this,' he said in German.

They exchanged curious glances and followed the man across the suite and down a corridor to a bedroom. A wood panel on the wall opposite the door stood ajar. Conrad's heart leapt. There was a steel safe in the brickwork behind it.

'I've seen similar set-ups in apartments like this one,' the technician explained. 'There's always a safety deposit box in these kinds of places.'

They crowded around the opening and observed the coded security panel on the strongbox.

'We might have to wait until morning before we can get one of our specialists to have a go at this,' said Peters pensively.

'Why don't we ask Maximilian Obenhaus?' Laura suggested. 'He might know the code.'

'Good idea,' said Conrad.

He borrowed her cell and made the call. 'Hi, Mr. Obenhaus? I'm sorry to bother you. I know this is the last thing you want to hear at the moment, but I'm with the police in Luther's apartment in Leipzig. We found his safe. Would you happen to know the code?'

'Try Wagner 050845,' said Maximilian Obenhaus after a thoughtful pause. 'Wagner was born less than a mile from that apartment building. He was Luther's favorite composer.'

'And the date?' said Conrad, curious.

'It's our mother's birthday,' the Obenhaus Group president explained. 'He's used that combination in the past for some of his other security details.' Muffled sobbing echoed in the background. 'Mr. Greene, please find the people who did this to my brother,' he added in a hard voice.

Conrad hesitated. 'I will.'

He ended the call and wondered whether he would be able to keep the second promise he had made to the German that day. He returned the phone to Laura, stepped up to the safe, and punched in the key. The strongbox clicked open with an electronic beep.

Inside were a wallet of documents and a stack of foreign currency. Peters carefully lifted out the folder. Something fluttered to the floor. Conrad bent and retrieved a small white card.

'What is it?' said the female detective curiously.

Conrad turned the card over in his gloved hand. There was a single, hand-drawn symbol on the front. It wasn't one he recognized.

'Would you mind if we take a picture of this?' he asked the detective.

Peters hesitated for a beat. 'Can't see what harm it'll do,' she said with a shrug. 'Let's take a look at the rest of this stuff.'

They returned to a reception room overlooking the terrace at the rear of the property. Peters emptied the document holder onto a dining table and spread the contents across the polished surface. They studied the handful of files.

A whistle left Anatole's lips. 'Wow. The dude was in deep shit.'

Satisfaction flared through Conrad. Yet another piece of the enigma had been solved; he had been correct in his assumption that Luther Obenhaus had been in it for the money.

The paperwork inside the safe was a summary of the man's financial accounts over the last five years. According to the figures, the former director of the Obenhaus Group had been in debt to the tune of ten million dollars, thanks to several poor investment choices and heavy gambling losses. His fiscal misfortune appeared to have started well before he stopped receiving income from his company shares.

Peters straightened and sighed. 'Well, I think this is it for the time being. We'll take a look at his banking transactions when we get back to head office.'

Schulze turned to Conrad. 'I'll call you if we find anything.'

Conrad gave him a brief smile. 'Thanks, that would be—'

The sound of shattering glass came a second before a blue and white, antique porcelain vase exploded on a console table next to them.

'What the—?' Peters started, her eyes widening.

Another bullet punched through the terrace doors and smacked into Laura's thigh. She gasped and jerked backward. Conrad slammed into her and carried both of them to the floor just as the third bullet skimmed inches past his temple and struck a chair.

The others dove to the ground around him and scrambled for cover as the glazing collapsed in glittering fragments.

'Get down!' Peters shouted at the shocked crime scene tech standing frozen near the window.

More shots whined through the air and thudded into the furniture and floorboards. A mirror disintegrated on the opposite wall and showered the room with deadly shards. Feathers from perforated cushions and upholstery filled the air with white down.

Conrad unwrapped his arms from around his and Laura's heads, his pulse jackhammering in his throat.

'I'm okay,' she breathed, dark pupils dilating in a green expanse inches below him. Her heart thudded rapidly against his chest, while her breath warmed his cheek, sending a tingle down his spine.

Conrad pulled her to a sitting position. His eyes shrank into slits when he saw the blood staining her trouser leg. They shuffled back against the wall.

Anatole scuttled next to them. 'They must be on the roof!' he shouted as he reached for his gun.

Bullets continued to pound the room. Debris clouded the air. The fine art on the walls was being shredded to a pulp.

Peters grabbed the radio unit at her waist and barked an emergency alert in German as she staunched the bleeding from a cut on her head. 'Control, we have one or more shooters at the following address! Please send backup! I repeat, shots have been fired at the following address!'

Conrad slipped Laura's belt from around her waist and tied it swiftly around her bleeding leg. The bullet had travelled straight through muscle and exited the back of her thigh. Further shots struck the furnishings next to them, raising a billow of fluff and foam.

Laura's hand closed on Conrad's wrist. 'I'm fine!' she said between clenched teeth. 'Go stop those bastards!'

His fingers stilled on her leg. 'Okay. But let me take a look at that later.'

She bit her lip and nodded reluctantly. Conrad turned and grabbed a fragment of the broken mirror off the floor. There was a sudden lull in the hail of bullets. He put his arm out care-fully and angled the glass toward the terrace. His eyes opened wide at what he saw.

He dropped the mirror, rose, and sprinted toward the French doors.

CHAPTER EIGHTEEN

S CONRAD BOUNDED THROUGH THE BROKEN, GAPING FRAME and skidded to a halt on the stone terrace. He turned and looked wildly in the direction of the figure he had spotted in the mirror. The sniper was racing away along the rooftop of the building adjoining Obenhaus's apartment block at an angle, a rifle strapped to his back.

A hiss of fury escaped the immortal's lips. He scaled the metal table in the middle of the patio in one leap and jumped. His fingers closed on the edge of the flat overhang above the terrace. He swung himself up onto the roof with a grunt, climbed to his feet, and raced after the fleeing figure. He reached the adjacent complex in seconds, a cold wind whipping at his clothes and hair.

The sniper glanced over his shoulder at the sound of the immortal's footsteps. He vaulted over the narrow gap to another building and slid to a stop. He reached under his arm as he spun, yanked out a handgun, and fired.

Conrad swore and dove to the ground. Bullets winged past him and chipped the bitumen roofing. He rolled, reached behind his back, and came up with his gilded staff in hand. The sniper took off again.

The immortal followed and crossed the next apartment block after the retreating gunman. His eyes narrowed as he gauged the distance separating them. He twisted one of the rings on the staff, raised it behind his shoulder, and hurled it through the air.

The weapon whistled through the night, the twin spear blades gleaming in the moonlight as it sailed straight and true. It impaled the sniper's right calf a heartbeat later. A gurgled scream escaped the man's lips. He staggered down to one knee and looked at the spear embedded in his leg in disbelief. He reached for the shaft, pulled, and released the weapon almost immediately with a yelp of pain.

The sniper rose and lurched forward. Alarm tore through Conrad when he saw the man reach inside the utility belt at his waist. The immortal came up behind him and kicked him in his good leg just as the latter placed something inside his mouth.

The sniper started to fall to his knees. Conrad hooked a forearm around his throat and yanked sharply. The man gagged. A tiny capsule flew out from between his lips and landed on the roof. Conrad glanced at the pill with a scowl and maintained his chokehold.

The sniper twisted and bucked beneath him, hands scratching and pulling desperately at the immortal's unmoving arm. A moment later, the man's eyes rolled backward in his head.

Conrad stepped back and let the limp body fall to the ground. Running footsteps rose above the whistle of the wind. Anatole, Schulze, and Stevens appeared in the moonlit gloom and stumbled to a stop around him.

'You killed him?' panted Schulze. He stared at the motionless figure on the ground.

'I just knocked him out,' Conrad replied darkly. 'He was

about to take a poison.' He indicated the clear gel cap a few feet from the sniper's head.

Anatole glowered. He kicked the unconscious man lightly. 'Bastard!'

Schulze's eyes followed the pool of blood beneath the sniper's leg to the spear. 'Er, did you *always* have that with you?'

'Yes,' said Conrad.

'Ah,' the German agent uttered diplomatically.

Conrad bent and retrieved the weapon from the gunman's leg. It exited broken bone and torn flesh with a wet crunch that made Stevens pale.

Schulze slapped cuffs on the sniper's wrists after they divested the man of his weapons. They lifted the limp figure between the four of them and carried him across the rooftops to Luther Obenhaus's apartment building. A squad of armed police officers swarmed inside the suite just as they lowered the body to the terrace.

Peters spoke to the officer in charge of the assault team before coming out to meet them. She glared at the man lying still on the ground. 'Was he the only one?' she snapped.

'Yes,' said Conrad.

The sniper moaned and opened his eyes. Panic flared in the brown depths when he saw the ring of menacing figures surrounding him. He tried to sit up.

'You're not going anywhere, asshole,' said Peters as several officers moved in to restrain him. She watched the struggling man disappear inside the apartment.

'You're gonna want to get this analyzed quickly.' Schulze removed the carefully wrapped capsule from his pocket and placed his handkerchief in Peters's hand. 'We think it's a potent poison.' He hesitated. 'It might be the same one used by the bodyguard who killed the Russian president, so this is for your eyes only,' he added in a low voice.

Peters's eyebrows rose. She called one of the crime scene

technicians over and passed him the pill with strict instructions for its priority evaluation by their forensic toxicology department.

Conrad entered the condo and looked past the officers milling across the floor until he found the figure he was looking for. Laura was leaning against the wall on the other side of the room. Blood had soaked her trouser leg down to her knee. He headed toward her.

'Let me take a look at that.'

Laura flushed. 'You don't have to. It's only a scratch. It'll heal just fine in a few—'

'You told me you'd let me examine your wound,' Conrad cut in impatiently. 'Besides, I need you in good shape if you want to stay on this investigation team.'

It was a weak threat and they both knew it. Irritation flickered in the hazel gaze. Laura sighed and allowed him to guide her to a bullet-riddled couch. Conrad sat next to her and placed his hand on her thigh. Her muscles tautened beneath his touch. He ignored her reaction and released his healing power.

Heat flared under his hand as he concentrated on the tense flesh beneath his fingertips. It took but a moment for him to repair the damage caused by the bullet. Conrad exhaled slowly, looked up, and went still.

High color darkened Laura's cheeks. Her eyes were focused on his lips, and her chest moved rapidly with her breaths. This time there was no mistaking the naked desire in her gaze.

Conrad's mouth went dry. An unconscious sound left his throat. He moved toward her. Laura leaned in, as powerless as he to resist the magnetic force pulling them together.

'Er,' someone interjected above them.

They froze and blinked at each other.

'Not that I dislike seeing all this simmering, sexual tension. Honestly, it brings back wonderful memories of the two of you going at it like—' Anatole stopped and cleared his throat at their expressions. 'All I'm saying is this is not really the place to be exploring those feelings. You know, think of the innocent children.' He gestured vaguely at the busy crime scene, and the agents and police detectives looking curiously their way.

'He's right,' Laura murmured. Her eyes darted to Conrad's, a chagrined expression washing across her face. 'But still, this doesn't make me want to shoot him any less.'

'I might kill him first,' said Conrad.

'Hey, you guys are hurting my feelings here,' Anatole protested.

Conrad sighed. He rose to his feet and offered his hand to Laura. She allowed him to pull her up and let her fingers linger in his grasp for a moment. His skin burned where they touched.

It took all of Conrad's willpower to step away from her. If they remained in close proximity for another second, not even a stadium full of avid spectators was going to deter them from doing what they so desperately wanted to do.

He cleaned the gilded staff in one of Luther Obenhaus's bathrooms before they left the apartment. Schulze insisted on driving them back to Erfurt. They were nearly at the airport when Bauer rang them on the German agent's cell.

'I just heard from Peters,' said the policeman over the phone's speaker. 'The financial crime section found fifteen million dollars deposited last year into a Swiss account belonging to Herr Obenhaus.'

'Wow,' said Stevens, wide-eyed. 'That would more than cover his debt.'

'We've also identified the sniper as a Moroccan national by the name of Isaac El Ifrani,' Bauer continued. 'He's wanted by Interpol for the assassination of several prominent business and political figures around the world. He's refusing to talk.'

Lines creased Stevens's brow. 'Why would they send him after us?'

A mirthless smile lifted the corners of Conrad's mouth. 'They're getting anxious.'

'Which means we're getting close,' said Anatole thoughtfully.

Unease suddenly dampened the rush of excitement coursing through Conrad. How had the enemy known they were going to be in Leipzig?

'Can they trace where the bank transfer to Obenhaus's account came from?' said Laura, interrupting his troubled thoughts.

'They've already tried,' said Bauer. 'It looked like it could have come from at least a hundred separate servers located in China, Russia, and the US. There's no way of pinpointing the exact source.'

Conrad concentrated on the conversation at hand. 'How close are you to getting a result on the poison?' he asked the policeman.

'Our forensic specialists are examining it as we speak,' replied Bauer. 'They'll liaise with your guys in Quantico, as well as the Russians, to see if it's the same stuff you've both come across.'

'That's great,' said Conrad.

'No problem,' said Bauer. 'Oh, and Greene?'

'Yeah?' said the immortal.

'Thank you,' Bauer murmured. He disconnected.

The policeman's tone reminded Conrad of their conversation before they departed the Thüringer Forest earlier that evening.

'Did you do something to me?' Bauer had asked him hesitantly.

'What do you mean?' Conrad responded in a neutral voice.

'Somehow, I can't shake the feeling that I should be dead,' the policeman said with a small frown.

Conrad had watched him for a silent moment. 'You were lucky, that's all.'

Bauer had still looked unconvinced when they drove away from the ruins of Luther Obenhaus's lodge.

Schulze bade them goodbye on the airport tarmac in Erfurt and drove off. Conrad checked in with the White House as soon as he entered the Learjet. Connelly had stepped out for a few hours, and he got the Sit Room director instead. There had been no further developments on the US end; their hunt for the mole was still ongoing. He briefed the man about the Leipzig incident and told him to give Lewis and the FBI forensics labs a heads-up. He called Victor Dvorsky next.

'How did Westwood and the UN Security Council take it?' Conrad asked after they greeted each other.

'Considering the circumstances, better than I thought they would,' the leader of the Bastians replied over the cabin speakers. 'The Head of the Order of Crovir Hunters provided details about the sect Dimitri Reznak came across last year. He went to great lengths to explain how the matter had been dealt with internally by the immortals. The Security Council got pretty twitchy when they realized what would have happened had that sect achieved its goals.' A guarded pause followed. 'The humans are willing to give us the benefit of the doubt for the time being, but I don't know how much longer this state of affairs will continue if we don't stop the group behind the current debacle. The two immortal societies have plenty on their plates as it is without making more enemies.'

Conrad frowned at the noble's words. He was aware of the heavy burden they both shared. The responsibility for this mission lay as much at Victor's feet as it did his.

'We should have another lead by the morning,' Conrad said quietly. He glanced at the others. 'We're going to stay put and see where it'll take us next.' He ended the call.

Stevens shifted restlessly. 'Is that likely ever to happen? A war between humans and immortals?' he mumbled after a short silence.

Conrad shared impassive looks with Anatole and Laura. 'I doubt it,' he replied. 'The current human population exceeds the immortal one by a factor of several thousand.'

Relief flashed in the agent's eyes.

'However, we can die up to seventeen times, have superior healing abilities and combat skills, and own more than half the world's wealth,' Conrad continued.

A wave of weariness suddenly washed over the immortal. He had seen more than enough battles during his existence to last dozens of lifetimes. He didn't think he could stomach one as terrible as an all-out war between humans and immortals.

'The physical numbers won't match on the battlefield, but the immortals would likely still win,' he told the suddenly despondent agent.

A stilted hush followed. Anatole broke it a moment later.

'I've booked us rooms in a hotel in town,' he announced, slipping his cell back inside his suit.

Conrad raised an eyebrow. 'When did you do that?'

'Just now, via the magic of phone texting,' replied Anatole. 'Seeing how you've been stuck in the jungle for so long, you may not have heard of it. I'll teach you.'

A car drove onto the tarmac and pulled up outside the Learjet before Conrad could tell the red-haired immortal exactly what he could do with that proposal.

Anatole grinned at his expression. 'And that must be our ride.'

Conrad bit back his words. He strolled to the cockpit and told the pilot their plans for the evening. They exited the plane with their bags in hand.

The private car dropped them off at a sleek, glass and concrete building in the center of Erfurt. They checked in at the reception and took the lift to the eighth floor.

Conrad stopped in front of his suite and watched the others stroll down the corridor. 'Goodnight,' he called out.

Laura nodded curtly and disappeared across the threshold of her room. Stevens was in the suite next to her. Conrad became aware of a hot stare from the opposite side of the corridor.

Anatole glowered at him. 'What is *wrong* with you?' he hissed. 'Barely two hours ago, you looked like you were about to tear each other's clothes off, and now—'

'Oh shut up!' snapped Conrad. He closed the suite door forcefully behind him and stalked into the bathroom.

He was drying his head with a towel when a knock sounded at the main door. Conrad crossed the floor and yanked it open, lips parted to deliver a well-deserved tirade. His voice died in his throat.

Laura stood facing him in the passage outside. Moisture glistened in her hair under the muted glow of the spotlights in the ceiling. A sweet scent wafted from the coffee-colored curls. She was wearing a fresh change of clothes and a steadfast expression.

Heat flashed in her eyes as she took in his appearance. Her gaze moved from his bare chest to the towel around his waist. She stepped inside the room and slammed the door shut.

'We need to talk,' said Laura. 'But first, let's get this out of the way.'

She closed the distance between them, looped her arms around his neck, and planted her lips firmly on his.

Conrad remained rooted to the floor, shock immobilizing his limbs. A wave of desire rose through him, drowning out all reason. He unfroze, hands rising to clutch the sides of her head. He deepened the kiss, his tongue sweeping inside her mouth as he let out a low groan.

They came together frantically, their movements savage and uncontrolled. He tore at her clothes, a hiss of frustration leaving his lips when his fingers fumbled on the buttons of her trousers. She peeled off his towel and pulled her shirt over her head, her breaths coming hard and fast. She was naked in five seconds, and they were flat on the bed in the next two. His mouth closed greedily on hers, the force of the kiss almost painful. Her fingers clenched in his hair and she wrapped her legs around his hips.

The next hours were a blur of fevered, mindless hunger. They each knew what made the other moan and gasp. His lips on the curve of her left breast, her teeth on his ear, his fingers dancing up the inside of her thighs, her hands stroking his spine, the spot on her waist that made her shudder, the one on his abdomen that caused all his muscles to clench. They held each other desperately, their touches almost bruising; each sigh, each pant, each cry was a sweet sound that inflamed Conrad's senses further.

They made love until the small hours of the morning, finally collapsing in a tangle of sweaty limbs and damp sheets. Laura lay on top of Conrad and fell asleep with her head cradled against his shoulder.

He woke a while later to the wetness of her tears on his skin.

'If you had those powers then, would you have—?' she started tremulously.

Conrad brought his lips to her forehead and swallowed convulsively. 'In a heartbeat,' he whispered.

She cried then for the boy who had been more a son than a stepbrother to her. For Conrad knew Laura had raised William Hartwell as she would have their own child. She spoke falteringly of the anger and self-hatred she had felt for not having seen what her brother had been going through at the time, and for having failed him. Because the one she truly blamed for his death was none other than herself.

Conrad wrapped his arms in a vice-like grip around her

slender form as he listened to her broken sobs. His heart shattered all over again and a choked sound escaped him when she asked for his absolution for the centuries they had lost because of her willful foolishness.

He waited until her cries quieted before lifting her chin and staring into hazel depths he would happily drown in. 'There is nothing to forgive,' he breathed.

A fragile smile dawned on her face through the tears still clouding her gaze. Air froze in Conrad's lungs. Her radiance stole his breath away. He raised his head and gently captured her mouth with his lips.

It took only seconds for the kiss to turn feverish. He rolled and pinned her to the mattress, desire clawing at his insides once more. Her eyes darkened to the color of a storm-tossed sea. She clung to him, her hands digging possessively into the small of his back. His fingers traced her thigh where her wound had been mere hours ago. Rationality fled as they lost themselves in the other once more, their heated gasps filling the room while their bodies flowed in perfect synchrony.

It was Anatole's voice that roused them a couple of hours later. 'Hey, lovebirds, we gotta go!'

Laura blinked and gazed muzzily at Conrad.

There was banging on the door. 'You guys hear me in there?' shouted Anatole.

Conrad sighed. 'You have my permission to shoot him first.'

She grinned, kissed his chin, and wrinkled her nose at his stubble. 'We better go or Harry's gonna think I'm a complete hussy.' She leapt out of bed, grabbed her clothes from the floor, and strolled naked into the bathroom.

Conrad watched her seductive form disappear before he swung his legs to the carpet. He wrapped the discarded towel around his waist, crossed the room, and yanked open the door. 'What?' he barked.

Anatole paused with his fist raised mid-strike. A dirty smile dawned on his face.

Conrad glanced down the corridor. 'Where's Stevens?'

'He's checking us out. Lewis called him when he couldn't get through to you or Laura. They've got something on the poison.'

Conrad grunted. 'We'll be downstairs shortly.'

'*Rigghhht*,' said Anatole. 'There's no time for shower sex or any other kind of hanky-panky.'

Conrad glared at the red-haired immortal and slammed the door shut in his face. He looked down and slowly fingered the kiss marks on his chest. His lips curved in a grin. It took all his will power to shake off the warm glow overfilling the once frozen depths of his heart. His smile faded at the thought of the monumental task that still lay ahead.

They were at the airport half an hour later and linked up to the Sit Room within a minute of entering the Learjet. Connelly and Lewis stood framed inside the video screen.

'Hey,' greeted Connelly. 'The Germans sent us their analysis of the drug you got your hands on.' Her eyes shone as she glanced at Lewis. 'Like the FBI suspected, the only way to identify it was to obtain the original sample. The primary compound is a poison called Batrachotoxin.'

Conrad's fingers tightened on the backrest of a chair, a tremor of excitement shooting through him. 'Isn't that what the Columbian Indians of the Embera Choco region use to coat their blow darts?'

'Yes!' said Lewis. 'Although it's originally found in a specific family of beetles and some indigenous birds who ingest the insects, Batrachotoxin's most famous source is the Golden Poison Frog.' The FBI agent made a face. 'Our guy in Crystal City didn't stand a chance. Around one tenth of a milligram of the stuff is enough to kill an average-sized man. His muscles and heart would have seized up seconds after it hit his bloodstream. Now *this* is where things get intriguing. The mode of delivery was through a sophisticated film disc that dissolves at normal body temperature. More interestingly, the poison was combined with a second compound to help speed its absorption through the skin.'

Laura raised an eyebrow. 'I doubt that stuff is available over the counter.'

Lewis smiled mirthlessly. 'Correct again,' said the FBI agent. 'Batrachotoxin, or BTX, is sold by a number of companies around the world. The buyers are pharmaceutical corporations and medical research labs working on specific application areas such as anesthetic, antiarrhythmic, and anticonvulsant therapies. We've contacted the sellers who are known to trade in the poison to see whether they've had any new buyers on their books, or if any of their current clients have been requesting more BTX than usual.'

Conrad leaned forward tensely. 'And?'

'We got four hits,' said Lewis. 'The first one is a lab in Finland that's recently increased its demand for BTX. The next two are research institutes in California and Chicago with a similar rise in orders. The fourth one is a drug company in France that only started purchasing the toxin some eighteen months ago.'

The four locations flashed up on a world satellite map on the screen.

A thrill of anticipation ran through Conrad as he studied the monitor. 'Good work, Lewis. Can you send us the details of the European sites?'

Lewis grinned. 'Will do. We'll have our teams in LA and Chicago check out those two research institutes.'

Conrad's gaze switched to the Director of National Intelligence. 'Can I talk to you in private?'

Connelly arched an eyebrow in faint surprise. 'I'll call you on the Learjet's private line.'

The plane's phone rang seconds later. Conrad answered it.

'What is it?' said Connelly.

'Apart from the people who were in the Sit Room, who else knew we were going to Leipzig?' Conrad asked.

There was a brief silence at the other end of the line. 'No one.'

'The enemy knew we were going to be at Luther Obenhaus's apartment,' said Conrad. 'That's why they sent an assassin after us. Whoever the mole is, they heard our conversation last night.'

Connelly's voice was stiff when she spoke again. 'I'll look into it.'

Conrad ended the call and turned to Laura. 'Why don't you and Stevens take the lab in Finland? Anatole and I will check out the one in France.'

Laura asked Stevens for his satellite phone. She handed the cell to Conrad, her fingers lingering on his. 'That way, we can stay in touch,' she murmured.

Conrad smiled and squeezed her hand lightly.

The Learjet's pilot arranged for a private charter Sikorsky helicopter to take the two immortals to Paris. Minutes later, Conrad and Anatole stood on the tarmac and watched the plane lift off for Helsinki.

'I'm happy for you,' said Anatole after a while.

Conrad turned and observed his friend's serene expression. 'Thanks. That means a lot.'

~

CHAPTER NINETEEN

NADICA GLANCED AT HER WATCH, TEETH GNAWING AT HER lip. They had been inside the building for just under twenty minutes. A restless energy tautened her limbs as she observed her guards load the first of the consignment of metal crates onto the back of the trucks.

A curse erupted from the bed of one of the vehicles. It was followed by a loud clang. Nadica ran to the rear of the truck and saw the overturned container. She climbed aboard, strode to the dismayed figure standing next to it, and backhanded him across the face.

'You fool! The contents of that chest are worth more than all your miserable lives put together!' she hissed.

Red marks flared on the guard's pale cheek. He lowered his head and stared numbly at his feet. 'I'm sorry, mistress,' he mumbled. 'It slipped from my grasp. I'll be more careful.'

A savage thrill surged through Nadica as she watched the man tremble. 'Next time, I'll cut off your hands.'

She turned and leapt down from the bed of the truck. The service elevator opposite the loading bay opened. Six men walked out with another three steel containers. She headed for the lift.

CONRAD AND ANATOLE LANDED AT THE INTERNATIONAL airport in Orly just before noon. With Connelly having alerted the French Intelligence agencies, the Ministry of Interior, and the Judicial Police to the potential US operation inside their territory, they passed through security without a hitch.

A pair of navy blue Merc sedans stood waiting at the curb outside the main terminal building. Victor Dvorsky had also dispatched a team of local Bastian Hunters to assist them.

Anatole made a private phone call as they strolled toward the vehicles. Conrad caught him smiling and eyed the immortal curiously while the driver of the first car got out. Anatole took the keys and a pair of fake IDs off the Hunter. The man nodded curtly, twisted on his heels, and headed for the second vehicle. Conrad would only ask the Bastians for help if he desperately needed the backup.

Anatole slipped behind the steering wheel of the sedan and glanced at the badges. 'Says here we're French Central Intelligence.' He beheld the dashboard and console with a grin. 'Oh good. It's a stick.'

Conrad hesitated as he closed the passenger door. 'Maybe I should drive,' he muttered.

Anatole gaped. 'Do you even know how? You were in that jungle an awfully long time!'

Conrad glared at him and clipped the seatbelt in forcefully. 'I swear you say this stuff to piss me off.'

Anatole's cell phone chimed an alert. He checked the screen, smirked, and slipped the phone back in his jacket.

'Who was that?' said Conrad, curious.

'Horatio,' came the nonchalant reply.

Conrad looked at the clock on the control panel. It was six fifty in the morning in Rio de Janeiro. He cocked an eyebrow at his second in command. 'What did he want?'

Anatole shrugged. 'He's mad that he lost a bet.'

Suspicion flared inside Conrad. He scrutinized the red-haired immortal with probing eyes. 'What bet?'

Anatole maneuvered the car onto an expressway. 'It's not important. Let's just say he owes me a crate of that expensive cachaca he likes so much.'

The drug company's headquarters were located in the business district of La Défense, at the western end of Paris's six-mile-long Voie Triomphale. Anatole guided the sedan onto the busy Boulevard Périphérique and through a series of underground tunnels, before exiting the motorway close to Charles de Gaulle Avenue. Though it was well past morning peak traffic time, the boulevard was a gridlock of slow moving vehicles.

The immortals snaked through the crowded lanes and blissfully ignored the horns and angry shouts peppering the air around them.

Glittering glass and steel sky-rises loomed on the horizon as they approached the River Seine. The facade of La Grande Arche glowed in the distance, the pale marble reflecting the midday sun. Conrad was seeing it for the first time.

A phone rang as they started across the Pont de Neuilly. Conrad removed Stevens's cell from his jacket and answered the call.

'Hi,' said Laura.

The sound of her voice sent a small shiver down his spine. Conrad suppressed the wave of yearning that rose through his body and concentrated on the green waters beyond the window. 'What's up?'

'The research facility in Helsinki is clean,' said Laura.

Conrad could practically see the frown puckering her brow.

'Stevens and I have been through the place with a fine-tooth

comb,' she continued. 'They're doing advanced work in anes-
thetics, hence their need for bucket loads of BTX in the last
couple of years. Their story makes sense. Our intelligence
analysts can't find any red flags in their history or financial
activities.'

Anatole left the bridge and headed up an exit, the second
Merc close on their tail.

'Okay,' said Conrad. 'We're almost at the French company's
location. We'll keep you updated.'

'Be careful,' warned Laura. 'Lewis just called. They've
cleared the labs in Chicago and LA.' She paused. 'We'll be
taking off within the hour. I'll see you at the airport.'

Anatole negotiated a series of access roads and swerved ille-
gally into a service lane at the back of a group of buildings. He
drove down a slope and parked in the shadows of a trio of
skyscrapers.

Conrad stepped out and strolled to the Bastian Hunters'
vehicle as it rolled to a stop behind them. 'Stay put,' he told the
driver. 'We'll yell if we need you.'

The man handed over a couple of flesh-colored, pea-sized
earpieces and tiny, wireless Bluetooth transmitters. 'These are
hooked up on the same frequency we're using,' he said.

Conrad put on the devices and gave the second pair to
Anatole. They followed a path to a flight of concrete steps and
climbed up to a courtyard containing a modern water feature. A
white high-rise soared on the other side of the piazza beyond it.

They entered the building through a side entrance and went
up an escalator. Moments later, they reached a gigantic, airy,
glass-covered courtyard connecting a complex of interlinked
towers. They headed into the lobby of the tallest building and
took a lift to the twentieth floor.

The elevator opened silently onto a carpeted corridor. A
pair of frosted doors stood at the end of the empty passage.
They stopped in front of the glass entrance and contemplated

the security panel on the wall. Conrad glanced at the discreet cameras in the corners of the ceiling before studying the words etched on the doors.

"'Societé Strabo,'" he spelled out slowly.

Anatole pressed the buzzer on the panel. A small burst of static preceded a pleasant female voice. 'Hello, how can I help you?' the woman said in French.

'We're with the Security Service,' Anatole declared in a somber voice, his accent flawless. 'We have reason to believe that a crime has been committed on the premises that poses a threat to national security. Let us in.'

A gasp travelled over the intercom. 'Pl—please wait a moment!' the woman stammered. An electronic buzz sounded seconds later.

Conrad pushed through the doors and strode along a hall that opened onto a circular foyer. Steel-reinforced security doors with biometric locks radiated off the round space. He stopped in front of the pale blonde in the white dress suit seated behind the curved reception desk. The woman was placing a phone back on its cradle.

'Our security chief will be with you in a moment,' she said in a flustered tone, her cheeks flushed a bright pink. 'Please take a seat.' She indicated the brightly colored, modular chairs behind them.

'I'm afraid we don't have time for that,' said Conrad bluntly. 'We need to talk with whoever is in charge of—'

'Good afternoon, gentlemen,' someone cut in smoothly from the left.

Conrad turned and watched a tall, heavily built man in a crisp, black suit cross the floor toward them. 'And you are?' asked the immortal.

The man bristled at his tone. 'I'm the head of security at Strabo Corp.,' he snapped. 'May I see your credentials?' He extended a hand rudely.

They showed the man their IDs. He scrutinized the badges for some time. Conrad knew the delay was deliberate. Anatole's eyes glinted with a cold light as he studied the Strabo Corp. security chief.

'How may I be of assistance?' the man finally grunted.

'We have reason to believe that a poison used to assassinate an American prisoner and a Soviet agent may have been manufactured by this company,' said Conrad. 'We would like to talk to your director.'

The man sneered. 'I'm afraid that's impossible. Mr. Sahin is with Professor Kadir. They are otherwise engaged at the moment.'

'Oh.' Conrad smiled. His patience was wearing thin. 'Doing what, exactly?'

The security chief squared his shoulders. 'Not that it's any of your business,' he said coldly, 'but they're attending to one of our most important clients.'

Unease shot through Conrad at the look that flashed in the man's eyes. 'Anatole?' he said quietly.

'Yeah?' Though anger radiated off the red-haired immortal in waves, he grinned apologetically at the blonde behind the desk.

'Open that door.' Conrad indicated the opening through which the security head had entered the foyer.

The man glared at him. 'What the—?'

'Sorry, lady.' Anatole strode around the receptionist's station and gently moved her wheeled chair back from the desk. He took her place in front of a sleek computer, his fingers dancing nimbly over the keyboard. The woman's mouth opened and closed soundlessly behind him.

The security head reached inside his suit jacket and took a step toward the reception. He stopped dead in his tracks when the barrel of a gun kissed the skin at his temple, his own weapon frozen in his grip.

'Don't make this any harder than it needs to be,' Conrad murmured at the other end of the HK P8 pistol.

Nadica studied the contents of the metal case. 'Is that all of them?'

'Yes,' said Professor Ridvan Kadir. The head of R&D for Strabo Corp. pushed his glasses up the bridge of his nose. His eyes gleamed with a zealous light as he observed the black boxes stacked neatly inside the padded briefcase. 'They've been tuned to the specific C-band microwave frequency of the satellites and are ready to be deployed. I would advise a trial run. One of the smaller targets, maybe.' His lips compressed in a thin line. 'The people you have at your disposal should be more than capable of taking care of such a task.'

The director of the company bowed. 'Please let us know if you require more products,' Volkan Sahin said ingratiatingly. 'Your will is our command, mistress.'

Nadica smiled crisply at the Strabo Corp. scientist and CEO. She knew that the two men both feared and lusted after her. Her face and physique were nearly as stunning as those of Ariana Rajkovic, a combination that had proven lethal on more occasions than she could count during the nine decades of her existence to date. Still, none of the men Nadica had attracted in that time could ever hope to match her brother's physical and intellectual greatness; she was more committed to her sibling than she could ever be to a lover. She engaged the security lock on the case, dipped her head imperiously at the men, and turned on her heels.

The company's secret research facility occupied three levels of the tower block. The walls and floors had been reinforced with extra steel and concrete to mask the presence of the experimental lab in the middle of what was effectively a business complex.

Her eyes skimmed dismissively over rooms of expensive equipment and scores of white-coated staff as she headed for the stairs that would take her back to the goods lift. As far as she was concerned, Strabo Corp. existed for a single purpose: to make the components of the devices that would help Zoran Rajkovic become the ruler of a new empire.

She went down two flights of steps and entered a small foyer holding the elevator. A security door opened at the end of the passage to her right just as she pressed the call button.

CONRAD FROZE WHEN HE SAW THE WOMAN STANDING WITH A metal briefcase in front of a lift some twenty feet away. Shock flared in her slate-colored gaze. It was replaced by a flash of recognition and anger. Her free hand moved to the small of her back.

'Hey, isn't that—?' Anatole started to say behind him.

Conrad bolted down the corridor a split second before she raised her gun. She squeezed the trigger repeatedly. Bullets whispered past his head. A grunt sounded behind him. Anatole swore. A soft 'ping' chimed. The lift doors opened. The woman darted inside the cabin.

Conrad staggered to a stop in front of the closing elevator. 'Help me!' he shouted. He dug his fingers in the gap between the panels and pulled.

Anatole joined him, blood blossoming on his left temple where a bullet had grazed his head. Harsh grunts left their lips as they forced the outer doors apart. Conrad looked down the shaft, aimed his gun at the power unit on the roof of the rapidly disappearing car, and fired rapidly. The bullets struck metal with loud cracks.

Something exploded inside the electric motor; a high-pitched whine followed as the unit controlling the lift's inner doors failed. The elevator slowed and stopped, its automatic safety measures engaging.

'Take the stairs!' Conrad barked. 'And warn the Bastians!' He jammed his pistol in his waistband, pulled out the gilded staff, and twisted the first ring.

Anatole gaped at him, his eyes shifting from the weapon to the yawning elevator opening. 'Hey! Where the hell do you think you're—?'

Conrad leaned inside the shaft and weaved the double-ended spear through the hoist ropes. He jammed the ends into the guide rails on the walls, braced one foot on a cable, and stepped into empty space.

The weapon shuddered in his hands as he slid some thirty feet down, the spear blades raising hot sparks from friction against the steel supports.

His boots struck the roof of the car hard, the shock of the landing reverberating up his legs. He yanked the staff from the cables, broke the locking mechanism on the ceiling exit hatch with a blow from one of the spear blades, and wrenched the trapdoor open. Brightly lit paneling appeared beneath him. He kicked through the frosted surface. The panel fell toward the floor of the lift.

Conrad kneeled and poked his head through the opening. He pulled back sharply. A bullet winged past his left cheek and struck the masonry wall of the elevator shaft above his head. A tortuous whine of metal reached his ears from below.

'Oh no you don't!' he hissed.

He closed the staff, swapped it for the HK P8, and dropped inside the cabin.

The elevator had stopped partway between two levels. The woman had already forced the inner doors apart and was prizing the outer panels open onto an uneven landing. She spun around when the car juddered under the impact of his feet. Her eyes shrank into slits.

She cast the briefcase through the gap between the cabin transom and the adjacent floor, twisted on one leg, and aimed a high-kick at his head. Conrad blocked the blow with his forearm and staggered back a step.

The woman turned and jumped toward the opening. The immortal lunged forward. His fingers closed around her right calf. She gripped the edge of the landing, glared at him over her shoulder, and kicked out. Her boot connected sharply with his head.

Conrad stumbled, bright spots bursting across his vision. He shook his head dazedly and looked up in time to see her disappear through the breach. He swallowed a curse and put the gun away before scaling the exposed concrete wall.

Alarmed cries resonated close by as he rolled past the opening. He leapt to his feet and looked around. The woman was racing down a passage on the left, the briefcase and gun in her hands. Heads appeared in the doorways lining the corridor. Conrad clenched his teeth and bolted after her. He glimpsed rows of shocked faces as he sprinted past the startled office workers.

The hallway ended in a panoramic glass wall overlooking a vista of glimmering towers. The Arc de Triomphe rose along Charles de Gaulle Avenue in the far distance. The woman reached a fire door adjacent to the large window. Her fingers stilled on the handle and her head whipped around when she sensed his looming presence.

Conrad slammed into her with a harsh cry. His momentum carried them inexorably forward. They smashed sideways into the glass wall, hoarse grunts escaping their lips. The glazing shattered under the force of their combined impact.

Conrad froze. The woman's eyes rounded. Wind whistled in his ears as they tipped through the expanding breach in the facade of the building. They fell outside in a rain of sparkling shards. Sunlight struck Conrad's face. A kaleidoscope of white clouds, blue sky, and glittering walls flashed across his vision during the moment of weightlessness that followed.

He hit the roof of the atrium on his right side. Air fled his body in a guttural wheeze. Numbness enveloped him as his senses shut down from the pain of the impact.

He lay winded for long seconds, his throat and chest locked in a spasm of shock. He opened his mouth and heard a labored rasp whistle past his lips. Blood thundered in his ears, drowning all other sounds. A choked cough finally tore up his windpipe.

Conrad shuddered and gasped as oxygen flooded his lungs. The roar in his head faded. The panicked shouts rising from below finally registered.

He rolled onto his stomach and started to push himself up on his elbows. His right arm throbbed. He winced and looked down. His forearm was broken. He pressed his lips together and sent a burst of healing energy to the injured limb as he staggered to his feet. By the time he stood up, the angled bone had snapped back into place and repaired itself, along with the damaged flesh around it.

He looked for the woman.

CHAPTER TWENTY

NADICA SPAT OUT CRIMSON DROPS AND CRAWLED TO HER knees. Pain stabbed through her left flank from a pair of broken ribs. The ringing in her head subsided to a dull thrum. She inhaled shallowly and looked up.

They had plummeted two floors onto the roof of the glass-covered courtyard that connected the complex of towers. Distant figures milled about more than a hundred feet below, their fingers pointed agitatedly in her direction. The metal briefcase and the gun had escaped her grip during the fall and lay some fifteen feet away.

Movement caught Nadica's eyes. She swung her head, her instincts on high alert. Conrad Greene was rising a short distance from where she stooped on all fours, his broken arm hanging limply at his side.

Nadica stiffened at what she witnessed next. Greene's limb straightened itself with a low crack. The red swelling deforming his skin vanished before her eyes. He lurched upright and glared at her.

'Give yourself up!' he shouted. 'There's nowhere for you to go!'

Nadica stared into the gray-blue irises and felt a shiver run down her spine. A cold conviction flooded her consciousness.

Conrad Greene was no ordinary man.

An unexpected thrill followed that thought; here was someone who could be her brother's equal. She wiped blood from her mouth, rose in a low crouch, and reached for the short kilij saber tucked in a scabbard under her jacket. Her amulet fell out of the neckline of her shirt.

Greene's stare focused briefly on the pendant before shifting to the Turkish sword in her grip. He removed a gilded staff from his back and twisted a ring in the middle of the shaft. Twin blades sprung out from the ends of the weapon.

Nadica observed the spear and its holder appraisingly, a quiver of lust shooting through her. Her lips parted in a savage smile. She darted toward Greene, slipped to the side, and thrust the curved blade toward his gut. He deflected the strike.

She whirled around him and came in for another stab. He spun the staff expertly between his fingers, the weapon hitting her arm and wrist in rapid succession. The edge of the spear sliced across her skin.

Nadica sprang back and stared incredulously at the crimson beads blooming on the shallow gash on the back of her hand. No one had ever wounded her in battle. She stroked a thumb across the cut and licked the end of her bloody finger; her gaze hooded as her temper flared.

'You're mine!' she hissed.

Sunlight gleamed on the sharpened edge of the kilij as she attacked, the crescent blade flowing seamlessly through the air in a rain of deadly stabs and thrusts. Greene parried her blows just as skillfully with his spear staff, his jaw set in a forbidding line.

Sparks erupted where their weapons collided. Seconds later, the kilij slipped past his guard and carved a deep line along his cheek. Nadica gasped.

The wound healed immediately, the damaged skin and muscle knitting seamlessly together in front of her eyes, not a single drop of blood spilled.

A sliver of fear skittered through her veins, dampening her rage. She straightened and took a step back. 'Who are you?' she whispered.

A dark smile dawned on Greene's lips. His eyes glittered with the light of an arctic storm. 'I'm the son of a bitch who's going to stop you,' he said coldly.

Automatic gunfire suddenly erupted behind them. Bullets peppered the roof of the atrium with sharp pops. A shot thudded into Greene's leg. Terrified cries replaced the shocked silence from the crowd in the courtyard below.

Nadica looked up and saw the Strabo Corp. security head standing at the broken glass wall two floors above them. She turned and ran, her heart thundering inside her breast. Greene started after her. He skidded to a stop a split second later as more bullets riddled the transparent floor around him.

Nadica swooped down, grabbed the metal briefcase and her pistol, and raced for the tower wall. She glanced over her shoulder. Greene had exchanged the staff weapon for a gun and was running in a zigzag to avoid the hailstorm of shots from above. She smiled grimly and accelerated, the pain in her chest drowned by the murderous fury pouring inside her.

A crowd of horrified faces loomed behind the window of the office in front of her. Nadica raised her weapon and fired rapidly, hoping her bullets would maim, blind, kill. The only thing that could satisfy her wrath in that moment was a bloodbath of death.

The figures scattered as her shots smashed into the glass. The glazing collapsed in shimmering fragments. She dove through the opening, rolled when she hit the floor of the room beyond, and rose to her feet.

~

CONRAD WEAVED A RANDOM PATH ACROSS THE ROOF OF THE atrium, his heart in his throat. He had already ejected the bullet from the gunshot wound on his thigh and repaired the injury. A further burst from the automatic rifle whistled past his ears. He lifted the HK P8 in the direction of the Strabo Corp. security chief, hesitated, and cursed. He jammed the pistol viciously in his waistband; he could not shoot at the tower without the risk of one of his bullets striking an innocent bystander.

The gunfire ended abruptly. Conrad looked up and saw Anatole struggling with the security head. He clenched his teeth and changed direction, boots pounding the glass roof as he sprinted toward the broken window where the woman had disappeared.

He launched himself through the gaping hole, landed hard on a bed of shards, and slid some twenty feet across a polished floor. Blood blossomed from dozens of cuts on his body as he spun to a stop. He leapt to his feet and looked around wildly.

'Where did she go?' Conrad bellowed at the people cowering on the ground.

A man pointed shakily to a door on the other side of a row of cubicles. Conrad turned and ran toward it. A wide corridor lay beyond. He spotted drops of blood on the marble floor and followed the scarlet trail to a foyer with a service lift. His eyes darted to the operating panel. It showed the elevator opening on an underground car park.

Conrad swore and slammed his fist against the steel door. He scanned the lobby and saw a fire exit in the corner. He barged through it and started down the stairs beyond, the tower's rear facade a solid wall of glass to his left.

'They're in the garage under the main building!' he barked into his Bluetooth transmitter as he glanced out to the back of the complex.

'Gotcha!' responded the Bastian Hunter through the earpiece.

Conrad gripped the steel handrails and bounded swiftly from landing to landing, his chest heaving with his rapid breaths. Motion outside drew his gaze. A line of trucks with dark canvas roofs emerged from beneath the high-rise several floors down and headed rapidly for the road behind the building.

'No,' he breathed.

A screech of tires brought his eyes up. The Bastian Hunters' sedan came into view some two hundred feet up the thoroughfare. The vehicle shot through the contraflow, juddered onto the curb, and slewed sideways across the garage exit.

Conrad's heart stuttered against his ribs. The lead truck had accelerated. It plowed mercilessly into the Merc, the force of the collision loud enough to penetrate through the glazing of the tower wall. The car spun across the lanes.

Fury filled the immortal. He raced down the stairs, his blood a thunderous roar in his ears.

By the time he located an external door and reached the access road to the underground parking, the trucks had disappeared. Traffic had piled to a stop behind the heavily mangled wreckage of the sedan. Both sides of the vehicle had been smashed in repeatedly. Steam curled up from under the hood. The figures inside were ominously still.

Conrad bolted toward the car. Sirens sounded dimly in the distance. He skidded to a stop by the driver's door and looked through the cracked window. Bile flooded the back of his throat.

He grabbed the handle and pulled. A whiff of diesel reached his nostrils. Metal shrieked in the distorted frame under his grip; the panel was jammed. He ignored the shouts of alarm from the growing crowd on the sidewalks, braced one foot against the center pillar, and tugged with all his might.

Veins and muscles bulged in his neck, and a harsh cry left his lips as the door finally gave way with a tortuous creak. Conrad reached inside the sedan and heaved the heavily bleeding driver and front passenger to the safety of the opposite sidewalk. He returned to the vehicle, air leaving his lips in tortured gasps. He ducked inside the car in time to see one of the Hunters in the back stir.

'Open the door!' he shouted. The immortal blinked at him.

Conrad raced around to the other side and saw the Hunter push weakly against the damaged rear door. Sparks flashed under the vehicle's carriage. Icy fear danced down Conrad's spine as he tugged on the door handle in vain. The stench of diesel grew stronger. A dark trail of fuel flamed up.

His eyes flared. 'Shit!'

About the only two things immortals could not survive were decapitation and being pulverized into tiny pieces by an explosion.

The crowd scattered amid panicked screams as the blaze took hold of the rear of the sedan. Conrad finally managed to wrench the back door open and helped the dazed Hunter grab the last two men under their shoulders. The roar of the flames drowned the sound of their wheezing breaths as they hauled the inert figures out of the sedan and staggered backward across the asphalt.

They got twenty feet away from the vehicle before the fuel tank exploded.

Heat scorched Conrad's face and chest. He caught the smell of singed hair.

The pressure wave from the blast wrapped around their bodies and hurled them a dozen feet through the air. They landed hard on the road and rolled over several times before finally rocking to a stop.

Further detonations erupted from the direction of the burning sedan. Conrad blinked at the smoke trails blurring the patch of blue sky above him, the explosions echoing dully in his ears. He lifted his head and stared at the blazing remains of the car.

On the other side of the flames, the two Bastians who had been in the front of the vehicle were rising to their feet.

Conrad pushed himself up slowly, his chest heaving with painful pants. He looked down at his trembling, bloodied hands, stunned that he had somehow managed to rescue the five men.

'You okay?' gasped someone beside him. It was the Hunter he had pulled out from the rear of the car.

'Yeah,' muttered Conrad. He climbed unsteadily to his knees. 'You?'

The Hunter groaned. 'I've been better.'

The two men they had pulled out of the sedan started to come around. The Bastian driver and passenger stumbled across the road to join them. Conrad ignored the simmering anger still plaguing him and quickly assessed the Hunters' injuries. He healed one man's lacerated liver and spleen, another's shattered pelvis and torn gut, and a third man's contused lung. The rest he deemed their immortal bodies able to repair.

He ignored the flashing lights and sirens of the police vehicles and ambulances hurtling down the road, and headed back inside the complex of towers. Streams of people surged past him when he reached the glass atrium; the buildings were being cleared. Conrad marched against the living tide and negotiated a path to the bank of lifts in the main tower. His bloodied clothes earned him a few fearful glances. He turned a blind eye and took the elevator to the twentieth floor.

The frosted entrance to Strabo Corp. lay wide open as he jogged toward it a moment later, his gun held low in his hands. The security panel on the wall had acquired several spiderweb fractures from a spray of bullets.

Conrad slowed when he reached the foyer of the drug

company. He glanced at the blonde cowering on the ground behind the bullet-riddled reception desk, loaded a fresh magazine in his pistol, and barged through the open door on the left. He stopped at the scene that met his eyes.

Anatole was leaning casually against the wall backing a metal walkway some ten feet ahead, a pair of AK74 assault rifles sitting comfortably in his grip and a makeshift tourniquet wrapped around a wound on his thigh. Blood oozed from dozens of grazes and cuts on his face and hands. The skin over his knuckles was raw.

Although he looked relaxed, the dangerous glint in his eyes told Conrad that his friend had had one of his infamous "moments."

A roomful of people sprawled quietly on their bellies on the floor of a lab some fifteen feet below, their interlinked fingers resting submissively on the back of their heads. Conrad gaped. By the looks of things, Anatole had detained the entire company. A familiar figure caught Conrad's eye.

The Strabo Corp. security chief was lying on the ground at the bottom of a short flight of stairs to the right, amid a group of similarly unconscious and battered uniformed guards. Drying blood caked the man's face from a broken nose and torn lips, while the bruised swelling on his left cheek suggested a fractured jaw. A dark pool congealed beneath his leg, evidence of bullet wounds.

A thin, dusky man with white hair and glasses sat behind the security men, alongside another dark-skinned individual in a suit. Both of them gripped bleeding arms where they had been injured.

Anatole looked around at the sound of Conrad's footsteps. He smiled, uncrossed his legs, and straightened from the wall. 'Ah, the prodigal son returns! Did you catch her?'

Conrad shook his head, bitterness rising in his throat once

more. Anatole's expression sobered. Conrad indicated the silent figures beneath them. 'What happened?'

Anatole glanced over the railing. 'Oh, that? I made a citizen's arrest.'

Conrad raised an eyebrow. 'And them?' He cocked a thumb at the gunshot victims at the bottom of the steps.

Anatole shrugged, unrepentant. 'What can I say? They resisted.'

'That—that man is a *lunatic*!' spat the old guy with the glasses and white hair. 'How dare you savages—!' A short burst of gunfire interrupted his tirade. He blanched and looked at the fresh line of bullet marks dotting the floor next to his leg.

'Don't tempt me, grandpa,' Anatole growled. He raised the barrel of an AK74 back toward the ceiling.

Conrad swallowed a sigh and studied the rifles in the red-haired immortal's hands. 'Where did you get those?'

A fierce smile lit Anatole's face. 'Would you believe they had an armory in their security room?'

French Judicial Police arrived at the scene minutes later, on the heels of two local SWAT teams. Conrad and Anatole were briefly detained before someone from the French Ministry of Interior approved their release.

By one thirty in the afternoon, the headquarters of Strabo Corp. was swarming with police officers, French Central Intelligence agents, and an Interpol Incident Response Team.

The two immortals were standing in the middle of a lab on the twenty-first floor when a tall detective with brown hair and eyes came up to them.

'It's Anatole, isn't it?' he said hesitantly. His English was good, with a trace of a Lyon accent.

Anatole's face brightened in recognition. 'Hey. Long time no see, Lacroix.'

The man sighed. He looked around guardedly and leaned

closer. 'I take it by your presence here that your—*people* are involved in this international fiasco?' he murmured.

Anatole pulled a face. 'Yeah, sorry about that. President Westwood put this guy here in charge of the US investigation.' He indicated Conrad.

The French detective observed Conrad for a beat. His gaze shifted back to Anatole. 'How's Soul?'

A grin stretched Anatole's lips. 'Busy changing diapers,' he said with a low chuckle. 'He just had twins.'

The man arched an eyebrow in evident disbelief. 'Somehow, I can't quite imagine that.' Someone called his name from across the room.

'I've got to go,' the detective said tersely. He started to walk away, paused, and looked over his shoulder. 'Is it true that you arrested the entire company?'

Anatole's ears reddened. He shuffled his feet. 'Er, yeah.'

'I see.' The man muttered something under his breath and headed toward his colleague.

'I don't think that was a compliment,' said Conrad. He cast a quizzical frown at his second in command. 'Who was that?'

'His name's Christophe Lacroix,' said Anatole. 'He helped us out last year, during the incident with the Crovirs.'

Conrad recalled what Horatio had told him in Rio as he watched the figure disappearing across the floor. 'Was that the one that resulted in the deaths of Agatha Vellacrus and Felix Thorne?'

'Uh-huh.'

Conrad hesitated, troubled. 'He said Soul. Did he mean—?'

'Yes,' Anatole interjected. 'He was referring to *the* Lucas Soul.' The immortal's pale eyes considered him. 'Actually, in some ways, you kinda remind me of him. Especially with that stunt you pulled in the elevator shaft. He was always doing shit like that.'

'What about you? I thought you'd mellowed,' retorted Conrad.

'Oh, come on!' Anatole protested. 'A hundred years ago, I would have riddled these bastards with bullets until they looked like Swiss cheese!'

It didn't take long to determine that the two olive-skinned men whose arms Anatole had grazed with bullets were the Strabo Corp. head of research and development, and the company director. It was another hour before they were allowed to question the pair.

'Who is she?' Conrad demanded. He indicated the video display on the wall.

They were inside the Strabo Corp. security office, on the twentieth floor of the tower. A row of monitors dominated a workstation spanning the curved wall of the ergonomically designed chamber. The upscale impression of sleek efficiency was somewhat spoiled by the broken door of the weapons and ammunition cage at the back of the room.

Volkan Sahin sat with his hands cuffed behind his back in front of the terminal. He stared blankly at the screen in front of him and remained silent.

The security camera recording had been frozen to show a shot of the woman who had escaped from the facility. She was standing in one of the underground garages, where she watched workers loading a truck with steel crates.

'What's her name?' asked Conrad.

Sahin stayed mute.

Conrad quelled a flicker of irritation. He leaned against the console and crossed his arms. 'Does she work for you?' he said, his tone still deadly calm.

A smirk flitted across the company director's features, as if the question amused him.

Conrad studied Sahin thoughtfully. 'I have it the wrong way round, don't I?' he mused. 'You work for *her*.'

Sahin leaned back in the chair and assumed a bored expression. Conrad noted the infinitesimal flash in the man's eyes with a degree of satisfaction. He was right; the director of Strabo Corp. was employed by the enemy.

The immortal decided to change tactics and pointed at the containers being stored inside the truck. 'What was in those crates?'

Sahin glanced at him and kept tight-lipped. Several minutes later, he had still not spoken a word. Conrad scowled. This was getting them nowhere. He stepped in front of the company director, leaned down, and gripped the armrests of the chair.

'The only thing stopping me from putting a bullet in you right now are these gentlemen,' the immortal hissed inches from the man's face. His eyes moved briefly to the French agents and detectives at the back of the room. 'Once we confirm that your company had something to do with the assassination attempt on their president, I don't think they're gonna give a damn. After the French have finished with you, we'll have you extradited to the US to face charges concerning the FedEx Field incident. You'll be behind bars for a long time while awaiting trial, Sahin.' Conrad stood back. 'It's a shame how often accidents happen in prison. And not just accidents,' he added with a mirthless smile.

Trepidation darted across the man's face. Despite this brief show of anxiety, Volkan Sahin refused to answer any of Conrad's or the French officers' questions.

To the immortal's growing frustration, Ridvan Kadir was just as taciturn when he was brought in for interrogation. Following fifteen minutes of fruitless questioning, the head of R&D for Strabo Corp. was taken away by French police. He sneered and spat at Conrad as he disappeared through the door, a litany of hate-filled, foreign words finally escaping his lips.

Moreau, the lead French Central Intelligence agent overseeing the local investigation with the Judicial Police, stared at the departing man. 'What was that?'

Conrad watched the empty doorway, startled by what Ridvan Kadir had revealed in that one sentence.

'"Soon, the Rightful Heir will rise and walk over your bloodied corpses,"' the immortal translated slowly. 'It was Turkish,' he explained at the agent's puzzled expression. He glanced at Anatole. 'Did you notice?'

'Yes,' said Anatole. 'He used the ancient Ottoman Turkish word for "heir."'

Anatole's troubled tone mirrored Conrad's own unease. He could not help but think of the haiku that had led him to uncover the assassination attempt on Westwood's life; it had also used the words "Rightful Heir." He ran a hand through his hair and let out a sigh of frustration. 'Shit! Looks like we have no option but to go through this place inch by inch.'

Anatole gave him a look. 'Gee, that sounds like fun.'

Conrad turned to one of the French detectives. 'Any luck tracing those trucks?'

The man placed a hand over the mouthpiece of his cell and shook his head, a dejected look on his face. 'Cameras lost them somewhere in the tunnels. We have no idea where they went.'

Conrad clenched his teeth. 'And the number plates?'

'They were all fakes. There's no way to trace where the vehicles came from,' came the glum reply.

'Goddammit!' hissed the immortal.

The door opened. Harry Stevens entered the room. Relief flooded Conrad when he saw the woman behind the agent.

'What have you got?' said Laura.

CHAPTER TWENTY-ONE

S

'VOLKAN SAHIN WAS BORN IN MANISA, IN WEST TURKEY, IN 1958. Parents deceased, no siblings. He is unmarried and has no dependents. He has diplomas and degrees from several internationally renowned business schools and worked in senior managerial roles in the US and Switzerland before being appointed executive director of Strabo Corp. in 1995.' The French Central Intelligence agent scrutinized the paperwork in his hand. 'According to this, he has no prior felony or criminal convictions and is not a subject of interest to any intelligence community or counterintelligence organization.'

The fax machine next to him spat out another sheet. Moreau lifted it off the tray and perused the contents with a tiny frown.

'Says here Ridvan Kadir was also born in Manisa, in 1953. Parents deceased. He had an older brother who died in a car accident in 1970. He's divorced with no children and holds PhDs in medicinal and organic chemistry. He became the head of Strabo Corp.'s R&D program in 1995. Prior to that, he held high-ranking scientific positions in a number of organizations.' The agent paused. 'Hmm.'

'What?' said Conrad.

'He was briefly investigated by Mossad in 1984, when he was seen in the company of a weapons dealer. The case was closed by the Israelis after two months. They thought he was clean.' Moreau placed the record on the table.

Conrad studied the passport photographs on the intelligence reports of the two Strabo Corp. employees. He could not help but feel that the Anatolian Peninsula had a key role to play in their investigation.

'So we have two men born in the same city a few years apart who end up working for the same company several decades later. Somehow I doubt it's a simple coincidence.' Conrad glanced at Moreau. 'Did they know each other before they joined Strabo Corp.?'

'This is just the basic data we have on them,' said Moreau. 'We'll have to contact the Turkish authorities if we want further details on their backgrounds.'

'What about the company?' said Laura.

'Strabo Corp. was registered as a non-stock corporation in 1995,' said a French detective in heavy English. He was leafing through the documents they had confiscated from Sahin's office. 'It appears to be a niche enterprise specializing in cardiovascular and anesthetic drugs.'

Anatole rubbed his chin thoughtfully. 'So Sahin and Kadir came on board when the company was formed.'

Conrad drummed his fingers on the table. 'Does Strabo Corp. have a board of directors?'

'Yes,' replied the police detective. He studied the paperwork in front of him. 'There were ten names listed at the time it was established.'

'You should have them checked out and bring them in for questioning,' Laura suggested to Moreau.

Lines creased the French agent's brow. 'I agree,' he said gruffly. He turned to the detective. 'Why don't you ring around?

I'll see what our intelligence network has on them.' He glanced at the Interpol agent. 'I think you guys should do the same.'

The Interpol agent nodded. The detective took out his cell.

It was four in the afternoon by the time they stumbled upon the first of several crucial discoveries. Having traced the orders of BTX to a Strabo Corp. lab on the twenty-second floor of the tower, Conrad had asked the Judicial Police to call in a forensic chemist to analyze the drugs manufactured in that particular facility. Satisfaction darted through the immortal when the scientist confirmed that the poison identified by the Germans was among them.

'I came across something else,' the woman added after she finished explaining her findings. She indicated the Strabo Corp. computer in front of her with a faint frown. 'This poison was made by a process called co-crystallization, something I'm told your FBI experts already discovered when they analyzed traces of the sample they got their hands on?'

Conrad nodded, intrigued.

'Co-crystallization is not a new science,' the woman continued. 'It's been around for more than a century and is principally used in the field of pharmaceutics. The technique has recently seen a revival in interest, however, and is being extensively researched for its potential application in other industries.'

'And?' said Laura.

'Well, there's a hell of a lot of stuff on co-crystallization in the Strabo Corp.'s databases,' said the scientist. 'Seems to me that they were working on something pretty big to do with that process.'

'Like what?' asked Conrad.

The woman hesitated. Her eyes swung from the computer to the confines of the lab. 'I think they were conducting experiments on a new co-crystal product beside this poison,' she finally admitted. 'Have any of you heard of PETN?'

'No.'

'It stands for pentaerythritol tetranitrate. It's an organic compound with a similar chemical structure to nitroglycerin. It's all over their research files.' The scientist paused. 'The presence of PETN in a pharmaceutical lab is not unusual per se, since it's a major ingredient of vasodilator drugs used to treat heart conditions like angina. However...' The scientist trailed off and bit her lip.

'Yes?' prompted Conrad, masking his impatience.

'It's also an exceedingly powerful commercial explosive,' she said.

Coldness spread through Conrad as a memory reared its head. 'Pentolite,' he breathed.

Anatole swore. Laura's face darkened.

The Interpol agent studied their expressions with a raised eyebrow. 'What's Pentolite?'

'It's a military explosive made of 50 percent nitropenta and 50 percent TNT,' Laura explained in a forbidding tone. 'It was one of the most commonly used explosives during the Second World War.'

'Nitropenta is the other name for PETN,' said the forensic chemist. 'These days, you know it more commonly as a main ingredient of Semtex.'

A bleak silence descended on the lab. 'Are you suggesting these guys were making Semtex?' said Moreau, his lips pressed in a thin line.

The scientist shrugged. 'I'm not saying anything of the sort.' She indicated the computer. 'But there are a number of drives on there that I can't access. The data they contain may tell you why Strabo Corp. was so interested in PETN.' She showed them the locations of the drives on the company's private network.

Conrad studied the screen for some time. If Strabo Corp. had deemed it necessary to lock these partitions with such advanced security protocols, it meant they contained important information. They had to access the data—fast.

'Call Vienna,' he told Anatole in a low voice.

A tiny smile flitted across the other immortal's face; he nodded once and exited the lab.

'What's in Vienna?' asked Moreau with a curious frown.

'A friend.' Conrad gazed steadily at the agent. 'Time is of the essence here. I want our analysts in Washington to look at the Strabo Corp.'s network. The US government has some of the world's best hackers at its disposal. It will speed up the task.'

'He's right,' Laura concurred as mutters broke out among the French officers. 'They may crack these codes faster.'

It was the Interpol agent who convinced the other agencies to agree to Conrad's demand. Twenty minutes later, Moreau obtained the approval of the Ministry of Interior to allow the US to access the French company's systems. They returned to the security office, where Laura linked them up to the White House Sit Room.

A familiar face blinked into view on the display of the laptop they had borrowed from the Interpol agent.

'Hey,' said Connelly. Dark circles underscored the eyes of the Director of National Intelligence; she looked like she hadn't slept in weeks. 'How are you guys holding up at your end?'

'We're surviving,' said Conrad.

Connelly made a face. 'Really? I saw a video of that fight on the roof. There's also one of you pulling some men out of a car just before it exploded. You've not exactly being the definition of subtlety, Greene.'

Conrad shrugged. 'Call it collateral damage.' He saw Laura smile out the corner of his eye. As he updated Connelly with their most recent findings and what he wanted the Sit Room analysts to do next, the screen on the Strabo Corp. computer next to the laptop flickered.

Anatole walked back in the room and dipped his chin

slightly. Tension eased out of Conrad's shoulders. The immortals running the sophisticated intelligence network supporting the Bastian Councils had successfully infiltrated the Strabo Corp.'s computer systems.

Stevens had left to join the French agents and police officers investigating the other levels of the secret research facility. He returned moments after Conrad ended the call to the White House, his expression guarded.

'There's something upstairs you need to look at,' said the agent.

Conrad's pulse jumped at Stevens's tone. They followed him to a lab that took up almost the entire twenty-third floor of the tower. Stevens guided them past rows of abandoned workstations and cubicles before stopping in front of a sealed entrance at the back of the facility.

'At first, we thought this was just another sterile workroom,' he explained as he punched a key into the security panel on the steel door. 'Once we found the access code though, we discovered it was something else entirely.'

He grabbed the handle and pulled. There was a low hiss of escaping air. The door swung open on thick hinges. Stevens stepped across the threshold and entered a sizable chamber lit with bright, fluorescent strips.

'There's about two feet of reinforced concrete above us,' he said, indicating the low ceiling. 'Walls and floor are the same.'

Unease filled Conrad as he followed the agent. Although it looked for all intents and purposes like a normal lab, this space had more in common with an industrial unit than with the other facilities he had seen inside Strabo Corp. so far. His eyes roamed over the heavy production machinery crowding the floor and work surfaces before landing on a dark gray, tank-like structure on the far side of the room.

Conrad headed toward the metal cabin with leaden steps and stopped in front of the heavy containment door set in the curved wall. A faint, acrid odor reached his nostrils. He peered through the narrow, glazed window near the top and observed the black marks staining the surfaces inside with a sinking feeling. Something to the left caught and held his gaze.

Footsteps sounded behind him. Laura appeared at his side. 'What is it?'

'It's a detonation chamber,' Conrad replied in a low voice.

An undefined fear filled the immortal as he stared at the ominous device propped on a thick metal support fixed to the floor. He glanced at Laura and saw the same dread reflected in her eyes. There was a sudden clatter from the other side of the lab. They turned and saw Stevens lugging a waist-high, metal cylinder across the concrete floor.

'I found this as well,' huffed the agent. He lifted the heavy canister onto a worktop, laid it on its side, and unscrewed the lid. 'There's another one in a locked compartment at the back.'

They joined him and studied the fat, red rods filling the container.

Anatole reached over and carefully pulled one out. 'What the hell is this?'

Conrad took the rod off him and rolled the cold, smooth bar between his fingers, his pulse racing.

'One of the Strabo Corp. scientists said she saw the woman who got away talking to Kadir and Sahin just outside this place,' said Stevens. 'The stuff inside the containers that went on those trucks all came out of this room. Kadir also gave her a metal briefcase.'

Hope flared inside Conrad. 'Did she know what was in those crates?'

Stevens shook his head, dashing the immortal's newborn expectations. 'No. Kadir and Sahin were the only ones who had access to this chamber. It took us a while to unearth the code from their security system.' He reached for the canister lid and was about to twist it back on when Conrad grabbed his wrist. The agent froze. 'What?'

Conrad's eyes did not shift from the faint engraving on the inside surface of the metal cap. 'That symbol,' he breathed.

Anatole squinted and leaned in for a closer look. 'Isn't that the one we found on that card inside Luther Obenhaus's safe?'

Conrad's heart thudded wildly inside his chest. 'Yes. It was also on the amulet that woman was wearing around her neck.'

They stared at the complex of curved lines for long seconds.

'Send a shot of the canister lid and one of these rods through to Washington and the Bastian intelligence network,' Conrad instructed, a buzz of excitement underscoring his voice. 'I want to see what they make of them.'

They conferred briefly with the French agents and detectives before leaving Strabo Corp. a short while later. Halfway to Orly Airport, Laura's cell rang.

'Agent Hartwell here,' she answered in a crisp tone. Her brow furrowed slightly. 'Wait, I'll put you on speaker.' She tapped the touch screen and held the phone face-up in her hand. 'It's Moreau.'

'Can you guys hear me okay?' came the Frenchman's voice.

'Yes,' said Conrad.

'I have some news,' said the agent.

A flicker of apprehension blossomed inside Conrad at the man's bitter tone. 'What is it, Moreau?' he said tensely.

'The board of directors of Strabo Corp. is fake,' said Moreau.

Conrad glanced at the immortals and the Secret Service agent and read the same concern in their eyes. 'What do you mean it's fake?'

'You know the list we got from the company records?' said Moreau. 'Well, Judicial Police crosschecked the data provided by Strabo Corp. to the Register of Commerce in 1995. All the documents, including the passports and ID cards of the

members of the board of directors, were well-executed forg-
eries. These people are frauds.'

Conrad detected the Frenchman's frustration in the lull that
followed.

'French Central Intelligence just confirmed this as well,'
Moreau continued. 'The addresses provided were anonymous
mailboxes in Paris. Of the board members who supplied French
birth certificates, none were on the Civil Register. If these
people did in fact ever exist, they were not who they said
they were.'

Conrad's nails bit into his palms. 'Then who the hell is
running that company?'

'I don't know.' Moreau sighed. 'We'll keep digging, Greene.
Kadir and Sahin already have their lawyers barking at the doors
of the Judicial Police. I wouldn't be surprised if they were
released on bail in the next twenty-four hours.' He ended
the call.

Conrad gazed blindly through the windscreen of the sedan
as it sped along the French motorway. Planes rose and sank on
the horizon to the right, distant white specks against a pale
blue sky.

'Let's run those names through our intelligence network in
Washington,' he told Laura in a hard voice. 'I want to know if
these people are on any other company listings elsewhere in the
world.' He frowned. 'Let Vienna know as well.'

They rolled into the airport moments later. Conrad thanked
the Bastian Hunters who had driven them there, before heading
for the Learjet parked on the tarmac with the others. They had
just stepped inside the cabin when the pilot came out of the
cockpit.

'A Detective Lacroix just rang. He said to call him on this
number.' He handed them a note.

Conrad glanced at Anatole. 'Any idea what he might want?'
he said, perplexed.

Anatole shrugged. 'Nope. Not a clue.'

Conrad turned to the pilot. 'Call him.'

The man nodded and returned to the cockpit. Lacroix's voice soon came over the cabin speakers.

'I'm at Ridvan Kadir's home in the 7ème arrondissement,' the French detective explained after Conrad greeted him. 'There's something you need to see. You got access to a computer?'

'Yes,' Conrad replied.

Stevens logged onto the aircraft's desktop.

'Good,' said Lacroix. 'This is a secure site where you can view the pictures.' He gave them a web address followed by a username and password.

'This guy's apartment is as clean as a whistle,' the French detective continued as they accessed the site and waited for three files to load up. Voices rose in the background behind Lacroix; the local crime scene investigators were still working the place. 'I'm afraid that apart from the items I've uncovered, we're not going to find much else here to help you.' He paused. 'You have those items yet?'

Stevens clicked on a document.

'We're opening the first one,' said Conrad.

An image unfurled across the screen.

'That one is pretty self-explanatory,' said Lacroix. 'Call it pride or stupidity on Kadir's part, but considering that this is not on his official CV, I was surprised to find it in his study.'

Conrad's mouth went dry. The photograph was of a picture frame sitting on a wall. Inside it was a certificate proclaiming that Ridvan Kadir held a postgraduate degree in physics from MIT.

'He's a physicist as well?' the immortal said in a stunned voice.

Blood thundered inside his head as he thought of the sealed tank on the twenty-third floor of Strabo Corp. and the heavy production machinery inside the isolation chamber. Stevens opened the remaining attachments.

'The last two files are the front and back of a picture I found tucked inside his desk,' said Lacroix. 'I'm hardly a forensic facial mapping expert, but I thought I recognized Kadir and Sahin among the faces.'

The display filled with two adjacent images. The one on the left was a faded, black and white photograph depicting a group of children and teenagers standing and sitting in an orderly fashion around a central figure seated regally in a beautifully sculptured, high-back chair.

'What the—?' Anatole exclaimed.

'Is that *her*?' snapped Laura.

Conrad stared at the woman in the middle of the picture. Although the image was a monochrome, there was no denying that she was stunning. Her complexion was creamy and flaw-less, with lips that glistened in the light and pale eyes that seemed to drill into the camera. Her expression was one of serene pride, with a hint of cruelty in the lines of her mouth.

She bore an uncanny resemblance to the woman he had fought with several hours ago on the glass rooftop in La Défense.

'No, that's not her,' Conrad said slowly. 'But they sure as hell look alike.'

A teenager and an older child, who could have been Kadir and Sahin, stood on either side of the woman in the picture.

'Guess we have the answer to the question of whether those two knew each other before Strabo Corp.,' Conrad murmured.

His eyes switched to the second image. It was a shot of an inscription on the back of the picture.

'Is that Ottoman Turkish?' said Anatole warily.

'Yes.' Conrad peered at the handwriting. '"To my little soldiers. Signed, Ariana,"' he translated. His pulse accelerated as he considered the meaning behind those words. Soldiers meant an army—and Donaghy's undercover operative had seen plenty evidence of that.

'I hope that helped,' said Lacroix in the heavy silence that followed. 'I'll get in touch if we find anything else.'

'What the hell is going on?' Stevens muttered after the French detective ended the call.

They were still pondering their worrisome discoveries when an alert signaling an incoming connection sounded on the computer at around six that evening. The video link to Washington flashed open on the screen.

'Victor Dvorsky got in touch with us just over an hour ago,' Connelly announced in a harassed tone. Conrad straightened in the executive chair.

The Sit Room was a hive of activity. Agents and White House staff crowded around the command console behind the Director of National Intelligence, their voices raised in a hubbub of conversation.

A muscle jumped visibly in Connelly's cheek. Conrad had a sinking feeling there was more to her agitation than him getting the Bastian Councils' intelligence team involved in the matter at hand without her permission.

'What's wrong, Sarah?' he said quietly.

CHAPTER TWENTY-TWO

CONNELLY BLINKED AT THE SOUND OF HER NAME. SHE TOOK A deep breath and looked more composed when she spoke again.

'The situation here and abroad is getting more fraught by the hour, Greene. Congress is baying for Westwood's blood and wants the FAA ban lifted. They're claiming that Westwood is playing Russian roulette with the economic future of the United States.' A frown darkened her features. 'The political situations in Europe and Asia are no better. Tension is still running high between the White House and the Kremlin. Berlin, Paris, London, and Beijing are also at loggerheads, while North Korea is starting to make some noise. Pyongyang has increased the numbers of short-range, guided missiles along the country's borders and coasts, and NORAD has confirmed that North Korean submarines with ballistic and cruise missile capabilities are being mobilized in the Sea of Japan.' Bitterness sharpened her voice. 'Although the evidence your team and the Germans have come up with vindicates our claims that external forces beyond the targeted nations are at work here, everyone is too busy playing the blame game to see the wood for the trees.' She closed her eyes briefly and rubbed her temples in slow circular motions. 'We're still at DEFCON 4. The Joint Chiefs are recommending Westwood increase the alert state of the US Armed Forces to DEFCON 3. At this rate, all we'll need is someone to blink faster than the others and we'll have an all-out nuclear war on our hands.'

Coldness spread through Conrad. The situation was deteriorating by the hour. He had to agree with Connelly's conclusion; war was looking more and more likely. 'What did Victor have to say?'

Connelly brightened slightly. 'He sent us some information our cryptanalysts were able to use to access the data on the secured drives on the Strabo Corp. systems.' The corners of her mouth turned down. 'But we couldn't capture everything. It seems the company's computer framework was functioning as a database server on a large-scale, virtual private network. The drives were in the process of being erased when we got to them. Our techs couldn't trace the remote locations accessing the VPN connections. Not only did those appear to require multi-factor authentication, the links were severed shortly after our presence within the network was detected.'

Conrad went still. Not only was the enemy's goal of global unrest becoming a reality, they were also moving faster than he could have anticipated. 'What's in the data you retrieved?' he said between clenched teeth.

Connelly sighed. 'I'm afraid the material was too complex even for our forensic scientists to fully grasp, so we got in touch with a couple of experts in the field,' she said in a worn out voice. 'I have Professors Bradley Janssen and Akihito Itaka, from the universities of Michigan and Case Western, waiting online at the moment. Both of them specialize in chemistry and macromolecular science. They've been briefed on the sensitive nature of the information we're about to discuss and have agreed to give us their professional opinion on what it means.'

A troubled light dawned in her eyes. 'Their area of special interest is explosives engineering,' she added quietly.

Tension formed a leaden knot in the pit of Conrad's stomach. An image of the detonation tank inside the isolation chamber in Strabo Corp. flashed before his eyes.

The video link split into three windows. Janssen looked about forty years old and was wearing a faded University of Michigan sweatshirt. His blue eyes shone with keen intelligence behind the glasses perched on his nose as he stared into the webcam of his laptop.

Itaka's disheveled, gray-streaked hair put him about a decade ahead of Janssen. There was a garish, yellow Scooby-Doo tie clipped to his shirt and a Garfield mug next to his desktop. Despite the distance separating him from the two men, Conrad detected the nervous excitement in their postures.

'Go ahead, gentlemen,' Connelly ordered from the main window.

Janssen blinked and cleared his throat. 'Please bear in mind that, without knowing the context in which this data was obtained, it's difficult to tell you for certain what the people behind it were intending to achieve,' he warned.

'That's okay,' said Connelly, a trace of impatience modulating her tone. 'Time is of the essence here. We just want you to put this stuff to us in plain terms.'

Janssen inhaled shallowly. 'All right,' he mumbled. 'The gist of it is this: from the formulations and processes described in the files you showed us, it seems someone may have invented a new explosive.'

There was an audible intake of breath from Connelly.

Itaka leaned closer to his desktop camera. 'I concur,' said the Cleveland professor, his head bobbing vigorously. 'Though the final production method is missing, the data indicates the successful co-crystallization of PETN with a chemically modified nitroamine compound to create a liquid high explosive with a significant RE factor.'

'RE factor?' said Laura, puzzled.

'Relative effectiveness factor,' Itaka explained. 'It's a measurement of an explosive's power as compared to 1 kilogram of TNT. For example, Semtex has an RE factor of 1.66, meaning you'd need 0.6 kilogram of Semtex to achieve the same destructive effect as 1 kilogram of TNT. This product has an apparent RE factor of 4.9.' The professor hesitated, his face losing some of its initial thrill. 'That's higher than any non-nuclear material currently in existence today.'

'If this stuff has indeed been made, it'll be the biggest innovation the explosives industry has seen in decades.' Janssen's face gleamed with a fine sheen of sweat. 'The engineering applications in the military and mining fields alone for a liquid substance with this kind of sensitivity, detonation velocity, and stability will be almost infinite.'

Conrad's heart pounded painfully against his ribs. 'Can this thing be detonated by a high-intensity energy beam?'

Janssen blinked. 'Hmm. It's feasible, yes,' he admitted, surprise evident on his face.

'A Q-switched laser can initiate the detonation of PETN,' said Itaka.

'Connelly, show them the picture of the red bar Laura forwarded earlier,' Conrad requested in a stiff voice.

The Director of Intelligence puckered her brow slightly and barked out an instruction over her shoulder. The image of the object Stevens had discovered inside the metal canister in the isolation lab in Strabo Corp. appeared on the screen.

'Do you know what this is?' Conrad demanded of the two professors.

The scientists squinted at their respective cameras.

'That's a ruby laser rod,' said Janssen.

'Although I haven't seen one quite that size before,' muttered Itaka.

Conrad's hands balled into fists on the armrests of the chair. 'Could a physicist make a laser device using these rods?' he asked, dreading the answer he knew he would receive. 'One capable of detonating a liquid explosive?'

'Yes,' the two men replied simultaneously.

'Thank you,' Conrad murmured after a beat, his knuckles white.

Laura placed a hand on his shoulder. Although he was grateful for the warmth of her touch, Conrad detected the same rigid tension coursing through her.

'If that's all, I think we'll finish—' Connelly started in a brisk voice.

'Wait!' Itaka interrupted. He stared at the camera. 'Brad, did you notice something strange in the data we saw?'

'What do you mean?' said Janssen, perplexed.

'The formulae. Don't you think they look like the stuff Professor Hagen was working on before he died?' said Itaka, his tone insistent.

Conrad watched as Janssen clicked on his mouse and scrolled down the screen of his laptop. Light reflected off his lenses and highlighted his widening eyes. 'Gosh. I can't believe I didn't see that. You're right, Aki. These could be his experiments.'

'Who's Professor Hagen?' Connelly demanded of the two men.

Itaka tugged at his collar. 'Our apologies,' he said in a somber tone. 'Professor Svein Hagen was an esteemed colleague of ours who died in an accident in Hawaii eight years ago.'

'What kind of accident?' asked Conrad.

'His car plunged off a cliff into the sea.' Itaka's mouth drooped. 'His wife and eldest daughter also perished in the incident. Their bodies were never recovered.'

Conrad mulled this over for a moment. 'Could someone have stolen his work?' he said finally.

Itaka hesitated. 'I honestly don't know. But this data bears a remarkable similarity to the research he was engaged in before his accident.'

Connelly thanked the two men and disconnected their links, her face pale.

'I'll have to talk to Westwood and the Joint Chiefs,' she said. 'If there's a new bomb being made to target us, we need to be prepared. I'll pass the information to our allies across the Atlantic.'

She seemed to recall something. Some color returned to her cheeks.

'Incidentally, the NSA and CIA have uncovered subtle variations of the Strabo Corp. directors' names on the executive boards of more than forty companies around the world.' A bleak smile crossed her face. 'One of those enterprises owns a black MD520N helicopter. Another participated in the FedEx Field fundraiser event.' She leaned toward the webcam. 'The most interesting fact is this,' she added in a hardening voice. 'A CIA analyst ran that list through an anagram software and came up with a surprising hit. One of the Strabo Corp. directors was called Rojan Korviacz. We found someone by the name of Zoran Rajkovic mentioned in an old Obenhaus Group news archive. He was a former member of their board of directors. We've contacted Maximilian Obenhaus to obtain more information on the man.'

Shock reverberated through Conrad at this news. 'That could explain how they got to his brother,' he muttered.

One of the Sit Room analysts crossed the floor and wordlessly handed Connelly a sheet of paper. Her lips tightened in a thin line as she scanned its contents. She looked up at the camera. 'French Central Intelligence just called. The Turkish authorities have confirmed that Ridvan Kadir and Volkan Sahin attended the same private school in Manisa. Guess who owned the place?'

Conrad stared blankly at her for a couple of seconds. He pulled a face. 'The same people who were running Strabo Corp?' he hazarded.

'Bingo.' Connelly's eyes glinted dangerously.

The flare of satisfaction that coursed through the immortal was short-lived. 'But we still have no idea who these people really are or what they're planning.'

'No,' Connelly concurred, her face sobering. She hesitated, her eyes darting right and left. 'But, according to Victor Dvorsky, your kind may feature somewhere in their history,' she added in a low voice.

'We know they possess the knowledge and ability to make a powerful new explosive,' said Laura with a frown.

'And the capacity to detonate it, if they're making those laser devices,' added Stevens.

'Not to mention that they appear to be gathering a well-equipped army led by a battalion of ruthless mercenaries and warlords,' mused Anatole.

'But for what purpose?' Conrad exclaimed bitterly. 'I can't help but feel that a small group of individuals are masterminding all of this. And I fear their next step will make the events we've seen so far look like child's play.' He stared at his fisted hands for a moment before looking up at Connelly. 'I think we should go public.'

A blank expression washed across the face of the Director of National Intelligence. 'What do you mean?'

'Put out the picture of the woman from the FedEx Field to the world media. We don't need to release any confidential information. Just the fact that she's a prime suspect in the recent incidents in the US and Europe, and that she's wanted for questioning.'

Connelly steepled her fingers in front of her face and

watched him thoughtfully above them. 'You really think that's gonna work?'

Conrad shrugged. 'We've got nothing to lose.'

A strained silence followed while Connelly contemplated his suggestion. 'Okay,' she said finally. She called Petersen over and gave him brief instructions in a low voice.

The Homeland Security agent moved off camera, a faint frown on his face.

A phone suddenly chimed inside the Learjet cabin. They looked at Anatole as he took out his cell and answered the call.

'Hi,' said the immortal. His brow furrowed. 'We're talking to the team in Washington right now. You want to link up?' He paused. 'Okay.'

Anatole disconnected and leaned across the table. 'That was Victor,' he explained, fingers clattering on the keyboard of the plane's computer. 'He wants to talk.'

Another window opened up on the screen. Victor Dvorsky gazed solemnly into the webcam on the other side of the video link. He was seated at a desk inside a floating, glass office overlooking an enormous vaulted stone chamber milling with people. Conrad dimly recognized the background as the Bastian First Council's main command post in Vienna. It looked somewhat different from the last time he had set eyes on it, more than sixty years ago. Back then, the world's first computer had just been invented.

'Sarah, Conrad,' Victor greeted with a brisk nod. 'It's good I could catch you together. What's the latest from your end?'

Conrad swiftly apprised the Bastian leader of their most recent findings from Paris. Connelly did the same with the investigation's progress from Washington. Victor's face remained inscrutable while he listened.

'Have you got something for us?' said Conrad.

'Yes,' said the Bastian leader. 'It's about that symbol Laura sent through earlier, the one you found in Luther Obenhaus's safe and the Strabo Corp. lab.'

Conrad straightened. 'What about it?'

'It's a Tughra,' said Victor. 'I'm not surprised you didn't recognize it. It's been a few centuries since I've had any reason to set eyes on one myself.'

Connelly raised an eyebrow. 'What's a Tughra?'

'It's an imperial monogram used by the Sultans who ruled the Ottoman Empire,' said Conrad bitterly. 'Dammit, I can't believe I didn't see that!'

'Each Ottoman emperor had his own Tughra created at the start of his reign,' said Victor. 'This monogram became the royal signature and seal that went on every official document issued by that particular ruler.' The Bastian noble leaned back in his leather chair. 'The Ottoman Empire was dissolved in the early 1920s. The last Sultan to have an imperial monogram made was Mehmed VI. We've compared the symbol you discovered with all the Tughras that have ever existed.'

'And?' said Conrad, muscles tightening.

'It doesn't match any of them,' said Victor. 'This is a completely new Tughra.'

'What does that mean?' said Connelly in the silence that followed.

'The design of a Tughra is not without significance,' Victor explained. 'Each element that makes up the motif has a specific meaning. In combination, they spell out a message in Ottoman Turkish specific to the ruler the Tughra represents. This one is no different.' He paused. 'It says "Zoran, of the line of Suleiman and Mustafa, the Rightful Heir to the Empire."'

Conrad's mouth went dry.

'Zoran?' said Connelly sharply. 'Are you certain?'

'Absolutely,' said Victor in a steely voice.

'That ex-Obenhaus Group director was called Zoran Rajkovic,' said Stevens.

From the way the Bastian leader focused a calculated gaze on Conrad's face, he knew he was the only one who had grasped the extraordinary significance of the Tughra's message.

'When you said Suleiman, did you mean—?' Conrad started, hardly daring to believe his ears.

'Yes,' interrupted Victor. His eyes shone with a dangerous light. 'Suleiman bin Selim Khan; also known as Suleiman the Magnificent, one of the most powerful Ottoman Sultans who ever lived. I met the man on a couple of occasions.' He smiled humorlessly. 'He was one deviously smart bastard.'

'Holy crap,' Anatole said hoarsely in the frozen stillness that descended on the cabin.

Conrad gazed blindly at Victor, too stunned to speak.

'Was he...an immortal?' Connelly finally asked. A sheen of perspiration beaded her forehead.

Victor shook his head. 'Far from it. But he was one of a small group of human leaders who knew of our existence at the time.' A rueful sigh escaped the Bastian leader. 'One of the reasons Suleiman was so obsessed with expanding his empire was because he truly feared the immortal societies. In the end, we had no option but to go against him during his military campaigns in Europe.' He grimaced. 'He did, however, gain the support of the Crovirs in some of his greatest battles.'

Conrad stirred. 'Mustafa was one of his sons?'

'Yes,' replied Victor. 'Mustafa Muhlisi was Suleiman's first child with his concubine, Mahidevran Sultan, and his second son chronologically. He was charismatic, exceedingly talented in the arts of politics and war, and generally adored by his people and the Janissary army. He was recognized as a significant future threat by Europe's rulers, most of whom suspected he would be an even more fearsome leader than Suleiman.' He rubbed his chin thoughtfully. 'Incidentally, Mustafa was a Prince of Amasya, a city in the northern Ottoman Empire. It also happens to be the birthplace of the ancient Greek philosopher and geographer, Strabo.'

'Hence Strabo Corp.,' murmured Conrad.

'Although Mustafa was the favorite to take the throne after his father, it was one of his step-brothers who eventually succeeded Suleiman,' Victor continued. 'Mustafa was executed by order of the Sultan himself as a result of a political intrigue that had dominated the Ottoman court for years.'

'Was he married?' asked Laura. 'Did he leave behind any heirs?

'No,' said Victor. 'That's the strangest thing.' The Bastian leader's puzzlement was obvious from the lines that creased his brow. 'Although he had lovers, Mustafa was not known to have fathered a child, nor did he have a favorite concubine that was ever documented. I've asked the Bastian Immortal Culture & History Section to go over the information we have on the Ottoman Empire.'

'So, hang on a minute. Let me get this straight,' said Connelly, disbelief raising the pitch of her voice. 'Are you really suggesting that there might be someone out there who thinks he's the next ruler of a defunct world superpower? Someone who may incidentally also be a descendant of,' she leaned toward the camera and lowered her voice to a hiss, 'an *immortal?*'

Victor did not answer the question directly. He rested his elbows on the desk, propped his chin on his interlaced fingers, and watched them broodingly for some time.

'Consider this theory,' he said quietly. 'Suppose you were the last remaining scion of a dead empire. Imagine you wanted to restore the kingdom of your ancestors to its former glory.' He paused. 'What would you need to achieve that goal?'

'An army,' Anatole replied promptly.

'Weapons of power,' said Laura.

A chilly smile danced on Victor's lips as he observed understanding dawn on their faces. 'And what would you *have* to do to ensure your success?' His forceful gaze focused on Conrad's face once more.

Part of the enigma unraveled inside the immortal's head. An icy conviction formed in his heart. 'You'd have to take out the opposition,' Conrad stated grimly.

The color drained from Connelly's face. 'Oh God,' she whispered.

'I think we're starting to see a structure to their plans,' said Victor. 'The question is, what will they do next?'

CHAPTER TWENTY-THREE

THE RED VASE SAILED THROUGH THE AIR AND CRASHED against the wall of the yacht's main salon. Sharp fragments scratched the expensive wood as they exploded outward from the point of impact. Nadica's guttural cry of rage underscored the echo of the explosion.

'I will kill that man with my own hands!' She bit her lip so hard she drew blood.

Ariana frowned from where she sat in a chair. 'Calm down, child.'

'Ama is right, sister,' said Zoran Rajkovic. His gray eyes glittered darkly. 'Now, tell us exactly what happened.'

Nadica took a shuddering breath and described the events that had taken place in Paris. Ariana grew still when the young woman related her physical encounter with the man the US president had put in charge of the investigation into the FedEx Field assassination attempt.

'Are you certain of what you saw?' she asked sharply.

Nadica hesitated. 'Yes, Ama.'

Ariana gazed at her blindly before sinking back against the silk cushions. 'Then he must be an immortal,' she murmured.

Zoran froze. 'Are you sure?'

'That's the only explanation.' A flicker of unease flashed through Ariana's subconscious.

Although she knew of the Crovirs and the Bastians, she had deliberately kept herself beneath their radar since she first became aware of their existence more than four centuries ago.

Immortality had come as a shock to Ariana.

Her earliest memories were of living in a cage in the Ukrainian city of Kefe, which was home to one of the largest slave markets of sixteenth-century Europe. After years of abuse at the hands of the Crimean traders who had stolen her from her home when she was a baby, she was eventually sold to a rich merchant in Istanbul when she was nine years old.

Her new masters were more tolerant of their pretty child slave. In the years that followed, Ariana got a glimpse of a freedom that she had never before known in her short life. But all too soon, her burgeoning beauty made her a subject of desire to the youngest master of the house. When her mistress came upon her son raping Ariana, his hand choking the air from her throat to stifle her screams, the woman whipped the young girl to the point of unconsciousness and sold her to a passing tradesman.

That man turned out to be a principal provider of slaves to the Imperial Harem. Taking pity on the bruised and battered girl, he asked a palace chambermaid to take her into service. When she awoke from her beating a day later, Ariana found herself on her way to the fortified city of Amasya, as a servant to one of Mahidevran Sultan's ladies in waiting. Her wounds had almost healed, an observation that seemed irrelevant at the time, but would prove to be shockingly significant in the future.

She met Prince Mustafa more than a year after she settled into life at the Imperial Palace, upon his return from a long and arduous military campaign. Ariana had been sitting in the gardens that hugged the cliffs overlooking the moonlit

Yesilirmak River at the time, lost in her thoughts while she enjoyed a brief moment of peace. At the sound of forceful footsteps, she turned and beheld a tall, handsome man dressed in a tired Janissary uniform striding toward her. It wasn't until she saw the palace guards bowing and heard their happy greetings that she realized she was in the presence of Suleiman's heir.

Although tales of his kindness had reached her ears, Ariana was still unprepared for the warmth and affection the Prince so readily showed her from the moment they met. Mustafa was twenty-one years her senior and the first man she ever willingly lay with. Conscious of the political plot being hatched against her son, Mahidevran Sultan took the young concubine under her wing and begged the two lovers to keep their relationship a secret.

Mahidevran's fears were proved correct all too soon. Mustafa was assassinated a year later. Ariana was two months pregnant at the time.

Heartbroken and bereft of the one person she had ever pledged her life to, Ariana eventually agreed to Mahidevran's desperate plans to keep her existence and that of Mustafa's potential heir hidden from the eyes of the greater Ottoman Empire.

A fortnight after the fateful day when they received the news of Mustafa's death, Mahidevran took her to the Janissary barracks in the city to meet with Branimir Rajkovic, the young captain who had brought them tidings of the Prince's execution at the hands of his own father.

Ariana recalled hearing about Rajkovic from Mustafa and knew the captain to be as good a man as her lover had been. When Mahidevran expounded her idea on how they should proceed with regards to Ariana's pregnancy, Branimir was shocked and stammered out an immediate refusal. Mahidevran instructed him to think carefully over the matter.

A week later, Branimir Rajkovic climbed the steep road to

the palace and came to deliver his answer to the Sultan. The following day, Ariana became his wife in everything but the law, as Janissaries were not permitted to marry at the time.

Although they never consummated their relationship in the months that followed their union, Ariana was aware of how deeply Branimir had fallen in love with her while her belly still grew with Mustafa's child.

Her labor came four weeks earlier than expected. As the hours of the day dwindled into night, Ariana knew something was terribly wrong. Mahidevran and Branimir stayed at her side the whole time, their lips full of encouraging words while their hands comforted her during the spasms of unbearable agony that tore through her bloated body and made her scream until her voice grew hoarse.

At long last, when night turned into day once more, Ariana heard her child's faint cry for the first time. She lifted her head weakly from the sweat-soaked bed and tried to peer through the veil of blackness falling across her vision at the pink, squirming bundle in Branimir's hands.

But fate had other plans for her. With blood pouring uncontrollably from her hemorrhaging womb, Ariana's heart soon slowed to dull, weak thuds. She pressed her lips to her son's head and wheezed out her last breath minutes after giving birth. As she slipped into a yawning, cold darkness, Ariana had but a single prayer in her thoughts: that she would see her beloved Prince once more.

An hour later, she awoke with a gasp, the white shroud enveloping her freshly cleaned body slipping from her face.

At the other end of the room, Branimir sat with Mustafa's son in his arms, sobs shuddering through his body and his tears shimmering in the candlelight as they fell on the newborn baby's sleeping face. He looked up at the sound of her voice and almost fainted when he saw her.

It took them days to come to terms with the fact that she

had survived her death. Mahidevran swore the female attendant who had helped during the childbirth to secrecy and had Branimir's new family moved to a Janissary posting outside Amasya.

They decided to call the boy Kader, which meant "Fate" in Ottoman Turkish. Shortly after her son turned one, Ariana finally accepted Branimir into her bed and allowed herself to love the man who had been like a brother to Mustafa. More than a decade later, she finally became Branimir's wife in the eyes of the law and God, when the new Sultan lifted the ban that forbade Janissaries to marry. By then, she had given birth to two more sons and a daughter.

The years passed. Although the core of her still belonged to her Prince, Ariana tended happily to her family, her days full of love and laughter. Branimir progressed rapidly in his career, and they lived comfortably on his earnings.

But by the time Kader turned nineteen, Ariana still looked the same as she did the day she gave birth to him. The evidence of her agelessness horrified her; viewing it as a curse from the heavens, she tried to kill herself. She was successful.

She survived that death as well.

It was Mahidevran who finally allayed her fears and put her on the path to discovering the existence of the immortals. After receiving news of Ariana's suicide and seeing the physical proof of the young woman's enduring youth, Mustafa's mother cautiously related a tale Suleiman once told her one evening when they were in bed.

The story was of two races of powerful, supernatural beings who had walked the Earth as long as man himself had existed. According to Suleiman, they were the greatest threat humanity would ever face, for not only were their fighting skills and stamina in battle truly terrifying, they did not seem to age like ordinary men and possessed the capacity to defy Death himself.

Although the Sultan's voice trembled as he talked about these "fearful immortal creatures," Mahidevran had taken the tale for what it appeared to be—the fanciful imagination of a great man who wished to see enemies everywhere.

Ariana waited until Branimir retired from the Janissary army a few months later before traveling secretly to Europe in the company of her husband and her first-born son, on the trail of these legendary beings. By then, Branimir's status had grown considerably in the army, and he had become a significantly wealthy man in his own right, able to open doors in societies that would normally have shunned them. Because of her youthful appearance, Ariana posed as Branimir's daughter, with Kader acting as her brother.

It was almost three years before they uncovered evidence of the existence of the immortals, in one of the greatest cities in the world. As she gazed at the small group of elegantly dressed figures circulating through the ballroom of a magnificent palace, their intimidating presence easily commanding the respect and awe of the noblemen and women around them, Ariana felt a rapport she had never experienced before.

The knowledge that she had found her true kinsmen was carved into her very bones that day. Although she wished to make herself known to them that same night, Branimir and Kader held her back, cautious of these powerful strangers they knew nothing about. In hindsight, she was grateful for their instincts.

They returned from their travels half a decade after they had left, thoughtful and fearful of all they had learned about the immortals in the two years since they first encountered them, including the rumor that the Crovirs and Bastians could survive up to sixteen deaths.

During their absence, yet another Sultan had taken to the throne of the Ottoman Empire. As they passed through the port of Istanbul, Ariana observed the glimmering fortress of Topkapi Palace overlooking the resplendent city and felt the first seed of anger germinate in her heart. Here was the capital of the empire that rightfully belonged to her long-dead Prince and their son.

She did not speak to Branimir of her increasing resentment after they reached their home in Bursa, although she suspected her husband knew the truth of her feelings from the anxious way he often looked at her. While Branimir had been outraged for a long time about the way Suleiman Sultan had treated Mustafa, the passage of time had eased his ire. Knowing that he would not approve of the scheme blossoming in the core of her soul, Ariana approached Mahidevran and requested her counsel.

The former concubine of Suleiman the Magnificent listened attentively to the outrageous idea that had preoccupied Ariana's every waking moment since her return from Europe. The older woman studied her in silence for some time before asking her to leave and come back the next day. Ariana departed Mahidevran's residence uncertain of the older woman's intentions, and spent a restless night wondering whether the dream growing inside her would ever come true.

She returned as requested the morning after, her heart full of trepidation. After closing the doors of her chamber to watchful eyes and curious ears, Mahidevran went to her writing table and produced several sheets of paper from a drawer. On them were written the names of everyone Mahidevran knew would be faithful to Mustafa's heir and Ariana's cause. Half were former members of Mahidevran's court from Amasya. The rest were officers of the Janissary army.

In the year that preceded Mahidevran's death, the former Sultan accompanied Ariana and Kader on their campaign across the Ottoman Empire, where they secured the allegiance of more than four hundred men and women.

Though it was not enough to lead a campaign against the ruling Sultan, Ariana was not disappointed by the size of the devoted following they had gained. For it was only the beginning of her plans.

By the time Branimir passed away, it was evident that two of his children and Kader had inherited traits of her immortal bloodline; all three had outstanding fighting skills, accelerated powers of healing, and delayed aging. Although a strong fighter, Branimir's second son recovered from his injuries and aged like other humans. All had married and had offsprings of their own.

Over the next eighty years, Ariana secretly tested the mettle of her growing troops against the Sultans of the Ottoman Empire, beginning with her support of the Janissary uprising of the 1620s, in which the ruling emperor was captured and killed.

Other Sultans rapidly took the throne in the decades that followed, and Ariana could only watch in growing frustration as the beloved empire of the two loves of her life started to crumble around the edges under the increasingly ineffective and weak rule of the Ottoman government. By the time the Great Turkish War ended at the dawn of the eighteen century, large territories previously seized during long and bloody battles had been reclaimed by their European enemies.

Kader died in 1710, after falling from a horse and breaking his neck. When Ariana realized he would not wake again, as she so easily could, she wept for weeks; the realization that she had fifteen lives remaining and would likely be walking the Earth well after the deaths of all her children felt like purgatory. But Kader left behind a son and a daughter, and one grandchild. Two of them inherited the powers of her immortal ancestry.

After the fall of the Ottoman Empire, Ariana sat down with the progeny of Mustafa's and Branimir's bloodlines, as well as the generals of her flourishing army, all of whom were descendants of those who had pledged their loyalty to her and Mustafa's heir almost one and a half centuries previously. They spent months analyzing the changing landscape of power, politics, and economics across Europe, Asia, North Africa, and the Americas before finally deciding on a master strategy.

The next hundred years saw her lineage and that of their

faithful followers expand their reach across six continents and gradually accumulate the wealth, knowledge, and influence they would one day need to take back the lands that had been lost, and build a greater and more formidable Ottoman Empire— one that would have the world quaking in fear.

But it wasn't until the technological and scientific advances of the latter half of the twentieth century that the last pieces of their battle plan could be finalized. By then, they had enough assets to buy off several African countries, and their army counted almost a quarter of a million in number.

At the birth of the twenty-first century, only Zoran and Nadica remained of Mustafa's bloodline. Though they were cousins, they had been raised as siblings from an early age. They were the seventh generation to be born after Kader, and their thirst for power and justice more than matched Ariana's.

She looked up from her silent contemplation when Zoran spoke.

'If the immortals are helping the Americans, then they are likely to become a problem,' he observed.

'That's why we have a contingency plan,' Ariana said in a deadly voice. She had not come this close to achieving her dreams to have them snatched by the immortals. 'If they will not listen to reason when the time comes, then I will bury them so deep into the ground it will take them months to climb out of the hole.'

Nadica moved restlessly at her words. 'I think we should do it anyway. A preemptive strike will show them how serious we are.'

Ariana watched the young woman for a moment. Of the last two descendants of Mustafa's bloodline, Nadica was the one who had inherited the sadistic savagery of some of the most fearsome Ottoman rulers. Ariana was confident she had made the right choice by selecting Zoran to be the first ruler of their new empire. He possessed the same coolness of head Mustafa and Branimir had been blessed with; Nadica would make an excellent general and second in command.

'We shall see,' Ariana murmured finally. 'In the meantime, I think the trial run Ridvan suggested seems more than appropriate.'

'What of Kadir and Sahin?' said Zoran.

'Our lawyers should be able to get them out of French police custody,' said Ariana. She shrugged. 'If not, they will be more than happy to sacrifice themselves for our cause. They are devoted to their ancestry.'

Ridvan Kadir and Volkan Sahin were but two of hundreds of descendants of the original members of Mahidevran's court in Amasya.

Zoran rose from the couch and crossed the room to a desk holding a sleek laptop. He ran his fingers over the keyboard. A digital map of the world appeared on the wall monitor. Multiple dots flashed across several continents. A third were on yellow, indicating final preparations were still in progress at those sites.

'The most suitable target would be location 10. Though small-scale, its destruction will have an impact in terms of political and economic disruption for Central Europe.' His lips curved in a humorless smile. 'It will no doubt shock and scare them.'

Ariana stared at the city in question. 'What would the estimated death toll be?'

Zoran tapped a key and studied the table hovering over the map. 'Inside the strike zone? About four thousand to six thousand. Maybe more depending on the extent of the damage.'

Ariana pursed her lips. 'Make the arrangements,' she ordered after a short silence.

Nadica grinned, her eyes gleaming with savage glee.

'MAXIMILIAN OBENHAUS JUST SENT US A PICTURE OF THE EX-company director who went by the name of Zoran Rajkovic. It was taken at a social event held in Berlin several years ago.'

It was seven thirty in the evening, and the Learjet was still parked on the tarmac at Orly Airport.

'He believes someone hacked into the Obenhaus Group's network and erased all photographic documentation pertaining to Rajkovic from their database, including his human resources file,' Connelly continued. She was talking to them privately from a locked cubicle inside the Sit Room. 'He managed to find this single snapshot through a friend at a German news agency.' A grim smile crossed the face of the Director of National Intelligence. 'I think you'll agree it makes for interesting viewing.'

A JPEG file materialized on the computer display next to the video link. Conrad opened it.

'Shit,' Anatole muttered woodenly.

Three arresting figures dressed in expensive evening wear and holding champagne glasses stood next to each other in the middle of the frame. The man in the center was tall and striking, with bronzed skin and sharply defined Slavic features dominated by piercing, slate-gray eyes. He was smiling faintly.

The two women draped on his arms were equally stunning, with ivory complexions, ruby lips, and silver eyes. They could have been sisters.

The one on the left was their suspect from the FedEx Field, Crystal City, and more recently Paris. The second woman was the seated figure who had featured in Ridvan Kadir's childhood photograph.

Conrad clenched his jaw as he stared at the screen. The enemy finally had a face.

'Anyone hazard a guess as to who the immortal is?' Connelly asked in a derisive tone. ''Cause I sure can't tell. From what Victor told me, the human half-breeds previously encountered by the Crovirs visibly aged by about a year for every five to ten years of real time that they actually lived. Their aging process apparently slows from the onset of adulthood.'

Conrad studied the faces in the picture. 'It's the woman from Ridvan Kadir's school picture,' he said quietly.

'I agree,' murmured Anatole.

'So do I,' said Laura.

'How can you be so certain?' said Connelly, her tone skeptical.

'Her eyes are old,' replied Conrad. 'Only an immortal who has lived through centuries of hardship could have that look. From her appearance, I would put her at 460 to 500 years old.' He paused. 'She's in the prime of her existence.'

Connelly observed him blankly for a moment. She blew out a sigh. 'Jesus, Greene. There are times when I forget what you guys are. She doesn't look a day older than you.'

Conrad hesitated. 'I was born three years before Prince Mustafa's death.'

Connelly blanched. 'So Victor is—?'

'A lot older and wiser than me,' Conrad interrupted. He leaned impatiently across the table. 'Put all their shots out to the media. Let's see what we get. We take off for Washington within the hour.'

∼

PART THREE: VELOCITY

CHAPTER TWENTY-FOUR

THE NEXT PIECE OF THE PUZZLE CAME FROM AN UNEXPECTED source.

Somewhere over the North Atlantic, Conrad awoke to someone gently shaking his shoulder. He opened his eyes and blinked groggily at Laura's shadowy shape.

'Hey,' she said softly. 'Donaghy just called. She's got something for us.'

Conrad glanced at his watch. Three hours had passed since they left Paris. It was almost midnight, continental time.

Shortly after they lifted off, he had ordered the two immortals and the Secret Service agent to get some rest. Despite his strict instructions, it had taken him a while to drop off to sleep, his head too full of the day's events to be able to relax. He stifled a yawn and stretched his shoulders.

Laura's face grew thoughtful. She glanced furtively to where Anatole and Stevens slept at the rear of the cabin, grabbed the front of Conrad's shirt, leaned down, and kissed him hard.

Conrad's eyes slammed wide open before drooping half-closed. He made an inarticulate noise at the back of his throat, curled his fingers around her nape, and deepened the kiss.

Laura melted in his hold. 'Okay!' she gasped seconds later. She pulled back sharply. 'I think you're awake now!'

Conrad groaned and tried to quell the tide of lust sweeping through his body. 'Shit,' he whispered, knuckles whitening on the armrests, 'I really want to—'

'Trust me,' Laura murmured, 'nothing would give me greater pleasure than ripping your clothes off and testing out the tensile strength of this chair, but I'm afraid Harry might need therapy afterward.' She smiled and leaned in. 'You never were a morning person,' she said in a throaty voice. 'I recall having to do some terribly wicked things to wake you at times.'

Her breath in his ear raised goosebumps along his skin.

She has to be doing this deliberately, Conrad thought achingly. The playful light in her eyes was almost his undoing. He did his best to suppress the torrid memories her words evoked and crossed the aisle to the table holding the onboard computer. He brought up the White House link while she roused the two sleeping men.

'Hi,' said Donaghy on the screen. The CIA agent was in the seat usually occupied by the Director of National Intelligence. 'Connelly's upstairs with Westwood and the Joint Chiefs,' she explained at Conrad's questioning look. 'Looks like DEFCON 3 is seriously on the table. The North Koreans are making some pretty aggressive tactical maneuvers in the Sea of Japan.'

Anxiety twisted through Conrad's gut. This was the last piece of news he wished to hear.

'Anyway, reason I'm calling is because of that little stunt Connelly and you decided to pull with the suspects' photographs.' Donaghy grimaced. 'You won't believe the number of crazies coming out of the woodwork since we showed those to the media,' the CIA agent continued in a faintly accusing tone. 'One name came up that we felt warranted immediate attention.' She cocked a thumb to something on her left. 'From the big-ass digital flowchart on the wall monitor, I gathered the explosive engineering experts Connelly and you talked to earlier today mentioned a Professor Svein Hagen during their video call. Well, guess what? I have a Dawn Hagen on the line at the moment from London. She's the professor's only surviving child and is a physics undergrad at Imperial College. She says she has some important information for us. Seems she tried Homeland first and couldn't get anyone to put her through. She called the White House directly in the end. We've run a background check. She's the real deal.'

Conrad glanced at the two immortals and the Secret Service agent gathered around him. They looked as mystified as he felt. 'Put her through,' he ordered quietly.

A second link blinked open on the display. The woman occupying the center of the frame looked to be in her early twenties and sported shoulder-length blonde hair streaked with red, and a solid, blue-eyed stare. Science posters dotted the stark walls of the university lodging behind her.

'Hi,' said Conrad.

Dawn Hagen blinked. 'Hello,' she responded curtly. 'Are you the man the CIA lady wanted me to talk to?'

'Yes. My name is Conrad Greene.'

Dawn Hagen narrowed her eyes at the camera. 'I saw the photographs the US government put out an hour ago. I recognize one of the women.'

Conrad's pulse ratcheted up a notch. He leaned forward tensely. 'Which one?'

'Your FedEx Field suspect. I remember her from the day my family had the accident in Hawaii, eight years ago.' Dawn Hagen's cheeks flushed with color. 'I was supposed to go with them on the trip we had scheduled that day, but I wasn't feeling well and stayed back at the hotel. Bridget was going to keep me company. I insisted she go.' A haunted look rose on her face. 'I knew how much she wanted to see the national park.'

'Bridget?' asked Conrad, puzzled.

'My twin sister,' she replied huskily. 'We were sixteen at the time.' Her expression slowly hardened. 'From the bits of conversation I heard between my father and that woman, it seemed it wasn't the first time he had spoken to her. They had a terrible argument outside the restaurant, when we were having breakfast.' Her lips pressed into a grim line. 'My father was not a man who lost his temper easily, Mr. Greene. I had never seen him so angry in my life. He shouted at her to stop harassing him or he would call the police. She left the hotel right after.' Her eyes darkened. 'She looked like she wanted to kill him.'

Conrad studied the grave young woman for silent seconds while he recalled what Professor Akihito Itaka had said about the Strabo Corp. data.

'Did anything related to your father's work ever go missing at the time?' he said finally. 'Were there any break-ins at his lab or disturbances at your home that might have suggested somebody had tried to—?'

'No,' she cut in. A troubled expression clouded her features. She chewed the inside of her cheek.

'What is it?' Conrad prompted gently.

Dawn Hagen hesitated for a moment. She appeared to come to a decision.

'I've already reported what I'm about to tell you to the authorities in the US, but they chose to ignore it,' she said in a brittle tone. She stared unflinchingly into the laptop's camera. 'I have always felt that my family is still alive, Mr. Greene. Don't ask me how; I just know they are. The psychologists who counseled me after the accident said this feeling was survivor's guilt. A couple of years later, I was prescribed antipsychotics because they believed I was crazy.' A muscle twitched near her jawline. She took a deep breath. 'Thirteen months ago, I received an email from an account I didn't recognize. It went to my junk folder and I almost deleted it. But something made me stop and open that message.' Her shoulders lifted in a shrug. 'Call it a sixth sense.'

'What was in the email?' said Conrad.

'The first part was pretty self-explanatory. It said "We're alive, SH, Morocco." It was followed by three numbers.' Dawn Hagen frowned. 'The message was incomplete. I believe it was sent in haste.' A bitter expression twisted her features. 'I gave this information to the FBI and Homeland Security. They promised they would look into it. They never did.' She moved closer to the monitor at her end, her eyes gleaming in the light reflecting off the screen. 'That email was sent by my father, Mr. Greene. I would bet my life on it.'

Conrad stared at her, his mind racing with the possible implications of this fresh revelation.

'I believe you,' he said at last, his own conviction crystallizing as the words fell from his lips.

Dawn Hagen paled. Tears pooled in her eyes. She bowed her head and whispered, 'Thank you.'

'Can you forward that email to us?' Conrad requested in a soft voice.

She jerked her head in a nod. Five minutes later, they were staring at the email Dawn Hagen had received.

'She's right,' muttered Laura. 'Without the complete information, we have nothing to go on.'

Stevens started pacing the cabin.

'Do you guys really believe this stuff?' The agent's eyes reflected his growing incredulity. 'That the accident in Hawaii eight years ago was somehow a fake? That this professor and his family didn't die? I mean, why go that far? Also, what happened to his wife and daughter?' He blew out a frustrated sigh. 'Christ, what's to say this girl's not actually making this stuff up like the authorities probably suspected. She could be leading us on a wild goose chase!'

Donaghy pulled a face in the silence that followed. The CIA agent had stayed online while they spoke with Dawn Hagen. 'He's kinda got a point there, Greene.'

Conrad observed the two agents for silent seconds. The more he thought about it, the more what Dawn Hagen had asserted made sense. A professor in chemistry and macromolecular science with expertise in explosives engineering would be the ideal person to create a new bomb.

'Considering what these people have done to date, it wouldn't surprise me if they orchestrated that car crash,' said the immortal finally. 'Svein Hagen's research into explosives was obviously of great interest to them. If they couldn't persuade him to join them of his own free will, it seems logical they would resort to kidnapping him.' He pulled a face. 'We are after all talking about some seriously deranged minds here.'

'From the way his daughter described his interaction with that woman, I doubt Svein Hagen would have helped them if he was on his own,' Laura concurred. 'But if they were holding his wife and child hostage...'

'Still, that's a helluva speculation,' said Donaghy. 'And eight years is a long time. Even if we assume your supposition to be correct, what's to say they're still alive?'

'We believe the enemy we're facing has been around for some time,' said Conrad. He chose his words carefully; the only members of their team who knew of the immortals were Connelly and Stevens. 'What we're currently seeing are the key stages of a plan that may have been set in motion several decades ago.' He bit back a sigh. 'And you're right, Donaghy. Dawn Hagen's family could very well be dead. But I think they will be kept alive until the final act plays out, whatever that may be. It's what I would do if I were in the enemy's shoes.'

Stevens's shoulders drooped. 'Jesus,' he murmured in a dejected tone. 'Do we really have a chance against these—?'

'Don't give me that bullshit, Harry!' snapped Laura. 'The Service trained you better than this!' She glared at Stevens. The latter flushed a dull red.

Anatole patted him on the shoulder. 'Hang in there, kid. You haven't *really* seen us in action yet,' the immortal said with a dangerous glint in his pale eyes.

'Did you get any other leads from the pictures we put out?' Conrad asked Donaghy.

The CIA agent shook her head. 'Nope. None that seem relevant at the moment, anyway.'

Conrad rubbed his chin reflectively. 'How about the email Dawn Hagen sent through? Think you could trace the source?'

Donaghy looked doubtful. 'We can try, but I'm not promising anything.'

'Okay,' Conrad said. 'Let us know if anything else comes up.'

'Will do,' Donaghy replied. Her gaze shifted. 'Vassili, we still on for that drink?'

Conrad blinked, nonplussed.

'Honey, if the world hasn't ended in the next few days, I shall take you to this little place I know in New York and treat you to the most delicious Cosmopolitan you have ever tasted in your life,' Anatole drawled with a wicked grin. 'I'm hoping it will rob you of more than just your inhibitions.'

Claire Donaghy shook her head and chuckled. 'You're such an ass.' She grinned. 'I'll bring the gun in case you don't deliver on that promise.'

Anatole laughed. The window winked close. Stevens stared at the immortal, slack-jawed. Laura looked amused.

'Since when do you go out with CIA agents?' Conrad blurted out.

'Since none of your beeswax,' Anatole replied. The tips of his ears reddened.

Conrad gazed silently at his friend. Though he had never

lacked lovers in the centuries that Conrad had known him, Anatole had yet to find his soulmate, a common state of affairs for many immortals since the plague that decimated their numbers in the fourteenth century and rendered most survivors infertile. Conrad had never known him to date a human. Claire Donaghy's forceful personality had obviously made an impression.

He shook his head and drummed his fingers on the table, his mind returning to their current predicament. 'What time is it in Cleveland?'

Laura looked at her watch. 'Six thirty in the evening. Why?' she asked, puzzled.

'I think we should talk to Akihito Itaka,' Conrad replied pensively.

The Case Western professor was in the middle of dinner when they phoned. Conrad waited while he transferred the call to his study.

'I'm sorry for disturbing you, but I have an urgent question,' said the immortal.

'It's alright,' said Itaka over the cabin speakers. 'What can I do for you?'

'You mentioned earlier that the data we showed you contained strong elements of Professor Svein Hagen's work, correct?'

'Yes, I did,' affirmed Itaka.

'What I'm about to tell you also falls under the heading of secrecy that Director Connelly explained to you earlier today,' warned Conrad.

There was a thoughtful lull. 'Okay,' said Itaka cautiously.

'I just spoke to Dawn Hagen, Svein Hagen's surviving daughter,' said Conrad. 'She's convinced her family is still alive.'

Itaka inhaled sharply. 'How—?'

'She received an email from an unknown computer server

about a year ago,' Conrad interjected. 'She believes it was from her father.' The immortal hesitated, wondering how much he should reveal to the scientist. 'The content suggested he might be somewhere in North Africa.'

Itaka's gasp was audible across the connection.

'My God,' the Cleveland professor whispered. There was a faint thump and a squeak of wheels, as if he had sat down heavily in a chair.

'My question is simple: if Hagen is alive, could the data you saw be his work?' asked Conrad. '*Could* the new explosive have been made by him?'

A long silence followed.

Conrad straightened in his seat. 'Professor Itaka?' he said sharply.

'I'm here,' came the quiet reply. 'Yes. If Svein was alive, that could very well be his work.'

Conrad released the breath he had been holding. He had suspected as much. 'Thank you,' he said quietly. He bade the professor goodnight and disconnected.

A small frown wrinkled Laura's brow. 'What now?'

Conrad ran a hand through his hair, his head churning with the astonishing revelations of the last twelve hours. 'I don't know.' He sighed. 'We've followed all the leads we've had so far. It'll be up to our intelligence network to come up with the next clue.'

His words proved unerringly prophetic. He was still awake and gazing meditatively out of the porthole next to his seat when they got a phone call from West Virginia.

'Hey, it's Franklin here.'

Conrad recognized the NSA agent's voice over the Learjet's cabin speakers. 'Hi, Franklin,' he greeted. 'What's up?'

'I'm outside Charleston, at the headquarters of the firm that owns the MD helicopter from the Crystal City incident,' said the NSA agent. Static crackled faintly on the line. 'Petersen had apparently already cleared them. We were in the area, so we came to take a second look. Call it a gut instinct. Anyhow, turns out they operate hydraulic equipment manufacturing plants across several states. We're talking pretty large-scale stuff, Greene. Their clients feature among the biggest names in the oil and gas, offshore drilling, shipbuilding, and mining industries in the world. Anyway, they'd closed shop by the time we got here. One of their employees was a bit lax when it came to shutting down his computer. We found some financial records dating back to 1990 that show substantial holes in their accounting figures. Guess what?'

Conrad could almost hear the smile in Franklin's voice.

'It seems they've secretly been providing equipment to an oil and gas production facility in Morocco. The orders we've seen are on a massive scale,' said the NSA agent.

Conrad exchanged stunned glances with the immortals and the Secret Service agent. 'Morocco? Are you sure?' he asked sharply.

'Yeah,' said Franklin. 'The shipments were originally addressed to offshore drilling sites in the Middle East. They never made it to their destinations.' The agent paused. 'Sorry, Greene,' he continued in an apologetic tone, 'but this oil company's name didn't come up when we were searching for links to the Strabo Corp. board of directors. We had to dig through a shitload of bureaucratic red tape and I'm pretty certain I heard one of my agents promise her first newborn to the Moroccan authorities before they would give us a name. The outfit is called Khan Inc. It's owned by an Ariana Muhlisi Khan.'

Conrad saw the shocked looks dawning on the others' faces.

'It's all right Franklin, you've done a great job,' he said, unable to hide the urgency in his voice. 'Have you got an address for us?'

The NSA agent chuckled. 'I've got even better. Seeing that the site is in the middle of bloody nowhere, the Moroccans kindly provided us with the GPS coordinates. I'll send them through to Hartwell.'

Laura's phone beeped with an alert five minutes later. She tapped the screen and opened the new email. A gasp left her lips when she read the message.

'What?' said Conrad, alarmed.

'Dawn Hagen was right.' Laura stepped to the onboard computer and brought up a satellite map. 'That number she received in that email a year ago? It was the beginning of a set of geographic coordinates.' She typed in a series of numbers and stood back, her face hardening. 'Her father's in Morocco.'

They stared at the complex of lights etched starkly against a dark, desert background on the monitor. A thrill of excitement shot through Conrad. He detected the same nervous energy rising in the others. He stood and strode to the cockpit.

'Change of plans,' Conrad told the pilot.

Three hours later, they were on the ground at a military airport in southwest Morocco. It was four thirty in the morning in northwest Africa. A cold wind struck Conrad's face as he exited the aircraft. He glanced at the tiny sand devils whirling on the tarmac before studying a hulking shape some fifty feet away. The plane had taxied next to a gunmetal-gray, MV-22 tilt-rotor Osprey helicopter.

Conrad led the way down the cabin steps and jogged across to the two figures standing in the shadow of one of the prop rotors of the vertical takeoff and landing aircraft. He looked at the rank insignia pinned to the collars of the soldiers' utility uniforms and offered his hand to the woman with dark hair and green eyes. 'Hi. Conrad Greene.'

'First Lieutenant Avery, platoon commander, US AFRICOM,' she said perfunctorily and shook his hand. 'This is Moore, my staff sergeant.'

Conrad acknowledged the stocky blond man next to her with a curt nod and introduced the rest of his team.

US AFRICOM was the Unified Combatant Command of the United States Armed Forces in Africa. As such, it was responsible for all US Department of Defense operations, military exercises, and security relations on the continent.

It was yet another credit to Connelly's influence that she had managed to get the Secretary of Defense and the Combatant Commander to agree to the deployment of a US Marine Corps platoon to support Conrad and his team on their last-minute mission to the African continent. Westwood had also spoken to the Moroccan king and the country's prime minister to apprise them of the potentially explosive situation about to be played out.

The staff sergeant grabbed a couple of duffel bags by his feet and handed them to Conrad. 'These are yours.'

They changed into the uniforms and tactical gear the Marines had provided and boarded the Osprey. The helicopter lifted off a short time later.

Khan Inc. was located in the Tindouf Basin, in Moroccan-controlled Western Sahara. The oil and gas plant occupied a strategic position on a remote stretch of desert hedged on three sides by wide belts of folded rocks that spread for miles across the land. It was a considerable distance from any human habitation or highway infrastructure, and accessible by a narrow road that wound through wide stretches of inhospitable wasteland.

Avery's ground intelligence officer, a young corporal by the name of Gibbs, showed them the infrared satellite imagery and topographic data he had obtained from their geospatial intelligence.

'The compound is around three-quarters of a mile in length and about as wide. It's surrounded by a double-fenced perimeter and divided into three distinct zones,' he said into the microphone of his communication headset. 'Zone One is the largest section, to the north. It's the heart of the production facility and houses the drilling wells, processing plant, and storage tanks. Zone Two to the southwest is the living quarters. Zone Three to the east has a range of small outbuildings, a helipad, and an administrative office.' He pointed out the three areas on the computer on his lap. 'They've got pipes bringing in water from local aquifers outside the site.' He tapped the touch pad and zoomed out of the main satellite image. 'We've also identified these large belts of disturbed ground some two miles northwest of the site. They look like explosive craters of some sort.'

Conrad's stomach flipped at the soldier's words. 'Are you sure?' He stared at the irregular, gray depressions on the screen.

'Yes,' replied Gibbs.

Avery's brow puckered at Conrad's expression. 'What is it?'

The immortal glanced at her, a muscle dancing in his cheek. 'The man we're hoping to find at this facility is a professor in explosives engineering. We believe he's been coerced into making a new and exceedingly powerful liquid bomb for the enemy.' He cocked his head at the computer. 'I think we're looking at their test site.'

Avery went still. Her staff sergeant squared his shoulders next to her. The Osprey's rotors rumbled loudly in the stilted hush.

'What about security?' said Laura.

Gibbs's gaze moved back to the computer. 'We've counted five posts,' replied the corporal. 'One at each of the four corners of the compound, which includes the main gates to the northeast, and one in the center.'

'We'll drop off in a valley about a mile and a half west of the target,' said Avery. She indicated the spot on the satellite map. 'These ridges should shield us from curious eyes. We'll hike to the site on foot.' Her lips compressed into a thin line, just visible in the gloom of her helmet. 'We'll have approximately seventy minutes of darkness left in which to take action. Sunrise is at zero six forty.'

'We have a small, unmanned aerial vehicle on board,' added Gibbs. 'It'll give us more recon details after we land.'

Anatole raised his eyebrows. 'You've got a drone? Cool.'

CHAPTER TWENTY-FIVE

THE OSPREY CURVED SOME FIFTEEN MILES WEST OF THE
plant before winding toward it over an expanse of windswept,
undulating desert. The aircraft soon dropped altitude and
followed a tortuous path along an ancient riverbed.

Conrad gazed blindly at the low outcrops and narrow
canyons of prehistoric rock materializing through the nearest
porthole as the helicopter weaved through a barren landscape
lit by the stars and the moon. Dawn Hagen's face kept flashing
across his vision. His hands balled into fists in the dark interior
of the aircraft. He hoped to God that his gut feeling turned out
to be correct and that he would find her family alive.

Thirty-five minutes after they lifted off, the Osprey twisted
down and landed in a shallow bowl in the floor of the desert.
They exited the helicopter while its blades still spun above their
heads, whipping sand and dust around them. Stars painted the
heavens diamond-bright, and a cold desert wind raised goosebumps on exposed skin.

The Marines rapidly set up the ground control unit for the
UAV and deployed the hand-launched device a short distance

from the aircraft. They all gathered around the GCU computer. A real-time, thermal infrared video appeared on the display.

The lightweight aircraft followed the same path they would take over the land. A thousand-foot-wide gully unfurled over a ridge. Lights appeared in the center of the screen, faint at first, then brightening flares in a monochrome background.

The UAV made its first wide-angled pass over the facility. The security hut at the southwest corner of the inner perimeter fence came into view. The living quarters appeared eighty feet beyond it, a collection of one-story cabins and static mobile homes arranged in orderly rows on either side of a courtyard dominated by two larger constructions.

The UAV curved to the north. Conrad stared at the dazzling constellation of Khan Inc.'s main production plant as it grew rapidly in the distance. Oil derricks loomed among a conglomeration of flare stacks, pipes, and tanks; a metal maze sprouting from the desert. Despite the late hour, there were still workers visible on the ground and metal walkways connecting the various structures. The nightshift was in full swing.

The UAV looped half a mile ahead of the compound and turned to make its second approach. It swooped over the brightly lit main gates, the helipad, and the cluster of buildings to the east.

'They've got plenty of guards,' commented Avery.

Conrad frowned. The UAV's camera had picked out at least two men at each of the security stations, with an extra two at the main site entrance. He detected three more figures, armed with what looked like automatic rifles, patrolling the inner perimeter to the north, south, and east.

'If these guys are just the nightshift, we can assume there are that many, if not more, currently off duty on site,' said Moore.

Conrad turned to the ground intelligence officer. 'Can we take a look at those areas you identified to the northwest?'

'Sure,' said Gibbs. He gave the Marine operating the UAV fresh instructions.

The soldier looked down into the flight module and maneuvered the remote control stick by his right hand. The lightweight aircraft changed course once more and shot over the darkened landscape, a silent bullet speeding through the night.

The first of a dozen massive depressions appeared on the terrain moments later.

'Holy cow,' murmured the platoon staff sergeant. 'What the hell have they been doing?'

Conrad's gaze did not shift from the gigantic craters disrupting the natural contours of the desert sand and rock. Dismay flooded him when the last one came into view. It measured well over two football pitches in size and looked almost half as deep.

The UAV swung around and started back toward the plant. Troubled murmurs sounded from the assembled Marines.

'Hagen's made one hell of a powerful explosive,' muttered Anatole.

Conrad suddenly froze. 'Stop!' he barked.

Gibbs and Avery looked at him, alarmed. The Marines shifted, their grasps tightening on their M16 rifles.

'Can you go back?' Conrad asked the UAV operator tensely. 'I think I saw something.'

The Marine steered the aircraft out of its return trajectory and back toward the craters.

'Come in again from the west,' Conrad directed, his eyes glued to the GCU display.

They watched the desert unroll through the IR camera.

'There!' Conrad exclaimed. 'At ten o'clock!'

'What the—?' started Moore.

The UAV angled to the northeast. The faint flare of brightness the immortal had glimpsed became more distinct. They watched silently as the aircraft dropped altitude and circled what appeared to be a contoured rise in the land.

'Son of a bitch,' Avery said in a leaden tone. 'That's clever.'

Conrad's stomach knotted. Carefully camouflaged under a solid layer of black rock was a low-lying, dark building. Narrow windows were inset deep into its west-facing wall, under an irregular overhang that effectively made them invisible to high-flying aircrafts. There were no windows on the other walls.

The only way someone would spot the openings would be to approach the site on foot from the west, over miles of open desert and rocky terrain. A dim light had been left on somewhere inside the structure. It was the faint reflection on a glass pane that had drawn Conrad's attention.

'Well spotted,' said the platoon staff sergeant gruffly.

Conrad remained silent. Sixty years in the rainforest had sharpened his senses. There were many things willing and able to kill you in the Amazon if you didn't pay attention. A single question now dominated the immortal's thoughts, surpassing even his concern for Svein Hagen and his family.

What's inside that building?

'Ready to deploy?' Avery asked.

Conrad looked around. The Marines stood silently watching their platoon commander and him, automatic weapons and rifles at the ready.

Anticipation tightened the immortal's muscles. They were drawing closer to the truth; he could feel it in his bones. 'Yes. Let's go.'

They set off briskly in a westerly direction. The Osprey's pilots and flight engineers remained at the landing site, along with the two soldiers manning the UAV and the GCU; the drone would remain airborne during their operation. Despite having to cross a canyon and climb an incline, it took them just over ten minutes to get to within seven hundred feet of the facility's outer perimeter fence.

Moore had supplied Conrad's team with head-mounted, enhanced night vision devices employing the latest in multi-spectral fusion technology. The Marines had similar monocular scopes fixed to their helmets and mounted on rails atop their rifles.

Conrad experimented with the toggles on the device as they covered the uneven terrain. By the time he sank to the desert floor next to Avery, he had started to get accustomed to viewing the world in the faint green, phosphorus light of the image enhancement, as well as the black and white screen of the thermal imager through his non-dominant eye. Stevens was not faring as well; he had already stumbled twice.

'Target closing in, seven hundred feet and eighty degrees to the left,' said the platoon scout sniper quietly through his throat mike a short distance away. The Marine gazed steadily through the integrated infrared laser rangefinder on his rifle-scope, his finger on the trigger guard.

Conrad turned his head and adjusted his night vision device to fuse the thermal imager with the low-light image enhancement. The guard's figure became a crisp, bright shape in an eerie background.

The man was smoking a cigarette and strolling casually alongside the inner fence toward the southwest corner of the compound. He passed under one of the security lights mounted on tall steel posts positioned at four hundred feet intervals along the perimeter.

Conrad's gaze shifted to the security hut. He saw the head of a single guard through the glass window. A background light fluctuated against the walls above the man; he was watching TV.

'Ready for the decoy?' murmured Avery beside him.

Conrad took a deep breath and rose into a low, starting-block position. He glanced to his right. Laura, Anatole, and

Stevens were also up in crouches. The immortal nodded at Avery.

'Go for decoy,' the platoon commander ordered into her communication headset.

The scout sniper fired a single shot at the security light behind the ambling guard. The suppressor screwed on the end of the Marine's M16 rifle silenced the sound and muzzle-flash of the discharge.

The bulb burst with a low crack of breaking glass. Shadows deepened over a hundred-foot-wide circle across the ground. The guard stopped in his tracks, cigarette frozen halfway to his lips. He looked over his shoulder and hesitated, before turning and heading back toward the fresh pool of darkness.

A thrill coursed through Conrad. Their attempt at misdirection had worked.

'In three,' warned Avery.

Conrad's pulse jumped.

'One, two, *three!*' hissed Avery.

Conrad bolted across the ground toward the security perimeter with the two immortals and the Secret Service agent.

During their flight in the Osprey, Conrad and the platoon commander had decided that his team of four would infiltrate the facility first to try and determine the location of the missing professor and his family. Although Avery had initially been less than keen on the idea, her staff sergeant had advised her to agree to Conrad's suggestion. The Marines would only intervene if the Hagens could not be extracted without drawing the attention of the security guards.

They dropped down by the outer chain-link fence. Rolls of barbwire topped the ten-foot-high barrier. They had decided to go through it rather than over it.

Anatole and Stevens used small wire cutters to create a man-sized breach at the bottom of the fencing. They rolled the three-sided section up, crawled through the narrow opening, and pinned the cut edge to the sand-covered dirt with hooked tent stakes.

Conrad glanced to the left. The guard had reached the broken light. He was staring at the glass on the ground. They crossed the twelve-foot gap to the inner fence and repeated their procedure. Less than ninety seconds after the scout sniper had shot the security light, Conrad and the others were inside Khan Inc. They melted into the shadows and raced toward the southwest corner of the compound.

The security post was housed inside a small concrete structure with a single door to the south and two windows, one to the east and another to the west. The blare of the TV reached Conrad's ears as they closed in on the hut. He backed up against the wall, flicked up his night vision device, and peeked through the west-facing window.

The guard was sitting on a swivel chair with his back to them. His feet were up on a table and his eyes were glued to the small TV in front of him. He threw his head back and laughed at something on the screen.

Conrad signaled to the others and dropped to a squat. He scuttled beneath the window ledge and stopped at the corner of the building. Light washed across the ground to his left from the doorway. He located a suitably sized piece of rock and tossed it some ten feet in front of the opening. The rock thudded dully onto the ground. Conrad glanced over his shoulder.

Stevens peered through the window and shook his head. Conrad bit back a curse. The guard had not heard the sound.

Avery's voice came over the immortal's headset. 'You have twenty-five seconds before the second guard reaches you,' she warned.

'Copy that,' Conrad murmured into his throat mike. He looked around and grabbed another rock. He was about to throw it when he saw Anatole gesture from the other side of the doorway, where he lurked in the shadows alongside the building. Conrad hesitated and looked past the immortal. Laura shrugged behind Anatole. Conrad sighed and nodded once.

Anatole grinned. He raised his gun and fired twice. The bullets left the suppressor silently and struck the rock with sharp pings. It skipped noisily across the ground.

Conrad looked to Stevens. The agent flicked his thumb up. They heard the squeak of wheels as the guard shifted in his chair. Boots thudded to the ground. A shadow blocked the light coming through the door.

Conrad tensed as the guard took several steps outside, a rifle clasped in his grip. Anatole came up behind the man, clamped a hand over his mouth, and struck the back of his head with the butt of his pistol. The guard went down soundlessly, his gun falling at his feet.

Anatole hefted the unconscious figure up under the shoulders while Laura grabbed the man's legs. They hauled him away and melted into the night. Conrad and Stevens raced past the open door to the other side of the building.

Shuffling footsteps rose from the direction of the inner fence. The second guard had reached the security hut.

'Hey, one of the lights broke,' he started to say in French as he came around the corner. He stopped in the open doorway. 'Khaled?' he said in a puzzled voice.

The jingling music of an ad break on the TV was the only response he received in the lull that followed. Conrad waited tensely in the shadows a few feet away.

'The bastard. He must have gone for a piss,' the guard finally muttered under his breath. He twisted on his heels and walked a few feet toward the fence. A scratching noise sounded as he struck a match and lit another cigarette.

He had barely inhaled when Conrad rose from the darkness and closed his forearm in a vice-like grip around his throat. The guard choked, his cigarette falling to the sand. A strangled gurgle left his lips. The fingers of his right hand dug into Conrad's skin as he reached blindly for the rifle slung across his chest.

Conrad kneed him sharply in the small of his back, yanked the firearm out of his reach, and released the chokehold. He struck the base of the man's neck sharply with the edge of his hand. The guard crumpled with a low grunt.

Conrad and Stevens restrained the man's wrists and ankles with nylon straps before carrying him some eighty feet to where the other guard lay, bound in the darkness behind one of the trailers. Anatole had taped the first man's eyes and mouth shut. They did the same with the second guard and divested them of their radios before returning to the security hut.

Conrad found what he was looking for on a clipboard hanging on the wall. It was a manifest of the staff accommodation. His heart slammed rapidly against his ribs as he ran a finger down the first page. He flicked it over. His hand stilled halfway along the second sheet. Relief flooded him.

'Hagen's in trailer 21,' he told the others.

Laura checked one of the guards' radios, communicated the bandwidth to Avery, and disabled the devices. The Marines would now be able to keep track of the enemy's movements while outside the facility.

They exited the hut and headed swiftly back to the living quarters. Laura lobbed the radios under a mobile home just as they entered the network of passages that separated the cabins and trailers. Small plaques gleamed on the corner rear walls of the lodgings, denoting their numbers. They swerved into the corridor between the first two lines of mobile homes and paused in the lee of a caravan.

'Hmm,' murmured Anatole. 'I anticipate a problem.'

Conrad frowned as he studied the courtyard fifteen feet ahead. It was bathed in the glow of six security lights.

According to his calculations, Hagen's living quarters were directly across the brightly lit space, facing onto the square.

Conrad increased the magnification on his night vision device and scanned the line of dark structures. His gaze stopped on a lime-green mobile home. 'Third one from the north,' he murmured.

They considered their approach. They could either cut across the courtyard or go around it to the north or south, steering clear of the lights. The path to the north would put them directly in the line of sight of the security station in the middle of the compound.

They went south and crossed the shadowy strip of land between the fence and the living quarters at a dead run, their boots drumming the sand with a faint patter. They turned the corner into the corridor between the first and second rows of trailer houses on the east side and skidded to the ground almost immediately.

Someone was leaning out of the window of a trailer some twenty feet ahead. The orange glow of a cigarette flared in the gloom and cast an eldritch light across the man's face as he sucked on the stick. They waited breathlessly in the darkness. Conrad glanced at the face of his watch. It was 05:53. He gritted his teeth. They had less than forty minutes left to find Hagen and his family, and get them out.

A faint clatter sounded in the night. The man had tossed the cigarette butt to the ground and was closing the window. They were on their feet a heartbeat later.

Hagen's mobile home soon came into view. Lights from the security station in the middle of the compound glowed some five hundred feet to the northeast.

They staggered to a halt with their backs against the trailer. Conrad studied the rear wall. Four dark windows faced their way. There was no way of opening them from the outside without alarming the people inside the trailer and alerting the sleepers in the adjacent caravans. They would have to go in through the front door.

'Anatole, eyes to the north,' Conrad instructed. 'Laura, you've got the courtyard. Stevens, come with me.'

Anatole faded into the darkness toward the first two trailers. Laura darted down the passage south of the mobile home, while Conrad and Stevens crept alongside the north. They stopped at the corner and scrutinized the brightly lit square fronting the mobile home.

'Clear on my end,' said Laura over the headset.

'Same here,' murmured Anatole. 'The chickens are in the coop.' The immortal's breath suddenly hitched over the comm line.

Conrad froze. 'What is it?' he hissed into his throat mike.

'Those bastards are having pizza!' Anatole replied in an affronted tone. 'I can see them through the scope!'

Conrad bit back a curse and heard Laura mutter something unsavory. He signaled to Stevens. They darted around to the trailer steps.

It took ten seconds to pick the lock on the door. The immortal was aware of how terribly exposed they were throughout that time. All they needed was for someone to look out of a window or step outside a caravan and their presence would be detected.

The door opened with the faintest of squeaks. They darted across the threshold and closed it behind them. Conrad flicked down the night vision device. The mobile home's interior became visible in his left eye.

They were faced with a sparsely decorated, open lounge and a kitchen diner. A corridor to the right led toward the rest of the trailer.

Conrad scanned the front room. His gaze landed on an object atop a side table next to the couch. He crossed the floor and picked up the discarded badge. A grim smile of satisfaction dawned on his lips as he studied the photograph on the ID.

'His daughter was right after all,' said Stevens in a low voice behind the immortal. 'They're still alive.'

They had found Svein Hagen.

CHAPTER TWENTY-SIX

CONRAD TURNED AND HEADED TOWARD THE NARROW hallway leading to the rear of the trailer. He walked past a closet and reached an unlocked door. An empty twin bedroom lay beyond. He frowned, glanced into the bathroom, and stepped to the last door. He tried the handle; it turned easily in his grip. He entered the room, Stevens on his heels.

A man lay asleep under a thin cotton sheet on the bed taking up most of the floor space. He was alone. Conrad scowled. He had assumed that the scientist's wife and daughter would be inside the mobile home with him. He stood still for a moment before gesturing to Stevens. The agent crossed the room and closed the drapes on the rear window.

Conrad walked to the bed and sat on the edge of the mattress. He placed his hand an inch above the sleeping man's mouth, leaned toward him, and flicked up his night vision device. He reached over and switched on the lamp on the table next to the bed.

'Mr. Hagen?' he said in a low voice.

The man's eyes snapped open. Pupils dilated in the blue expanse before constricting in the light. Conrad clamped his fingers over the man's mouth just as he started to scream and struggle.

'It's alright!' the immortal said hastily. 'Dawn sent us! We're with the US government!'

Svein Hagen froze.

'I'm going to take my hand away,' Conrad warned after a second.

Hagen nodded wildly. The immortal uncovered the man's mouth.

The professor sat up, his gaze swinging between the silent agent and the immortal. 'Who are—? How did—? I don't understand!' he stammered.

'We don't have a lot of time,' Conrad said urgently.

Hagen glanced at the clock on the bedside table. It was six in the morning.

'We're on the trail of a group of people who are behind the assassination of the Russian premier and the attempts on the lives of several other prominent heads of state, including the US president,' Conrad continued.

Hagen paled. 'Oh God,' he whispered. 'It's started.'

Conrad stared at the scientist and swallowed the questions rising in his throat. There would be time for that later, if they made it out of there in one piece.

'We found evidence of your work concerning a powerful new explosive on the database of a company in Paris,' he added. 'A Professor Itaka from Case Western pointed us in your direction.'

'Aki?' Hagen whispered in a dazed tone.

'I don't have time to go into details; suffice it to say that I spoke to your daughter, Dawn, and she explained her suspicions concerning your accident in Hawaii,' said Conrad. 'She got your email.'

Tears glistened in Hagen's eyes. 'How is—?'

Conrad suddenly raised a hand in warning, cutting off the professor; Anatole's voice had just come over the headset.

'There's a guard coming this way from the central post,' warned the immortal.

'I've got movement here as well,' whispered Laura. 'Someone just stepped out of a building in the courtyard.'

'From the chatter on the radio, it looks like an early change of shift,' said Moore. 'The rest of them will swap places at sunrise,' he cautioned.

Alarm tore through Conrad. 'Your wife and daughter, Bridget, where are they?' he asked Hagen hurriedly.

'They're being held in one of the outbuildings next to the admin office!' said the professor. He had climbed out of the bed and was changing hastily into jeans and a T-shirt. 'The others are there as well!'

Conrad went still. He exchanged a startled glance with Stevens.

'What others?' the immortal asked slowly.

Hagen explained. Twenty seconds later, Conrad swore.

'What's wrong?' Laura hissed over the headset.

'It looks like we have a more complex situation on our hands than previously anticipated,' Conrad replied bitterly. 'Avery, I think we're gonna need that back up. We have Svein Hagen, but there are four more hostages to rescue.'

'Four?' said the platoon commander sharply.

'Yes. Hagen's wife and daughter, a Professor Alison Williams, and a Dr. Ed Henderson. The last two were also kidnapped by these guys and are being forced to work for them.' Conrad glanced at the disheveled professor. 'I'll have Stevens bring Hagen to you. Laura, Anatole, and I will proceed to Zone Three. The other hostages are locked up in a building there.'

'I'm not leaving without my wife and daughter!' Hagen blurted, blue eyes blazing with a stubborn light.

Lines creased Conrad's brow. 'We haven't got time to argue, professor,' he said coldly. 'Besides, you'll only slow us down and place this entire operation in jeopardy.'

Hagen's hands curled into fists. He opened his mouth to retort. His protest died on his lips when Conrad froze.

'Shit!' Avery exclaimed in the immortal's ear. 'Something's up! There are a whole bunch of guards heading to the empty coop you guys cleared earlier! They know we're here!'

Conrad's stomach twisted. 'How?'

'It looks like they might have gotten a tip-off, Greene,' said Moore grimly over the headset. 'We can't track their chatter anymore. They just changed their communication channel.'

Conrad scowled. *The mole!* He didn't have time to dwell on the matter further. They had to get Hagen out of there. 'Let's go!' he snapped to Stevens.

They herded Hagen to the far wall of the trailer.

'Laura, Anatole, we're coming out the back!' Conrad barked into the throat mike.

Stevens opened the window and climbed over the sill. He landed lightly on his feet and helped Hagen down to the ground. Conrad joined the two men. Laura and Anatole crowded around them, weapons covering the dark passage. A faint light in the sky to the east signaled the imminent arrival of dawn. They had run out of time.

Conrad turned to the professor. 'Tell me exactly where they are!' he ordered in a low voice.

Hagen gave them the location of the prisoners, his voice stiff with fear but measured.

Conrad looked at Stevens. 'Think you can handle this?' he asked the agent.

A fierce smile stretched Stevens's lips. 'It'll be a walk in the park.'

'Please, save them,' Hagen whispered. He stared beseechingly at Conrad, his face ashen. 'They mean everything to me.'

Conrad hesitated. 'I'll do my best.'

Laura tapped Stevens lightly on the shoulder. 'Be safe, Harry. Your wife will kill me if I let anything happen to you.'

Stevens grinned. He faded into the darkness, the professor in tow. Conrad turned and headed east with the two immortals.

'He reminds me of William,' he said.

Laura glanced at him. 'I know,' she murmured. 'But he's not William.'

They had barely traveled two hundred feet from the living quarters when sudden shouts and the sharp cracks of automatic gunfire rose south of the compound. Conrad glanced over his shoulder. Lights were coming on in the trailers behind them. An alarm sounded from the direction of the production plant, the shrill sound tearing through the night.

'Avery?' Conrad hissed anxiously into his throat mike, boots pounding the ground as he sprinted toward the shadowy buildings in the distance.

'It's all right!' said the platoon commander. 'They spotted our two escaping friendlies. We're laying down cover fire!'

Relief rushed through the immortal at her words. His reprieve was to be short-lived.

'We've got company!' Laura barked to his right.

'Same here!' warned Anatole from the left.

Conrad glanced at the figures converging on them from the station to the southeast. In the opposite direction, the headlights of a Jeep cut through what remained of the night as the sentries from the main security post raced toward them. He made a swift calculation. From their numbers, it seemed all the guards inside the compound had been rallied to the cause.

'Anatole, you're rearguard!' Conrad shouted.

'Gotcha!' responded the immortal. He fell behind.

Conrad and Laura continued their desperate dash in the dark.

'This reminds me of the good old days!' she said, her breaths coming fast but steady.

Conrad glanced at her and saw teeth flash in the gloom. He smiled. Despite the dangers they faced, it felt good to be fighting with his soulmate at his side once more.

Bullets pelted the ground ahead of them. Another group of men was fast approaching from the north. Conrad raised the M16 rifle strapped across his chest and let loose a volley of shots. One of the figures staggered and fell to the ground.

The administration building loomed in front of them. Conrad spotted the lights of the helipad as they bolted into the cover of its rear wall. His gaze switched to the three smaller structures several hundred feet ahead.

Shadows shifted on his left. A shot whistled past his head. Laura dropped back and exchanged fire with the two men coming around the corner of the building.

An explosion ripped the air behind them. Conrad looked over his shoulder and saw the Jeep rolling to a slow stop, its hood ablaze. Guards were leaping out of the vehicle, their panicked screams audible over the roar of the flames. They fell under Anatole's bullets.

Conrad turned, his eyes focusing on the middle outbuilding. He reached it seconds later and tried the door. It was locked. He whipped out his handgun and shot at the metal insert beneath the handle.

There was movement to his right. Conrad's head whipped around. He dropped to the ground and barely avoided a spray of bullets as the guard who had been hiding behind the wall squeezed the trigger of his automatic weapon. The immortal rolled and brought his leg around in a sweeping kick that took his adversary to the ground. He straddled the guard's chest and punched him twice in the face before grabbing his head and slamming it repeatedly against the ground, a guttural snarl ripping from his throat. The man's eyes rolled back in his skull and he went limp.

Conrad rose to his feet just as Laura and Anatole reached his side.

'Cover me!' he yelled above the screaming siren from the production plant and the sharp reports of gunfire.

He was inside the outbuilding a heartbeat later. A dingy corridor stretched out ahead of him. A pale light streamed through a narrow window at the far end and outlined the row of cells to the left.

Three women shrank against the wall next to their cots, their faces ashen; their shoulders jerked in tandem to the shots blasting across the compound. A man pushed himself up shakily onto an elbow and blinked at the immortal.

Conrad's lips tightened when he saw the conditions inside the jailhouse. 'I'm with the US government! We've come to get you out of here!'

Shocked gasps echoed against the bare concrete. One of the women ran toward her cell door, her fingers closing around the bars in a white-knuckled grip. Conrad recognized Dawn Hagen's features in her thin, haggard face. The blonde woman in the next cell was an older version of her.

'Stand back!' Conrad ordered grimly.

He raised his gun and fired at the padlocks holding the cell doors close. A faint whimper escaped one of the women as the shots reverberated thunderously inside the enclosed space. The locks broke.

Conrad strode inside the cell where the man with the brown hair and eyes was swinging his legs to the floor. Tremors racked his frame as he leaned on the edge of the bed.

The immortal gazed at him in dismay. 'Dr. Henderson?'

'His wound is infected,' said a voice behind him. 'They shot him two days ago, when we tried to make a run for it.'

The woman who had spoken had dark hair and eyes the

color of a stormy sky. An ugly bruise discolored her jawline where she had been beaten. Conrad saw other bruises around her neck and on her exposed limbs. He took a shallow breath and suppressed the wave of rage threatening to overwhelm him.

The woman crossed the cell and crouched by the silent, trembling figure on the bed.

'Come on, Ed! We've got to go!' she urged and grabbed his arm.

Henderson looked up, sweat dampening his face. 'I don't think I can, Alison.' His accent was distinctly English. He winced and clutched his flank before looking past her shoulder to where the Hagen women stood watching them anxiously. 'Erica, take Bridget and go,' he whispered.

'Not without you,' Erica Hagen retorted in a hard voice.

Conrad knelt by the man's side and lifted his soiled shirt. Blood-soaked bandages circled Henderson's abdomen. The stench of infected flesh filled the cell. Henderson's skin was burning to the touch. The immortal wrapped his hand around the man's wrist.

The gunfire had abated outside. The alarm from the main plant still echoed shrilly across the compound. Footsteps sounded in the corridor. Laura appeared in the doorway of the cell.

'Avery's men are inside the compound. They have control of the site. Moroccan police and army are on their way.' She stopped, her eyes darkening when she saw the group gathered by the cot.

'He's septic,' Conrad explained grimly, answering the silent question in her anxious gaze. His fingers were on Henderson's thready pulse. 'He won't make it to the landing site.' He peeled off the dirty dressings and examined the gunshot wound in the man's flank with his left hand.

The bullet had ripped through Henderson's abdominal muscles and nicked his large intestine and the edge of his liver.

Whoever had dug out the shot had missed the small tear in the gut; peritonitis was setting in. Conscious of the watchful eyes of the Hagen women and Alison Williams, Conrad carefully let his healing powers loose.

'Avery, one of the hostages is injured,' Laura said into her throat mike. 'Any chance the Osprey can use the facility's helipad to evacuate all of them?'

'Sure,' replied the platoon commander over the headset.

By the time the helicopter landed inside the grounds of Khan Inc., the sun was a bright ball on the horizon.

Hot air washed over Conrad as he helped Henderson through the door of the jailhouse. Color was already returning to the man's cheeks, and his fever had started to subside. Although he was still weak from the infection, he was no longer at risk of dying. Alison Williams held Henderson on the other side, her arm wrapped around his waist. Conrad could not help but admire the woman's silent resilience.

They passed the admin building and saw the silent crowd assembled to the left. The plant's guards and staff had been rounded up in the middle of the compound. They sat on the desert floor, inside a ring of hard-faced Marines. Several of the workers looked scared and were crying. The majority bore mutinous expressions. Conrad suspected most were steadfast supporters of Ariana Muhlisi Khan.

Avery and the platoon's corpsman stood waiting under the Osprey's spinning blades. They jogged toward the small group approaching the aircraft.

Erica Hagen turned to Conrad. 'My husband?' she asked, fear making her voice tremble.

A shout erupted behind them before he could reply. They turned and saw Svein Hagen bolting across the compound from the south. The Hagen women stumbled toward the running man.

Stevens strolled a few dozen feet behind the scientist. Dirt and sand stained the agent's skin and clothes. He was smiling wearily.

'Glad to see you're still in one piece,' said Conrad when the agent was within earshot. They watched the Hagens embrace in a flood of laughter and tears.

'Like I said, a walk in the park,' muttered Stevens, satisfaction evident in his gleaming eyes.

A Puma helicopter from the Royal Moroccan Air Force descended on the site an hour later. It took the rest of the authorities another forty minutes to reach the desolate location over land. By then, the Osprey had also returned from ferrying the hostages to the Marines' military base a hundred and fifty miles away.

Conrad stepped out of the low-lying structure concealed under a blanket of black rock two miles northwest of the plant and looked up at the azure sky. They had already examined the explosive craters carved in the landscape some distance from the secret facility. As suggested by the UAV's images, the last one had proven the most alarming of all. Despite the blazing heat of the day, the immortal could not help the cold frisson of fear that danced down his spine. He turned to the three figures that followed him out of the building.

'Shit,' said Avery. The platoon commander's lips were pinched in a thin line. 'We need to tell Washington about this straightaway.'

'That's some bad juju in there,' said Anatole darkly.

Laura stared out across the desert, a scowl clouding her features. 'We have to stop these bastards!'

Conrad's suspicions had been on the mark once more. Their enemy appeared to be getting ready to launch a devastating campaign of destruction on the world. Frustration clawed at the immortal's insides. They still had no idea where and how they were going to strike. His eyes moved to the shimmering buildings of Khan Inc. He recalled Hagen's words inside the trailer. He had to speak to the three scientists.

They climbed inside the Jeep they had commandeered from the plant and drove back in grim silence. Stevens was talking to Gibbs in the shadow of the Osprey when they rolled to a stop next to the helicopter. Moore stood a dozen feet away, in conversation with a Moroccan military police officer and an army lieutenant.

Stevens turned when he heard their vehicle brake. Conrad's stomach knotted at his expression. Gibbs looked similarly troubled.

The immortal hopped out of the Jeep and jogged toward the ashen-faced agent. 'What's wrong?' he demanded.

Stevens swallowed hard. 'Something's happened in Luxembourg.'

CHAPTER TWENTY-SEVEN

'THE DETONATIONS HIT THE CAPITAL AT EIGHT FORTY, WHEN the place was at its busiest,' said Connelly. 'At first, everybody thought it was a major earthquake. The last time Luxembourg City experienced any kind of seismic activity was more than a decade ago. Once the tremors died down, reports started coming in from the less affected areas surrounding the impact zone about possible underground explosions being heard at several locations.' She scowled. 'That's when we got suspicious.'

Conrad stared at the computer, his mouth dry. The first window on the screen showed the Sit Room link. The second featured live coverage of the disaster that had struck the European city that morning, shortly after the gunfight at the Khan Inc. plant had abated.

'Could they have been gas explosions?' said Laura. She glanced distractedly at the squad of Marines running past.

They were standing in front of an improvised command post inside a hangar at a US military base in southwest Morocco. Avery's boss had granted Conrad and his team permission to use the Marines' facilities. The site had been a hive of activity ever since they landed there a quarter of an hour ago; US Armed Forces were being mobilized in view of a probable impending threat.

Connelly shook her head, lines of tension pinching her mouth. 'Not on this scale. Gas companies have plenty of failsafes in place to stop catastrophes of this nature happening. No, this was probably a bomb. Or a number of bombs, according to the experts who've looked at the initial data. The European Seismic Center has confirmed that no earthquake foreshocks or precursors were detected for the region in the last year. They also think the seismic waves they identified this morning are more in keeping with explosions than genuine quake activity.'

A video clip from a hovering helicopter flashed on the news channel. Dismay lowered the pitch of the reporter's voice as he commented on what he was seeing in French. 'This is unbelievable, people. Luxembourg City is no longer recognizable! A third of the capital is now a disaster zone centered on the Kirchberg Plateau, to the northeast of the town. Large sections of the old city walls have crumbled into the Alzette River, crushing buildings in their path! It's—it's like nothing I've ever seen before!'

Blood throbbed dully inside Conrad's head as he stared at the scale of the destruction. The rubble of collapsed buildings and roads filled most of the wide crater that took up the screen. A few fires had broken out among the wreckage of homes and businesses. Emergency vehicles dotted the lip of the basin. Hundreds of figures could be seen scrambling across the uneven terrain in their attempts to rescue survivors. Body bags were already piling up on the fringes of the devastation.

Although the Luxembourg impact zone was marked by the presence of crumbled human constructions, there was no denying that the shape and size of the depression matched those he had seen in the desert floor outside Khan Inc. under an hour ago. He had yet to tell Connelly of their shocking findings at the concealed facility close to the explosive craters.

'The death toll is predicted to be around 4,700,' the Director of Intelligence stated leadenly. 'It gets worse. Kirchberg was the site of several major European institutions, among them the European Parliament Secretariat, the European Commission, and the European Investment Bank. This calamity has dealt a severe blow to the EU as a whole. Not only have they lost a lot of their key staff and data, the financial ramification alone is likely to set them back a couple of years.' She sighed. 'It might be a day or two until we can determine where and what kind of explosives were used. We'll send the information we obtained from the Strabo Corp. databases about that new liquid explosive to the experts on the ground.'

'That won't be necessary,' said someone behind Conrad. 'I can give them its exact composition and the chemical signature of its residues.'

The immortal turned and saw Svein Hagen heading across the floor of the hangar toward them. He was helping Ed Henderson along. Alison Williams walked on the other side of the frail British engineer, her shoulder supporting his hand.

Conrad waited until the three scientists joined them at the command post before making introductions to the puzzled Director of National Intelligence across the video link.

'Professor Hagen you were already aware of,' the immortal said in a voice underscored by tension. 'This is Professor Alison Williams, geotechnical engineer from Berkeley, and Dr. Ed Henderson, a British civil engineer with expertise in directional boring and trenchless technology.'

Surprise flared across Connelly's face.

'Professor Williams was kidnapped five years ago, during an exploratory expedition to South America,' said Conrad. 'Her team's caravan was attacked en route to a mining site in Chile. She is suspected to be missing, presumed dead. Dr. Henderson was similarly abducted during an inspection of one of his firm's projects in China. Again, since no ransom was ever made for his release, he is presumed to be dead.'

Silence fell across the communication line. Connelly's brow became a mass of lines.

'I don't understand,' she said.

'Ed and I were captured shortly after the Rajkovics lost their own experts during an accident at their research site in Morocco,' Alison Williams explained in clipped tones. 'They had us take over their dead scientists' work under the threat that they would kill our families if we didn't cooperate.' She clenched her jaw. 'It wasn't an empty promise. They provided us with detailed images and videos they had taken of our relatives.' She glanced at Hagen and Henderson, anger clouding her eyes. 'The three of us were under no illusions that we would be killed after we had fulfilled our roles in their strategy.'

Connelly straightened. 'So all three of them are called Rajkovic,' she muttered.

'Yes,' said Conrad, impatience creeping into his tone. 'Nadica, Zoran, and Ariana Rajkovic. They go by many other names, including Muhlisi Khan, but from the conversations Hagen, Williams, and Henderson overheard between their guards, those are their true identities.'

Connelly leaned toward the camera and addressed the three scientists. 'Do you possess any information about their intentions?'

The two men and the woman looked at each other, dread evident in their eyes.

'We don't know all the details,' Williams said finally. 'They anonymized most of the data they gave us to work with, especially the particulars of specific locations. But I recognized the natural geology of some of the sites.'

'They're digging tunnels, Sarah,' Conrad said in a deadly voice. 'And filling them up with Hagen's liquid explosive.'

Connelly blinked, her eyes displaying dull incomprehension. 'What do you mean?'

Henderson rested one hand against the computer console. 'Mr. Greene is right, Director Connelly,' said the British engineer. 'From the materials we inherited from our predecessors on the project, we believe they've been drilling for years, if not decades. Borehole technology has been around forever, with the first ever recorded well being made by the Chinese more than two millennia ago. In more recent memory, we've had the Americans' Project Mohole off the coast of Mexico and the Kola Superdeep Borehole in northwest Russia.'

'The facility where Hagen, Williams, and Henderson were being forced to carry out the Rajkovics' research outside Khan Inc. was filled with schematics of networks of channels buried deep under at least thirty locations,' Conrad added. 'We suspect all of them of being major cities around the world.'

'They've had us working out the best geological formations in which to place the micro-tunnels so as to achieve the most destructive results,' said Williams bitterly.

Blood drained from Connelly's face. Silence descended in the Sit Room as agents and White House staff stopped their activities and gathered behind her, their expressions displaying alarm and fear.

'You mean, what happened in Luxembourg—?' the Director of National Intelligence said in a shaky voice.

'Yes,' Conrad cut in. 'They're quite likely planning to do the same to other cities.'

Connelly propped her elbows on the Sit Room conference table and held her head in her hands, her eyes directed blindly at the polished surface. She looked up slowly.

'But—I still don't get how they could have been digging for so long without anyone having prior knowledge of it,' she said, incredulous.

'Think about it.' Conrad glanced at the three scientists. 'We know these guys have been around for some time,' he said in a low voice. 'Remember, they *have* the resources to do this.'

Connelly stared at him, a flash of comprehension darting across her face. 'Of course,' she murmured in a sour tone.

'There *are* a couple of reasons why no one else would have been aware of these tunnels,' said Henderson. 'First, most of their digging projects started some time ago. Second, they went deep. They used standard oil and gas equipment to bore vertically into the ground, and added on directional drill strings to carve out the horizontal shafts. The drilling mud then sealed the walls of the tunnels, as it would an oil well.'

'We think they disguised the original boreholes under regular construction works,' said Williams. 'It's the only way they could have continued to work at them for all these years. You're not going to find any open drilling sites marked with an X. These wells are likely to be beneath buildings.'

'That's why they needed all the hydraulic equipment from the company outside Charleston,' said Conrad grimly. 'From the size and number of orders Franklin came across, it explains why we found only a few such machines at Khan Inc.'

Connelly clenched her jaw. 'And the explosives?' she said. 'Surely, they couldn't get their hands on that much—'

'They had access to massive stockpiles of disused Second World War explosives containing PETN,' interrupted Hagen. 'They also procured vast amounts legally for their legitimate mining ventures.' The professor ran a hand through his hair. 'I suspect they have a PETN manufacturing site somewhere else. We were given data from simulations taking place at other facilities.' He grimaced. 'They initially intended to use a combination of PETN and its derivative Semtex to achieve their goals. Unfortunately, one of their scientists came across my work. The Rajkovics realized they could have an even more powerful weapon at their disposal, one that would be more practical for their intentions as well, considering it would be in liquid form.'

'Sweet Jesus,' murmured the gray-faced Sit Room director on the video link. 'I'm calling Westwood and the Joint Chiefs.'

Connelly glanced at the man and inclined her head.

Hagen took an urgent step toward the makeshift command post. 'Tell the investigators in Luxembourg to look for evidence of a primary borehole within the disaster zone,' he advised in a low voice. 'I doubt they'll find the remains of the laser device used to detonate Cetrilium 24.'

'Cetrilium 24?' said Connelly in a puzzled tone.

Hagen flushed. 'That's the name of the new explosive.'

The scientists left the hangar a short while later. Conrad rubbed the knots on the back of his neck, still reeling from the recent revelations. His hand suddenly stilled as he recalled a crucial detail.

'There's something else,' he said in a hard voice.

Connelly sighed. 'I suspect we have enough on our plate as it is, but go on.'

'Someone tipped off the guards at Khan Inc. about our operation,' said Conrad. 'We were already inside the compound at the time.'

Consternation darkened Connelly's expression. 'You think it was our mole?'

'I'm betting on it.'

Connelly drummed her fingers on the table. 'Let's see. The Sit Room staff knew of the mission. Lewis and Donaghy were with me when I spoke to the Secretary of Defense and the US AFRICOM Commander.' Her eyes narrowed. 'Franklin was still on his way back from West Virginia—'

'It's not Franklin,' Conrad cut in. 'He's the one who gave us the lead in the first place. And I doubt it's Lewis or Donaghy.'

Connelly chewed her lip, fingers still tapping the table. Her hand suddenly stopped mid-air. 'Petersen,' she breathed.

Conrad's stomach plummeted as he stared at the Director

of National Intelligence. 'He cleared the company in Charleston.'

'He was also the last one who got told about the mission,' said Connelly grimly. 'It would have been around the time you infiltrated the plant in Morocco. Shit!' She turned to the Sit Room communications assistant. 'Phone Homeland! I want to know where Agent Petersen is *right now*!'

~

'HOW DID THEY FIND IT IN THE FIRST PLACE?' HISSED Ariana. She glared at the video images being relayed on a Moroccan news channel.

Khan Inc., one of their oil and gas companies, had come under siege by the Moroccan army and military police. The clip playing on the screen showed the plant's workers climbing onboard buses guarded by scores of armed officers. The official story to the media was that there had been a terrorist threat at the site.

Ariana knew it was only a cover. Their spy inside the White House had warned them of the US operation taking place at the compound. It was led by that infernal immortal—the one who had almost thwarted Nadica in Paris.

'They uncovered our hydraulic manufacturing business in West Virginia,' said Zoran in a strained voice. 'One of the employees had left unencrypted data in a computer at the head-quarters. It led them to the Tindouf Basin.' Rage flushed his cheeks. His nails had scored the skin of his palms, drawing blood.

It was the first time Ariana had seen him so angry. She rubbed her throbbing temples. Although she was irritated at having lost the plant and the small group of faithful followers stationed there, she was far more annoyed that the three engineers had been snatched from under her very nose and that the hidden research facility had been uncovered.

'We should teach those scientists a lesson,' said Nadica between gritted teeth.

Ariana glanced at the younger woman. Zoran's sister had gone beyond simple fury. Bloodlust radiated off her body in waves. For once, Ariana shared her descendant's ire. She had not made so many sacrifices and shed so much blood over the last four centuries to come this far to fail on the very cusp of success. It was time the people of this world learned their truthful place.

'Make it so,' Ariana ordered coldly. 'Dispatch contractors to take care of their families.'

Nadica picked up her phone and started to dial a number.

Ariana turned to Zoran. 'Are the target locations ready?'

'They will be in the next eight hours.'

'Good,' Ariana said in steely tones. 'We start our operations as soon as the last one is prepped.'

Zoran glanced at the digital map on the wall. 'What about locations 25 and 26?'

Ariana studied the sites in Germany and Austria with a calculated stare. 'Activate those as well,' she said finally. 'I was hoping to convince them to join ranks with us once they realized what we were capable of, but I see that they also have to learn their position in this future world order.'

CHAPTER TWENTY-EIGHT

CONRAD STARED OUT OF THE LEARJET'S WINDOW, FINGERS restlessly rapping the armrest of the executive chair. Almost four hours had passed since his last conversation with the White House. So far, they had had no further leads on the possible locations of the other primary boreholes.

They were on their way back to Washington to regroup their forces with the other agencies. Shortly before they left Morocco, he had called Victor and briefed him on their progress. Although they could think of at least a dozen cities that would make ideal targets for the enemy's destructive plans, they did not have any definitive proof to corroborate their theories. Even if they did identify the relevant sites, pinpointing the exact whereabouts of the boreholes would be a proverbial needle-in-a-haystack job. Conrad could not ward off the feeling of imminent dread stealing over him.

They were running out of time again. He was certain of it.

Footsteps rose along the aisle. Laura appeared and handed him a steaming cup. He murmured a thanks and took a sip of the strong coffee.

'Why don't you get some shuteye?' she suggested. 'There's

not a lot we can do at the moment, so now would be a good time to rest.'

Conrad gave her a strained look.

'I don't think I can sleep right now.'

Laura's lips curved in a small smile.

'I know one sure way to get you to relax,' she murmured.

Conrad raised an eyebrow and glanced at the immortal and agent at the rear of the plane.

Laura made a tutting noise. 'There are ways and means, Greene.' She leaned over and trailed a seductive finger down his chest, igniting sparks on his skin.

Conrad recalled some of the less conventional places they had made love in the past. He swallowed.

'Sheesh,' someone muttered behind them. 'How you can even think about sex right now, I have no idea.' Anatole strolled up the aisle, a red-eared Stevens in tow.

Laura glared at the immortal. She was about to deliver a retort when her phone rang. She stared at the number on the display.

'It's Moreau,' she said, looking at them with a puzzled frown. She answered the call and put the French Central Intelligence agent on speaker. 'Hi, Moreau. It's Hartwell here. I've got the others with me.'

'Hey,' Moreau greeted. 'Word on the grapevine is that you guys have been having some fun in Morocco.'

Conrad grimaced.

'Your definition of fun is not quite the same as ours. What can we do for you?'

'Christophe Lacroix persuaded us to chase up Ridvan Kadir's Mossad incident from 1984,' Moreau replied. 'That cop's got good instincts. We asked the Israelis to dig further. They came up with a surprising connection. Kadir reappeared on the scene a few years after that initial episode. He was heavily disguised and used an alias, but the retired arms dealer the

Mossad agents spoke to was convinced it was our man. Kadir was looking for information on anyone who might be able to provide black market Scuds.'

'Scuds?' Laura repeated, fingers tightening on the phone.

'Yes, as in tactical ballistic missiles,' confirmed Moreau in a somber tone.

Fresh fear formed a hard lump in Conrad's throat. He gazed blindly at the cell, the Frenchman's words ringing in his ears. *What the hell would the Rajkovics want ballistic missiles for?*

'Did he get his hands on any?' he asked anxiously.

'Yes,' replied the agent. 'The arms dealer said Kadir had appropriated scores of disused Scud-Bs and Cs over a period of ten years or so.'

'Shit,' Anatole muttered dully.

'That's all I've got for the time being,' said Moreau. 'I'll let you know if we come up with anything else.'

'Thanks,' said Laura. She ended the call, her face pale.

'Now what?' said Stevens. The agent had a haunted look.

Conrad glanced at him distractedly, stunned by this latest news. 'We let the White House and the other countries know.' He could not fathom the Rajkovics' need for the missiles, not when they had Hagen's powerful explosive at their disposal.

We must be missing something.

Laura had taken the seat at the onboard computer. She opened the video link to the Sit Room. The window blinked into life. Connelly and Donaghy appeared in the middle of the screen. They stood in close conversation, their expressions grave. The place was teeming with agents and White House staff.

Connelly turned when the video connection pinged.

'Oh!' She crossed over to the conference table. 'I was just about to call you.'

Donaghy followed in Connelly's footsteps.

'Ridvan Kadir has been buying Scud missiles on the

weapons black market since the late 1980s,' Laura announced in a hard voice. 'French Central Intelligence just heard from Mossad.'

Connelly and Donaghy looked at each other.

'We know,' said the CIA agent with a dark expression. 'Petersen told us.'

'You caught him?' exclaimed Conrad.

Donaghy's lips twisted in a bitter smile.

'Yes. Bastard was boarding a plane to Alaska. Airport security scanned his face and tipped us off.'

'It seems Petersen was in it purely for the money, Greene,' said Connelly in a level tone. 'He had no other links with the Rajkovics.'

Conrad grasped the silent message behind her words. Petersen was not of the Ottoman-Crovir lineage. 'Has he talked?'

The two women exchanged guarded glances once more.

'We had to cut a deal,' Connelly admitted, her voice tight with anger. 'Life imprisonment rather than the death penalty he justly deserves for treason.'

Conrad's heart pounded dully inside his chest.

'What did he say?'

'He admitted to passing on Westwood's security details for the FedEx Field fundraiser event and feeding the Rajkovics particulars of the investigation, which came as no real surprise to anyone,' said Connelly.

'No, the humdinger was this,' said Donaghy. She leaned toward the camera. 'He also gave them comprehensive reports on the locations and blueprints of US military bases here and abroad.'

Conrad stared at her blankly for a couple of seconds. His brain finally made the connection. Ice filled his veins. 'The Scuds.'

'Yes, the Scuds,' said Connelly. 'It would be virtually impossible for the Rajkovics to dig tunnels under an established army base; they would have been spotted a mile away. Instead, Petersen helped those bastards identify sites free from our geospatial intelligence's scrutiny, from which they could launch their ballistic missiles against our armed forces. Most of them are abandoned barns and isolated woodland.' She bit her lip. 'We have to assume they've done the same in other countries.'

'That traitorous son of a bitch!' Laura hissed in the stunned silence that followed.

'They're going to take out cities and military bases at the same time,' muttered Stevens, his face waxy.

Conrad's fingers dug into his palms. This was even worse than he had imagined.

'Did Petersen give you the details of those locations?'

'He said he wasn't sure which ones they'd decided on,' replied Donaghy with a disgusted grimace. 'He gave them the list a few years ago.'

Connelly's face darkened. 'I've spoken to the Joint Chiefs and the Secretary of Defense. We're going through them one goddamned site at a time.'

Fear flooded Conrad. He suspected they would be too late to prevent the loss of more human lives.

'Petersen overheard snatches of a conversation when he was on the phone to Zoran Rajkovic last week,' said Donaghy. 'Nadica Rajkovic was talking to someone in the background about satellite-linked remote controls she was going to pick up.'

Conrad went still. Images of the incident in Paris flashed across his vision.

'The briefcase,' he said hoarsely. 'Nadica Rajkovic escaped with a metal case that Ridvan Kadir had given her!'

Shocked comprehension washed across the others' faces.

'They must be for the laser detonation devices,' said Stevens.

'Wow.' Anatole shook his head in amazement. 'You gotta

admire them. The bastards are going to blow up the world by remote control.'

'One more thing,' added the grim-faced CIA agent. 'Petersen heard an air horn just before the call ended. He thought the Rajkovics might have been at sea.'

A flicker of hope burst into life in the depths of Conrad's soul.

'Do any of the companies the Rajkovics own have links with the shipping industry?'

'Not that we know of,' said Connelly. 'We're checking them out anyway for connections to any kind of ship.'

Conrad swallowed a wave of disappointment. 'That's great. Let me know as soon as you find—'

A voice suddenly shouted excitedly somewhere off-screen.

Connelly's head whipped around. 'What is it?' She stared over her shoulder. A man jogged into view.

It was the Sit Room analyst.

'You know how we put a call out to all the agencies investigating those forty-odd businesses we think the Rajkovics own?' he said breathlessly.

'Yes. What about it?' said Connelly, impatient.

The man grinned. 'FBI just came back with a doozy. They found an electronic fuel receipt at an abandoned brokerage firm yesterday. It was for a luxury yacht called "*The Ariana*." She stopped over in Crown Bay on St. Thomas, in the US Virgin Islands.'

Conrad's pulse speeded up.

'When was this?'

The Sit Room analyst glanced at the paper in his hand.

'Two days ago!'

'Can we get satellites over the area?' said Conrad urgently. 'We need to find that boat. They probably have those remote controls on board!'

'Already on it,' said the Sit Room analyst with a sharp dip of his head. 'We should have images coming through in the next few minutes. We're checking to see if the yacht has an automatic identification system. It should be easy to locate them if they do.'

It turned out *The Ariana* did not have the tracking system installed.

Conrad paced the Learjet cabin while they waited for the NGA to work out a search grid based on the information they had obtained on the vessel's average speed and a forty-eight-hour window from St. Thomas. Laura called Victor on her cell and asked him to put the immortals' own satellite network into play.

It was almost an hour before a sharp-eyed Bastian intelligence analyst finally picked out the super yacht.

'They're in the Sargasso Sea, about 850 miles northeast of the US Virgin Islands,' announced Victor.

They were in a conference call with the White House. Conrad stared unblinkingly at the white and navy-blue shape moving seamlessly against a cobalt background on the enhanced satellite video. A buzz of anticipation flared into life inside him.

'Laura, can you ask the pilot where we are in relation to that yacht?' he said quietly. He saw her startled reaction out of the corner of his eye.

'Okay.' She disappeared in the direction of the cockpit.

A slow grin lit up Anatole's face.

'Time to have some fun.'

The red-haired immortal's gleaming gaze matched the thrill dancing through Conrad's veins.

There was a sharp intake of breath from the Sit Room video link.

'Hang on a minute!' Connelly blurted. 'You're not thinking of intercepting them, are you?'

'That's exactly what I'm going to do,' Conrad affirmed with a dark smile.

Connelly gaped at him.

'You're in a Learjet thousands of feet in the air over the bloody North Atlantic! How the hell do you think you're—?'

'We're about seven hundred miles northeast of them,' interrupted Laura as she came down the aisle.

'Your closest land mass is Bermuda,' said Victor crisply on the second link. 'Connelly, I believe the US Navy has a Nimitz class aircraft carrier in the vicinity. They could have a Seahawk helicopter waiting at the airport on St. David's island.'

Shocked silence came from the White House. Conrad suppressed a smile. Victor Dvorsky could still surprise him.

Connelly opened and closed her mouth soundlessly. She turned to the Sit Room analyst.

'Is that true?' she asked stiffly.

The man tapped a couple keys, checked the data on the screen, and nodded sheepishly.

Connelly's gaze shifted to the camera. She glared at Victor before letting out an exasperated sigh.

'Shit. I don't even want to know how you know that.'

She chewed her lip as she mulled over the Bastian leader's suggestion.

'Goddammit!' she finally snapped. She looked to the Sit Room analyst. 'Talk to the Navy.'

Laura twisted on her heels and headed back to the cockpit.

THEY LANDED IN BERMUDA JUST OVER AN HOUR LATER AND taxied toward a gray Sikorsky Seahawk helicopter squatting at the edge of the tarmac. Conrad had just exited the Learjet when the pilot called out to him from the top of the steps.

'There's an urgent video call from Vienna!' he shouted.

Conrad hurried back inside the plane, alarm shooting through him. He reached the onboard computer and saw Victor in the center of the link on the screen. The Bastian leader was standing at the desk inside his glass office, his expression grim. The command post below him was a hub of agitated activity.

Conrad's stomach sank.

'What's wrong?'

Laura, Anatole, and Stevens appeared beside him, apprehension evident in their tense postures.

'The investigators in Luxembourg found the primary borehole at the source of the disaster,' Victor said darkly. 'It was under a building belonging to one of the Strabo Corp. directors.'

Blood thumped dully in Conrad's ears as he suddenly recalled Alison Williams's words. *These wells are likely to be beneath buildings.* The Berkeley engineer had been bang on the money. They just hadn't thought one step further.

'Shit,' he whispered leadenly.

Anatole swore under his breath while Laura scowled.

'I can see from your expressions that you've reached the same conclusion I did,' said Victor. A digital map of the world flashed up next to the window. 'These are the locations of all the companies owned by the Rajkovics.'

Conrad's heart slammed erratically against his ribs as he stared at the display.

'God! Most of them are in the middle of major cities!' exclaimed Stevens, horror draining the color from his face.

'Thirty-seven of them are, to be precise,' said Victor. 'That's if you count Luxembourg as well.'

Conrad slammed his fist on the table. Frustration raged inside him. How could he not have foreseen this?

'Franklin and the FBI mentioned that the premises they investigated in the last couple days were abandoned,' said Laura bitterly. 'The reason must be because the primary boreholes are underneath most of them.'

Anatole drew in a breath sharply.

'Hey! Two of those sites are near the headquarters of the—'

'I know,' Victor cut in. He clenched his jaw. 'I've already contacted the Crovir First Council. They're sending teams out to the suspect location in Dresden to seek and destroy the laser device. We're doing the same here.' He glanced over his shoulder at the busy command center. 'We're clearing out anyway. There are hundreds of items pertaining to our cultural heritage stored underneath this facility, never mind the centuries' worth of Bastian knowledge and intelligence data. We *cannot* let them be destroyed.'

The Bastian leader's words were still echoing in Conrad's head when they crossed the tarmac to the helicopter. The Seahawk's tactical officer greeted them at the cabin door and ushered them inside the aircraft just as the rotors started up.

The gunner nodded an acknowledgement and indicated the communication headsets hooked to the wall. The tactical officer's voice came through their earpieces seconds later.

'We're tracking the yacht,' he told them. 'We expect to rendezvous in approximately thirty to forty minutes.'

The Seahawk lifted off and rose rapidly toward the azure sky. After checking their weapons and familiarizing themselves with the equipment they would use to drop down to the boat, Conrad and the others sat back in tense silence.

'Harry, you going to be okay?' Laura asked a while later.

Stevens had gotten steadily grayer over the half hour they'd been in the aircraft. He nodded shakily and wiped a film of sweat from his face, his eyes straying to the open cabin door and the ocean below.

'He doesn't do heights,' Laura explained at Conrad's questioning look.

Stevens made a heaving sound.

'I don't think he does Seahawks either,' the door gunner muttered as the agent lurched past him and emptied the contents of his stomach into the sea. Anatole shook his head pityingly.

The words Conrad had been waiting for finally came over the headset.

'Target in sight.'

CHAPTER TWENTY-NINE

THE HELICOPTER DID A WIDE-ARCED SWOOP AND BORE DOWN on *The Ariana* from the south. The vessel's crisp lines came into focus, her navy blue hull gleaming in the sunlight. Powerful thrusters churned the waves in her wake, stirring up a foaming, white backwash.

Conrad frowned when he made out the black shape of the MD520N aircraft on the yacht's sun deck. Figures appeared aft of the boat. A dim staccato reached them above the roar of the Seahawk's rotors.

Anatole squinted. 'Are they shooting at us?'

'I'm afraid so!' said the door gunner with a grin. He swung the barrel of his pintle-mounted machine gun, charged the weapon, and looked down his sights. 'Ready when in range!'

The Seahawk dropped in altitude and reduced speed.

'Two thousand meters!' said the tactical officer.

Arcs of automatic gunfire greeted the helicopter's approach. The bullets fell harmlessly into the water.

Conrad adjusted the staff strapped to his back and the M16 rifle slung across his chest. A familiar sense of calmness stole over him. He glanced at Laura and Anatole and observed the same cool composure in their eyes and the lines of their bodies. They were in battle mode.

'One thousand meters!' warned the tactical officer.

Though no shots reached the Seahawk, the helicopter came under increasing attack from the gunmen on *The Ariana*.

'Eight hundred meters!'

'In range!' said the gunner a second later.

'Fire!' yelled the tactical officer.

The machine gun juddered as the gunner pulled the trigger. Bullets tore into the yacht, chipping the wooden decks and aluminum superstructure. Sun-lounger beds and armchair cushions exploded in a shower of sponge and foam. Splinters fogged the air. The gunmen fell back.

The Seahawk swung closer to the vessel.

'Get ready!' the tactical officer shouted at the three immortals and the agent. He raised his hand in the air as they swiftly discarded their headsets.

The gunner continued to lay down bursts of suppressive fire. Glass shattered below, fragments sparkling in the sun.

The tactical officer dropped his hand sharply. 'And *go, go, go!*'

Conrad kicked the cord hooked to the external hoist over the edge of the open door, wrapped his gloved hands and feet around the thick cable, and fast-roped to the yacht. His boots struck the sun deck of *The Ariana* seconds later.

Shots sprayed the wooden boards several feet ahead of him. He raised the M16 rifle and returned fire as the others came down behind him. The gunmen retreated toward the stairs on the starboard side.

A cry suddenly shattered the air.

'Harry!' Laura screamed a heartbeat later.

Conrad's head whipped round, fear squeezing his chest in a tight vice. Stevens had been shot in the leg. Though he clung grimly to the rope, the agent slid down too fast and hit the deck hard. He crumpled to his knees, his face a mask of agony. Laura rushed toward him.

'No!' yelled Conrad. 'Cover me!'

She faltered.

Conrad raced past her and reached the crippled agent. He grabbed the man under the shoulders and heaved him into the cover of a large bed lounger. Laura turned and joined Anatole as he discharged his M16 at the armed crewmen on the opposite side of the deck.

Conrad ignored the hail of gunfire and tugged his gloves off, his pulse racing wildly. He pressed his left hand against Stevens's bleeding thigh and unleashed his immortal powers. The agent released a hiss of pain as the bullet migrated forcefully back along its entry path. The bloodstained shot dropped to the ground while the immortal concentrated on repairing the torn muscles and soft tissues beneath his fingers.

He moved his hand down Stevens's legs and fixed the two hairline fractures in his right tibia. The man suddenly relaxed beneath his touch. Conrad looked up into his stunned gaze.

'That—that was—' Stevens stammered.

'Save it for later!' snapped Conrad. He rose to his feet, pulled Stevens up, and jerked him close by the front of his tactical uniform. 'I swear to God, kid, if you dare die and make Laura cry, I'll bring you back just so that I can kill you myself!' he threatened. Stevens smiled shakily and bobbed his head.

They stepped around the bodies of four gunmen and joined Laura and Anatole where the two crouched at the top of the staircase leading to the lower levels of the ship.

The Seahawk pulled up in the sky behind them and headed away from *The Ariana*.

NADICA PACED NEAR THE OUTER DOORS OF THE MAIN SALON,

a Glock 19 in hand. Zoran saw a shiver of rage dance along her limbs as she studied the damage inflicted to the yacht by the Navy helicopter. Gunfire sounded above, where the crewmen of *The Ariana* engaged the enemy who had landed on the boat.

Her knuckles whitened on the gun. '*How dare they!*' she hissed.

Zoran's gaze switched to the laptop in front of him. 'I don't understand,' he said between clenched teeth. 'The explosives at the first four targets failed to detonate.' He glanced at the remote controls inside the briefcase on the desk.

'Is it Ridvan's equipment?' snapped Ariana.

Zoran shook his head. 'No.' Trepidation filled him. For the first time in decades, he felt they might not achieve their goals. 'I think they may have discovered the locations of the boreholes.'

CONRAD GASPED AND BENT BACK SHARPLY AT THE WAIST. THE tip of a Turkish sword skimmed the air inches from his chest. He blocked the next two strikes with the handguard of the M16. The man on the other end of the sword glowered at him. Conrad's eyes darted across the deck, his breathing hard and fast.

From the way the crew of *The Ariana* fought, it was obvious they were willing to lay down their lives for Mustafa Muhlisi's bloodline. Judging by the array of scimitars and sabers that had suddenly appeared in their hands, it was also evident they were gifted swordsmen.

Conrad leapt out of the way of the swinging blade, dropped his rifle, and yanked his staff weapon from his back. He twisted the second ring and unsheathed the short swords.

The crewman's eyes gleamed as he studied the shimmering steel. He raised his own sword and charged. Conrad warded off his strikes, the short blades moving seamlessly in his grip. The man growled and continued his relentless attack. Although he had talent, the crewman was still no match for the immortal. Conrad yanked the bloodied, twin swords out of the man's body a moment later. The crewman crumpled to the ground, eyes wide in a pale face as he gazed unseeingly at the blue sky. The immortal scanned the deck beyond his still form.

Anatole had appropriated a saber from one of his victims and was fighting two armed figures on the other side of an external dining space. The blade glinted in his grip as he wielded it in deadly arcs.

Some eight feet to his left, Laura used the stock of her M16 rifle to deflect the thrusts from a large carving knife held by *The Ariana's* glowering cook.

Conrad retrieved the sword at his feet. 'Laura!' he yelled and pitched the blade in the air.

She kneed the cook in the groin, raised her hand, and caught the sword by the hilt. A fierce smile flashed across her lips as she glanced at him.

Stevens stood braced near the port railing, his empty rifle lying at his feet while he clasped his FN Five-seveN in a double-handed grip and steadily picked off one crewman at a time.

Conrad grabbed his discarded M16 and cast the weapon toward the agent as he ran past him to the spiral stairs leading to the main deck. Bullets scored the treads when he was halfway down the steps. He cursed, jumped over the handrail, and landed nimbly on the floor below.

More shots winged through the air toward him. Conrad darted into the limited cover of the staircase as the bullets thudded into the steel frame. He peered through a gap in the structure.

Nadica Rajkovic stood framed by a pair of sliding doors some twenty feet away, the barrel of her Glock flaring repeatedly as she fired the weapon. Her face was livid with fury.

Conrad crouched behind the center pole of the spiral stairs and gripped the short swords tightly, blood pounding in his ears. Chips of wood rained down on him while he waited for the telltale click of the empty magazine. It came in a matter of seconds.

He rose and bolted across the deck.

The woman's eyes shrunk into slits. She tossed the Glock away and backed up, her hands reaching under her jacket. A pair of kilij blades materialized in her grasp. Swords met sabers a heartbeat later. Conrad fended off a flurry of blows and cast a glance at the figures in the room behind her.

Ariana Rajkovic was pulling a pair of gilded, curved swords from their wall mounts, her face flushed with anger. She turned and threw one of the blades to Zoran Rajkovic, who fielded it smoothly.

Conrad's gaze landed briefly on the metal briefcase atop the table next to Mustafa's heir. It was the one Nadica Rajkovic had taken into her possession in Paris.

A kilij sailed past his face and sliced a sliver of hair from his temple. Conrad staggered back and almost lost his footing on the wooden floor.

A wild smile distorted Nadica Rajkovic's face. She stooped and lunged forward, her arm swinging up in a lethal arc. The kilij sliced Conrad's abdomen from his left hip to his right ribcage. He gasped as searing pain flared across his body. Laura's enraged cry sounded somewhere on the steps behind him. Conrad gritted his teeth and retreated from Nadica Rajkovic's fast-moving blades while he healed the gaping wound in his stomach.

Laura appeared beside him and swung her sword at Nadica, hazel eyes blazing like the sun. 'Go!' she yelled at Conrad.

He darted through the doors behind the fighting women and headed for the metal briefcase. Ariana Rajkovic stepped into his path. The Crovir immortal glared at him, her lips pinched in a pale line. She brandished her sword in a practiced move. Conrad parried with the twin short blades. Their weapons locked.

Ariana leaned toward him, her fingers white on the handle of her sword. 'Why couldn't you leave well alone?' she hissed. 'Our kind could have shared this world!'

Conrad studied her grimly between the interlocked blades. 'The immortals would never engage in mass genocide!'

Ariana smiled thinly. 'From what I know of your *immortals*, they have been guilty of much worse in the past!'

Conrad scowled. The woman was right. 'That might be so, but they know better now!' he retorted. 'The world has changed and we with it. Both Suleiman and Mustafa would know that if they were alive today!'

Ariana's eyes turned to molten silver. 'How *dare* you speak his name!'

She attacked, the blade flowing skillfully in her grasp with each brutal move. Conrad countered with deft swings of his twin swords, heart thrumming rapidly in his chest as they moved across the salon. She was a better swordswoman than her descendant.

A startled gasp suddenly sounded to the right, where Anatole clashed swords with Zoran Rajkovic. Ariana inhaled sharply.

Mustafa's heir gripped his arm and retreated a couple of steps. Crimson drops fell to the pale floor from the wound the red-haired immortal had inflicted.

A howl of rage erupted from the direction of the sliding doors. Nadica spun beneath Laura's blade, kicked the immortal hard in the stomach, and raced across the room toward Zoran.

Laura staggered across the deck. Stevens came up behind her and caught her before she fell. The agent twisted on his heels, dropped to one knee, and fired at the crewmen charging down the spiral staircase.

Nadica raised the sabers and rushed Anatole. Sparks rose where she struck his sword with the kilij blades. The immortal grunted and backed up under her savage assault.

Ariana wielded her sword in a tempestuous swirl. Conrad took an unconscious step back as the edge of the blade hummed past his skin, his short swords up to ward off the wild blows. His legs struck the edge of a low table and he stumbled to the floor, a curse bubbling up his throat. Instead of striking him where he lay, Ariana ran to where her descendants now fought Anatole and Laura.

'Take the case and leave!' Ariana barked. She grabbed Zoran's blade and stepped in the path of the two immortals' swords.

Nadica and Zoran Rajkovic faltered, their gray eyes filled with anger and a trace of fear.

'I'll be fine!' Ariana said between gritted teeth, the swords dancing in her grip as she fended off multiple blows. 'Now, *go!*'

Nadica whispered a tortured 'Ama!' from pale lips. Zoran snatched the metal briefcase from the table and grabbed the younger woman's arm. He pulled her toward a doorway to the rear of the room.

Conrad jumped to his feet and went after them. He saw Ariana's eyes widen in alarm and heard her mumbled '*No!*' as he flashed through the arch.

He cleared an empty dining room and reached a small foyer with a spiral staircase. Footsteps faded toward the upper deck. Conrad scaled the stairs at a dead run, air leaving his lungs in harsh pants.

He reached the landing and looked around wildly, sweat dripping past his eyes. A door swung close to his right. He barged through it and was greeted with a burst of close-range gunfire. Bullets slammed into his chest and legs. Numbness bloomed along his skin as his body reacted defensively to the multiple injuries.

Conrad clenched his teeth and charged the crewman wielding the machine gun, his immortal powers surging from his core. The man's eyes grew round; a low grunt wheezed out of his lips as a short sword impaled his heart.

Conrad yanked the blade out and started up a staircase in the corner of the narrow space. Slugs fell to the floor in a sharp staccato as his wounds healed and closed.

Brightness flooded the landing at the top of the steps. The slow whirr of rotors rose from somewhere outside. Icy fear gripped Conrad. *They're taking the helicopter!*

He pushed through a door and stepped into bright sunlight. A floating, glass swimming pool shimmered to his right, the water rippling with waves from the increasing revolution of the nearby rotors. Conrad bolted up the steps beside the pool and saw the black helicopter some twenty-five feet ahead. Zoran was at the controls of the aircraft, while Nadica sat in the seat next to him.

Conrad raced across the sun deck, a single thought blazing through him: he had to get that briefcase.

Nadica's eyes betrayed her alarm when she spotted him. She grabbed her brother's gun from where it lay on the metal case by her feet, kicked open the door, and raised the weapon.

Conrad darted sideways as bullets pelted the aluminum superstructure. He sheathed the swords, exchanged the staff weapon for the HK P8, and fired at the helicopter.

'*Go!*' Nadica screamed at Zoran.

Mustafa's heir adjusted the throttle.

Conrad put his head down and sprinted toward the aircraft, his heart in his mouth. He leapt onto the starboard skid and yanked the rear door open just as the chopper lifted off the sun deck. A bullet whistled past his head and slammed into the rear wall of the cabin as he lunged inside. The helicopter cleared the yacht and accelerated out to sea.

Conrad landed in the rear footwell with a harsh grunt. He

twisted on his back and rolled sharply to avoid another shot. Nadica aimed the gun at his head once more. He sat up and grabbed her hands just as she pulled the trigger. The bullet punctured the roof of the helicopter.

A tortured whine rose from the engine mounted to the rear of the cabin pod.

'Nadica!' Zoran shouted, horror raising the pitch of his voice as he glanced at the young woman.

Conrad gritted his teeth as Nadica struggled against him. He twisted her wrists further and pushed her arms away. The gun shifted wildly in her grasp a second before she pressed the trigger once more.

The bullet flashed out of the barrel and entered Zoran Rajkovic's head just below his ear. Fragments of bloodied skull and brain splattered onto the window as the shot exited the other side. He slumped over the controls, his eyes wide open.

'*No!*' screamed Nadica.

Her grip loosened on the gun. The weapon fell in the gap between the seats as she lunged toward Zoran. She wrapped her arms around his lifeless body, an agonizing sob rising from the very depths of her soul.

The helicopter pitched sharply toward the blue expanse below, engine shrieking.

Conrad was dimly aware of the Seahawk approaching rapidly from the west. His stomach rose in his throat as he watched the sea grow closer through the transparent cabin wall.

The helicopter smashed into the ocean with a deafening boom. A million cracks blossomed across the curved surface of the windshield. The aircraft sank beneath the waves, rotors still spinning and driving its descent into the deepening blue.

Conrad swung his legs around and kicked at the rear door. Cold water started to flood the aircraft, and the sharp smell of brine inundated the enclosed space. He cursed when the panel refused to budge. The pressure outside was already too great.

He lunged to the other side of the pod and tried the second door, desperation making his movements awkward. Twilight enveloped the aircraft.

Nadica Rajkovic sat frozen in the front compartment, her arms still folded around Mustafa's dead heir. She gazed at the growing fractures in the cabin wall without a sound. The windshield imploded a second later.

Conrad took a few giant gulps of air as the sea rushed inside the aircraft. Water filled his ears and dulled the gushing roar. Coldness stung his eyes and skin. He blinked, grabbed the back of the front passenger seat, and pulled himself toward the gaping hole where the windshield used to be.

A hand closed around his leg as he passed through the opening. Conrad looked over his shoulder and saw Nadica's fingers wrapped around his ankle. The woman stared at him blankly, her other hand clamped on the edge of her seat. Panic swamped Conrad. He kicked out sharply. Nadica Rajkovic's grasp grew tighter.

Darkness shrouded them as the helicopter continued its plunge into the ocean depths.

～

Deep in the bowels of the Amazon rainforest, Roxanne woke up from her afternoon nap to the sound of Rocky howling.

Alarm tore through the old woman and she straightened in her chair. Her eyes darted around the small clearing at the bottom of the porch, looking for what had frightened the animal. Her brow furrowed when she found nothing threatening. Her puzzled gaze shifted to the dog.

Rocky stood on the bank of the river, his body shaking uncontrollably. He threw his head back and bayed at the sun-dappled branches above his head once more.

Apprehension replaced bewilderment in Roxanne's chest as she listened to the heartbreaking sound. 'What have you done, *Deus Demônio?*' she whispered to the muggy air.

Down by the water, Rocky continued to cry.

Nine hundred and seventy miles from the Sargasso Sea, James Anthony Westwood clutched at his chest.

'Mr. President!' The Secretary of Defense lunged from his seat. 'Are you okay, sir?'

'James!' Sarah Connelly leaned toward Westwood, her eyes wide with concern.

Westwood raised a hand and winced. 'I'm okay,' he murmured. 'Just—give me a moment.'

He was in the back of an armored car heading out of Washington D.C., as part of the emergency evacuation of the capital. He rubbed the painful spot over his heart. He was as healthy as a horse, so he doubted this was a heart attack. On the other hand, considering the events of the last week, having a coronary would not be in the least bit surprising.

His hand stilled as his consciousness finally registered what his body was telling him. Something had changed.

He could no longer feel the man who had granted him a piece of his immortal soul.

'Greene.' Westwood stared at Connelly, fear knotting his stomach. 'Something's happened to him!'

CHAPTER THIRTY

NOVEMBER 2011. ONE HUNDRED MILES NORTHEAST OF Hamilton Harbor. Bermuda.

GEORGE TUCKER CHOMPED DOWN ON HIS CIGAR AND adjusted his captain's hat. He watched the waves through the glass windows of *The Beaver*'s wheelhouse with a satisfied smile.

His fifty-four-foot seiner had been camped out in these waters for three days, ever since he heard of the hurricane that would soon pass through this part of the Atlantic. After studying the patterns of the winds, tides, and currents, he decided to bring *The Beaver* out to this remote stretch of the Sargasso Sea, where instinct told him the best catch would be. He had seen other seiners and trawlers scrambling out of Hamilton Harbor on the day he set off, though none had followed the course he laid out for *The Beaver*; fishing ahead of the storm would produce a heavier bounty than several normal trips combined. *The Beaver*'s keel already sat deeper in the water, its aluminum-tanked hold heavy with some fifteen tons of yellowfin tuna.

Tucker removed his cigar and lifted the VHF radio to his mouth. 'All right Tom, close her up.'

His skiffman's voice came over the airwaves. 'Closing the net, captain.'

Tucker stepped out of the wheelhouse and was about to call down to the deckhands when Tom Fairbanks's voice came over the radio once more.

'Hey George, tell the boys to be ready for the mother of a haul,' warned the skiffman. 'Fish are going stir crazy here!'

Tucker turned and watched the expanse of ocean separating *The Beaver* from the skiff. Thousands of small ripples sparkled across the surface, against the prevailing wind and current. A few boobies and seagulls hovered in the sky, ready to plunge-dive for prey.

The captain's heart thumped with rising excitement as he stared at the dancing water. *There has to be eight tons in that one catch alone!*

Tucker had rarely seen anything like it in his forty-odd-year fishing career. He grinned and shouted down to *The Beaver*'s deck. 'Get ready to haul gear! It's a *big* one!'

The crew of four put on their waterproof coats and gloves, eager chatter ringing out among them. This was to be their last set of the day. They would be back in Hamilton Harbor by sundown, ahead of the black clouds staining the sky to the east.

Fairbanks's skiff chugged steadily toward the seiner. He handed over the end of the dragnet to the deck crew and circled to the other side of the large boat to attach the second towline. A deckhand operated the winch to pull closed the heavy, lead-woven purse line at the bottom of the seine. Minutes later, another man engaged the power block to haul it in. The crew got to work at the business end of the boat, stacking the lines and webbing quickly and efficiently onto the deck.

Tucker waited until a third of it was on board before

reversing *The Beaver* to submerge the float line. This would allow any large creatures captured inside the net to escape at the top of the safety panels in the webbing. He watched the bobbing corks closely and repeated the backdown maneuver several times. His lips curved in a contented smile when he saw the small, gray shapes of a couple of porpoises slip over the line.

Thousands of gleaming, thrashing bodies finally broke clear of the water as the yellowfin tuna surfaced inside the mesh. The crew gradually emptied it onto the deck and started to sort through the haul.

Tucker left the wheelhouse and headed down the bridge ladder. He grabbed the galoshes on the walkway at the bottom and started to climb in them. They would need all hands on deck to deal with this catch.

A horrified shout reached his ears as he stepped inside the second rubber boot. Tucker froze, alarm darting through him. *Holy hell! Did we catch a barracuda? Or a young marlin?!*

He knew all too well the damage those creatures could inflict to fishermen; he had several scars on his legs to prove it. The captain rose and stumbled aft of the boat.

Fairbanks and the deckhands were gathered in a half circle in the middle of the main deck. Tucker spotted a large, black shape lying in the midst of a mass of twitching, yellowfin tuna between their legs.

'What is it?' he called out sharply as he made his way toward the crew.

Fairbanks turned, his face grim. 'It's a man.'

Tucker's stomach dropped. He reached his skiffman's side and looked down at a lifeless body dressed in a faded, army-style, black tactical uniform. The wet slaps of fish bodies convulsing against the deck was a ghastly soundtrack to the macabre finding.

'We better alert the coastguards,' Fairbanks said in a low voice.

Tucker's mouth had gone dry. He had only ever come across a floater once. He'd lost his appetite for days after.

'I wonder if he's the guy they've been looking for,' muttered the youngest deckhand.

'What d'you mean?' asked *The Beaver*'s engineer.

The deckhand waved vaguely out to sea. 'I mean the Navy. That US aircraft carrier's been sending out search and rescue helicopters most days now for the last month. Apparently, some big-shot crashed their helicopter in the sea.'

The engineer made a face. 'I doubt the US government would go to that much effort just to find a VIP.' His gaze shifted to the body. 'Anyway, whoever the poor guy is, no one deserves to die like this.'

Tucker stared. Although the grayish color of the man's skin indicated he had been dead a while, the captain could see no signs of lividity or bloating. A black snake symbol twisted out from under the left cuff of the man's long-sleeved shirt. The creature's forked tongue stood out starkly against his pale wrist.

'What's that in his fingers?'

He squatted and cleared away a few fat tuna fish. A gilded staff appeared in the man's left hand. Tucker gripped one end of it and pulled.

The staff didn't budge.

~

SARAH CONNELLY STARED THROUGH THE TINTED WINDOW OF the SUV, her fingers clasped tightly on her lap.

Castle Harbor was a patchwork of dazzling blues and greens beyond the parapet of the low stone bridge the vehicle was travelling on. In the sky to the east, the white shape of an airliner grew steadily in size as it prepared to land at the island's only airport.

It was a balmy eighty degrees Fahrenheit, and the sun blazed brightly down on the islands of Bermuda. Despite the SUV's air conditioning, a thin sheen of perspiration already peppered her brow.

It had been eighteen hours since they found Conrad Greene's body.

Connelly swallowed the lump in her throat as she recalled Westwood's words the day before.

'I know you're busy with all the stuff going on at the moment, but you're the only one I trust to do this,' the president had told her somberly on the steps of Air Force One.

Sarah Connelly had stared at Westwood for some time before finally agreeing to his request; she knew full well he would have come himself had he not been traveling to Europe for an important meeting with several heads of state, including the new Russian premier.

She gazed blindly outside as the SUV rolled through the outskirts of Hamilton town. The two agents in front had remained silent throughout the ride. Half an hour after landing on the island, they pulled into the circular drive in front of the capital's main hospital.

The agent in the passenger seat jumped out before the vehicle had rolled to a complete stop. He scanned the surroundings through his sunglasses. The driver joined him and opened her door.

Connelly thanked the man and stepped out onto the asphalt. Sultry warmth washed over her. A trickle of sweat pooled at the base of her neck and ran down her spine. She shivered despite the heat and looked up at the pale facade of the building. She squared her shoulders and headed for the main entrance, the two agents in tow.

A gaggle of journalists crowded inside the hospital lobby. Excited murmurs rose from the group when they saw the dark-suited men. Connelly blanked the mikes and cameras angling toward her and carried on briskly down the corridor. The police officers drafted in for added security formed a defensive wall in front of the rowdy reporters.

Connelly walked past the sign for the morgue and pressed the call button for a lift. She stepped inside the steel cabin with the two agents. The doors closed and the lift started to rise. Tension knotted her stomach as they drew closer to the third floor.

They exited the elevator and strolled down a busy corridor to the entrance of a private ward. Connelly gave her name at the door. It buzzed open a second later. She walked in and acknowledged the agent at the nurses' station with a brief nod.

'Where is he?' she asked.

'Last one on the left,' said the man. He indicated the corridor to the south.

Connelly headed down the passage. All of the rooms bar one had been cleared of patients. She stopped in front of the final cubicle. The blinds were down in the glass inset in the top half of the door.

She signaled to the two agents. They took up guard position outside the doorway. Connelly inhaled deeply and twisted the door handle. It opened smoothly in her grip. She entered the room.

Her eyes were immediately drawn to the billowing white curtains at the window. She caught a glimpse of turquoise waters between the swaying fronds of palm trees. Her gaze shifted to the empty bed. She closed the door and looked toward the sound of running water coming from the closed bathroom to the right.

Connelly crossed the floor and sat in the armchair next to the bed. She eyed the gilded staff on the nightstand and lifted it gingerly in her hands. She fingered the rings in the middle.

She was studying the spear blades that had almost impaled her when the bathroom door opened. Conrad Greene stepped out.

He was buttoning up a clean shirt, a towel slung around his neck. He stopped in his tracks when he saw her by the bed. Apart from seeming thinner than the last time she had seen him, Conrad Greene looked to be, if not a picture of health, then at least a fairly realistic sketch of it.

'Oh,' said Greene. 'Hi, Sarah.' An unspoken question dawned in the immortal's gray-blue eyes. He hesitated and glanced at the door.

'Hartwell isn't with me,' said Connelly. She placed the double-bladed spear on the bed. 'She took an extended leave of absence shortly after you went missing.' She looked up at Greene. 'She said you'd know where to find her.'

Greene went still. Surprise flared in his gaze. His lips curved in an arresting smile.

Connelly ignored the mild quickening of her pulse, crossed her knees primly, and propped her chin in the palm of her hand. 'So, care to tell me what the hell happened?'

Greene's expression grew sober. He walked to the bed and sat on the edge of the mattress.

As the helicopter continued its deadly dive toward the ocean floor, Conrad reached down and unclasped Nadica Rajkovic's fingers from around his ankle. She resisted him for precious seconds, her nails biting into his skin with steely determination. He jabbed desperately at her with his free leg and felt his boot connect sharply with her head. Her grip finally loosened.

Conrad kicked away from the aircraft and turned to watch the looming darkness swallow its shape. Bubbles of air escaped Nadica's lips as she reached toward him, her features distorted in a mask of rage and her mouth open on a silent scream. She disappeared from view.

Conrad looked to the distant surface and started to swim, his arms swinging out in strong, steady strokes while his legs scissored through the cold water.

His vision started to flicker with dark spots when he was halfway to the glimmering, sunlit ceiling. The lack of oxygen became a physical, growing pain at the back of his throat, and the urge to take a breath an even stronger one. His movements grew steadily more sluggish. A chilling numbness soon enveloped him and spread to his fingers and toes.

Something sparkled in the gloom next to him. Conrad blinked and made out the gilded staff floating in an underwater current. He reached out and wrapped a hand around the weapon.

The immortal gazed up and felt Death's shadow walk toward him once more. Resignation flooded his diminishing consciousness. He was not going to make it to the surface.

Conrad sank in the eddies and dimly wondered how many deaths an immortal could survive at the bottom of the sea. His eyes fluttered close. They popped open a moment later as a startlingly clear thought suddenly flashed through him.

He said a silent prayer, clasped his staff to his chest, and unleashed the full force of his immortal powers. Heat exploded inside him and burned a fiery path across his soul. As the murkiness of the ocean depths engulfed him, Conrad thought he saw his birthmark glow, the snake's body a shimmering ribbon of unearthly energy.

Then, awareness faded and he plunged deeper into his watery grave.

~

'WHAT? AND THAT'S IT?' SAID CONNELLY PRESENTLY, HER tone full of skepticism. 'Twenty-eight days later, you pop up in a fisherman's net some two hundred and fifty miles from where you crashed?'

Conrad sighed. 'Not exactly.' He ran a hand through his damp hair and grimaced. 'It seemed I managed to slow down every single process in my body.'

Lines creased Connelly's brow. 'What do you mean?'

'Someone who drowns in icy water has better preservation of organ function than someone who drowns in a milder environment,' Conrad explained. 'I released my powers as I lost consciousness out of pure instinct, to try and achieve the effects of those very conditions.' He paused. 'What they did was effectively put me in a hypothermic state close enough to death that my body would need minimal energy to operate and survive.'

Although the details were still hazy, Conrad also suspected that the healing energy of his immortal legacy went on a continuous loop, repairing his damaged tissues until he finally surfaced days later, his body dragged up from the oceanic abyss by a powerful eddy.

He'd awoken an immeasurable length of time after he emerged from the fathomless grasp of the Sargasso Sea and drifted in and out of consciousness on its surface, suffering the scorching hot days and freezing nights that followed. Thirst and hunger became secondary concerns, as did the sunburns that healed almost instantly.

At times, the immortal had been aware of large, dark shapes swimming close to him, their postures displaying curiosity. Though none of them bumped him, Conrad had hoped they weren't sharks. He wasn't in a fit state to fight a gnat, let alone dangerous creatures of the deep.

When George Tucker finally hauled him up in his net, the immortal had slipped into one of his comatose sleeps. It was the captain of *The Beaver* who first realized that he was still alive, when Conrad wouldn't let go of the staff weapon he had gripped in his left hand for twenty-eight days. Tucker was also the one who detected the sluggish twenty-beats-per-minute pulse at his wrist.

Conrad had woken up in a cabin on *The Beaver* just as Hamilton Harbor came in sight. After congratulating him on his miraculous survival, Tucker offered him his first drink of the month. It was a glass of expensive Irish whisky. The immortal managed to keep it down for all of sixty seconds.

He had dispatched a case of the stuff to Tucker's home address that very morning, after making a phone call from his private room in Hamilton town's main hospital.

'Did you recover Nadica's and Zoran's bodies?' Conrad asked Connelly.

The Director of Intelligence shook her head, her expression chagrined. 'I'm afraid not. Westwood had Navy search and rescue looking for you practically every single day since the accident. He refused to believe that you were dead.' She sighed. 'The Bastians also participated in the search, with Victor just as adamant that you were still alive. We've had the NGA satellites scanning the sea for debris for the last month.'

Conrad swallowed the lump in his throat. He had spoken to Victor briefly during the night, in between being poked and prodded by the hospital staff; the Bastian leader hadn't managed to go into a great deal of detail before the first reporter descended on the hospital grounds. Several others followed after receiving the tip-off about the sole survivor of the fatal helicopter accident that had taken place during a covert military assault on a private yacht a month ago.

The immortal recalled what the captain of *The Beaver* had told him the previous day. The helicopter had crashed in a region of the Sargasso Sea dominated by the North Atlantic Gyre, one of several enormous systems of rotating oceanic currents stretching thousands of miles across the Earth's surface. It was not surprising that he had been found some distance from where the aircraft had impacted into the sea.

The fact that Westwood and Victor never stopped looking humbled him.

Connelly opened her mouth. She hesitated. 'Did you see them—?'

'Yes,' Conrad cut in. 'They didn't survive the crash.' He studied his hands.

Zoran Rajkovic had been dead before they hit the water. Conrad knew without a doubt that Nadica had followed him to his grave at the bottom of the Sargasso Sea.

'I take it you heard about Ariana?' said Connelly. Her expression darkened.

Conrad nodded. It was one of the few things Victor had told him the night before. Ariana Rajkovic was now in the custody of the Bastian First Council. His mentor had mentioned the diaries they had found on the yacht, which chronicled her long history and her associations with the Ottoman Empire. The Bastian leader had quietly pondered what an asset she would have been to the Crovir immortal society had she lived her lives within it.

Although Westwood and the other heads of state had demanded Ariana be tried in a human court of law, the Bastians and the Crovirs had convinced them otherwise.

'It would look strange if she survived the death penalty,' said Conrad.

Connelly grunted noncommittally.

'What's been happening in Washington and abroad?' said Conrad.

'You trying to distract me, Greene?' Connelly asked, suspicious.

'No,' Conrad replied with a faint smile. 'I didn't get a complete update from Victor.'

Connelly spent the next half hour recounting the events

following the helicopter crash. In the time it had taken for Conrad and his team to travel to the Rajkovics' luxury yacht, six cities had managed to identify and destroy the laser devices above the primary boreholes that were meant to destroy them.

In the hours that followed, another twenty eliminated the threat to their territories. Four military bases, two in the US, one in Italy, and one in Germany, were destroyed by Scud missiles; the artillery trucks from which they were launched had been manned by devoted followers of the Rajkovics. There had been no loss of life, however, with the sites having already been cleared of all personnel following Petersen's confession.

Over the next day, the FBI and the CIA also apprehended the assassins Ariana had dispatched to kill the families of the three scientists Conrad and his team had rescued from Morocco.

The governments of the world were still rounding up members of Ariana Rajkovic's thousands-strong army of descendants, followers, mercenaries, and drug lords scattered to the four winds.

'What will happen to her?' Connelly finally asked.

Conrad observed the Director of National Intelligence for a moment. 'She will be tried and likely executed,' he said quietly.

Some color drained from Connelly's face at his words. 'How many times?'

'However many it takes,' said Conrad.

Awkward silence fell between them. It was broken by raised voices outside the door.

'Seriously, you guys need to take a chill pill!' someone roared. 'I'm his best friend. Now, let me in!'

'Excuse me,' Conrad told Connelly. He rose from the bed, crossed the floor, and opened the door. 'Get in here,' he told the man framed by the two agents.

Anatole's eyes widened. He barged inside the room and engulfed Conrad in a fierce hug. 'You bastard!' he said, his voice husky with emotion. Elated laughter shook his chest. 'I *knew* you'd make it!'

Victor Dvorsky appeared in the doorway. The agents glanced at Connelly. She sighed and inclined her head. The Bastian leader walked in and studied Conrad for silent seconds. 'You look good,' he said.

Conrad smiled. From Victor, this was the equivalent of a welcome parade.

~

Laura Hartwell wiped her brow with the back of her hand and blinked at the dazzling midday sun. She took a sip of the bottled water on the worktable, grabbed another handful of nails, and raised the mallet. The sound of steady hammering echoed around the clearing once more, breaking the jabber from the squirrel monkeys in the trees around the swamp.

Floorboards rattled under Laura's boots. She paused in the middle of striking a nail, turned her head, and eyed the dog loping toward her. Rocky slid to a stop on the porch, claws digging into the wood. He dropped a stick at her feet and sat down heavily, his loud pants warming the skin on her legs. He watched her with an expectant expression.

Laura resisted the lure of the shiny, brown eyes. 'Look, pooch,' she said in a no-nonsense voice, 'until you master the ability to hold a hammer, I suggest you let me carry on with the construction work.'

Rocky whined and nudged her leg with his head. Laura sighed. She was as much putty in the dog's paws as she suspected Conrad had been.

She picked up the stick, strode to the edge of the porch, and pitched it toward the trees. Rocky bolted across the clearing and disappeared under the canopy, his tail rotating fast enough to achieve vertical lift-off. The immortal grinned and returned to the task of rebuilding the house that had been destroyed by the plane crash more than a month ago.

When she first arrived in Alvarães, nine days after the events in the Sargasso Sea, Laura had been surprised to discover that the burnt ruins of Conrad's home had been cleared from the land. It was Matheus Diaz, the police officer who took her out to the site, who explained how he and Roxanne, Conrad's closest neighbor and friend, had taken care of removing the remains of the plane's wreckage and the damaged cabin. They were both convinced that the man who had lived there would return one day.

Laura had Diaz introduce her to the old lady later that very evening. Roxanne had studied her above the drifting wisps of smoke from her mapacho cigarette for a long time, before telling her she should take Rocky into her care. Laura still visited the old woman most days and listened to her tales about the one she loved to call *Deus Demônio*. Diaz sometimes joined them.

They were all pleased with how Rocky had progressed since Laura's arrival. When she first met the dog, he had been solemn and withdrawn. Although he seemed to recognize Conrad's scent on her, his eyes were dull and his tail drooped constantly. Roxanne explained that he had barely eaten in a week.

As the days passed, the dog gradually came out of his shell. Then, about a fortnight ago, his whole demeanor changed. Laura awoke to his excited yips early one morning. She crawled out of her tent to find him jumping and barking at the sky, tremors of excitement rippling through his body. She sat on the ground and cried then, the flame of hope that had lived inside her in the dark days following the helicopter crash blazing into life and filling her soul.

The dog's behavior could only mean one thing. Conrad Greene was alive.

With the help of Diaz and Roxanne, Laura doubled her

efforts to erect a new house for the man she loved while she waited for his return.

The chatter from the monkeys grew louder. Branches swayed in the canopy as they disappeared into the shadows of the forest. Laura stopped, hammer in hand. She turned to study the clearing and spotted the cause of the monkeys' agitation further up the swamp. A black jaguar was curled up on the roots of a kapok tree, golden eyes fixed unblinkingly on the immortal.

'Hey girl,' Laura called out softly.

The creature acknowledged her greeting with a lazy blink.

Laura lifted a plank of wood from the pile on the ground and heaved it between two posts. She had just finished securing it to the pillars when Rocky's animated barks suddenly rose in the distance. She frowned and put the hammer on the table before walking to the edge of the porch, one hand raised above her eyes to block out the glare of the sun.

She wasn't expecting a delivery of hardware for another week. Her gaze shifted briefly to the swamp. Diaz or one of his men would normally come from Alvarães by boat anyway.

Rocky's barks were coming from the opposite direction to the water.

Laura's heart started to thud erratically in her breast when she registered the sheer joy in the dog's voice. She stepped to the ground, her mouth suddenly dry and her legs shaking. Shadows shifted under the trees to the east.

A man walked out of the jungle, a backpack strapped to his shoulders. Rocky leapt excitedly around the tall, thin figure, his head occasionally bumping the man's legs while his tail moved in an invisible blur.

Conrad Greene stopped on the edge of the clearing and scratched the dog behind the ears. He straightened and looked at Laura across the lush expanse of vegetation. His eyes were unreadable from the distance.

'You building a mansion?' he asked lightly.

Laura glanced over her shoulder at the large footprint of the new house, sweat dampening her palms.

'I thought we could do with something bigger,' she said, barely masking the tremor in her voice. 'Besides, we need space for the hot tub.'

Conrad raised an eyebrow. 'It's gonna have a hot tub?'

'Yep. And we need the extra rooms.'

'We do?' he said, puzzled.

'Uh-huh,' said Laura. 'For the babies.'

Conrad paled. 'We're having babies?' he asked hoarsely.

Laura stuck her hands on her hips and glared at him, her eyes misting up. 'Well, if you get your ass over here and kiss me, we could start on it straightaway!'

'Yes, ma'am,' said Conrad, a slow grin splitting his face.

They met halfway across the clearing.

Laura leapt into Conrad's arms and wrapped her legs around his waist. He grunted, his breath choking with laughter as he fell back. They landed heavily on the ground. Rocky ran circles around them, delighted yips leaving his throat while he drowned them in licks.

Laura's tears spilled over and fell on Conrad's face as they kissed each other fervently. She ran her hands hungrily over his body, relishing the heat of his skin. Her fingers stilled when she registered his thin ribs and arms. A low sob escaped her lips.

Conrad cradled her head against his neck.

'It's okay,' he whispered brokenly in her ear. 'I'm not going anywhere.' He raised her face in his hands and pressed his mouth to her brow reverently, blinking back tears. 'I'm all yours.'

Laura read the undying promise in his blazing eyes and smiled.

～

EPILOGUE

S

They parked the rental a couple of blocks down from the address they had been given and walked the rest of the way. Five minutes after they left the car, they were standing in front of a nondescript apartment building.

'Is this the place?' said Laura.

'Uh-huh.' Conrad glanced at the piece of paper in his hand.

In contrast to its exterior, the building's lobby was warm and classy, with pale marble walls and golden lighting. They took an elevator to the tenth floor.

The lift doors opened on a silent corridor. They headed along the carpeted floor and stopped in front of an apartment in the middle of the passage. No sound escaped from the other side of the black door. Conrad pressed the buzzer on the call box next to it.

'Yes?' answered a male voice he didn't recognize. Low murmurs were audible in the background. A dog barked.

'It's Greene and Hartwell,' said Conrad. 'I believe you're expecting us.'

'Hang on,' said the man.

Locks soon turned on the inside of the door. It opened to reveal Victor Dvorsky.

A golden retriever stuck his head around the Bastian noble's legs and looked at them curiously, bushy tail thumping the wall. He huffed a welcome and padded back inside the apartment.

'New place?' said Conrad with an arched eyebrow.

'You got a dog?' Laura asked, deadpan.

'Very funny,' Victor muttered at their expressions. 'Come on in.'

Conrad and Laura exchanged curious glances before walking through the entrance.

Victor had called them ten days ago, when they were visiting Horatio and Anatole in Rio for the New Year celebrations. The Bastian leader explained he had some vital information to impart to Conrad that couldn't be relayed over the phone. He had insisted they travel to Boston to meet with him at their earliest convenience. Conrad and Laura had taken the red-eye flight to Massachusetts via New York the previous day.

Victor closed the door and led them down an elegant hallway that opened onto a sizable living room. A fire burned in a large hearth to the right. The flames reflected off the thick, polished, walnut mantelpiece and the painting of Monet's 1906 "Water Lilies" above it. The decor was pleasant and sophisticated.

Two women sat on a couch to the left. They each cradled a baby in their arms and spoke in soft voices, their faces relaxed in easy smiles. The dog lay quietly at their feet, a silver tabby perched on his back in a Sphinx-like pose. The cat turned its head and watched Conrad and Laura unblinkingly.

A thickset figure stood by the large bay window ahead, a cell phone cradled to his ear. A jolt of surprise darted through Conrad when he recognized Dimitri Reznak, the Crovir noble.

Footsteps rose on the right. A man strolled out of a corridor, a feeding bowl in each hand.

'Grub's up, kids,' he said in a business-like tone. The babies looked around at his voice and let out high-pitched squeals.

Conrad froze. Laura inhaled sharply.

Lucas Soul stopped and looked at them. 'Hey,' he murmured, blue eyes glinting with an unreadable expression.

Conrad stared at the immortal who had once been the most wanted and feared man in all of Bastian and Crovir societies. His gaze shifted to Victor Dvorsky.

'What is this?' he said in a low voice. He stepped in front of Laura, aware of the weight of his staff in the small of his back.

Dimitri Reznak ended his phone call and turned to face them, his eyes hooded.

'It's okay,' said one of the women on the couch. She waited until Soul put the dishes down on the coffee table and handed him the baby. Chestnut curls danced around her striking face and olive-green eyes as she rose to her feet and crossed the floor toward them. 'We mean you no harm.'

Lucas Soul gently cradled the child in his arms. The boy giggled.

'Sit,' Victor ordered. He indicated a pair of leather armchairs.

Conrad hesitated and looked at Laura. She bit her lip and inclined her head. They walked over and sat down carefully. The woman with the green eyes smiled and returned to her seat. She kissed Soul and took the child off him. Silence descended on the room.

Conrad became aware of a laser-like stare from the second woman on the couch. She was even more stunning than her companion, with short, onyx-black hair and silver eyes. Though she was spoon-feeding the gurgling baby girl in her arms while making encouraging coos, he could not help but feel that she had just picked out ten ways in which to kill him. A diamond engagement ring glinted on her left hand.

Conrad looked at Victor. 'Okay, I'm sitting,' he said gruffly. 'What the hell's going on?'

The woman with the deadly aura narrowed her pale eyes. 'We do not say bad words in front of the b-a-b-i-e-s,' she admonished.

Conrad cocked an eyebrow. 'They're like what, six mon—?' he started to say in a sarcastic voice.

On cue, the baby boy said, 'Hel!'

'Oh crap,' muttered the silver-eyed woman.

The child in her arms came out with an enthusiastic, 'Cap!' and sprayed mashed carrot and potato across her expensive leather jacket. Lucas Soul sighed.

A dry smile curved the lips of the woman with the green eyes. 'Well, at least we're raising them on the island,' she told Soul. 'They won't get kicked out of nursery for using offensive language.'

Conrad stared.

'Lucas Soul and Dimitri you already know,' Victor stated crisply. 'This is Anna Soul, Lucas's wife, and their children, Tomas and Lily.' He indicated the woman with the green eyes and the babies. 'And this is Alexa King, Dimitri's goddaughter.' He paused. 'They know who the two of you are.'

Conrad studied the woman with the silver eyes guardedly. He had heard King's name before. The Crovir agent had a fearsome reputation, even among Bastian Hunters.

'Why did you never tell me you were a pureblood?' Victor asked him brusquely.

Conrad startled, surprised at the question. 'It never came up,' he muttered after several seconds. 'Besides, stuff like that doesn't matter to me.'

'It should!' snapped Victor. 'If I had known that fact and

made the connection with your immortal abilities, we could have had this meeting last year. Christ, I would have dragged your stubborn ass out of that goddamned swamp myself!'

Tomas Soul punched the air with a plump fist and went, 'Gada!' while his sister uttered a more dubious, 'Ath?'

'Well, at least we know what *their* first immortal ability's going to be,' muttered Alexa King in the uncomfortable hush that followed.

Conrad narrowed his eyes at his old mentor. 'You *knew* where I was?'

Victor snorted. 'Of course! Once Anatole let it slip that you were visiting Horatio, I arranged to have you tailed!'

Conrad silently cursed his absent friend. 'What the he—?' He stopped, glanced at the rapt babies, and corrected himself. 'What does my lineage have to do with any of this?'

It was Dimitri Reznak who answered his question with another one. 'Does the name Rafael mean anything to you?'

Conrad frowned. 'No, it doesn't.'

Dimitri Reznak spent the next hour recounting the most fantastical tale Conrad had ever heard in his entire existence. It was a story that dated back more than five thousand years, about a man called Romerus and the extraordinary fates that would befall the children he had borne.

Conrad listened with rising incredulity while the Crovir noble related his centuries-long quest to discover a truth that had been consigned to oblivion and how this crusade had come to fruition just over fourteen months ago, when he discovered a pair of caves in the mountains of the Eastern Desert, in Egypt. The body of evidence he uncovered finally started to yield the answers he had long sought about the origins of the two immortal races. Victor interjected from time to time, in support of Reznak's words.

Halfway through their account, Conrad felt Laura's hand slide on his. He turned his palm over until their fingers intertwined. He didn't have to look at his soulmate to feel the shock reverberating through her.

As if their narrative wasn't enough of a bombshell in itself, the nobles' next two stories rocked Conrad to the core. By the time they finished retelling the extraordinary tales of Lucas and Anna Soul's origins, as well as the formidable history of Alexa King, the immortal knew his world would never be the same again.

Conrad turned to the three figures on the couch, blood pounding dully in his ears. 'We're cousins?' he breathed.

Lucas and Anna Soul smiled.

'In a very distant sense, yes,' said Alexa King, a trace of wariness still evident in her gaze.

'But...how can you be so sure?' Conrad turned to Victor, still reeling from everything he had just been told.

An embarrassed expression flashed across the Bastian leader's face.

'I stole the blood samples the doctors in Bermuda took from you and had them analyzed for your genetics,' Victor admitted, his tone somewhat defensive. 'They matched those from the samples Dimitri found in Egypt.'

Conrad's jaw sagged in the stunned silence that followed. He wasn't sure whether to be furious or appalled.

'Seriously, the two of you need to stop this nasty habit you have of stealing other people's blood,' said Alexa. She was frowning at Reznak and Victor.

Anna sighed. Lucas muttered something under his breath.

Reznak crossed the room and stopped by Conrad's chair. 'May I?' he said quietly. He indicated the immortal's left arm.

Conrad swallowed the lump in his throat and pulled back his sleeve. The light from the fire flickered across the black Aesculapian snake on his forearm. For a breathless moment, the creature appeared to dance on his skin. Alexa leaned forward and scrutinized the birthmark.

'Fascinating,' murmured Reznak. 'Most human historians know these creatures as being related to the healing arts practiced by the followers of the Greek God of medicine, Asclepius. They were said to be found freely roaming popular healing temples built during the fourth century BC for the deity.' His gaze shifted to Conrad's face. 'The Aesculapian snake wrapped around a rod is still the most recognized symbol of medicine to this day.'

The Crovir noble indicated his goddaughter. 'Alexa has a trishula birthmark, a symbol of her own unique lineage.' He gestured to Soul. 'Lucas has an alpha and omega one, a legacy of his original bloodlines.'

Conrad digested this information in silence. Reznak's words about the rod of Asclepius resonated in his ears. The immortal hesitated and glanced at the woman beside him. Laura inclined her head. Conrad reached behind his back and took out his staff. He handed it to Reznak.

The Crovir noble carefully took the weapon off him. He examined it for some time before manipulating the rings. Conrad felt grudging approval radiate from Alexa when the spear blades and short swords appeared. Reznak looked thoughtful as he slid the blades back inside the shaft.

'From the scriptures we found in Egypt and in the Ural mountains, the pureblood immortal from whom you, and all the men in your family who came before you, inherited your powers was said to carry a staff,' said the Crovir. 'Some of the writings mentioned that he used it as a walking stick, whereas others professed that he fought with it.' He paused, his expression solemn. 'He was known as the greatest healer who ever lived in those times and was said to use snakes in his rites. He also kept them as pets.'

'This is the...*Rafael* you referred to at the beginning?' Laura asked haltingly.

'Yes,' said Reznak.

Conrad stared at his hands, his head buzzing from the incredible revelations of the last hour. He thought of all that he had ever done with his immortal powers in the four hundred and sixty years of his existence and what he had more recently achieved, first with Rocky, then with Westwood. He had never heard of another immortal pulling off something like it in the past, in either his own bloodline or the rest of Bastian society.

'Could Rafael...*give* life?' Conrad said finally. He looked up at Reznak and Victor.

The Crovir noble appeared puzzled. 'What, you mean as in procreate? Well, he obviously had children, otherwise you wouldn't be—'

'He doesn't know?' Conrad interjected. This time, he addressed the question squarely to Victor.

The Bastian noble shook his head. 'I didn't think it was my prerogative to tell him.'

'What are you talking about?' said Reznak.

Conrad took a deep breath. 'I can do more than heal.' He hesitated. 'I can also gift one of my seventeen lives if I wish to do so.'

'What?' exclaimed Anna Soul. Her green eyes reflected shock and a glimmer of intellectual interest. Lucas and Alexa went still.

'The seventeen pieces of an immortal's soul reside in their heart,' said Conrad. He heard Alexa inhale sharply and glanced at her pale expression. 'I can feel all of mine and manipulate them. It's not easy, but it's doable.'

Reznak was quiet for some time. 'As far as we know from the scriptures we have in our possessions, Rafael never gave away any of his lives,' he said finally. He exchanged a troubled glance with Victor. 'It seems that all your powers have evolved in some way or another. None of your ancestors could do what you can.'

'Are there others?' said Laura.

'You mean other pureblood descendants of the original immortals?' said Reznak.

Laura nodded shakily.

The answer came from Victor Dvorsky. 'Yes. Based on the genealogy of the bloodlines, there may be two more. We don't know for sure. As far as Dimitri and I are aware, it isn't anybody in our current societies.'

Conrad's mouth went dry at this news. He possibly had two more cousins out there.

An excited gurgle drew his eyes to the couch. Lily Soul was bouncing up and down on Alexa's knees and wriggling her hands toward him in a demanding gesture.

'Looks like she wants to get to know you,' Alexa said wryly. She rose and came over.

Conrad suddenly found himself holding the baby.

Alexa frowned. 'She's not a bomb.'

'Oh,' blurted Conrad when he realized that he was holding his niece at arms' length. He savored the word as he cradled the tiny body against his chest. *Niece*. It had a nice ring to it.

Lily Soul had inherited her father's eyes and her mother's complexion. She looked at him solemnly for a moment before reaching up. Plump fingers closed on his cheek. Conrad grinned at the warmth of her skin.

Lily's lips curved in an answering beam as dazzling as the sun. 'Karad,' she said.

Laura gasped.

Conrad looked up, dazed. 'Did she just try to say my—?'

Anna nodded with a tremulous smile. Conrad's heart thudded wildly inside his chest. None of them had uttered his name since he entered the room.

Tomas sat on Lucas's knees and watched Conrad with an identical grin to his sister, his green eyes bright. 'Gada! Hel!' he contributed enthusiastically.

Victor laughed.

'I suspect Lily is going to be the brains of this outfit,' said Alexa as chuckles rang around the room.

A sudden premonition blasted through Conrad as he gazed into the eyes of the twins. These children were special. He could feel it in the very marrow of his being.

He sensed the same awed awareness in the others' expressions.

Laura reached across and gently stroked Lily's face, hazel eyes gleaming with unshed tears. Lily grabbed her hand and cooed. In that instant, Conrad Greene felt the bonds of destiny irrevocably seal themselves around the immortals in that room. He thought of the two who still remained to be found, the missing links of their extraordinary circle.

They were out there.

He was certain of it.

THE END

THANK YOU

Thank you for reading EMPIRE.

I would be really grateful if you could consider leaving a review on Amazon, Goodreads, or other platforms where you buy your books. Reviews are vital for authors and all reviews, even a couple of short sentences, can help readers decide whether to pick up one of my books.

WANT FREE BOOKS AND EXCLUSIVE EXTRAS?

Join my reader list today for free books, exclusive bonus content, new release alerts, giveaways, and more.

Go to the link below to find out more.

www.ADStarrling.com/free-download-offer

ACKNOWLEDGMENTS

To Kat, Wendy, Lorraine, and Shaheel, my beta-readers. Without your kickass comments, this book would not be what it is today.

To Liam Carnahan from Invisible Ink Editing and Sara Litchfield from Right Ink On The Wall. Your critiques and feedback make me a better writer everyday. Thank you for helping me overcome my bad writing habits!

To my friends Dawn and Ali, and to Ed and the Hagen family. Apologies for being accidental victims of my imagination. At least I didn't kill you.

To Kriss Morton, who loved Anatole Vassili so much, I just had to bring the man back.

To Deranged Doctor Design, for the amazing new cover.

FACTS AND FICTIONS

Now, for one of my favorite parts of writing my books. Here are the facts and fictions behind the story.

Suleiman The Magnificent

The historical events behind the prologue and the first chapter are factual. Suleiman the Magnificent had his first-born son with Mahidevran Sultan and later had him killed, for fear of a coup during the Persian campaign in the 1500s. Captain Branimir Rajkovic and the young Ariana are purely fictional characters.

Treaty of the Union

The Treaty of the Union is factual and was established in London in July 1706, under the patronage of Queen Anne. The talks between the English and Scottish commissioners assigned to the negotiations took place in the Royal Cockpit theatre, close to Whitehall and the Banqueting House.

Aesculapian Snake

Conrad's birthmark, the Aesculapian snake, is inspired by

the Rod of Asclepius, the most recognized symbol of medicine to this day. At the end of the book, I introduce the notion that Rafael, Conrad's pureblood-immortal ancestor and Bastian's second-born son, is the original "healer" upon whom all subsequent mythological figures, such as the Greek God Asclepius, are based. Giving Conrad a staff weapon to fight with was a logical step to complete the symbolism of the Rod of Asclepius.

Typhoon Freda

The 1962 Columbus Day storm, Typhoon Freda, is factual and was perfect inspiration for a haiku.

US Secret Service

Researching the structure of the US Secret Service and how these agents would protect the President during a public function, such as the FedEx Field fundraiser event, was hard work. It was only after trawling through dozens of newspaper articles, pictures, and the highly-instructive websites of several US government agencies, including that of the US Secret Service itself, that I managed to write those scenes. The White House Situation Room exists and is usually managed by a Sit Room director, as depicted in the book. Description of the physical layout and the idea of having the US Director of National Intelligence take over its operation are purely fictional. From my research, I gathered that mobile phones and other such devices are not normally allowed in the Sit Room, which is why I have everyone using landlines. Again, I took a lot of liberties with how the US intelligence community as a whole would coordinate their efforts if a similar crisis as the one depicted in the novel was to arise in real life. I hope it would mimic what I described in the book. The Crystal City US Secret Service detention facility is purely fictional.

Vehicles of Heads of State

The current US President travels in a custom-made Cadillac that contains a blood bank of his specific blood type in the trunk. The full resuscitation kit I included in the book is fictional. The current Chancellor of Germany counts an Audi A8 among her state cars.

Plastic Guns

The technology to make carbon-fiber-reinforced plastic guns and ceramic bullets that can evade metal detectors is factual. The first publicly known plastic gun was shown to the world in 2013.

Polymer Material

The fictional Obenhaus Group is loosely based on a very famous and innovative manufacturer of polymer materials which started life in the German state of Bavaria. The plastic polymer OG1140 is fictional, although the methods used to produce it are factual.

Co-crystallization

The co-crystallization process used to make the poison and liquid super explosive in the book is factual. As described in the novel, it is an area of increasing interest with regard to its applications in other industries besides pharmaceutics, including mining and explosives engineering. PETN and its derivative Pentolite were used extensively during the Second World War and large amounts remain leftover in old weapon stockpiles. The R.E. factor used to describe the power of the liquid explosive invented by Svein Hagen is factual. Cetrilium 24 is fictional.

US Marines

The details of U.S. AFRICOM, the UAV, and the composition, hierarchy, and weapons of the US Marines Corps platoon, are based on factual research. Any mistakes in accurately depicting these are mine alone.

Boreholes

The Kola Superdeep Borehole and Project Mohole are factual, as are directional or horizontal boring and trenchless technology.

Super yacht

The Rajkovics' yacht *The Ariana* is based on the super yacht *Anastasia*, designed by Sam Sorgiovanni Designs and made by Oceanco in 2008.

And that's it for the science and technology lesson folks! Want to check out more Extras? Then visit my website at www.adstarrling.com

ABOUT THE AUTHOR

AD Starrling's bestselling supernatural thriller series **Seventeen** combines action, suspense, and a dose of fantasy to make each book an explosive, adrenaline-fueled ride. If you prefer your action hot and your heroes sexy and strong-willed, then check out her military thriller series Division Eight.

When she's not busy writing, AD can be found looking up exciting international locations and cool science and technology to put in her books, eating Thai food, being tortured by her back therapists, drooling over gadgets, working part-time as a doctor on a Neonatal Intensive Care unit somewhere in the UK, reading manga, and watching action and sci-fi flicks. She has occasionally been accused of committing art with a charcoal stick and some drawing paper.

Find   out   more   about   AD   on   her   website

<u>www.adstarrling.com</u> where you can sign up for her awesome newsletter, get exclusive freebies, and never miss her latest release. You'll also have a chance to see sneak previews of her work, participate in exclusive giveaways, and hear about special promotional offers first.

Here are some other places where you can connect with her:

<u>www.adstarrling.com</u>
Email: <u>ads@adstarrling.com</u>

ALSO BY A. D. STARRLING

Hunted (A Seventeen Series Novel) Book One

'My name is Lucas Soul. Today, I died again. This is my fifteenth death in the last four hundred and fifty years. And I'm determined that it will be the last.'

National Indie Excellence Awards Winner Fantasy 2013

National Indie Excellence Awards Finalist Adventure 2013

Next Generation Indie Book Awards Finalist Action-Adventure 2013

Hollywood Book Festival 2013 Honorable Mention General Fiction

Warrior (A Seventeen Series Novel) Book Two

The perfect Immortal warrior. A set of stolen, priceless artifacts. An ancient sect determined to bring about the downfall of human civilization.

Next Generation Indie Book Awards Winner Action-Adventure 2014

Shelf Unbound Competition for Best Independently Published Book Finalist 2014

Empire (A Seventeen Series Novel) Book Three

An Immortal healer. An ancient empire reborn. A chain of cataclysmic events that threatens to change the fate of the world.

Next Generation Indie Book Awards Finalist General Fiction 2015

Legacy (A Seventeen Series Novel) Book Four

The Hunter who should have been king. The Elemental who fears love. The Seer who is yet to embrace her powers.

Three immortals whose fates are entwined with that of the oldest and most formidable enemy the world has ever faced.

Origins (A Seventeen Series Novel) Book Five

The gifts bestowed by One not of this world, to the Man who had lived longer than most.

The Empire ruled by a King who would swallow the world in his madness.

The Warrior who chose to rise against her own kind in order to defeat him.

Discover the extraordinary beginnings of the Immortals and the unforgettable story of the Princess who would become a Legend.

Destiny (A Seventeen Series Novel) Book Six

An enemy they never anticipated.

A brutal attack that tears them apart.

A chain of immutable events that will forever alter the future.

Discover the destiny that was always theirs to claim.

The Seventeen Collection 1: Books 1-3

Boxset featuring Hunted, Warrior, and Empire.

The Seventeen Collection 2: Books 4-6

Boxset featuring Legacy, Origins, and Destiny.

The Seventeen Complete Collection: Books 1-6

Boxset featuring Hunted, Warrior, Empire, Legacy, Origins, and Destiny.

First Death (A Seventeen Series Short Story) #1

Discover where it all started...

Dancing Blades (A Seventeen Series Short Story) #2

Join Lucas Soul on his quest to become a warrior.

The Meeting (A Seventeen Series Short Story) #3

Discover the origins of the incredible friendship between the protagonists of Hunted.

The Warrior Monk (A Seventeen Series Short Story) #4

Experience Warrior from the eyes of one of the most beloved characters in Seventeen.

The Hunger (A Seventeen Series Short Story) #5

Discover the origin of the love story behind Empire.

The Bank Job (A Seventeen Series Short Story) #6

Join two of the protagonists from Legacy on their very first adventure.

The Seventeen Series Short Story Collection 1 (#1-3)

Boxset featuring First Death, Dancing Blades, and The Meeting.

The Seventeen Series Short Story Collection 2 (#4-6)

Boxset featuring The Warrior Monk, The Hunger, and The Bank Job.

The Seventeen Series Ultimate Short Story Collection

Boxset featuring First Death, Dancing Blades, The Meeting, The Warrior Monk, The Hunger, and The Bank Job.

Mission:Black (A Division Eight Thriller)

A broken agent. A once in a lifetime chance. A new mission that threatens to destroy her again.

Mission: Armor (A Division Eight Thriller)

A man tortured by his past. A woman determined to save him. A deadly assignment that threatens to rip them apart.

Mission:Anaconda (A Division Eight Thriller)

It should have been a simple mission. They should have been in and out in a day. Except it wasn't. And they didn't.

Void (A Sci-fi Horror Short Story)

2065. Humans start terraforming Mars.

2070. The Mars Baker2 outpost is established on the Acidalia Planitia.

2084. The first colonist goes missing.

The Other Side of the Wall (A Short Horror Story)

Have you ever seen flashes of darkness where there should only be light? Ever seen shadows skitter past out of the corner of your eyes and looked, only to find nothing there?

AUDIOBOOKS

Hunted (A Seventeen Series Novel) Book One

Warrior (A Seventeen Series Novel) Book Two

Empire (A Seventeen Seres Novel) Book Three

First Death (A Seventeen Series Short Story) #1

Dancing Blades (A Seventeen Series Short Story) #2

The Meeting (A Seventeen Series Short Story) #3

The Warrior Monk (A Seventeen Series Short Story) #4

LEGACY EXTRACT

PROLOGUE

January 1599. Polar Urals. Western Russia.

The immortal bit back a curse as his boots sank in a snowdrift. He struggled out of the icy clutches of the land and carried on climbing, his eyes never leaving the dark shape moving between the trees above him. The figure suddenly stopped and turned. A flash bloomed in the gloom of the evergreen forest.

The immortal heard the crack of the pistol's discharge a moment before the lead ball thudded into the trunk of a birch, just inches from his head. He dropped to the ground, wood chips raining down around him and the sulfurous smell of burning gunpowder tainting the crisp, cold air. A further bang drowned out the agitated barks of the sled dogs in the outbuilding next to the log cabin at the bottom of the rise. The second shot smacked through the tightly-packed snow next to his hand. He swore and rolled behind a cluster of bushes. He rocked to a stop and peered around the edge of the snow-laden branches as the echo of the blast died down.

His prey was disappearing into the shadows beneath the canopy.

The immortal jumped to his feet and gave chase once more, his breath leaving his lips in white plumes. A bitter wind whistled down the flank of the mountain and stung his frost-crusted eyes and exposed skin. Down below, the sled dogs started to howl. The immortal clenched his jaw against the burning pain in his lungs and legs and willed his body forward.

Dazzling light greeted him at the summit of the rise. He staggered to a halt in calf-deep snow and squinted in the glare. His stomach lurched.

The forest ended abruptly on the edge of a rising ice field. Beyond it, a glacier rose to the summit of the peak, a white scar spread across miles of jagged, dark rocks. Sunlight reflected off towering cliffs and precipitous valleys, the shimmering brilliance masking the deadliness of the hostile landscape. Some hundred feet ahead, barely visible in the blinding radiance, the man he had been hunting for nearly two centuries scaled the treacherous incline.

The immortal removed the musket rifle strapped to his backpack, his gaze locked on the running figure. He shouldered the weapon, cocked the hammer, and carefully sighted down the barrel. Blood pounded in his ears as he held his breath and pulled the trigger.

Flint struck steel. Sparks flared as gunpowder ignited. The lead shot erupted from the muzzle of the gun and flashed through the air, its path straight and true.

The man he was chasing jerked and cried out. He stumbled down to one knee and clamped a hand to his right flank. He swayed for a moment, pushed himself up, and turned to fire his weapon once more. The shot whistled harmlessly into the treetops. He threw the pistol to the ground and started to climb again.

Rage darkened the immortal's vision. He had waded through thousands of miles of godforsaken wilderness before finally tracking down the man who had killed his lover and who posed the greatest threat the immortal societies had ever known. Having lost precious moments dispatching the bodyguards who stood watch over the remote hideout in the Urals, he had come within seconds of killing his enemy when the man escaped his grasp once more, rescued by the same uncanny luck that had been his savior for the last two hundred years.

The immortal shoved the rifle into its straps and headed over the ice.

Despite the wound, his prey accelerated and angled for a black outcrop rising out of the glacier to the far left.

Cold air seared the immortal's throat as he pursued the bleeding figure. He had just reached the crimson trail staining the pristine snow when a distant boom reached his ears. He stopped and looked up.

Movement on the slope some six thousand feet above him caught his gaze. A wall of whiteness slowly detached itself from the face of the mountain.

The wounded man froze in his tracks. He stared at the approaching avalanche before moving once more, his legs pumping awkwardly through the snow as he raced for the shelter of the spur of rock.

The immortal followed, despair sending a fresh burst of energy through his body. *No, not now, not when I am this close!*

The deluge rushed inexorably closer, a tidal wave of death dancing gracefully down the incline.

The immortal staggered after his prey, his resolve unshaken, air leaving his body in harsh gasps. The land rocked violently beneath his feet. He floundered and lost his footing. A thunderous explosion tore the air as he fell to his knees. A large crack appeared in the glacier in front of him.

The immortal's eyes widened. A cold blast knocked him sideways and sent him tumbling along the incline. He rolled and slid to a stop on his stomach some twenty feet down the slope. The roar of the approaching maelstrom of snow and ice echoed against the looming peaks and vales. The fissure lengthened. He blinked and saw a jagged line dart inches past his right hand before snaking toward the distant tree line behind him.

He scrambled backward as a dark crevasse opened in the ice sheet. The ground crumbled beneath him. His stomach dropped. He yanked his sword from the scabbard on his back and stabbed the blade frantically upward.

It sank into the edge of the ice just as he started to fall. He dangled from the hilt for a shocked moment before slowly looking down at the yawning darkness between his legs. His breath froze in his throat, the fear that gripped him almost paralyzing in its intensity. He gritted his teeth and reached up with his free hand, his flailing fingers searching desperately for purchase. They closed on the lip of the widening chasm.

The avalanche became a deafening howl that eclipsed the rapid drumbeat of his pulse. He looked over his shoulder.

His prey had reached the rocky outcrop and was crouched beneath it, his body braced for impact. Their eyes met through a thickening mist of fine snow. The wounded man smiled, his gaze full of dark triumph.

The immortal closed his eyes. Despair formed a tightening band around his heart as he steeled himself for what was to come.

The white torrent washed over the crevasse, pounding him with a cold, deadly weight that knocked the air out of his lungs. A rock smashed into his fingers, breaking skin and bone. He choked back a cry and swallowed a mouthful of snow.

The sword shuddered in his grasp. He let go of the edge of the chasm and clung to the hilt with both hands. Blood made his grip slippery. Another crack reached his ears. He looked up through the gray haze and glimpsed the fracture tearing through the ice holding the blade. It collapsed a second later.

He fell into the abyss, sword in hand.

Wind whistled in his ears. White walls rushed past him. The light faded as the deluge followed him into the gulf.

Soaring cliffs of black rock replaced the walls of ice as he fell through the crevasse into the very bowels of the mountain itself. Then the rock disappeared.

He had a vague impression of a gaping, empty void before he struck the ground.

Pain exploded through his consciousness, blocking out sight and sound. He felt his bones shatter. The earth shifted beneath him once more. Icy liquid suddenly flooded his throat. He gasped and choked. As freezing numbness engulfed his body, dulling the agony searing his senses, the immortal blinked and registered the clear waters surrounding him in dull incomprehension.

Darkness descended from above. The rest of the avalanche crashed down around him.

His fingers slowly loosened on the hilt of his sword. His final thought before darkness and silence locked him in the icy grave of the underground lake was that no one in the immortal societies knew of the danger that was still to come.

∼

Get the book now!
Legacy (A Seventeen Series Novel) Book Four

Ingram Content Group UK Ltd.
Milton Keynes UK
UKHW041313100423
419921UK00001B/131